Miss Molly Robbins Designs a Seduction

JAYNE FRESINA

sourcebooks
casablanca

Published by Sourcebooks Casablanca, an imprint of Sourcebooks,
Inc.
P.O. Box 4410, Naperville, Illinois 60567-4410
(630) 961-3900
Fax: (630) 961-2168
www.sourcebooks.com

Printed and bound in The United States of America.

VG 10 9 8 7 6 5 4 3 2 1

To Johanna

One

SHE WAS A SELFISH, UNFEELING, UNFAITHFUL YOUNG woman, and she wouldn't be at all surprised if she met her demise in some horrid, bloody end. Certain folk familiar with her story would say she had received entirely what she deserved.

At the rate these carriage wheels spun, they wouldn't have long to wait for the satisfaction, either.

"Moll Robbins?" they would exclaim. *"Isn't she the one who jilted that poor, honest lad at the altar and ran off to gamble her life on a rake's offer?"* Her fate would become a cautionary tale for young women all over the country.

Molly felt sick. Oh, what was she thinking to disappoint everyone like this? Rafe Hartley would never forgive her for calling off the wedding at the last minute. He was a most affable young fellow until he thought he'd been wronged, and then he could hold a grudge the way a farmyard mutt guarded a bone. Now she'd left him in the care of her best friend, Lady Mercy Danforthe, while she, a woman who had spent most of her life in service to others, suddenly decided to do something new. Something unexpected.

Alone in a jostling carriage, hurtling along at run-away speed—a fitting adjective, she mused—Molly would have two entire days to consider what she'd done, and where, exactly, she was likely to end up.

Carted off to the devil in a wheelbarrow, her mother would have said.

Chaos was an unfamiliar element in the life of Molly Robbins, lady's maid. She'd always expected that her epitaph, when she finally went tranquilly to her maker, would read simply, "She caused very little harm." That, indeed, was her plan for the first twenty years or so of her life, but there remained the lingering problem of an imagination that sometimes led her mind off on a meandering path. As a child, she'd been known to go missing for hours, often to be found much later lying on her back in the meadow, counting all the colors she could find in the clouds above.

"For pity's sake, dozy child," her ma would say, impatient and cross. "Clouds are white, and that's all there is to it."

But Molly saw more than white. Not wanting to dismay her mother, she learned to keep that to herself.

Today, outside the carriage window, the clouds were mottled with gray, yellow, pink, and mauve. Occasionally they were heavy with a storm brewing and hung low over the spring-blossoming trees, but if rain fell, she did not hear it. Perhaps the carriage was going too fast, outpacing the raindrops. She slid about, bouncing every so often like a rubber ball, not having enough heft to keep contact with the seat.

And with every bone-shaking jolt, she heard the question again, running through her mind.

Margaret "Molly" Robbins, what have you done?

As one of eleven children born to poor but hard-working parents and a mother who never suffered fools gladly, she'd discovered, early in life, that drawing less attention to oneself was often the best course of action. With her mother's stout and sensible opinions to guide her in those early years, Molly formed the belief that mayhem happened to other people when they daydreamed, drank too much Madeira, or loosened their stays. It was their own fault for not having any self-control. Inhibitions and bosoms, as she witnessed during her time in London as a lady's maid, seldom did credit to their owners when allowed to wander freely. As an adult, strictly holding her own occasional yearning for mischief in check, she maintained moderate enjoyment in the rare glass of fortifying wine, kept prudent guard over her body parts, and never imagined finding herself suddenly at the center of pandemonium.

Until now.

In a slightly dazed state, tossed from left to right as that recklessly driven carriage raced along narrow, uneven country lanes, Molly glanced down at herself and slowly realized she still wore her wedding gown. Such a sad garment it seemed. Impractical, purely decorative, a needless extravagance so her mother would say, if she were there to see it. Perhaps it was a good thing she was not, thought Molly. Fashion was not something her poor mother had known anything about, and Molly became aware of it herself only when befriended by Lady Mercy Danforthe, who taught her that wealthy people of Society, unlike the villagers of

Sydney Dovedale, did not dress themselves merely to stay warm and give the appearance of decency.

Thank goodness Lady Mercy had the foresight to pack her off with a trunk of clothes when she left the village in shameful haste. But then Lady Mercy was always sensible, always practical. In a state of emergency, she was the very best sort of no-nonsense person to have around.

It was a dozen years since Lady Mercy plucked "thin and plain" Molly Robbins up out of that little country village and whisked her off to London as her maid and companion. That was when Molly discovered how her speedy skill with a needle could be combined with her previously curbed creativity. And when those ideas were finally given rein to leap and stretch their legs inside her, the ambition for more in her life—for change—became a voice that refused to be stifled.

"Moll, my girl," her ma used to say, "you've got the neatest, fastest sewing fingers the Good Lord ever gave out."

But her prudent mother never meant for Molly to use those fingers for anything other than practical garments. Nan Robbins would not comprehend the extent of her daughter's secret, thrusting ambition to design elegant clothes for ladies of the *ton*, any more than she understood that clouds could be anything beyond white. But Nan Robbins had died in poverty, having devoted her life to eleven children, many of whom drove her to distraction and probably contributed to the illness that put her in her grave at the age of six and thirty. Molly did not want that for herself. She felt wicked and ungrateful and an unloving daughter to think that way, but it didn't stop her from wanting something different.

"You're a rotten, selfish girl, Robbins," Molly chided, staring at herself in the carriage window.

Despite tears, the face looking back at her was shockingly defiant.

"Don't you care?" she demanded breathlessly. "Are you, after all, such a heartless wench that you let Rafe and many good people down, just to run off and chase a foolish dream? What has got into you?"

Two brown eyes stared back at her, unflinching but wet. The tight lips gave no reply. Perhaps it was not "what" had got into her, but "who."

Who else but Carver Danforthe, the Earl of Everscham, scoundrel of the first order? A seducer, reckless and unbound by any form of self-control.

"I can set you up in that little dressmaking business, Robbins. All you need do is ask," he'd said to her only a few days ago, before she had left London for her wedding in Sydney Dovedale.

Thus the devil threw down that temptation before her like a gauntlet.

How had he known of the ambition she nursed in her heart? She didn't think he ever really paid attention to anyone's desires but his own.

The carriage wheels bumped over a hard rut, and Molly grabbed the leather strap above the door to prevent herself from being tossed out through the carriage window. Clearly the driver had forgotten he had a passenger.

Suddenly she thought of the very first time she rode in a grand carriage like this one, the very first time she left the village of Sydney Dovedale. Back then, at thirteen years of age, she'd had doubts about her decision too, just as she did now. But twelve years ago on that journey, she had Lady Mercy Danforthe chattering away beside her on the plush velvet seat, and the little madam would not have been at all pleased if her new lady's maid suddenly expressed a desire to go home again. The copper-headed, bossy girl was a few years younger than Molly but much older in some ways and always in the right. At least, in her own mind.

"I'm very advanced for my age," had been the diminutive lady's first proud words to Molly, followed by, "You're very thin and plain. You should eat more cake, curl your hair, and never wear brown. People with brown eyes, like yours, should wear bright blues and greens. And don't stoop. You look almost ashamed of yourself just for standing there. At least you have good teeth and elegant hands. You're not completely a lost cause."

Molly had never met anyone quite so self-assured, colorful, and unstoppable. She could not help but admire the bold little girl and wish some of that brazen confidence was her own.

She smiled as the memory came back to her of that first strange journey to London. How young she had been, and how brave she had tried to look. The opinionated young Lady Mercy was not her only companion on that ride to London twelve years ago, for they shared the carriage with Mercy's brother.

Having put aside his usual entertainments to chase his sister into the country and bring her home again, Carver Danforthe, the Earl of Everscham, had not been in the best of moods. Sprawled in his seat, head back as far as it would go, he'd closed his stormy gray eyes and snored rudely, one foot propped up on the seat between the other two passengers. He had long legs, as young Molly had already observed, and no wonder he liked to stretch out on a journey of some distance, but he might at least have apologized for setting his heel down on part of her coat. Even if her coat was shabby and much mended, it did not deserve to be marked by his muddy boot. And even if he was a peer of the realm and terrifyingly beautiful, like a drawing she saw once of a sleek black panther stalking its prey, that gave him no license, in her opinion, for inconsiderate, surly behavior.

The carriage tilted sharply as they rounded a curve at speed, and Molly was momentarily bounced out of her daydream. She glanced at the opposite seat where there was no Carver Danforthe today, but a hatbox and her shattered, wilted bridal bouquet of orange blossoms. For some reason she had not wanted to leave that behind, although it was a silly thing to bring with her and, in her agitation, she'd plucked most of the petals off it.

She turned her head to look out again at the scenery as it flew by in a sun-dappled, colorful print.

Twelve years ago, rattling along this same road, but under a star-peppered, ink-blot sky, she'd worn a tiny posy of pressed flowers pinned to the collar of her coat. Rafe Hartley had given it to her when they said their good-byes. She knew the boy was probably prompted into it by his aunt, but even so, it pleased her that he bothered. On her journey, she had brushed the posy with her fingertips, hoping to release some good luck into the air and boost her spirits.

Molly closed her eyes and sank into the memory again.

She pictured the Earl of Everscham as he was that night, all those years ago, seated across the carriage, letting out a loud snort, gusty enough to disturb a slightly curled lock of ebony hair fallen to his brow. At first glance his eyelids appeared shut, but there was a thin slit of silver between his black lashes, and Molly had suspected he slyly watched her with those scornful eyes. Rafe's aunt, Sophie, had whispered that eyes like those belonged on a circus wild cat—the sort that broke free of their trainer and terrorized the audience until it was recaptured, causing a lurid, illustrated tale in the newspaper the next day. Molly had never seen a wild cat or a circus, but was nevertheless obliged to agree, for she could tell, from the very beginning, that there was a bit of the bloodthirsty and untamable about Carver Danforthe. He wore only an outer shell of civilization the way his footmen—riding on the outside of the carriage—wore their livery. Good thing she was a country girl, grew up around beasts, and wasn't afraid of him.

With a quick tug, she'd tried to move her coat from beneath his muddied heel, but his foot was too heavy. If anything, it seemed as if he pressed his boot down even harder to keep her coat trapped.

Oh, why had she agreed to become Lady Mercy's maid and travel all the way to London in the company of that arrogant, uncivil young man?

For the wage, of course. That was the simple, practical answer. Then came the clothes, the fashion she had just begun to discover with the help of Lady Mercy's enthusiasm. Molly had never seen such luxurious garments as that girl wore, even when she went to bed. She was fascinated by the rich fabrics, the vibrant new dyes and printed patterns. In Sydney Dovedale, folk dressed according to their work and wore their best only on Sundays. But even their "best" was plain.

Molly opened her eyes and looked down at her wedding gown, the finest dress she'd ever owned. She ran her fingers over the soft silk where it rippled onto the seat by her thigh, and she pictured Carver Danforthe's boot heel resting there, as it once did, the heel marking the shabby old coat she wore at the time.

Whenever he moved his foot, it almost touched her leg, but if she spoke and asked him to move it, Molly knew the earl would continue feigning sleep. He did not think her worthy of his attention. She'd heard him warn his sister before they set off, "Don't think I'll have anything to do with this. The country wench is your pet. You can feed her and walk her and make sure she's trained to go outside. This is *your* project. When she chews up your laces and ribbons, don't come crying to me."

Molly had made several attempts to slide her coat free of the earl's foot, but in vain. She could have sworn she caught his lips turning up, an extra gleam shining under his lowered lashes. Quickly she had unpinned Rafe's posy from her collar. The earl had a small hole worn in the toe of his boot. It surprised her when she saw it, for the Danforthes were one of the richest families in England, and he could surely afford a new pair of boots for every day of the week if he wanted them.

She took the pin from her little posy, stuck it through that hole, and jabbed him in the toe.

With a yelp, he sat bolt upright and slammed his foot to the floor of the carriage. He had glared at her with all the wrath of the devil. "You just poked me with a pin."

Young Molly had stared back, unblinking.

"Don't be silly, Carver," Lady Mercy exclaimed with a yawn. "How tiresome you are."

"*Me* tiresome?" he snapped at his sister. "Perhaps you ought to give that tongue a rest. It's hardly stopped since I found you. And bear in mind, the next time you go running off on one of your adventures, don't expect me to come after you again." He folded his arms over his chest. "I shall leave you to your own damn devices."

"Don't say damn in front of Molly Robbins."

"I'll say what I like. This is my carriage, and I'm paying her wage."

His steel-blade eyes slashed back to Molly, but despite his haughty bluster, something in her countenance caused him to move his feet even farther away from her. It took all her willpower not to laugh at his red face. He was wide awake now for sure.

But in her eagerness to prick the young man's foot, Molly had accidentally dropped Rafe's gift, and it was immediately found by another.

"Oh look!" Lady Mercy had cried excitedly. "How pretty. I shall keep it as a souvenir of my country adventure." Never noticing the flowers pinned to Molly's collar earlier, she did not hesitate to claim the decoration for herself.

The carriage bumped and swerved, knocking Molly sideways in her seat, waking the runaway bride from her ponderings again. She gripped the leather strap tighter and stared across the carriage to where Carver Danforthe once sat and accused her of wounding him.

How long ago it was, yet she could see it all as if he was still there with her now.

The young earl had stretched his arms along the back of his seat and observed Molly in a cross and wary manner, as if she might stick that pin in him again, given half the chance.

What on earth would have made him think that?

When she caught her reflection this time in the window, she was smiling, so Molly slid back in the seat rather than witness her own irreverence for which there could be no excuse in light of the awfulness of her situation. She had given up a husband, a home, and a future family, and she was on her way to the devil in his own carriage.

Best stock up on pins.

❦

What was that damnable scratching in the wainscoting?

Carver Danforthe paused, halfway down the stairs to the servants' hall, listening intently for those tiny sounds he could have sworn followed him all over his house. No. Quiet again now.

He stumbled down the remaining steps and looked about for signs of other life. Surely someone should be up, although he actually had no earthly idea what time it was. Usually whenever he came home very late—or very early, depending upon your point of view—he found at least one soul down here, pottering about in the scullery or the kitchen.

But as he stood at the foot of the stairs, looking around, he finally remembered that *she* was gone.

Robbins, his sister's lady's maid, who was often the person he encountered down here so late—or early— had left his household to get married. Of all the bloody ridiculous things for her to do.

He stared at the empty chair by the long table, where he was accustomed to seeing her bent over a patch of mending or fighting with a stubborn stain on one of his sister's gowns. She would look up, put her work aside, and fetch him whatever he wanted. He wouldn't even have to tell her. There was no exchange of words. She just knew what he needed.

Funny, plain little girl. Or woman, as he supposed she was now. It was hard to recall how long she'd been a part of his household. Not exchanging words with him.

Suddenly a door opened, and the well-padded cook waddled in from the larder with a large ham on a tray. When she saw him, there she almost dropped her burden.

"My lord. I did not know you were—you should have rung the bell, sir, and someone would tend to you."

"Ah…yes." *Should have rung the bell, numbskull.* Larkin, his valet, or Richards, the butler, would have come in answer to it. "What time is it, Mrs. Jakes?"

"Why, 'tis just eleven, my lord." She gestured with a nod at the clock on the wall.

"In the morning?" He thought he'd better check. One could never be entirely sure, and he was still dressed in evening clothes.

The stout cook set her tray on the table and smiled indulgently. "Indeed it is, my lord."

Robbins wouldn't have smiled like that, he thought, staring again at her empty chair. She would have given him one of her looks that made him feel thirteen again, instead of three and thirty. Impertinent young woman, really. Jolly good thing she was gone. Her preposterous piety, communicated almost entirely with glances, chafed something chronic. No one other than his father had ever made him feel quite so inadequate. When Robbins made one of her disapproving faces, it read as if she, like his father, hoped to see someone else standing before her and, upon finding him there instead, could only give herself up to resigned disappointment.

"Did you require anything, my lord?" the cook asked.

Yes. But he could no longer remember what it was. Robbins probably would have known, he thought.

How dare she up and leave his household? He was accustomed to her being there. She might be a dreadful prig, but she was steady and dependable.

Odd how that happened—that she became a part of his life when she clearly did not want to be and he didn't want her there either.

The cook, he realized, was still waiting to know what he wanted. Hastily searching for an excuse to be below stairs, he finally muttered, "Have you seen any mice about, Mrs. Jakes?"

"*Mice?*" She paled, her round knuckles hastily gathering bundles of skirt, swiping it aside to check around her feet.

"I thought I heard...no matter. Carry on as you were. Excellent work, Mrs. Jakes." He turned and made his unsteady way back up to the main floor of the house.

Why had he gone down there? Well, if he should remember, he'd ring the bell. As Mrs. Jakes said, someone would tend to him. Didn't matter who it was. Even though one woman was gone, he still had a house full of good servants. He was—whether his father had thought he was the best man for the post or not—the Earl of Everscham. As such, he had everything he could ever want at his disposal. What did the absence of one woman matter?

Cherishing this thought the way a little boy clutches at marbles won against a bitter enemy, Carver Danforthe went to his chamber, dropped to his bed, and jerked the counterpane over his head. Shutting out the sunny April day, he dismissed likewise a fear of sly, swift, brown-eyed creatures hiding in his walls, disapproving of him with a twitch of their tiny pink noses.

Two

Three days later

THE TROUBLE WITH WEARING ONE'S BEST DRAWERS was that nobody else ever got to admire them. As a young woman of frugal sensibilities, that unfortunate fact always grated on Molly's nerves, but there were certain days that required the wearing of elegant underpinnings, even when she was the only soul who knew she wore them—and even though some would consider her "fast" just to be wearing drawers at all.

This was one such day. For Miss Molly Robbins was about to begin a new chapter and hopefully become that rarest of all things: a woman of independent means. Not to put too fine a point upon it, she was about to seize her world by the unmentionables.

Unfortunately, she must first find the courage to walk up a set of grand steps to the pilasters of Danforthe House and pull on that bell cord. Her fancy drawers weren't about to do it for her.

Paused in the street, one hand resting on wrought iron railings, she looked up again, squinting against the rain. Here before her was the elegant Portland stone facade of the house in which she'd lived and worked for just over a dozen years. Within those walls she'd transformed from girl to young woman, emerging like a butterfly from a chrysalis. Perhaps not a butterfly, she reconsidered, more like a dull brown moth. Which was perfectly adequate for her purposes. Not everyone was meant to be a great beauty, and God had given her other talents, which, as her mother had said, would last longer than a pretty face.

Danforthe House looked different today, more forbidding, with dingy, tattered clouds snagged around the chimneys. No sun shone on the windows this morning, and they stared down at her—dark, hollow eyes in a ghostly white face. The master of that house was probably still fast asleep, his cheek stuck to a fat pillow, his mind wallowing in those empty dreams of the rich and idle. But he was in for a surprise. Molly had often thought a few sound shocks might do her former employer some benefit, and she was in a position now to be the purveyor of one such rousing poke in the breeches—another pinprick in his toe. The jaded rake might not be her ideal source of coin, but he was the only one she had. At least, he was the only one from whom she could accept a loan with no danger of him meddling in her spending of it.

Just a week ago he had made his offer, throwing a handful of spice into the bland pudding mixture she stirred with her good intentions.

"Well, Mouse," he'd slurred to her, grabbing a newel post to maintain a semiperpendicular stance as he leaned over her, "ponder my offer and remember—it's your last chance. I'll never make another, and once you're married to that farmer, I shan't be able to help you." He hiccupped, swaying dangerously before her in his fine evening clothes, a lick of dark curl falling over his brow. "The Earl of Everscham never makes propositions to lady's maids, especially those with"—he waved one pointed finger at her nose—"damnably grim faces." Then he turned to the side, tried to take a step up, and missed. They were at the foot of the kitchen stairs, and it was very late. He had come home from an evening at his club and stumbled down to the servants' hall, looking for a glass of cordial water.

How lonely the earl had seemed to her. A lost boy. If she was not there to put her hands on his arm, he would have fallen chin first to the wooden stairs. As she steadied his leaning form, he'd put his gloved hand on her waist—contact that should never have been, after a conversation that should never have taken place. Between master and servant there should always be distance, but in that moment the space was breached, and neither corrected the error.

He had lowered his lips toward her. It was not accidental; she was almost certain.

"Mouse," he'd whispered, staring down at her mouth the way a beggar might stare at a pie shop window. "Do you never smile?"

"Not if it can be helped," she'd replied.

His smoky eyes darkened, and the rugged lines of his face seemed accentuated, sharpened. "Smile at me now, Mouse. I insist. I command."

"I cannot smile at you, my lord."

"Why not?"

"I see nothing amusing to smile at in a grown man who doesn't know his own limits." Since she was leaving his house the next day to be married, Molly had seen no detriment to expressing her opinion. There might even be some worth in it, if he actually paid heed to her words, she thought.

A quizzical line had formed across his brow. He bent over her, one hand still claiming her waist with surprising steadiness for one in his cups.

"Mouse," he said again.

"Yes, my lord?" She'd thought, for one awful moment, that he would ask for something else she could not give. Preparing herself to let him down— possibly the first and only woman ever to do so—she was saved the trouble when he said simply, "Do tell Larkin to make sure he tends my new boots with linseed oil." Hiccup. "They squeak dreadfully."

The spell was broken. Apparently looking at her had reminded the man of his boots.

She could still feel the fine cloth of the earl's sleeve sliding beneath her palm as she'd let her hand linger on his arm. Could still remember the warmth of his flexing muscle.

Squeaking boots indeed!

He was a rake and a cad, tempting her with an offer she should have declined at once. Instead, here she was, having raced back to the wretched man.

Mouse, indeed! She'd teach him a thing or two about mice.

Unfortunately, there were very few things in life that Danforthe took seriously, and he may already have forgotten the promise he made in one of his capricious moods, when he was most certainly in liquor.

But Molly Robbins, sober and strong willed, had not forgotten.

That determined spirit growing inside would not allow her to ignore this chance. Although it should have been housed inside a man, seven foot tall with the shoulders of a prize seed ox, a most obstinate force lived in her lean frame and had suddenly decided to cause a vast deal of havoc, pushing her to be bold. There was nothing she could do about it now; the damage was done. One man was jilted at the altar, an entire village left to gossip about her, and her best friend, Lady Mercy Danforthe, thought she'd discarded her wits as well as her groom. If this plan fell through, she may as well throw herself off Tower Bridge and just hope she didn't float like a cork, which is what happened to witches, according to her brothers, who insisted she was one just because she always knew what they were thinking. As if that should be hard to discern. Men's minds were sheer gauze and just as impractical to make anything out of.

Well, this was it. Once again she'd come too far to go back now. Best get it over with.

About to take her first step up, she stopped again. No good. She simply couldn't bring herself to use the entrance of the house, where the family and other important folk came and went. Instead, she spun around, ran back along the pavement, and dashed down the other, more familiar set of steps used by delivery men and milkmaids.

❧

Slowly and with ominous smugness, like water dripping through a crack in the ceiling, unavoidable morning made itself felt and heard. The valet's voice— which had probably been talking for some time before

Carver became conscious of it—informed him of three things. It was ten o'clock, it was raining, and a young woman waited below for an appointment she seemed to think she had with the Earl of Everscham.

Carver cracked open one eye. "Young woman?"

He tried to think if he'd made any rash promises last night. It wouldn't be the first time he woke to the discovery of a stray female in his proximity—one whose name, had he ever known it, escaped him, and whose face was only distantly familiar.

"It is, I believe, my lord, Miss Robbins."

"Who?" He raised his head from the drool-dampened pillow.

"The Lady Mercy's former maid."

Blinking slowly, he tried to clear the haze that currently blurred his sight. Hadn't his sister's maid just left to be married?

Scraping fingertips leisurely over his rough cheek, he waited for the room to cease spinning, his thoughts to steady likewise. A heavy ache in his skull and the fact that he was still partially dressed in last night's clothes would usually be reason enough to lower his head back to the pillow for a few more hours. Ten o'clock was an unearthly hour to be woken. But as his face prepared to meet the comfort of goose down again, his head suddenly jerked back. "*Robbins?* Are you quite sure?"

"Yes, my lord. She still goes by the name, so I would assume the marriage did not take place. Miss Robbins arrived here alone, in the carriage that previously took Lady Mercy into the country, but she was observed hovering outside the house for some time before she came to the door."

His mind began to slot the pieces together, working sluggishly.

So the little Mouse was back. Aha! He knew that wedding would never go off. He'd warned his sister before she left for the country four days ago.

"I wouldn't be at all shocked if Robbins called off this wedding at the last minute. If she has any wits about her, she would."

But Carver's smug pleasure at being proven right in this instance was short-lived, crowded out as the last pieces came together in his head and presented the full picture.

"Bloody hell," he exhaled lavishly.

If the Mouse was downstairs waiting to see him, it could mean only that spur-of-the-moment suggestion he'd teasingly tossed her way was actually accepted as a solid offer. But surely she knew he wasn't the sort to be taken with any degree of sincerity. She'd worked there long enough to know his personality by now, and there wasn't much more he could do to discourage any good opinion of him. He still vividly recalled the incident when she had walked up to him in the hall and silently handed over two ladies' slippers she'd recovered from a privet bush in the walled garden behind the house. She hadn't said a word, just held them out for him, as if she knew it must be his fault and no one else's.

Rain threw itself at his window now, like diamonds pelted by an angry, abandoned mistress. Carver felt the intense urge to curl up in bed again, shutting out the day and with it any unpleasantness he might otherwise be obliged to face. Alas, the moment he laid his head down again and shut his eyes, he'd see *her* small, frowning face with pinched lips, mutely confronting him. A quiet creature with a gloomy disposition, Robbins need apply only one very subtle tightening of the mouth to convey an entire barrage of sheer disgust at his behavior without a single word exhaled. As a boy, he'd endured nannies with less stern power in their stout bodies than whip-slender young Robbins had in the tiniest change of expression.

There was nothing else for it. The day and the Mouse must be faced. And his own stupidity explained away on drink, mischief, and...well, he was Carver Danforthe. Surely that was reason enough. It usually was for most people.

❦

Having cast an unhappy gaze up and down her bedraggled length, the butler intoned somberly, "The earl is indisposed today, Robbins. You should have sent a note first and waited for a summons. Especially in this weather. What could you be thinking to traipse about in it?"

"I could not delay my visit another day, Mr. Richards. Life goes on whether it rains or not. You must excuse me, but I will wait here until his lordship's lazy posterior is up and out of bed."

The butler's nostrils widened, and that haughty nose tipped so far back that she feared being sucked up by his horrified inhale. "I did not say he was still abed, Robbins."

"I know what you said, Mr. Richards. I have two good ears and very shrewd powers of deduction."

The earl must be suffering the effects of a long night of carousing. Even on the best of days, he was seldom out of bed before noon, but she couldn't risk the fellow leaving his house again before she caught him, so she was early. Better that than too late. Carver Danforthe could be a slippery creature when he wished to avoid a person, but he certainly wouldn't slip by her today.

She dropped her backside—secretly clad in those emboldening fancy drawers—to the old bench by the fire and warmed her boots in the heat. "Unless you feel inclined to lift me up bodily and throw me out into the pouring rain, you'll have to tell his lordship I'm here, won't you, Mr. Richards?" She took a kerchief from her reticule and blew her nose soundly. "I daresay Lady Mercy won't be too cross to hear how you forced me back out into this foul weather."

Eventually one of the kitchen maids, risking the butler's displeasure but on the cook's urging, brought her a cup of tea. After a wait of forty-five minutes and two more cups of tea, she was taken upstairs, marched across the hall, and shown into the earl's library.

"Mind your manners," the butler muttered before closing the door behind her. It was as if he had to say something to put Molly in her place, but he wasn't really certain what her place must be anymore. She barely knew herself.

Mind *her* manners? She was not the one who kept a person waiting this long. At least she was dry now—almost—and those cups of tea would keep her stomach from grumbling in the presence of the almighty Lord Sloth, Earl of Lazybones.

She looked across the room. A fire in the grate provided a wavering, bronze glow to one area of the library, but had evidently not been ignited long enough to completely chase away the damp chill. The curtains were only half-open, allowing a thin, lackluster shaft of foggy light to trickle across the blotter on his desk. But the man himself sat back, hiding his face in a shroud of darkness. A cup of tea waited before him, untouched, and she could just make out his hands spread upon the blotter, the ring on his little finger winking at her in the flickering shadows.

Molly waited, listening to the steady patter of raindrops on glass and the quickening sizzle of coal in his fire. Apparently he was not going to speak. Had they propped him up in his chair while he still slept? Time to find out.

She gave a bob curtsy.

"I've come to accept your proposition, my lord." She felt the air change and heard his long legs fidget under the desk.

Sakes! Movement! And it was not quite eleven. Should *The Times* be notified?

"I would like to take you up on the offer of a loan." Reaching into her reticule, she withdrew two folded squares of paper. Rain had smudged some of the ink, but the words were still readable. She'd worked on them while the carriage stopped at the Barley Mow on the road back to London. Now she placed both on the blotter for his perusal.

"What's this?" he demanded gruffly.

Molly sneezed into her handkerchief. "As you suggested that night by the stairs in the kitchen, I have written a letter of agreement and calculated interest to be returned to you with the principle—" She snapped her lips shut while his opened in a long yawn. His fingers finally stretched, moving like large, slow centipedes toward the paper she'd laid before him.

"I've got eyes to read for myself," he grumbled.

Only if they stayed open long enough, she mused.

But Molly kept that thought to herself. She was still getting accustomed to the sound of her own voice in places where it was never formerly allowed to venture out, and it seemed especially loud and dreadful in his library. This was his sanctuary, a masculine place devoid of pretty, whimsical ornament, and imbued with a sense of rough-edged, stubborn contentment, as if to say that here he did as he pleased—truly as he pleased—and no one could force their way in to tidy or decorate it or rearrange a single piece of furniture. It was, she realized, the only main-floor room in the house that was not formally laid out, spotlessly clean, and prepared for guests to admire first, people to live in second. This was the only room he might call his, away from his sister's influence. Apart, of course, from his bedchamber. Whatever that might look like.

As the silence lengthened, she began to wonder if the earl had fallen asleep in his chair. Finally he creaked forward into the slender beam of pale, shimmering light, and his starless midnight gaze took her in slowly. Like his library, the earl's eyes had yet to know warmth this morning. One moment they were steel gray, and the next, black as pitch. Fortunately, Molly was not the superstitious sort, or she might have thought it was some special and terrifying magic from within that made them change color. But he was just a man with shortcomings like any other, not a frightening, mythical ogre. No matter how he managed to convince certain folk otherwise. Or what he believed of himself.

She once heard a young lady of questionable sense and evident moral turpitude giggling breathlessly about him. "Carver Danforthe is very, very bad, and when he's not wicked, he's awful."

It was a reputation he apparently enjoyed maintaining.

Now those cold eyes turned to the paper. Whether or not he read the words inked upon it, she couldn't tell. He was very still. Unlike her, he had no need to follow the words with his finger, but she supposed it would not say much for a university education if he did.

Rain blew hard at his window, reedy shadows casting a mottled, ever-changing pattern over his bent head. His dark hair stood on end, as if not even fingers had combed through it yet. She wondered what would happen if she straightened that hair for him, but since this thought led to a very unnecessary warmth under her skin, it was dismissed at once.

Molly refused to be distracted from her purpose by lusty thoughts. This was a practical matter, and she could afford no more pangs of mortifying, misplaced partiality for a man to whom she was merely a "mouse."

Sorely tempted fingers clasped tight around her reticule, she took a quick survey of his library. A plate, perched precariously on one corner of his desk, held remnants of a pork piecrust and a brown apple core. A half-empty wine glass stood near with two drowned flies floating in it. She'd already noted his hat and scarf left in a chair by the hearth, and several lumps of mud on the carpet where he must not have scraped his boots properly before he staggered in the night before. One glove had been abandoned on the mantel, above the poker he must have used to stir up the fire when he came in. It was a savage, ill-tempered stirring too, from the amount of coal and ash spilled haphazardly over the grate and across the hearth tiles.

Crumpled pages of a newspaper lay on the carpet by his desk, as if tossed aside in frustration. A waistcoat, discarded here for some reason instead of his dressing room, hung over the winged back of the chair in which he sat. Molly tried to imagine the circumstances that might cause a gentleman to unbutton his waistcoat and shrug out of it before he even went upstairs to bed. But then she decided it had better be none of her business.

Although it was she who invaded *his* private, intimate place, Molly was now the one surrounded and in danger of breathing too much of it in. Too much of him in. The heady essence of a seductive brute. It was somehow even worse, she realized, when he was in repose, not even trying.

Just like now, for instance, as he bent over his desk, and that dark lock of unbrushed hair tumbled carelessly over his brow.

"What are you looking at, Mouse?" He spoke without glancing up from his desk. "Lady Mercy would be appalled by my untidy habits, would she not?"

"You do seem to be taking advantage of your sister's absence, my lord. A dust rag and a broom would not go amiss."

He sniffed, still studying the contract, his wide, strong shoulders hunched forward over the desk.

"But what you do and the state of your library is not my concern," she added. "All I want from you"— she took a deep breath—"is the coin."

Now he looked up, fixing her in a stare that was potent, definitely heated this time. It almost drained the strength out of her knees. "A remarkably mercenary attitude, Mouse."

"Yes, my lord." She sighed. "I would feel ashamed of it, if I could afford the sentiment."

Three

She wasn't the first woman to want him for the money, of course, but she was the first to admit that was *all* she wanted. It was refreshingly honest, actually.

Carver was amused, and that seldom happened so early in his day.

The Mouse had drunk in every joking word he'd said and drawn up a contract in workmanlike fashion, also producing a copy so they could both keep one. Several misspellings and some odd punctuation, he noted, but for a country girl with no formal education, she had a neat hand. Obviously she picked things up as she went along, absorbed them quickly, and was determined to lift herself up out of the sphere in which she was born, even to the extent of abandoning her own wedding.

"Most women of your age and in your position," he pointed out, "want a husband to make fat and miserable, and a litter of screaming, snot-nosed brats to herd about."

"Then clearly I'm not *most women*, my lord. With your financial assistance, I won't have to be."

She drooped—yes, drooped, no other word for it—before him in a weather-beaten hat and coat, her small face solemn as an undertaker. But the eyes were large and bright, full of more hope than he'd ever felt directed at him before.

"You'll amount to naught, boy," he could still hear his father hissing in his ear. *"It is my greatest regret that I must leave this estate in your hands, but such is God's punishment for me."*

That was when he was expelled from boarding school for fighting. The second time. His father never wanted to know why the fights happened. His only concern was that Carver had an unpredictable side, a temper he could not hold, and he did not seem to have much respect for rules or punishment.

"That school was supposed to turn you into a gentleman!"

To which ten year-old Carver had replied, *"But nobody asked me whether I want to be a gentleman. I'd rather be a blacksmith or a carpenter. At least they make things."*

As the blows came down around his ears, his father shouted until he was hoarse. *"You will bring shame to this family. I might have known, but what choice do I have? Worthless boy! Good-for-naught!"*

He heard that name so often it ceased to hurt. Yet this plain wisp of a girl, who looked as if a strong gust of air might shatter her bones and leave naught but a pair of boots and a crumpled frock on his carpet, regarded him with something new. With hope.

She sneezed again, loudly. Although she quickly buried her face in an oversized kerchief, it was too late to catch the fine mist that shot out of her and into the air of his library. Carver winced, leaning farther back in his chair.

"I know most folk—my own family, for instance— will say I'm getting above my place," she mumbled

into her handkerchief, "but I can't help thinking that
life should move forward, my lord, not lie stagnant.
Isn't progress the very essence of being alive?"

She must have picked that up somewhere on a
seditious pamphlet. "Perhaps I should be more diligent
about the reading matter allowed inside my house,"
he muttered. "Servants who learn to read have done
themselves a disservice. It will end only in discord,
because it puts ideas in their heads, and they can no
longer be trusted not to pry into their master's business." It was something his father would say, and it
came out of him like anything else learned by rote—a
conjugated Latin verb or a mathematical formula.

"Rest assured, I wouldn't want to pry into *your*
business," she replied tartly. "As for ideas—my own
are plentiful. Believe it or not, they occur to me
without being put there by some man." Pausing for
another fretful sigh, she added, "I often wish they did
not. I wish I could be ignorant and oblivious of things.
Like the colors in clouds."

"Clouds?" He was trying to follow but had
briefly become lost in the dewy, shimmering depths
of her eyes.

"It is quite a burden for a poor, lowly but honest
girl like me to have any thoughts at all, especially when
they do not coincide with the ideas of other folk."

Carver studied her somber face. Her countenance
was calm, but there was a lot going on beneath that
placid surface. He'd never heard her speak much before
this, and now she was, he suspected, testing her new
boundaries, kicking up the grass like a filly released
from its bridle and let out in the paddock to run. Yes,
a long-legged pony. She was tall for a woman. The

length of her bones had outgrown her clothes and outpaced her ability to put much flesh upon them. It was one of the first things he'd ever noticed about Molly Robbins, because it made him nervous to think she might eventually grow tall enough to look him directly in the eye. Who knew what parts of him she could one day reach to prick with her sly pins?

He pressed his aching head into the chair back, lifted her contract with one hand, and glanced over it again in the light from his window. Surely she'd underestimated the costs.

"Two hundred pounds will not get you far," he muttered, although he really had no idea how much a dressmaker charged for her services. If his mistress desired new clothes, he told her to charge it to his account, and then the matter was taken care of by Edward Hobbs, who handled all such affairs. In fact, Carver didn't really know what anything cost, except for a good racehorse. Since there was little the Danforthe coffers couldn't afford, prices were mostly moot.

"I did not want to ask for more than I could pay back in a reasonable amount of time," she replied. "The sum I request from you is just enough to help with rent and materials until I am established. If I asked for more, you might expect something in return, and I have my virtue to consider."

He almost dropped the contract. "Your virtue?"

"That's right, my lord. I don't suppose you come across one often, but I'd like to keep mine unbesmirched."

A sudden ripple of laughter threatened his stern composure, but somehow he thwarted its determined progress up his throat and returned his gaze to the contract, where his attention was caught by a line of words, thickly underscored in the last clause. "What's this?" he demanded.

"No Tomfoolery, my lord. You needn't try to seduce me. Ours will be a business arrangement and nothing more. In light of your reputation, I thought I'd better put that in, so there could be no misunder—"

"Hush, woman!"

The threat of laughter successfully vanquished now, Carver scowled at the paper and felt that throbbing ache pounding in his temple with renewed force. For this he got out of bed? He ought to toss her damnable contract into the fire, send her away with a few stern words about never darkening his doorstep again, and then go back to his warm and cozy bed. When he looked up once more, the sanctimonious wench was suddenly at the side of his desk, closer than before. She'd moved with such stealth that when he saw her suddenly in a new place, his pulse quickened. It was as if he'd just found a spider on his blotter.

"I think you'll find it all quite in order, my lord."

No Tomfoolery, indeed! As if *he* might be tempted by her—his sister's former servant, and a dull, scrawny bag of bones into the bargain! Carver had his pick of society beauties and certainly would never choose a melancholy creature, adaptable to dark corners, and in possession of a sinister ability to move from one spot to another without sound. Carver preferred noisy, colorful women who were too loud to creep up on him and take him by surprise, too shallow to require more than a few expensive presents to keep them content. Spinsters with iron petticoats were of no interest to him.

Why, he wondered suddenly, had he ever suggested

he might loan this Mouse money? He didn't even know how he'd learned about her aspirations of starting a business. Surprising what he picked up around his own house, like lint.

"Didn't I pay you enough when you were my sister's lady's maid?" he muttered. "You ought to have some savings, surely."

"Much of what I earned went home to my family in Sydney Dovedale," she replied, looking down at her hands where they clasped around her reticule. "I saved a little, on Lady Mercy's urging, but there was always something at home to be paid for."

He knew she came from a very large family where the children were all sent out to work as soon as possible. Molly's wage, so his sister told him once, was greatly relied upon by a sick mother after the father was killed—run over by a speeding carriage one evening as he stumbled home from the local tavern. Carver seldom listened to his sister's gossip, but whenever she spoke to him about her lady's maid it sank in. Probably, he mused, because Molly Robbins was such a mysterious creature and would never volunteer information about herself. Neither could he let anyone see him interested enough to inquire. Yet he felt as if he needed to amass these little pieces of knowledge about her, merely to prepare himself.

For what he had no idea. Possibly against another attack upon his person.

"If you no longer wish to loan me the money, my lord, I'll understand, of course. If you don't feel up to the risk of investment. If, when you made the offer that evening, you thought to get something from me that I am not prepared to give. Or if you have lost your courage." She pressed her lips together. They were well-shaped, softly—one might even say invitingly—curved when she allowed them to relax. But it was as if she was afraid of what they might say or do when given too much freedom, so she kept them under close guard. "I wouldn't want to impose upon you. I daresay there are other places for a girl to find investors in this town."

"Indeed. Now you've dragged me out of bed at this unholy hour just to be impertinent to my face, I suppose you can be content, traipse back out again, and sully my name to all and sundry."

She continued somberly, "Since I am no longer employed here, I am not your responsibility, and you have no obligation toward my welfare."

"Quite. Let the rejoicing commence."

"I ask only that"—she paused for a quick sneeze—"should the peelers return my drowned body here to Danforthe House, you take pity on me and don't tell my brothers that I was driven, out of desperation, to end my own life."

"Wait, do I hear violins?"

"I wouldn't want to be buried outside the church wall with the sinners and those unbaptized. For then I might have to come back and haunt…somebody."

She already did, he mused, thinking of the scratching inside his wainscoting. But she didn't hide from him today. She'd stepped out of the shadows to get his attention. Her bonnet he vaguely recognized now as one that previously belonged to his sister. Molly Robbins must have altered it slightly, taken away some of the decoration and restyled it to fit her less flamboyant personality. Her cheeks were thinner than his sister's, the skin a little darker. Dimples, pouts, and fluttery lashes had no place on Miss Robbins's face. There was no artifice, such as he often detected painting the features of his mistress. Molly didn't need anything of that sort; hers was an honest face, unwavering, composed, fearless.

Carver watched her thoughtfully. Perhaps she was not so very plain after all. Or perhaps he had simply never observed her closely enough.

"Is there something amiss?" she inquired, very polite. This slender girl, sneezing all over his library, dampening his air with her germs, had the gall to ask if there was anything wrong with *him*. "You look a trifle pale, my lord."

He stabbed a finger at the *No Tomfoolery* clause in her contract. "This won't be necessary."

"I'd like it there all the same. Just to be sure." Bloody woman didn't even blink.

"Well, it's your ink wasted." He smirked. "Mouse."

"Better be safe than sorry, my lord. Like I said, if you don't feel up to it. If you prefer that I seek funds elsewhere, from some other gentleman who—"

"Hush, woman!"

He would never hear the last of it from his sister if he turned Robbins away from his door, and to be perfectly honest, he didn't like the idea of her going to others for assistance. He supposed this strange pinch of anxiety might have something to do with being dragged up and out of his own bed so blasted early, but he could not allow her to go to anyone else. Not with those wise-beyond-their-years brown eyes and lips that grew bolder by the minute.

Grabbing his pen, he scrawled an angry signature across the bottom of both copies, ending with a hard press to the last upward swing of the "m" in Everscham. A fat blot of ink blossomed on the paper— almost, much to his embarrassment, in the shape of a heart—and then he dropped the quill back into the ink well.

"You have somewhere to live?" he demanded gruffly.

"I will find lodgings, my lord."

Carver picked up his letter opener and tapped it on the desk, watching as she signed her name to the papers beside his own unwieldy blots. "My solicitor, Edward Hobbs, can be of assistance with that. Seek him out in his offices. Bishopsgate. My carriage can take you there this morning. I will write you a note to give him."

"Thank you, my lord. That is most kind."

Kind? Humph. "Well, I wouldn't know about that," he muttered. He was merely thinking he should know where she went in case any of the silver was later discovered missing and he needed to track her down. That, he assured himself briskly, was the only reason why he bothered to involve Hobbs.

He glanced at her neat signature. Margaret "Molly" Robbins might masquerade as a mouse, but her only similarities to such a creature were speed and hunger. While stealing cheese from the kitchen, she would never be crushed under the cook's feet or flattened by a rolling pin. She certainly knew what she was doing when she bearded him in his lair so early in the day and before he was properly awake.

The contract completed, she flashed her dark, spirited eyes back up at him, and he got the distinct impression she was celebrating. Slyly.

He'd have to correct her about something. Anything to restore order. After searching for several moments, Carver found a point to make. "Oh, and Robbins, since you are no longer my servant, the correct address is *your lordship*, not *my lord*. Try to remember the distinction."

"Yes, my—your lordship."

No longer his servant. The words echoed inside his skull. "Good gracious, Robbins, is that a smile I see attempting to meander across your prim lips with the stealth and ease of a leprous cripple?"

"No, your lordship. It was an exhale of relief."

"Relief?"

"Since you are infamously all bluster and breeches, I thought you might claim that you were in your cups before, and that you didn't mean what you said when you offered me a loan. That you were merely being mischievous, tempting me to abandon my wedding plans just to see if I would. Fancy me having such doubts that you would keep to your word! You, the Earl of Everscham. Of course you would not let me down."

Her steady gaze reached right inside his head and, like a thief in the night, turned everything upside down and rifled through it. For all her upright manners, Molly Robbins secretly nurtured the steely temperament and cunning demeanor of a grave robber. But just when he thought she might smile at last, there went the familiar tightening of her damned lips, denying any sign of it. Wretched, self-righteous creature. Cluttering up his library with her...her scornfulness. Forcing him out of bed at a decent hour.

Carver Danforthe suspected he'd signed away far more than two hundred pounds. Perhaps even a few body parts. Now she was leaving his household, just when he'd begun to realize that Molly Robbins might be a creature of some wit and worth keeping around.

She'd even talked Carver into paying her for leaving him.

So much for her "honest" face. It was, he thought—with the peevish anger of a man newly and reluctantly awakened to the fact that he'd been bested by a woman—as honest as it was plain.

Four

ANXIOUS TO KNOW WHY HIS SISTER HAD NOT returned to London with Molly Robbins, Carver wrote immediately to the Hartleys, with whom she would stay while in the country. She had known the Hartleys as long as she'd known Molly, and since they were the parents of the jilted groom, they should know everything that had happened. He did not wish to ask the runaway bride more than he had already, and she was reticent with her answers, as if it was none of his business when, of course, it was very much his business. Not only was this abandoned wedding connected to a former member of his household staff, but Molly Robbins was also his sister's closest friend and confidant. Perhaps the most important fact was that the groom, Rafe Hartley, was once married—for three hours—to Carver's sister.

Fortunately he was able to get the marriage annulled, as both Mercy and Rafe were too young, and neither had permission to marry. But Carver now worried that his sister's heart was not quite as free of the matter as she'd let him believe. He'd allowed her to attend Rafe and Molly's wedding in Sydney Dovedale because she was now engaged to another, and he thought she was old enough not to make another mistake of that nature. Edward Hobbs, the Danforthe family solicitor, and the only other soul who knew about Mercy's past elopement with Rafe Hartley, had suggested someone ought to travel with her into the country.

"My sister can look after herself," Carver had replied to the solicitor's quiet concern.

Perhaps, he thought now, chagrinned, he had misjudged both the situation and his sister, but he *had* been right about Molly Robbins. He'd warned his sister that Robbins could not be happy with marriage to a country farmer. Curious, but it seemed as if he understood the workings of that maid's mind more than he knew the thoughts of his own sister. From that first scowl, that first stab with a pin, Molly Robbins had told him where she stood and what she thought of his nonsense. She apparently never felt the need to lie to him or flatter with false words of admiration. She was a unique presence in his life.

He had not realized how unique until the day she left his house.

❧

"You've done *what?*" His friend Sinjun Rothespur, Earl of Saxonby, was incredulous and already slightly drunk. Swaying in his chair, he demanded Carver repeat what he'd just said. "My ears must be playing tricks upon me."

"I have loaned money to my sister's maid to start a business." He paused to let the words land and settle this time, but it was still no earthly good. They continued to make less and less sense the more often he uttered them. He had not meant to speak a word of it to anyone, yet here he was spilling the secret to his oldest friend. It could not be contained any longer. Carver downed another gulp of brandy and fell back into the warm embrace of a leather chair. "Dressmaking. Apparently she's very talented."

"Talented, eh?" Sinjun chuckled drowsily and winked. "So this is the maid who ran away from her own wedding. Now I see!"

"No, you do not see. It's not like that." Rolling his head against the dimpled chair back, he tried to get his thoughts in order. "It's not like that at all. Absolutely not. She's a grim creature, dull and drear. But I'm assured she has a very neat stitch and a good eye for design."

Who had told him that, he wondered. His sister? The Mouse herself perhaps, although it seemed unlikely. She was not the boasting sort. He kept seeing her unfolding the contract and placing it before him— her clause "No Tomfoolery" underlined in thick ink. Except she'd misspelled the word as Tomfollerie. Had he been more awake when she brought that contract to him, he would have teased her and asked who the devil Tom Follerie was. But hers had been a surprise attack and, of course, even misspelled, her disapproval of his varied activities with the ladies could not be mistaken for anything else.

"She's ambitious," he muttered. "Dedicated. Quite determined."

"*What*?" His friend sputtered with amusement. "But she's a woman. I've never heard you speak so admirably of the enemy."

"Nonsense." Attempting to hoist himself more

upright in his chair, he found it too much work and slipped down again, even farther. "I give credit where 'tis due. And she is far from a usual woman."

Life should move forward, my lord, not lie stagnant. Isn't progress the very essence of being alive? Her snuffled question had stayed with him as if imprinted on his mind, along with the unwanted Mr. Tom Follerie. She was right, of course. One must move in order to live.

He thought then of his father, who had given up on moving forward and on life. A once vital man, he wasted away only a few years after their mother's death. His sister liked to think their father died of a broken heart, but Carver recalled it differently. Their father was a selfish man who had no patience for sickness or frailty, not even his own. Forced to end his days in a wheelchair, he spent his last few years staring out of a window, shouting at everyone because he was miserable and wretched, angry at his lost youth, frustrated with an aging body that let him down daily. He saw no point in life anymore if he could only watch it happen around him. So he'd commanded that everything inside the country house remain exactly as it was when his wife died. Nothing was allowed to change. From that day, the Everscham Sussex estate was sealed in time. All very dramatic and befitting one of those romantic novels his sister liked to read, but it was truly their father's own youth he mourned, as much as—perhaps more than—the loss of his wife.

Carver had spent twenty years in that house on the Sussex estate, struggling for his stern father's approval, and almost as many years hoping for his busy, glamorous mother's attention. She'd barely looked at him. He knew an older brother, a precious firstborn son—doted upon by both parents—had died suddenly in childhood, so Carver grew up with the knowledge that he was the heir by tragic default. Anxious for paternal approval, he'd struggled to measure his own feet to his father's steps, but there was always a barrier in his way, an invisible wall between them that prevented any affection showing through. The old earl believed in raising his remaining son with the help of a stern rod. Nothing Carver did was ever quite good enough to escape the swing of that cane, and after a while, he gave up trying so hard. By the time his father died, Carver had given up altogether, accepting his role as a disappointment, the default son and heir. The whipping boy.

When he came into his title on the death of their father, he left the estate and purchased the London house, making it his primary residence even out of Season. He now returned to the country for brief visits, mostly to the horse stud farm in which he had the most interest, but he was never comfortable at that grand estate, for it felt as if his father's spirit roamed the extensive corridors, still ready to faintly disapprove of anything Carver said or did. Still mourning for the favored son.

Now he considered his preference for Town and realized that after his father's death he'd gravitated toward life—activities, people, and noise. Here in London, things changed, moved forward, and he—shocking as it might be—liked that. Did it make him a revolutionary? Heaven Forbid. He could hear his father's bones grinding as he turned in his grave.

Carver had begun to look at things differently. He was restless.

"The world is moving," he mused aloud to Sinjun, "and we must too, or be left behind."

"Zounds! Next thing we know, you'll actually be taking up your seat in the House of Lords, and not just on those occasions when you need somewhere to sleep undisturbed for a few hours."

"I must ask you to desist, Rothespur, before my breeches split from the hilarity."

"When I heard about parliament burning down last autumn, I imagined they'd find you, the sleeping culprit, spread out on a bench, charred to a crisp with the remnants of a cigar in your mouth."

"And I'm sure you got out the mourning black."

"No. I would have celebrated in your honor, old chap. I know how you despised the place. I've heard you, more than once, declare the House of Lords in need of fireworks to wake it up. Naturally, I thought you'd finally done something about it."

Carver smirked into his brandy. "You know me better than that, Rothespur. I'm all bluster and breeches, according to some. Never get anything done."

"True," his friend replied amiably. "But now you've invested in this business venture, I hope you realize you'll get all sorts begging at your door for similar assistance. The Everscham Benevolent Fund for Runaway Brides."

Carver was barely listening, too intrigued by thoughts of one particular runaway bride. What did one do with a woman who made it clear from the start that he needn't try flirting with her?

"I suppose she might be a useful acquisition," Sinjun exclaimed. "Your own personal dressmaker for the women always in and out of your life, someone to discreetly mend ravaged frocks. I'm sure there's no other fellow who can lay claim to a tame *modiste* at their disposal, all hours of the day…and night."

Clearly, despite protests to the contrary, Sinjun still thought there was more to this than a business investment. Perhaps there was.

Raising his glass to the candlelight, Carver thoughtfully observed the gleaming amber twinkle through the cut crystal. This was a rare, fine brandy. He'd thought it bitter at first, but the taste mellowed going down and lit a glowing warmth in his gut. The brandy's effects had crept up on him. Like she did.

"One thing is certain," he muttered, "if I want that loan repaid, she'd better find some customers." Of course, two hundred pounds was not a great loss. He'd forfeited more than that in one night of wagers at White's. Truth be told, he was concerned about the country mouse. She was thin enough already, and lack of regular meals would do her no good whatsoever. He also suspected she was too proud to admit herself in the wrong and return to Sydney Dovedale. There was a wild spark in her. He'd seen and felt it. An animal snared in a cruel trap would try to bite off its own leg to escape, and there was something of that same savage determination inside Molly Robbins. Carver recognized the flame that burned strongly inside her. He felt that warmth when she looked at him and tried not to smile.

Fate had put her in his way, as if he, the "good-fornaught," could actually be of some use.

Hope.

He looked at his glass again, slightly bemused. Was it brandy that made him think this way?

Or was it the Mouse?

When Lady Mercy Danforthe first offered to make her a companion and lady's maid, Molly had never traveled more than a few miles beyond the village of Sydney Dovedale. A wide-eyed girl, prone to bouts of muteness, she'd arrived in the great metropolis with her new mistress at her side to point out all the attractions and hazards of Town. It was the noise that hit her first. The crisp clatter of countless iron-ringed pattens in the street, the seemingly endless charge of horses and carriages, the sing-song of tradesmen and flower sellers, church bells ringing out in every corner of the place. Eventually she grew accustomed to it, and then the quiet of her old village, whenever she returned to visit her family, became the stranger of the two.

All these years later, returning to London for a new adventure, she did not have Lady Mercy to lead the way or "guide" her in that indomitable fashion. This time Molly was on her own, but she was not afraid. She might be a woman of little consequence and no beauty, but her bones—however thin—were hardy, and she'd been told she had a quick mind. Now she was a moving part of the finest metropolis in the world, a little cog in the great mechanism of London. The place where all classes of life bubbled and brewed together, where there were folk she would never meet if she'd stayed in Sydney Dovedale. She was no longer just a person to whom things happened; she made the happenings for herself.

Her hopes, in those first days, were high indeed.

The rooms she leased with Mr. Edward Hobbs's assistance were small and damp, leaning so close to the next house that by reaching through her small side window she might shake hands with her neighbor—if she could bear to open the shutters and suffer the foul odors that rose from the alley beneath. A second dormer window peeked out through the slate roof and overlooked the street, where the smells were not exactly sweet either, but certainly more tolerable and often fast moving, as opposed to the stagnant air of the side alley. Through this window the lively sounds of the town churned away, from the first song of a street vendor to the last call of the night watchman on his rounds. An elderly lady sold salop from her still on the pavement outside, and she was often there from the late to the early hours, providing her drink for its restorative qualities to those suffering the bad effects of too much liquor, as well as for sober customers in need of a morning jolt of vigor before they went about the business of the day. With so much life going on in the street outside at all hours, Molly never had the chance to feel lonely.

She spent hours at her window, watching the people pass, assessing their garments with a quick eye. Often she could imagine the entire life of a woman walking by just from the cut of her coat or the decoration in her bonnet. She saw no one as well dressed as Lady Mercy, her former mistress, but witnessed quite a few ladies rather overdressed and definitely overpainted. Few people Molly had ever seen used color and pattern as eagerly or with as much confidence as Lady Mercy, whose love of fashion had introduced a whole new world to Molly when she was a young girl handed her first copy of *La Belle Assemblee*.

One morning, while seated at her window with

a small breakfast of bread and cheese, Molly spied
a familiar gentleman on a fine black horse. He
approached along the other side of the street and
paused, watching the building with a frown.

The Earl of Lazybones. Looking directly up at her
window.

Molly gazed around in a panic, for the decoration
of her room left much to be desired. Wall plaster had
flaked away in several patches, showing the wooden
slats beneath, and the ceiling was mottled with yel-
lowish stains where rain, if it came hard and from a
particular angle, leaked through the broken slates. Her
furnishings consisted of a small table with a candlestick
holder, and two brittle chairs. It was all very different
from the life she'd led at Danforthe House, but for the
rent of two shillings a week she could not complain,
and Mr. Hobbs assured her it was a safe place where
she would be among good, honest people.

At least, living on the top level—which was really
the attic of the house—she benefited from the heat
escaping the lower rooms. She had no fire and was
glad warmer months were on their way. Hopefully,
by winter, she might be able to afford better accom-
modation. For now, she'd cheered the grim walls as
best she could, covering them with pinned sketches
and designs. She'd decorated her table with a vase of
dried lavender stalks, brought with her from Sydney
Dovedale, where it grew in abundance. It was a bit-
tersweet reminder of her childhood home, of the place
and the people she'd left behind.

But despite these attempts to improve her lodgings,
she could not bear for Carver Danforthe to see them.
He would turn up his noble nose in disdain. Glancing

down through the window again, she saw his horse proceeding across the busy road, coming closer. Wasting no more time in somber reflection, she leapt up, tossed a shawl around her shoulders, and raced down the stairs to intervene before he could arrive at the front door. He had not yet dismounted when she dashed out onto the cobbled street.

"Miss Robbins." He swept off his hat. "I trust you are in health?"

"I am, sir." *Goodness, what could he be doing there?* His fingers fidgeted with the brim of his hat, but he watched her with clear gray eyes, steady and thoughtful. "And you…sir?"

Now that frown reappeared. "I manage. Since I have been abandoned by those who once professed to have concern for me. I am left to my own devices, and I muddle on as best I can."

Molly almost laughed at that, but he seemed quite serious, so she pressed her lips together and waited for more. Nothing came, however. He was silent, his hands restlessly turning the brim of his hat. Apparently she had done something to make him cross. Or someone had. "You have not had word from her ladyship?" she ventured.

"I have not," he snapped, his gaze straying up and down her figure with neither discretion nor apology. "She extends her stay in Norfolk with no thought for me."

Her mind raced as she gathered the ends of her shawl tight against her bosom. Why would he care to see where she lived? Why would it matter to her if he did?

But it was his money funding this enterprise. He

might insist on seeing inside. If he knew she had no customers, he would laugh at her, or, worse still, he might pity her. Molly never knew how much pride she had until that moment. She wanted to prove herself. Especially to him.

As that fact dawned bright and spitefully clear to her, Molly felt her lips unclenching, falling apart in faint horror at her situation. His eyes were now heated steel, scalding her flesh.

"You were going out, Miss Robbins?"

Out? Out where? She couldn't think. Finally she blurted, "Yes. I like to walk for exercise every day."

He frowned. "But it is cold out, and you wear only a thin woolen shawl."

Her lips flapped wordlessly for a moment. It was so unusual to hear him express concern for anyone, yet he now did so for her. "I like the chill," she wheezed. "It sharpens the mind."

Carver pursed his lips and shook his head. "Which way do you go? Perhaps I might walk with you."

People passing along the street turned to look at the fine gentleman on the horse. A man like the Earl of Everscham was a rarity there, and they were understandably curious. Molly felt her face heat up, despite the weather.

"Which way do you go?" he repeated, his horse moving restlessly under him.

She stepped back. "I...think I go whichever way you do not."

"I beg your pardon."

"I prefer to walk alone, sir." Molly did not know how to deal with his sudden attention. It frightened her and yet thrilled her too.

"Far be it from me to spoil your solitude, Miss Robbins," he growled, glaring down at her. "At least now I can be satisfied, having seen you looking so well. Although you did not care how *I* might be managing without you."

"You still have Mr. Richards, your lordship, and Mrs. Jakes, and Larkin, your valet. And—"

"But I don't have you," he pointed out, churlish. Even when he sulked, he was handsome, she thought. Once again her panic dissolved in the temptation to laugh. He could be very amusing when he chose, but of course she knew that. Molly had seen how seductive he could be, the effect he had on women who did not know better.

She, fortunately, knew better. "Strictly speaking, your lordship, you never did have me."

He bent his head forward, and that stubbornly rebellious lock of hair, with which she already had some familiarity, trickled onto his brow. "True," he said. "More's the pity."

Molly swallowed hard, her fingers tangled in the holes of that knitted shawl. She was aware of the old lady by the salop still, looking over at them, grinning as she eavesdropped.

"Did you have some business in this part of town, your lordship?" Her fingers picked at the wool of her shawl. "I was surprised to see you here. I could not think what might have brought you so far from your usual playground."

He raised an eyebrow. "I was unaware I had been forbidden from venturing into this part of Town, now you reside in it. I am duly chastised."

"Of course, if you want to come here, I can't stop you." It did not sound the way she meant it, but in her fretful state it leapt out before she could think twice.

"Well," he huffed, "I wouldn't want to be in anybody's way."

"I didn't mean to suggest—"

"Oy, Mister!" A little lad with a dirty face and boots that were several sizes too big for his feet had decided to take his chance with the fine gent on the horse. He came tripping along the street and pulled on Carver's coat with an insistent fist. "Oy, Mister, spare a penny for a poor boy, will ya?"

Carver glanced down at the street urchin.

"I can 'old yer 'orse for yer, Mister."

"I'm sure you could steal it too, boy."

"Not me, Mister. Honest as the day is long, me."

Rolling his eyes, Carver reached inside a pocket of his waistcoat, took out a coin, and passed it to the boy.

The lad was, at that moment and surprisingly enough, more interested in the horse. "It's a fine beast, Mister. Do you race 'im?"

Carver's brow quirked. "No. Not formally. But he's fast."

The boy stretched to pat the horse's sleek black neck, and the animal whinnied appreciatively. "Aye, he's a beauty. Straight hocks, strong legs, good balance in the proportion. What is he, Mister, sixteen hands?"

"Yes," replied Carver, frowning faintly.

"Neck tied in well at the withers, and look how alert he is. Good feller. I bet yer run like the wind." He patted the horse again and ran his grimy fingers soothingly along the veined, satiny neck.

"You know about horses, boy?"

"I 'ad an uncle once what worked as a farrier on a

big estate. And I 'elp take care o' the dray horses up at the brewery." Finally the boy took the coin he was offered and looked at it.

"See that you buy something to eat," Carver muttered sternly.

"Thanks, Mister!" The boy's eyes opened wide. "That's a whole shillin'!"

"Yes…well…don't spend it on the cockfights. Put food in your stomach and don't—"

The boy would have dashed off, but Carver's long arm reached down and grabbed him by the collar so he stopped abruptly, almost falling over his too-big boots.

"Don't give it to your mother for gin or your father for gambling."

"I ain't got no ma, Mister. No pa neither. Jus' me and me sister."

"A sister?"

Sniffing loudly, the boy wiped his nose on his sleeve. "She's littler 'an me. I look after 'er."

"I see. Sisters can be a handful."

"They can that, Mister."

With his free hand, Carver retrieved another coin and gave it to the boy. "Where do you live?"

"Here and there." The boy's eyes became wary. "Round an' about. Why? I ain't done nuffin'."

Molly watched Carver's face soften slightly, but he said nothing, just let the boy go, watching as he tripped and shuffled down the street, yelling for his friends to see what he'd got from the "rich toff."

"Now you've done it," Molly remarked. "Any moment now you'll be surrounded with begging hands. They'll strip you of your fob watch and that fine silk handkerchief before you know it."

"Do you know that boy?"

"Only by sight. He's a regular on this street. There are a lot of children like that one, orphaned or as good as, doing whatever they can to get a few coins here and there."

He shook his head. "Something should be done about it." Carver was still looking in the direction of the disappearing boy. Perhaps the fact that he mentioned a sister had struck a chord with the earl, who always complained about his own. Of course, his problems with Mercy were very different to the sort the ragamuffin knew. But still it was a connection, she supposed. "Next time you see him, send him to me, or to Edward Hobbs. I'm sure we can find an apprenticeship for the boy. He looks strong and capable, knows about horses…whatever is the matter, Miss Robbins?"

"Naught, your lordship." She didn't feel the cold as much now. It was as if a little patch of sun had come out, although she couldn't see it yet through the leaden clouds.

"Your face is doing odd things," he snapped.

She bit her lip.

"There…again. Is something amiss?"

Molly took a breath. "No, your lordship. It just seems strange to hear you being…concerned for others." She shrugged awkwardly. Oh dear, that didn't sound right either. "I don't mean to say that you never are…it's just that…" What could she say to make it better? She was shocked to see him up and out of bed at this hour? That confession would hardly help improve things. The truth was, her sightings of him for the past twelve years had mostly occurred as he came home or went out in his evening clothes.

It was unusual for her to see the handsome but nocturnal creature out in daylight, being civil and sober, noticing the world around him. As all this ran through her mind, it must somehow have shown on her face.

"How nice to know you still think so highly of me," he remarked tersely. "Excuse me, Miss Robbins, I can't stand here all day talking to my little sister's former lady's maid. I must go before I am besieged with street urchins and their grubby hands, ready to fleece me of every item in my possession."

In the next sigh of a haughty exhale, he was gone, turning his horse sharply and trotting off down the street. Molly watched for a while in case he glanced back at her, but he did not. He had ventured so far from his usual haunts and changed his long-ingrained habits, just to find her. What could be the meaning of it?

Five

MOLLY HAD WAITED OUTSIDE LADY CECELIA Montague's house for almost an hour before the woman finally emerged with a female companion, both dressed in walking gowns and lavishly trimmed bonnets. Lady Cecelia's outfit was the grander of the two, her sleeves puffier, the hem decorated with an overabundance of frills and rosettes. But the style shortened her height and squared off her figure. It always hurt Molly's eyes to see a woman treat her shape so poorly and fall victim to fashion's less flattering foibles. Her friend, dressed in a simpler style, was lighter and more elegant. As Molly had often observed, those with the coin did not always have the taste to go with it. Fortunately, she was there to change all that.

At least the rain had stopped today, and spring was in the air. Molly hoped it might make her ladyship think of new dresses and a refreshing change of style.

Dashing across the street, she slipped between passing carriages and managed to align herself directly in the lady's route. Some encounter was now unavoidable. Unless, of course, the lady chose to snub her completely, as she well might. But Molly was quite desperate and prepared to make this mad attempt, even at the risk of her own humiliation.

Heart beating steadily, she approached along the path.

It would not be proper to speak unless she was noticed and acknowledged, but it seemed as if that would not happen. There was only one thing to be done. Molly gathered a deep breath and then exhaled in a low squeal of distress. Fanning her hands around her bonnet, she danced in a rapid circle.

"A wasp, a wasp. Oh!"

Her anxious gaze following the invisible path of the fantasy insect, she cried out for Lady Cecelia to be mindful of it. Instantly the other woman and her companion twisted about in a similar state of panic, Molly's performance being so gravely convincing that they both swore they heard the villainous buzzing around their bonnets. In fact, the effect was far greater than she'd expected, and as those two ladies spun like children's tops, another small group walking behind them were stirred into the same action. Not even knowing the cause of their plight, they became infected by fear of something unseen.

Molly hurried forward, removed her glove, and slapped it against Lady Cecelia's skirt and then her sleeve. "Begging your pardon, your ladyship, but I should not like you to be stung." She stamped her foot hard upon the pavement. "There! You are saved."

The lady's friend had almost staggered dizzily into the path of a passing curricle, but Molly grabbed her hand just in time, pulling her to safety by the width of a bonnet ribbon.

"Robbins, is it not?" Lady Cecelia muttered breathlessly, straightening her gown. "You are back in London? I thought you had gone into the country."

"Did you not receive my card, your ladyship? I left one with your footman at the door some days ago."

"I…do not remember it, but I—"

"I returned to open my own dressmaking business." Molly briskly pulled on her glove and looked away down the street, as if she were Lady Mercy dealing with a passing acquaintance. "In fact, I am on my way now to a fitting for a special client."

Lady Cecelia blinked against the bright sun. "Indeed?"

"I did not expect such a demand for my services, but it seems there are many ladies in Town eager for something different, a daring change of style." She gave the highly decorated lady a hasty up-and-down glance and then turned her eyes back to her glove. "They are quite bored by the usual overdone fashions, and…well, it was most pleasant to see you, Lady Cecelia. You must forgive me, but I am in rather a hurry."

"I see." Lady Cecelia managed a tight smile, and as Molly moved to pass, she touched her arm lightly. "You may call upon me, Robbins, now that you are returned. I was planning a new wardrobe for the summer myself."

Molly granted her a little smile but made no commitment. She prepared to move on, but the lady stopped her again.

"I daresay I know your client."

"I daresay. But she would not like me to disclose her identity. And I am always discreet." With a nod, Molly hurried onward, leaving both ladies on the pavement behind her.

The next morning she was surprised by a visitor. It was not quite twelve when her awestruck landlady, with lace cap askew and flour on her hands, brought the guest to her room and announced, "Lady Anne Rothespur to see Miss Margaret Robbins."

A slender creature with a piquant face, shining blue eyes, and a short dark fringe of hair under her bonnet came swiftly through the door, already talking. "So sorry to disturb you this early, Miss Robbins, and my governess says I should have sent a card first, but since I have more than thirty balls and dinner parties to attend already this Season, you can see I'm desperate for your services. Do say you'll have time to take me on. I'm afraid I'm rather an odd shape—like a damn plum pudding, my brother says."

Eyeing the tiny sash at the visitor's waist, Molly could only conclude her brother, whoever he was, liked to tease.

"Jumping Jacks, what a small room you have here. Are these your designs? How perfectly precious."

At first, Molly had no idea how the young lady had found her. Then she remembered that St. John Rothespur, the Earl of Saxonby, was a close friend of Carver Danforthe's. This must be the younger sister who was sixteen and had come up to London to make her debut that Season. Obviously she would have had gowns already made, but *someone* had sent her to Molly for more. The chirpy creature dashed about the room as if she had wheels upon her feet, examining the sketches on the wall and the vase of dried lavender stalks, even the prospect from the window.

"Well, this is very…quaint, Miss Robbins." She

stared at the flaking wall plaster, shivered, and rubbed her arms under a ruffled tippet. "Very…cozy."

Molly urged her to sit while they discussed designs, but the lady preferred to move about in busy circles, talking the entire time. "I really don't have any opinions on color or material, so I'll leave that up to you, and since my brother doesn't want me to embarrass him, he'd better be prepared to pay any price. He doesn't care much for these wide collars. He says they make me look like a bat."

"You mean the *pelerine en ailes d'oiseau*. It can broaden the shoulders too much, but I like to soften the shape with a few layers."

"Oh, that is the Princess Victoria on your wall. She's just a little younger than me, you know. I hear she's very amiable and accomplished. But, of course, my brother says everyone is amiable compared to me. He says I'm a damn inconvenience. He says 'damn' quite a lot."

Eventually she stood still long enough for Molly to take down a few measurements.

"I want to look sultry and sophisticated," she exclaimed. "Do you think it's possible? Is there any hope? My brother says I'm not in the least ladylike, and that it would take an entire team of fairy godmothers to turn me into a Society belle. I do so want to prove him wrong."

Molly finally squeezed some words in. "We can but try, my lady."

The customer stayed for half an hour and then left as suddenly as she'd arrived, clasping Molly's hand warmly and exclaiming that she had the greatest confidence in her abilities, since she'd come so highly recommended.

Bemused, standing by her window, Molly watched the young lady being gently chided by a thin-faced, elderly woman—probably the disapproving governess she'd mentioned—and then the two figures climbed into the Rothespurs' carriage and departed. She'd never expected clients to come to her lodgings in that decidedly less-than-fashionable part of Town, but clearly Lady Anne was too young and inexperienced yet to know all the proper etiquette. The governess must have her hands full with such a lively charge.

That day Molly also received a card asking her to attend the Baroness Schofield at her house in Grosvenor Square. The baroness was a young widow with portrait-worthy beauty and a curvaceous figure. She had come out of mourning six months before and was now making up for it. There appeared to be no budget to restrain her, and not much in the way of taste either. Indeed, the baroness had to be reined in, for her extravagant ideas were not in keeping with Molly's designs.

"I can assure you, madam, the fashion for too much trim at the hem is soon to pass," she told the lady. "The wide silhouette of the gigot sleeve has also had its day. You will be ahead of the trends with a less cluttered design." And she showed, by way of a sketch, how a simple cut would lengthen and lighten the figure, while also flattering the best features. Whenever she had the chance to talk of fashion and design, Molly enjoyed a burst of confidence and completely forgot to be reserved or timid. She loved to talk of fabric and trimmings, for in these subjects she was fluent, having amassed a vast amount of knowledge over her years of friendship with Lady Mercy. When she spoke with authority on her favorite subject, people listened to her for once, as if she had something of value to share and did not simply exist to do their bidding.

The Baroness Schofield, however, was not easily convinced. Like many, she was accustomed to following whatever style was taken up by members of Society's elite, even when it was not necessarily suited to her size and shape. She was also excessively proud of her fine bosom and showed it off at every opportunity. When Molly gently suggested that the baroness need not display herself to be noticed, the remark was treated with the same indignation as might be faced if she told a war hero that he wore too many medals on his uniform.

Eventually, after much careful handling and subtle persuasion, the client sulkily allowed a pared-down design. She reminded Molly of a pedigreed, self-contented cat. If she possessed a tail, it would definitely be up as she walked. Molly was quite relieved when the meeting was over and she could leave the lady's purring, humorless laugh and suffocating perfume behind. But as she passed through the hall on her way out, she turned her gaze to an elegant little console table with cabriole legs and, while her designing eye admired the softly curved lines of the craftsman's work, noted a man's scarf dropped in a crumpled snake upon it. Recognition was swift. She had sewn those initials upon it herself some six months ago for the Earl of Everscham.

She imagined her mother looking down from heaven and shaking her head.

Molly's sigh was so loud and gusty that the footman charged with showing her to the door threw her a wary look. She simply shook her head and walked out into the sun.

Soon after this, Lady Cecelia Montague sent for her to discuss a new gown, and once again Molly donned her best coat and bonnet to travel across town in a hansom cab.

After a few stiff pleasantries and inquiries into the health of Lady Mercy Danforthe—which they both knew was merely an attempt to find out why Molly's former mistress remained in the country—Lady Cecelia informed her that she would condescend to hire her services. "We approach the fashionable season, as you know, Robbins, and I need a number of new gowns. I do not like to burden my regular seamstress with too much work. I suppose"—and here she paused while giving Molly's coat a disdainful perusal that stopped just short of a sneer—"I *suppose* I can give you a trial."

As she knew it would, the patronage of Lady Cecelia granted the necessary mark of approval for other women to seek her services, and Molly became happily busy. It was important she begin dressing herself with more style, as everywhere she went she was an advertisement for her own business. In the past, her skills and services were reserved for her mistress—a good servant was not meant to be seen or heard. Now, however, Molly could no longer hide in the wall paneling, hoping to be forgotten. A transformation must take place if she was to be welcomed into those grand houses and not endure every footman and lady's maid looking down their nose at her.

❧

"I want you to round up as many of those able lads

as can be found and, if they show interest, send them to the Sussex estate," Carver explained to the startled Edward Hobbs. "They can join the other boys there."

"More children, my lord? The estate has already taken in a large number of orphans since you became earl. As it is, Phipps struggles to find work for all of them until the harvest."

"Then Phipps needs to use his imagination and initiative. The boys can learn valuable skills on the stud farm, or around the house if they are not working the land. I'm sure many of these children show aptitude for other lines of work where they can earn a wage. They need a fresh start, away from these streets where bad influences are rife."

"There are indeed a great many homeless children running about the streets of London," Hobbs replied steadily, and yet with a tone of weary acceptance, as if he knew the pointlessness of his own words. "I hope you do not think to help them all."

"I mean to help as many as I can. I'll get Rothespur involved. I'm sure he could find work for a few hands on that massive estate of his. Someone has to start somewhere, or nothing will ever be done. We must move forward, Hobbs, and stop merely discussing the problems. Change is the essence of life."

The solicitor shuffled his papers worriedly. "Indeed, my lord."

"Since parliament takes so bloody long to move its feet, someone has to take matters personally in hand."

"Yes, my lord, that was what you said ten years ago when you began the enterprise. The estate has now helped a great many more than one child, but they all enjoy it there so much they seldom move on. Where Phipps manages to put them all, I can't imagine."

"Nonsense. It's a six hundred-acre plot of land, Hobbs."

"The last time Lady Mercy paid a visit, she was increasingly perplexed by the number of small children running about the place. Phipps was obliged to make up some outlandish stories about a spate of sudden births in the village. And I believe it led to her lecturing quite a few confused inhabitants on the subject of abstinence."

Carver laughed at that. "Yes, well. I can't have her knowing what I'm up to. She'll only try to meddle and tell me I'm doing it all wrong."

Hobbs sighed. "No doubt."

"I'm sure you and Phipps can find somewhere to put them all." Carver waved his hand through the air, dismissing the counselor's concerns. "You can do anything, Hobbs."

"If you say so, my lord."

"And I'm thinking about a school too," Carver muttered, rubbing his chin. "Somewhere these children can go for a basic education, but not in subjects like Latin, that will be of no use to them."

This was far enough for poor Hobbs, who had been caught in the midst of his breakfast. "My lord, your father would never have condoned a school for the poor."

"Exactly. My father was stuck, Hobbs my good fellow, in the past." And he was not. Not anymore.

Six

SHE CAME TO HIM AT THE END OF THE MONTH. CARVER
had just returned from a ride with the Baroness Schofield
and had not yet wiped the mud of Hyde Park off his
boots. Or grass stains from the knees of his breeches. As
he marched into the drawing room, she stood from the
chair in which she'd waited and gave the usual bob curtsy.

The butler's warning had prepared him, of course,
but he was still startled by her appearance in a jaunty
green bonnet and matching coat. Today she had
shaken off the guise of a servant. Cheerful spring sun,
beaming through the tall window, cast her in a far
better light than the gloomy, rain-patterned shadows
of their meeting in his library.

Everything improved in sunlight, he supposed,
searching for a reason why she should cause his pulse
to quicken, his hands to lose their grip on his riding
crop so suddenly. That warm shade of her emerald
coat and the hint of verdigris lace inside her bonnet
made her small face glow today.

"Miss Robbins." He set his gloves over the seat of
a nearby chair before she made him drop those too.

"Your lordship." He caught her glance at his ·

muddied knees, and then saw her lips squeeze together in that familiar way, while her impertinent right brow rose half an inch. She never missed a chance to look at him with scorn. The burden of carrying that halo around must make her head hurt.

Carver straightened his shoulders and snapped, "To what do I owe this dubious honor? Are you allowed on this side of Town, Miss Robbins? It seems a trifle unfair, if I am not allowed on yours."

Her response was crisp, no-nonsense, ignoring his comment. "As promised, I have brought the first payment in person."

She could have left it with Richards, but apparently it was important to her that she put it directly into his hands. Since he did not reach for the notes in her hand, the Mouse finally placed them reverently on a small table by the window. She looked at his knees again, wayward sparks finding their way out from under her lowered lashes.

"Did you suffer a fall, your lordship? I hope you did not hurt yourself."

Carver scowled at her. He still hadn't forgiven this woman for leaving his household and forcing him to seek her out on the other side of Town, just for a glimpse of her damnably doubting face. "No," he snapped. "I was not hurt." The Baroness Schofield always provided an adequately soft landing.

"Those breeches should be tended to at once with white vinegar to remove the grass stain."

He wondered why the state of his breeches should concern her, since she was no longer his employee and clearly relished the fact. Bloody woman. "My valet will see to the matter."

Her gaze lifted to his, brown eyes apparently saved from the sun's glare by the peak of her bonnet. "I shall return the rest of the loan to you in due course. As stated in the agreement."

"Hmm." In truth, he could not remember much about that agreement. Except for one clause and the annoying Mr. Tom Follerie. She stood before him in a streak of sunlight, waiting for something, hovering on the tips of her toes. Any minute now she would turn and walk for the door. Who knew when he might see that frowning face again? He thought desperately for some way to delay her exit. "You recovered from your cold, Miss Robbins."

"Oh yes, your lordship. My landlady, Mrs. Lotterby, makes an exceedingly beneficial chicken broth. She looks after me very well."

Perhaps the landlady's broth was responsible for putting more color in her face and that extra curl in her hair. Margaret "Molly" Robbins bloomed with the spring, he concluded. "Business is going well, it seems," he muttered gruffly.

"Indeed, your lordship." Her face very solemn, she curtsied again and moved toward the door. Suddenly, she stopped and turned to him. "It was not necessary to involve your mistress, the Baroness Schofield. I am capable of finding my own clients."

"What makes you assume—"

"Do please credit me with some sense, your lordship. I may be a country wretch, raised by simple folk rather than among the *grand sophisticates* of Town, such as yourself"—she appeared to bite down on a chuckle, while her eyes once again studied his dirty knees— "but I am not naive. I have also borne witness to your high jinks for half my life."

He should have been angered by that remark, but something about her funny little face and her fascination with his breeches made it impossible to lose his infamous temper. Yet. A dent in her lower lip was in danger of absorbing his attention for too long. "Half your life?"

She sighed. "Yes."

"Then you know I am an unconscionable cad."

"Yes." No equivocation there.

"So why would I help by sending customers to you? Why should I care what becomes of an ingrate who abandons a good, steady, well-paid post in my household and has the gall to accuse me of—what was it—*high jinks*? You can hawk your wares on a street corner and down a quart of gin a day, and it won't make a ripple in my life."

"I assume you want your investment returned."

"Two hundred pounds? Do I strike you as a gentleman in need of it?"

"Do I strike you as a woman who lacks the determination and wherewithal to find her own customers and achieve her own success?"

There was a little feathery seed caught in her hair by her temple, just visible under the brim of her bonnet. Must have blown there in the spring breeze as she walked through the nearby park on her way to Danforthe House. Carver badly wanted to raise his hand and take the seed out for her, but then he would have to touch her hair. It would be soft, warmed by the sun. The curls would twist around his finger. He might not be able to stop there, and he didn't want his fingers bitten.

He felt a sharp pain, like a toothache. Wincing, he quickly lifted that same tempted hand to rub his cheek, and then it seemed as if she thought he was laughing at her, for the young woman's anger visibly mounted. When she stepped toward him, Carver could see more color in her face, more detail in the deep, warm, chocolaty depths of her eyes.

"And for your information, sir," she added indignantly, "I've never touched a drop of gin."

"Perhaps you should. Might make you smile for once."

"I do not believe in the overconsumption of alcohol. I've seen what fools it makes of people." Her face was pert, censorious. "Like you, for instance."

Oh, she was getting far too bold now, and he'd let her stretch her legs far enough. It was time he reined her in. "I daresay you also learned a lesson from your father's misfortune."

That caused the prissy madam a jolt. Her eyes widened. "What can you mean by that, pray?"

"Was he not the village drunk?"

"He most certainly was not!"

"But he was drunk the night that carriage ran over him. Had he not just been tossed out of the local tavern?"

Her cheeks flushed a dainty shade of pink. "My father was on his way home from market that evening. It was late, and he was tired."

"And soused."

"How dare you!"

"It's true. My sister told me. She heard all about it from Rafe Hartley's aunt and uncle."

Her lips parted. Her lashes flickered. Some of the high color in her face drained away.

"Perhaps your mother wished to save you from the

truth," he added, realizing he might have gone too far in his eagerness to put her in her place again.

She turned away swiftly, and the fresh, sweet scent of lavender tickled his nose as the sway of her gown released a soft wave of fragrance into the air. He waited. What could he say now? It wasn't as if he had any experience in making apologies.

"In any case," she managed, recovering quickly, "had I wanted meddling in my business, your lordship, I would have asked your sister for a loan. Not you."

Meddling? *Meddling?* He was speechless and so annoyed that he forgot his toothache and any thought of apologizing.

Now came the thrust of her sharp tongue, getting her vengeance. "Please do not send any more of your women to me."

She made it sound as if he kept a tribe of them in the cellar, along with a collection of fine wines. An amusing idea and quite practical actually, when he considered it. Carver always swore he would never devote himself to just one woman. Far better to have lots of *Buffers*, as he liked to think of them.

After that brief loss when he mentioned her father's drunken mishap, his assailant was now getting her color back. Had she much bosom, it might have been heaving with the exertion of her temper, but her shape was carefully guarded from his assessment, securely buttoned up under the armor of her green coat. He considered that first button, imagined his long fingers slipping it free of the hole and then proceeding to the next. And the next.

"Get a hold of yourself," he muttered. "There is no occasion for hysterics."

"Clearly you don't understand the cause of my distress."

Her distress? Oh, she had no idea. "Well, there does seem to be a blasted lot of it, but then females are prone to exaggeration in general."

She sucked in her cheeks and stared at him.

"Is your corset too tight?" he offered politely. "That could be your problem." One he would willingly help her out of.

"Your lordship, let me explain *my problem* in plain terms. The baroness ordered three day gowns and three for evening. You will pay for those gowns, therefore, paying back your own loan. Which means, your lordship, that this is not a business loan to me at all, but a gift. That was not what I asked from you."

"So what? So it is a gift." Laughing uneasily, he rocked on his booted heels. "Most women would take it and be damned grateful."

"As we already ascertained, I am not *most* women."

No indeed, she was not, he thought bleakly. He could neither seduce nor frighten her. There went the jabbing pain in his tooth again.

"I don't want gifts from you," she continued. "I don't want anything I cannot repay promptly. Money may not be very important to you, as it has always been in your possession, but for me it is a serious matter. I certainly do not want anyone thinking I'm one of your women, taking you for every penny while your transitory, puppy-dog attention lasts."

"Puppy-dog?"

"I came to you for a loan because I thought that you… I mean *it*…would be simple."

"Aha! Now that was a slip of the tongue, was it not?

You assumed I would blithely give you money and forget about it the next day, because I am too stupid to take an interest."

"Not give. *Loan.* I don't want you to *give* me anything. I'm not another of your loose women. I was raised to have some self-respect."

"Ah yes, your blessed virtue. What bothers you more, Mouse? The money I spend, or the women I spend it on? Perhaps your real disdain is for them." Her lashes were very full and lush, he noted for the first time as they blinked impatiently. There! He caught her looking at his grass-stained knees again and, if he was not mistaken, something above them. Interesting. "Or...perhaps you're jealous."

Her eyes widened, flicked back up to him and dragged him closer. Carver found himself staring down into treacherous, bottomless wells. He very nearly lost his balance, but she was the first to retreat.

"Don't be nonsensical," she sputtered, taking two steps back. He followed with three. In her next movement she backed against a corner china cabinet. "As if I care how you throw your attentions about so indiscriminately. Your lack of a moral compass, or theirs, is not my concern. My reputation, however, is."

He laughed huskily, still thinking of her too-tight corset and what he might do to ease her distress. *"My moral compass?"*

"I don't suppose you know what that means. I doubt they teach you that at Eton and Oxford." Each breath shot out of her with a jagged edge, as if ripped out haphazardly. It was a rare display of temper that shredded her usually prim and cool demeanor.

"I'll be damned if my sister's lady's maid, one of

my household servants, is going to lecture me on my principles."

"I am no longer a servant." The words tumbled out in haste and filled the narrow space between them, making the air thick and hot.

"Then why take such an interest in the state of my breeches?"

She hesitated and then muttered sullenly, "Some habits are hard to break."

He arched an eyebrow. "Better get out of that one, Miss Robbins. If gentlemen find you staring at their breeches, they might get the wrong direction from your…moral compass."

She raised a hand between them, her palm inches from his chest. He could nibble upon her fingertips if they came several inches higher. "Kindly step back."

"This is my drawing room," he replied with more calmness than he felt, "and I'll stand where I choose."

"You will keep a discreet distance."

"Will I? And you, the little girl from a one-horse village, will set the rules for the Earl of Everscham? The man who took her in and gave her a position in the first place. Fed her, clothed her, and gave her a bed for a dozen years. You will tell me what to do, is that it?" He smiled, trying to take the sting off his words. Not that she ever bothered with her own. Carver could no longer recall how this quarrel began or who made the first strike. But it was like a runaway cart rapidly bumping downhill, unstoppable by any but the most desperate of measures. Unless it was left to crash and splinter into a hundred pieces.

"I am no longer in your employ," she replied, breathless. "I am a woman of business." She stuck her small twitching nose in the air. "And we have more than one horse in Sydney Dovedale."

He closed another step between them, and she was forced to lower her hand or else let it make contact with his lips. The more he fought the need to touch her, the more he warned himself of the danger, the more he wanted to do it. What would it feel like, he wondered, to hold this woman who was so very different than any other he knew? What would it be like to kiss her?

"If I desire to take more than passing interest in a business in which I have invested, then I shall," he snapped. "I am entitled. *Margaret*."

Finally, taking matters into his own hands and employing one of those desperate measures required to end the argument, he let his fingers find that seed lodged in her curl and brushed it free.

He expected this shocking gesture to silence her, but there was only a pause before her next words rushed out, tumbling over each other. "You mean the mere two hundred you invested? The two hundred that means nothing to a man of your wealth, as you just pointed out?" Apparently she meant to ignore the fact that he'd just touched her and called her by her first name. Ignore it, and it would go away, was that her plan? Well, he supposed there was nothing in that contract about touching—only flirting and *Tomfollerie*.

So his fingertips lingered to caress the high curve of her cheek, all the way down to her chin, and beneath, where the pale green ribbons of her bonnet were tied. Waiting to be untied.

Why not?

He wouldn't be the first peer of the realm to enjoy a dalliance with a lady's maid, would he?

But Miss Robbins was a different creature, unpredictable and prickly. She wasn't likely to fall into his arms unless she tripped over his feet. It was doubtful she'd come there unarmed, he thought, remembering that sharp pin once stuck in his toe.

A sudden, intense need for brandy quickly made its grip felt, but there was none in the room, and he already knew what her expression would be if he rang for some at this hour of the day. The other urge he suffered at that moment would probably meet with a slapped face, so in the interest of self-preservation, he turned away from her and rubbed his cheek where she already caused his tooth to ache spitefully.

Apparently his new desire to be useful, to make change, had not gone without a hitch. He'd had no practice at it, of course.

Pacing around the couch, he eventually conceded, "It seems good deeds are not my forte, Robbins. I am duly reprimanded for my intention to help you. No need to flay me alive for it." Carver returned to safer, familiar ground. "Good Lord, I preferred you when you were mute and invisible, as any good servant should be. I paid you less, at fifteen pounds per annum, to be silent and obedient, than I now pay you at two hundred pounds to clatter your tongue like a bitter scold."

He heard her draw a sharp breath and, when he looked, some of the sparkle in her eyes had died away.

"I shan't try to help you again," he assured her firmly. "From now on, madam, your life is yours, and mine…is mine."

"I'm glad we understand each other, your lordship."

He gave her a stiff bow, and by the time he was upright again, she'd gone.

Striding to the window, he irritably nudged the curtain aside and watched her hurrying across the street, one hand on her bonnet. A flash of mud-spattered stocking as she scuttled away from Danforthe House drew his gaze downward, past her hem to the teasing glimpse of slender leg. He could close his fingers around that narrow ankle. Could probably lift her entire person over his head with one hand, throw her onto his bed, and do her at least one good deed she wouldn't turn her nose up at.

But he couldn't. It was in that damnable contract she'd tricked him into signing before he was fully awake.

Grumbling under his breath, he turned away from the window then paced to the couch, where an embroidered cushion annoyed him so much it had to be picked up from one end and thrown to the other. He tugged on his neck cloth, needing some air.

Damn servants and women getting uppity. His father would never allow it.

Carver strode to the window again, and with one hand, swiped the curtain back to see where she'd gone. The sun was bright, shining meanly in his eyes. He swung away, repeated his pacing circle, and cursed into the empty room.

Puppy-dog? *Puppy-dog?*

He'd certainly never help her again.

Resting his hands on the back of the couch, he took a deeper breath and heaved his shoulders until they felt less tense.

Well, he'd never help her in any way that she knew about it. Unfortunately for her, he was acquiring a penchant for being helpful. And for insolent brown eyes framed with very long, very dark lashes.

Seven

MOLLY WAS OUT OF BED EVERY MORNING AS SOON AS the pigeons came to coo by her window. She had settled in now, getting to know her neighbors. Her landlady, Mrs. Lotterby, was an irrepressibly cheerful, robust lady trying to maintain her dignity in a ramshackle house and somehow making ends meet, despite the fact that her generous spirit was far greater than her means. She held weekly dinners for her tenants, taking great interest in their trials and troubles, eager to set their problems to rights before the pudding was consumed. She formed a special concern for Molly, treating her in a motherly way, making certain she ate well and advising her on the temperature and the state of the streets whenever she waylaid her on the stairs going out.

The landlady's husband, Herbert, was a short, small-boned fellow who seldom got a word in edgeways and tended to drop or break anything he was charged with mending. Molly got the impression that Herbert was yet another of the good lady's charitable causes, for—as his jolly wife freely admitted—he was no use for much beyond lacing her stays in the morning.

Living in the rooms below Molly were Mrs. Slater,

an army captain's widow coping with an eternally crying baby and her lazy, ill-tempered, unemployed brother, Arthur Wakely. Molly quickly befriended Mrs. Slater, who was not many years older than she, but whose circumstances were much worse since she had a child to care for and only a military pension on which to do it. Her brother was a complete and utter wastrel who drank too much and seemed to think the world owed him a living without him actually having to earn it.

When Arthur Wakely learned that Molly was a spinster with her own business, he predicted loudly and arrogantly that no good would come of it. "You should have married when you had the chance," he dolefully assured her. In his opinion, women were good only for a life in service to a large household, or for marriage and childbirth. "An unwed, independent woman is a blight upon society." Sprawled across the frayed, patched cushions of their landlady's sofa, taking up all the space so no one else could sit, and periodically snorting the contents of a snuffbox, he declared, "A female that chooses not to do her duty, marry and produce children, is superfluous and should go to a nunnery, as they did in the vastly more civilized days of old."

"Poor Arthur," his sister meekly apologized, as she did far too often for him, "you must excuse his harsh words. He has had a very hard time…since His Foot."

Apparently the hard times to which his sister referred amounted to no more than serving in the militia for a few months—twenty years ago—managing to get himself thrown out for being excessively in drink and in debt, then shooting himself accidentally in the foot.

He now limped about, waiting for someone to compensate him for the foolishness of his own actions. His foot, which was always mentioned as if it ought to be written about in the court circular, was the most honored and pampered part about him, as well as the most interesting and least repulsive. Which was not saying much. Molly had no time for him, but was civil for Mrs. Slater's sake. Once they got to know each other, she invited the lady up to her room in the afternoons, and even offered to take the baby for her from time to time, just to give the young mother some respite. In return, Mrs. Slater was happy to lend her services with some sewing, although her stitches usually had to be unpicked later when she was gone.

Occasionally, at night, Molly heard Arthur Wakely of The Foot arguing with his sister in the room below, their voices rising and falling until the softer of the two eventually stopped, conceding to whatever point the other made just to soothe the crying baby. Mrs. Slater never had much coin at hand. It seemed as if her brother took control of her widow's pension, using it to keep up his own appearance and gambling in seedy establishments. If he had success with a wager, he disappeared for a few days, and his sister's spirits would lift, but sooner or later, once his luck ran out, he returned again, and so would the poor lady's sad, wilted demeanor.

The landlady's sister, Mrs. Bathurst, who entertained with colorful, highly improbable tales of her lurid past, and an idealistic young artist named Frederick Dawes completed the residents of the house.

Frederick had moved into the lodgings just a week before Molly, and since they shared creative interests, as well as a need for extra candles, they formed a bond.

Often, when Molly was sewing late in her room, Frederick would see the light under the gap of her door and slide a note to her.

Fancy a tipple?

It was not proper, of course, not by any means, but she would open her door to him, and they sat together with a decanter of wine and some cake too, if the generous Mrs. Lotterby had made any that day.

Molly enjoyed their conversations—the freedom to discuss design and art, being asked her opinion instead of being told what she should think. Frederick was a young man who did not care much for rules, and in that respect, he reminded her of her former fiancé, Rafe Hartley. He joked with her in the same way, warning her, whenever he caught her pulling a particularly ugly expression, that if the wind changed, she'd stay that way.

"One day, Miss Robbins, you will let me paint that unique, remarkably expressive face of yours," he teased with one of his wide smiles.

"Why, pray tell, should you wish to paint me?"

"Because you are so much more interesting than the usual *belles* I'm commissioned to paint. There is character and intelligence in your features, something mysterious and melancholy."

At least he didn't try to tell her she was beautiful.

"You may dismiss that thought, Mr. Frederick Dawes. I have no desire to be reminded of how I look. The shock is bad enough when I catch my reflection in the washbasin every morning."

He laughed so hard he spat cake crumbs down his shirt and waistcoat.

"You should paint Mrs. Slater," she added, looking down at her sewing. "She has a sweetly pretty face."

"Mrs. Slater is *too* pretty. There is no challenge in painting her, for I couldn't make a bad picture if I tried. Now a face of age and experience like yours…"

"Well, thank you very much!" Molly chuckled. "It may surprise you to know, sir, Mrs. Slater is two years older than I."

"Really? I suppose she does look rather glum sometimes."

"I daresay if you had the burden of a baby, with no husband to help you and an indolent drunkard of a brother stealing from your purse at every turn, you too would be glum occasionally."

He shrugged. "Perhaps I should paint her brother's infamous foot, since we hear so much about it."

"Hush!" The walls and floors were thin in that house.

"But you will let me paint *you*, Miss Molly Robbins. One day."

"I promise you it will never happen."

Frederick's eyes twinkled mischievously. "Someone might commission your portrait."

"Who on earth would do that?"

He shrugged, but the twinkle remained. After a while, they changed the subject to talk of where they grew up. Frederick listened intently to her tale of a childhood in the country and how she came to be plucked away from it by an aristocratic young lady who needed a maid and a friend. When it was his turn, Frederick spoke without emotion of a hard, unloved youth.

"I was raised in the workhouse," he explained. "Left there as a babe to fend for myself. Later I was sold to a chimney sweep for sixpence, but when I grew too large for the flues, I ceased to be of use to him. Luckily I had this handsome face"—he gestured at it with a circling finger—"my art, and my wits. Those three things have kept me afloat in this town."

Molly thought how fortunate she had been as a child, raised in the countryside with clean-smelling air and fresh food growing in the little patch of garden behind their cottage. She had two poor but sober and respectable parents who cared about her upbringing. Well...she'd always believed they were both sober, until Carver Danforthe recently accused her father of being a drunk. Why should she believe anything that rake told her? She was still affronted by the comment so casually thrown at her.

But little Molly's early years were almost idyllic in comparison with those Frederick Dawes had spent in the workhouse and in the hands of villainous folk who sold children into labor. Rafe Hartley, too, had spent a period of his life in the workhouse when he was very young, but it was something he'd never liked to talk about. Molly's imagination had filled in the long gaps whenever her former fiancé went silent on the story of his childhood.

Frederick smiled at her. "I was very fortunate to stumble upon the good Mrs. Lotterby and win her sympathy, or I would never have moved in here and met such an interesting neighbor."

"Interesting? Me?"

"Of course you are, with your somber little face that seldom cracks a smile and your incredibly talented fingers. Your prim manners. And your mystery gentleman."

She stared at him. "My *what*?"

"The one who pays your rent here." He calmly poured more wine for them both, as she was too slow and distracted to cover her glass with one hand. "There is a gentleman, isn't there? You may as well confess it."

"Certainly not." She smoothed a stray lock of hair behind her ear. It had begun to tickle her. Just like a certain set of brazen fingertips recently. "Not in that sense."

"Fibber! I know there is. Or else why would you not fall in love with me by now?" He grinned. "Besides, we all have secrets. How else do you suppose I can afford this wine? Not to mention paint and canvas?"

"You mean, you have a…a…"

"A great lady patroness who once saved me from the gutter. Yes." He sighed. "Sadly, we parted company when her husband decided he did not want his funds going to my upkeep. It seems he thought my bills for the past year were simply part of the expensive maintenance of two spoiled lapdogs. When he awoke to the reality of his wife's hobby, I was given short shrift. Now I must seek another lady of means to keep me in the manner to which I would very much like to become accustomed." Catching Molly's expression, which she could not control despite a worthy struggle, he sputtered into his wine. "Don't look so appalled, Miss Robbins. We all do what we must to get by."

"Yes, but—"

"Of course, you are an innocent country maid." His eyes watched her above his glass.

She sat tall and straight, remembering her mother's many warnings about the pitfalls faced by young girls who did not maintain their self-control. "I am indeed, Mr. Dawes. I'll thank you to remember that."

"But this town will corrupt you sooner or later, no doubt. The world is a harsh place, Miss Robbins, and one must learn how to swim to survive. Everyone is looking for a way to use someone else. Why should you or I be any different? Swim, Miss Robbins, before the current takes you under."

But Molly had seen folk trying to swim in the stream back home in Sydney Dovedale, and it involved a vast deal of undignified kicking and splashing. Not to mention the removal of clothes. She preferred to retain her decorum. And her drawers.

So, changing the subject, she asked his opinion on a paisley-printed muslin acquired for a gown. One thing they could always discuss without fear of venturing into private, personal matters was their creative projects. They were soon lost in that conversation, and the subject of corruption, survival, and wealthy patrons was forgotten.

Although she feared her mother would not have approved of the young man's casual manners, his love of wine, or his lack of certain scruples, Molly's bond with him was quickly struck, for Frederick Dawes was one of those few folk she met who, like her, found more than white in the clouds.

❧

While Molly was with Lady Anne Rothespur for a fitting in her dressing chamber one afternoon, a sudden ruckus in the marble-tiled hall below warned of the arrival of Anne's elder brother, the Earl of Saxonby, who was supposed to be out enjoying a cricket match.

"Oh, I must show Sinjun!" Lady Anne exclaimed, dashing out, barefoot, onto the landing. "Brother! You're home early."

"Rain stopped play," he called up to her. "We came back for refreshments."

"Do you like my new gown? Is it not simply scrumptious?"

He laughed. "Quite so, Sister. What say you, Danforthe?"

Molly, standing back from the stair rail, felt her heart skip an entire verse and go straight to the chorus.

"Oh, he has no appreciation for gowns," Lady Anne replied airily.

The object of their discussion spoke up, causing Molly to grip the pleats of her skirt as if someone might try to strip it off her. "On the contrary." The sound of his voice, that deep, rolling, distant thunder brought back every moment of their last encounter and that heated quarrel. "I always appreciate a well-dressed figure," he added.

Appreciates the pleasure of undressing them, more like, she thought dourly.

Bearing more resemblance to a Whitechapel hoyden than a Mayfair miss, Lady Anne shouted over the banister, "The miracle worker herself is here to fix me. You can tell her in person how well you appreciate her work, Danforthe."

Molly pretended not to see the lady beckoning or to hear her saucy remark, but Lady Anne grabbed her hand, drawing her closer to the carved railings. She cautiously looked down into the hall.

Today he wore cricket whites, with his shirtsleeves rolled up and his hair, dampened with a mixture of perspiration and rain, flopped over his brow. How broad his naked forearms were as he rested his knuckles on his hips. To Molly's eye, he appeared almost indecently undressed and insufferably handsome—not in the pretty, dandified way, as was fashionable among his set, but in an unrepentant, unpretentious, unpracticed manner.

It made her dizzy, looking down the great distance into the hall and finding his eyes, a distinctly wicked shade of silver-gray today, looking up at her.

"I am acquainted with the lady, of course," he said. "Miss Robbins."

It felt muggy on the landing suddenly, the air hot and heavy and thick.

Margaret, he'd said, in that deep, firm, masterful voice as they argued in his drawing room the last time they had met. She'd expected no acknowledgement of her presence this time after her stern comments, but having dispensed with the formal greeting, he added, "And I believe the lady keeps some unflattering, uncalled-for ideas about me. How she came by them I couldn't say."

Molly could not retreat, for Lady Anne still gripped her hand. She felt cornered. To say nothing would look foolish. To simper and smile would be even worse. The young lady at her side ought to be shown how to handle arrogant gentlemen. So she gathered her courage to fight back. "I tend to have my eyes and ears open, your lordship. That is how I come by my ideas."

Carver smoothly returned her parry. "The problem, Miss Robbins, is that a woman's eyes and ears are generally receptive only to things that verify her ingrained opinions. A woman uses her senses selectively."

"At least she puts them to some use. Unlike a gentleman who deadens his with brandy and port so he need not feel or know anything."

Lady Anne exhaled a peal of tinkling laughter that vibrated even through her fingers where they gripped Molly's. "It seems Miss Robbins can match you for cynicism, Danforthe."

She caught his eye again, saw him raise a hand to his hair, fingers combing through it. "Miss Robbins is indeed a force to be reckoned with. Too clever for me, by far. Too upright and virtuous for an old devil like me." A sly smile lifted one side of his mouth, and Molly's heart almost ceased to drum its beat.

When the two gentlemen finally disappeared from view, Molly was able to coax Lady Anne back into her room, and spent the remainder of the visit desperately trying to coax her own mind likewise.

"Well, you put *him* in his place, Miss Robbins." The young lady giggled. "I've never heard anyone stand up to him so boldly."

Bold? No one had ever accused her of being bold before. "Perhaps you have not met his sister, your ladyship."

"No, I have not. When Danforthe came to visit, she was busy elsewhere and, of course, I was too young to be of any interest to her. I had hoped to be formally introduced this Season."

"She would, no doubt, make you one of her projects, Lady Anne. She would like you very much." The two ladies had a great deal in common, Molly thought, for they'd both been raised mostly by a brother only. Many folk thought Carver a lackadaisical guardian of his little sister, and it was true that he really put his foot down and lost his temper with Mercy only when she was so very bad that other people knew and it couldn't possibly be ignored. But Molly had seen his behavior as indulgence, not neglect. She'd witnessed how, when Mercy was young, he'd patted her on the head and laughed as she related some of her naughty deeds. He never entered the house after visiting friends in Brighton or Bath without bringing his sister a present. Any governess she didn't like was immediately dispatched from the premises. Any treat she fancied for dinner was instantly procured. Not long after Molly first arrived to live with them, she'd discovered that Lady Mercy's tales of how he spanked her with his shoe were all colorful fibs she made up for sympathy. The beastly Earl of Everscham was all bark. And far fonder of his sister than he liked anyone to know.

Later, while leaving the Rothespurs' house, Molly heard Carver's low voice in the drawing room to which the gentlemen had retreated and felt that same tempestuous beat overtaking her usually steady pulse. It was like the old days, she thought, when she worked in his house and heard him every day through walls and doors. She missed the sound of his voice, she realized with a sudden wrenching ache of nostalgia. She missed him.

No point dwelling upon that now. She had a new life and was no longer one of his minions. As he'd said, his life was his and hers was hers. Someone else would get his cordial water when he stumbled down to the kitchens in the small hours, forgetting to ring the bell.

But there was a delay in finding her coat. While the servants of the house were sent to find it and a footman was dispatched to ask the coachman for his patience,

Molly waited for her coat with a growing sense of some mischief afoot. Sure enough, Carver soon appeared with her missing garment slung over his arm.

"Miss Robbins. Would this belong to you, by chance?"

She frowned, reaching for it.

He held the coat away from her fingers, swiftly moving it behind his back. She glanced up to the landing and was relieved to find they were not being observed. The butler was off searching for her coat, and Lady Anne's brother was in the drawing room, out of sight. The footman holding the door had discreetly averted his gaze.

"I have a very busy day, your lordship," she muttered.

"Then you'd better take your coat, Miss Robbins." He finally held the coat out for her arms.

She didn't want to feel his touch, for she knew already how it had the power to render her bones soft and her will compliant. She wanted to run as fast as her feet could carry her. Instead, she bravely turned, slipping her arms into the sleeves while he held the coat for her.

"You try to ensnare me," he whispered in her ear, his hands resting lightly on her shoulders for the briefest of moments. "While your lips insult me, your eyes pull me closer. This is your design for my seduction, I think. You seek my attention, Mouse, by running under my feet at every opportunity."

"I can assure you nothing is further from my intentions," she replied hotly, tugging her collar out of his fingers and facing him again. Remembering the footman nearby, she lowered her voice. "Even if I should desire your attention, I couldn't fathom how to begin." Then she caught his smile and realized he merely teased her to get her temper up. "Have you no other woman to pester, sir?"

His eyes narrowed. "None like you."

"Yes, I daresay hardworking women of ambition are in short supply in the places you frequent, your lordship."

"As are virginal maids and determined spinsters."

"You should widen your hunting grounds and find some nice girls for a change."

"Good gracious, whatever would I want a nice girl for? I have a reputation to maintain."

Molly studied his face for a moment, noting all the signs of his smothered amusement at her expense.

"How funny you look when you're angry and trying to despise me," he whispered. "But you know what they say...that there is only a slender leap between anger and desire."

It was hopeless. If she stayed much longer in the presence of this wicked seducer, he would make her laugh, and that would never do.

Exasperated, she made for the door. He followed and walked with her to the fly waiting outside, as if it was an everyday occurrence for the Earl of Everscham to escort a dressmaker, or even know she existed. He offered his hand to help her up. To refuse would be pettish and another protest he would mock, so she laid her fingers lightly over his and stepped into the fly. He closed the door for her.

"Miss Robbins."

"Your lordship." She fixed her gaze directly ahead, and only when the horses finally pulled away from him did she relax.

Eight

IT WAS NOT TO BE THE LAST TIME SHE FOUND HIM IN her path. Arriving one afternoon soon after for a fitting at the Baroness Schofield's house in Grosvenor Square, Molly was horrified to find her client entertaining a guest. Who else but the Earl of Everscham, busily maintaining his reputation.

He sprawled on a chaise lounge in the lady's dressing room, hands behind his head, one booted foot on the floor, the other carelessly marking the silk cushions. As usual, his was a powerful presence, devouring the frilly room, swamping the light, feminine furnishings and darkening the space with his masculinity. At least he was not still in his evening clothes, Molly thought briskly when she walked in and saw him there. The fresh spring air clung to him as she walked by, so she guessed he had arrived not long before her.

Good. He had not spent the night there then. Although why she should care was anybody's guess. *His life was his, hers was hers*. They'd agreed. Molly set her sewing basket down and primly set to the task of ignoring his presence.

The baroness acted very differently on that day,

with her lover in attendance. She was twittery and flirtatious, puffing out her bosom as she paraded around in her petticoats and corset, making Molly chase her back and forth with the measuring tape. Her lady's maid stood nearby, looking bored and weary.

"Peters," the baroness exclaimed at one point, "don't just drip there against the wall leaving a stain, go and fetch the tea tray. His lordship must be parched. I know I am with all this dreadful standing about and being still so this woman doesn't stick me with pins."

Abruptly reminded of the time she poked Carver in the foot with a pin, Molly glanced up from her work very briefly and caught his eye. Saw a slight smile lift the corners of his mouth, a wicked gleam lighten his gaze. When he pressed two fingers to his lips, she recalled how those same two fingertips had stroked the side of her face. She supposed a cheek was nothing to him. He must be accustomed to touching a great deal more than a lady's cheek.

Now it was as if she felt his lips travel the same course. Molly hurriedly went back to her pinning.

For all the Baroness Schofield's complaints about the inconvenience of standing still, she did not trouble herself to do so for very long. Even her girlish, high-pitched laughter caused movement. She could not seem to do anything, even breathe, without exaggeration. Carver, on the other hand, was very still and mostly silent. Molly suspected he wasn't even listening to his mistress as she chattered about other women of her acquaintance, happily disparaging their hair, their skin, their nails—anything she could. Did the baroness not know how little he was interested in gossip, how thin his patience for spiteful women?

Molly knew. But then she'd known him for twelve years. Had lived in his house all that time and seen him daily avoid the gossiping women who came to visit his sister. She'd heard all his muttered complaints as he stormed by her with his long stride, his coattails flapping like the wings of an angry blackbird.

She chanced another upward glance at the man on the chaise and saw him rub his brow with those fingers now in a quick, irritable manner. He must have a headache, she thought. Keeping up that reputation of his was taking its toll.

"Ouch!" the baroness squealed, jerking away. "Do try to leave my skin unpierced, woman! You render me full of holes!" Before Molly could apologize, the customer walked over to the chaise, trailing the unfinished hem across the dressing-room carpet, care-less of Molly's efforts to follow on her knees. "Darling Carver, how bored you must be waiting for this clumsy girl to be done. Here, I shall give you a kiss to make up for it. I know how impatient you are." She laughed, and it sounded like the hanging drops of crystal on a chandelier tinkling together as they met the caress of a housemaid's feather duster.

Molly's temperature rose another notch, and she jabbed a pin into the small cushion tied around her wrist.

"Not now, Maria," she heard Carver exclaim gruffly.

"Why not?" Again she laughed, harder this time, shaking those crystals until they became chipped. "It's only a servant."

Whether there was eventually a kiss exchanged or not, Molly didn't see or hear. She kept her sight trained upon her sewing basket, throwing her seamstress tools back inside it with increasing speed and venom.

Peters soon returned with the tea and set it up on a small table beside the chaise. There was a large silver urn, delicate china cups, and a three-tiered platter full of enticingly pretty cakes. Molly's stomach rumbled, but she kept her head down. She was not invited to partake of the tea, naturally, and in any case, how could she have enjoyed it in that dreadful woman's company?

"Madam," she ventured, when it seemed her presence and her purpose there was forgotten, "if you are occupied with your guest, I will take my leave and return again another day." How badly she wanted to add that the baroness was not her only customer, and other gowns awaited her work and her time.

"Heavens above, woman, I hardly knew you were still here." The baroness was perched on the edge of the chaise, since Carver had not moved to make room for her ample buttocks. She stuck a slender, two-pronged fork into one of the little cakes. "Peters, I suppose you'd better tell the footman at the door to summon a hackney cab for the dressmaker. It seems she didn't think to ask the one that brought her here to wait."

"I could not ask the coach driver to wait for me, madam, especially not knowing how long the fitting would take." She could not afford it, was what she meant, but it would not be seemly to mention money.

Not that "seemly" would matter much to a woman who walked about in her underthings in front of a gentleman in her dressing room.

The man on the chaise suddenly leapt to his feet,

almost causing the baroness to lose her balance. "I must leave. I have an important engagement elsewhere this afternoon." Molly saw his boots walk by with that forceful stride. But they stopped at the door of the dressing room and swiveled with their toes toward her. "Miss Robbins, perhaps you would care for a ride across Town, since you are done here?"

The silence that greeted this remark was in danger of stretching into uncomfortable territory, until the baroness exclaimed, "But she came in a hackney. She can leave the same way. I'm sure that's good enough for a dressmaker."

Molly snapped the lid of her sewing basket shut and scrambled upright. "Certainly, madam. It is no trouble to go back as I came, your lordship. Thank you for the offer."

"Nonsense," he growled. "You'll come with me."

Again, silence. She couldn't even hear her heart beating.

"It looks like rain," he added crossly, as if the bad weather might be her fault. "So you'd better let me take you home rather than wait for the footman to find you a hackney."

Even his mistress knew not to argue when he used that tone of voice. Not that it stopped her from pouting.

A few moments later Molly was marched out to his carriage, where she sat very straight, knees together, sewing basket on her lap, the covered, unfinished gown carefully folded beside her. After shouting directions at the coachman, Carver dropped to the opposite seat.

"Here I am, doing you a favor again," he muttered. "What can I be thinking? It's surely a fool's errand to expect gratitude from you."

"Of course I am grateful, your lordship," she

replied stiffly, her fingers tightly gripping the basket, her knees pressed together so hard they hurt. "I just wish you wouldn't." She couldn't resist adding, "I'm only a servant."

"Believe me, I also wish I didn't feel the urge to help you." Then he grinned suddenly. "But I can't seem to stop doing it. Servant or not."

She pressed her knees even more firmly together, until they began to feel bruised.

"If it is not deemed meddling, Miss Robbins, may I ask how your business proceeds?"

"Very well, your lordship. I am kept busy with orders."

"You are in good health?"

"I am," she replied in a tone of tense civility. "And you are in health, your lordship?"

"As a matter of fact, I have not been feeling myself." He stretched out his legs, hands on his thighs, looking like one of the healthiest male specimens she'd ever seen. "I am...perturbed by some illness I cannot identify. A fever of some sort."

"Really?"

He leaned forward. "Feel my brow, Miss Robbins. See for yourself."

She pursed her lips.

"Go on," he urged, "touch me."

"No, thank you."

"You'll never forgive yourself, madam, if something terrible happens and you dismissed me so callously."

"What terrible thing could happen to you?" She clawed her sewing basket a little tighter, glancing around the comfortable interior of his very new, well-sprung, draft-free carriage.

He pulled a somber face. "It may already have happened, Miss Robbins." Raising a hand to his forehead, he sighed deeply. "With my sister gone off on one of her adventures, and your heartless desertion, who is there to witness my decline and ease my suffering?"

Again Molly felt the unfortunate desire to smile at him. His teasing words fumbled over her, looking for weak spots and ticklish places. Swiftly she removed one glove and, all business, reached over to place the back of her fingers against his brow. He was, in fact, slightly warmer than she expected. "I'm sure you'll live, your lordship. If your head aches, Mrs. Jakes can make you a restorative potion with powders she gets from the apothecary."

He looked up, his eyes searching her face, pausing a moment on her lips. Molly's pulse quickened. She retrieved her hand, having felt enough of his heat.

Reaching inside his coat, he withdrew a little parcel made from his own silk handkerchief and held it out toward her.

She eyed the offering hesitantly. "What is this?"

"Something I know you wanted, Miss Robbins. Now if you refuse it, I have committed a crime for nothing."

Eventually she took it and untied the knot. He had filched six small cakes for her from his mistress's tea tray. Molly didn't know what to say to this bounty. Her eyes felt sore, her palms sweaty inside her gloves.

"You may thank me," he said, hitching forward on his seat.

She darted a shy glance at his face. "How might I do that?" Oh, dear. Oh, no.

He turned to offer his cheek and pointed to it with one long finger.

Her heart thumped away like the back foot of a distressed rabbit looking to warn the rest of his warren. "I couldn't."

"Why not?"

"We just left the house of your mistress." What else might she expect from a rake like him?

"Why do you think I did not kiss her?"

She hadn't seen, of course, so she didn't know whether he spoke the truth or not. "I'm sure it doesn't matter to me if you did."

"I saved my kiss for you."

Molly rolled her eyes. "Please don't neglect your mistress on my account, your lordship. Better you spend your kisses on a woman who needs them."

"Ah, that's right, Miss Robbins, you are a cold-hearted mercenary in need only of my coin."

"I was quite frank with you in that regard."

"Good Lord!" he exclaimed. "At least the baroness doesn't force me to beg for her kisses like a wet-nosed street urchin."

"You make this very difficult, sir. Have you forgotten the contract we signed and your promise? No Tomfoolery. I cannot imagine what your purpose could be in—"

"Then give me the cakes back, and I'll eat them, ingrate." He reached across, swiped one, and stuffed it whole into his mouth. "Bloody women!" he exclaimed, spraying crumbs. "Why do I bother?"

Molly stared as he chewed viciously, his eyes gleaming.

The sweet almond scent of marzipan already tickled her nose and her taste buds. He was a devil, she decided, sent to tempt her from the rightful path. Her mother would despair.

He paused his chewing and swallowed hard. "You were very rude to me in front of my friend when we last met. Accusing me of deadening my feelings with brandy. When you are the one who has no feelings. Or denies them at least."

Did he not understand how she had to be that way? Foolish question. Of course he didn't. When he wanted something, he had it, regardless of any scruples or morals. He never had to work for anything, and he wouldn't understand the strength of her ambition, the need to keep a focused direction on her career, undistracted by this intense attraction for a gentleman so unsuitable. Carver could never know that her "No Tomfoolery" clause was as much a warning for herself as it was for him.

But he had stolen cake for her and arranged things so she wasn't forced to wait for a hackney. Was this his usual routine of seduction? Probably couldn't stop himself, she mused.

"One tiny kiss," he grumbled. "On the cheek. How much harm could there be in it?"

Molly said nothing, just looked at the spoiled boy. She wanted to kiss him; that was the sad truth of it. Despite all his faults, despite the fact that he'd just left his mistress, despite her desire to cause very little harm and never disappoint her mother.

She wanted to kiss him.

"One kiss, and I promise never to pester you again." He gestured with his arms out, his shoulders shrugged. "We're all alone here. No one will know."

He wasn't going to shut up otherwise, it seemed. So she slid forward on her seat, struggling to contain her awful excitement. One kiss was not an affair, was it?

"Oh, very well then…for pity's sake." She would get it over with, she decided. Once the mystique was gone, she could put the temptation behind her and, hopefully, so could he.

His eyelids lowered. "Only if you're sure you can spare it."

"Before I change my mind."

He parted his knees farther still to make room for hers between them. She couldn't breathe. To sit this close, this intimately, set her skin afire.

"Hurry, Miss Robbins, or *I* might change *my* mind and take the cakes back again."

Terribly aware of his strong thighs on either side of her, not to mention the other parts of him in such close proximity to her knees, she leaned in, closed her eyes, and pressed a kiss to his cheek. It was cool, a little rough. Before she could retreat, he turned his face, reached up with both hands to cup her chin, and returned the kiss. Sort of. It was more of a lick than a kiss. She felt his tongue—the tip of it—slide over her clenched lips, sampling the taste of her.

She pushed back, clutching her parcel of cake. "You tricked me!"

"Of course I did. I'm a rake. That's what rakes do." Another slow grin relaxed his expression. "You knew that. You'd be the first to tell me so. In fact, if I hadn't, you would have been disappointed. Insulted even."

"You, sir, are incorrigible!"

He laughed. "How many times have you thought that of me today already?"

She scowled. "Twice," she mumbled.

"Yet you still got into my carriage."

"That's three times I've thought it now," she

added peevishly. Pressing her spine to the back of the seat, she stared at him through the flickering, rain-streaked light.

Carver was still on the edge, teetering toward her. Tight fists rested now on his thighs. "Very well, so I tricked you. Just as you tricked me with that contract you made me sign before I was awake to what I gave up."

"Then let that be an end to it. No more trickery."

He nodded, pretending to be solemn and concerned. It didn't fool Molly for a moment, and he couldn't keep it up for long. Only seconds later, he was stifling another chuckle as he said, "I can feed the cake to you, if you like." His amused gaze licked over her mouth just as his tongue had moments before. She was burned by it, her lips throbbing. It felt as if everyone they passed in that carriage must have seen her give in to temptation and kiss him, although her lapse lasted merely seconds.

"I'll manage to feed myself," she replied tautly. Her stomach wasn't feeling empty any longer. A heaviness had settled there, need replaced with want. Wicked, foolish, impossible want. And not for cake. "Perhaps I'll save them until later." She couldn't forgive herself if she didn't share the cakes with her friends at the boarding house. With trembling fingers, she retied the handkerchief around her costly prizes.

"As you wish, Miss Robbins." He sat back, the panther retreating to his shadows. "Later."

❧

"I must say, she's a peculiar thing," the baroness remarked as they took their seats in his box at the opera. "Barely speaks above a whisper."

"Hmm?" Carver flung out the tails of his evening jacket and dropped heavily into the seat.

"Darling, do pay attention! That funny, dour little dressmaker."

"Don't be fooled, Maria. She has a backbone of steel, and a bloodthirsty bite when she decides to use it."

"But I'm very excited about the new gowns."

She leaned over to plant a small peck upon his cheek, and he eyed her warily. Earlier that same evening, she'd displayed a hot temper, furious with him about "other women" she suspected him of pursuing behind her back. Although Carver never promised exclusivity in his encounters with the fairer sex, the baroness had apparently expected it during his attachment to her. He vaguely remembered her pushing for such a fool's promise on a few occasions, but he'd ignored it. Carver would never tie himself to one woman. Monogamy, he'd decided long ago, was for those who were stuck, planted, and set like tree trunks to grow fat and become a target for pigeon excrement. "If I ever thought it possible to be content with one woman," he would say to his friend Sinjun, "I would bloody well get married, and that I shall never do. I might have to go in the ground one day, but I won't be buried while still alive."

He even had a wager in the book at White's that all his friends would marry before he did. The women of his acquaintance, therefore, ought to know where they stood. Carver was always completely straightforward in his pursuit of pleasure, which was just as determined as his escape from duty. Particularly "duty" as defined by other folk.

When the baroness saw that her display of jealous

temper had got her nowhere with him that evening, she resorted to tears. Now, having run out of that short supply, she tried a giddy, airy-brained act, including an excess of "darlings" that was no less irritating to his nerves than her previous sobs and threats.

Suddenly she said, "Lady Mercy is still in the country?"

"She is." A lot of people had begun showing interest in his sister's extended visit to Norfolk. When Mercy left to attend her maid's wedding, she expected to be gone only a few days, but that had now stretched into a month, with no hint of when she might show her face in London again. He'd had a letter from her at last. While she explained that she'd found some worthy mission to occupy her time in the country, his sister relayed no plans for any return. If not for the fact that he had much on his own mind just then, Carver might have felt more concern than he did; but the truth was he spent much of his time thinking about Miss Robbins and trying to find secret ways of helping her, not to mention engineering an occasional "accidental" meeting. While he refused to label this as a pursuit of any sort, the hours of his day were considerably taken up with these thoughts and schemes. It would only complicate matters once his meddling sister returned, and if she'd found some other cause to keep her busy, he was happy for her. Doubly so for himself.

Besides, he'd warned her before that his days of chasing after her whenever she ran off on an adventure were long over.

"Did your sister not go into the country for a wedding?" his companion inquired.

"Yes." It was more of a sigh than a word.

"Yet the wedding did not take place, and Lady Mercy remained to comfort the jilted groom, even with her own fiancé due back from Italy soon."

How quickly rumor spread, ruthless and greedy as fire in a dry forest. "My sister remained because she thought she could be of service to the groom's family. She has known the Hartleys many years."

"I do hope her fiancé, Viscount Grey, will understand," Maria exclaimed, her tone devoid of sincerity. "Your sister has waited this long to get a husband. I should hate to see her engagement fall through."

In a time when most young ladies were expected to catch a husband by the end of their first three London Seasons, Mercy had raised eyebrows by remaining unwed. But when she recently announced her sudden engagement to Viscount Grey, it was a surprise to many, and no more so, he suspected, than it was to Grey himself. The unfortunate fellow would never succeed in handling Mercy, not in a month of Sundays.

The baroness continued, "Lady Cecelia Montague told me that your odd little dressmaker is the very same runaway bride whose wedding was abandoned. That she and Lady Mercy had a falling out over the groom. That is why your sister stayed in the country and her former maid returned here."

Carver scowled down at the stage as the curtain rose. "Well, if Lady Cecelia says so, it must be true. The woman is a fount of information, I'm sure."

Lady Cecelia and his sister had been at war since they were children. As far as he recalled, it all began over a bonnet they both wanted, or some such nonsense. Ever since then, Cecelia Montague had longed for his sister's tumble from the top rung of the social ladder, and she would doubtless relish the slightest hint of a scandal.

The baroness, he realized, was still talking. "People are saying that Lady Mercy has decided to enjoy a tumble in the hayloft with this country lad before the Viscount Grey returns from Italy."

Carver snapped his head around and glared at the elegant woman beside him as she fanned herself daintily. "People? By that you mean Cecelia Montague. She certainly has a big enough mouth to count as a crowd."

She lifted her bare shoulders. "It is becoming quite the scandal."

Amusing how she spoke this way about his sister's behavior when she was there at his side, involved in a relationship that was certainly not "proper." But of course, as members of the aristocracy, they got away with it. King William himself had sired a number of bastards by his mistress, "Mrs. Jordan," an Irish actress. It was simply the way things were done. With most marriages in their social class arranged for financial reasons, it was inevitable that spouses would turn elsewhere for passion and other needs.

However, if Carver's unmarried sister chose to play with a man from base beginnings, that was another matter. Rafe Hartley was the illegitimate son of a housemaid. Although his natural father—a gentleman of wealth and consequence—had publicly recognized the young man a few years ago and made some attempt to raise him up, Rafe was a stubborn, hot-headed bastard who insisted on doing things the hard way. He turned his back on his father's assistance and preferred wallowing in the dirt of a farmyard, laboring with his hands.

The baroness resumed needling at Carver with a spiteful tongue. "I suppose you felt obliged to compensate the dressmaker when she returned here, because of your sister stealing away her groom."

"Is that what you suppose, Maria?"

She shrugged. "It's clear you sent me to her for a purpose, darling. She needed customers, and you wanted to help her." Her fan stilled. She peered over it in a flirty manner he supposed was meant to be alluring and distract him from the wheedling note of suspicion in her voice. "I have wracked my brains for any other reason why you should care about that odd little person's success."

"And so you believed the scurrilous tale you heard from Cecelia Montague—a story she is, no doubt, circulating merrily about Town, simply because my sister is not here to defend herself, and Miss Robbins has too much discretion to speak of her abandoned nuptials to all and sundry."

"*Miss* Robbins?" she exclaimed haughtily.

"That is her name."

Apparently she didn't care to know it. "As for your sister—"

"What about my sister?" He was being lethally polite. Again she ignored the warning.

"Can you defend her? Can you say she has not taken up with a young man far beneath her in consequence? A young man recently supposed to wed her own lady's maid?" There was a shrillness to her voice when she forgot her act.

"Although I need not tell you anything, madam, I will say that I have no proof she has done anything of the sort. Neither does that overprimped harpy, Cecelia Montague."

Maria closed her fan and held it in her lap, her gloved arms curved gracefully, her gaze apparently riveted on the stage below them. "I have also heard that this is not the first time. That your sister made this mistake once before with the same young man, but it was hushed up for years. And that this country lad is perhaps the reason why she has remained unwed into her twenty-second year and seventh London Season."

Carver clenched his hands into fists on his knees and felt heat rising in the pit of his stomach. He knew he'd been a lax guardian to Mercy. Inheriting his title and fortune before he was twenty-one had thrust him into many responsibilities before he was ready, the care of a contrary sister—ten years his junior—perhaps being the most daunting. So yes, he'd made mistakes. The memory of Mercy's elopement to Gretna Green five years ago with Rafe Hartley stuck like a thorn in his conscience. Luckily he'd found them before their hasty marriage could be consummated. He took Mercy back to London, and that was that. No one but the principle players in the scandal, and the long-suffering Edward Hobbs, knew what had happened.

Had Molly Robbins found out, from either Mercy or Rafe? Did the Mouse sit in her lodgings, pining for Rafe Hartley? Is that why she added the "No Tomfollerie" clause? That might also explain why she buried herself in work. According to Edward Hobbs, she stayed up all night with a candle burning in her window.

"I can assure you, madam," he muttered thoughtfully, "my desire to help Miss Robbins has nothing whatsoever to do with my sister's visit to friends in the country."

"Why then?" his mistress demanded, pouting. "Why would you care about that pinch-faced dressmaker?"

Her whining voice scraped like fingernails over his flesh, making it raw and bloody. He wanted to retaliate. Perhaps she'd learn not to question him if she did not like his answers. "Miss Robbins interests me."

"*Interests you?* That plain, spindle of a creature?"

"Her mind intrigues me. It's rare to find a female who puts time and effort into more than catching a husband."

The baroness fussed with her gown and her fan. "I would have imagined her to be the very last sort of woman in whom you'd find anything remotely interesting. She has no bosom to speak of, an unremarkable face, and no conversation. Her lips are too thin, her chin lacks definition, there is no brightness in her complexion, her nose gives her a stunted profile, and her eyes are completely devoid of sparkle."

"How did you find her teeth?" he snapped dryly.

"Merely regular," she replied without an ounce of perception. "But that means nothing. They say savages from the jungle have the best teeth."

Her very predictability had made the baroness an attractive companion. She was always utterly transparent, unsubtle in her demands for his attention. There was nothing about her that required puzzling over, no mystery. But that same predictability now made her tedious, banal company.

Very different to the prickly and witty Miss Robbins, who kept him on his toes without even trying and held his attention without wanting it.

Carver pressed a finger to his lips, feigning complete absorption in the performance on stage, ignoring the beautiful woman beside him and thinking instead about the disagreeable one who brazenly insulted him in his own drawing room and kept her knees held so tightly together in his presence that he was surprised she walked instead of hopped.

As his thoughts thus turned to Miss Robbins's legs, which were undoubtedly of some considerable length under her layers of petticoat, all concerns about his sister's antics and his irritable, gossiping mistress, were soon erased completely from his mind. He pictured his hands slowly making their way up Miss Robbins's stockings to her nervously clenched thighs and between them, where he would soon amend any doubts she might have about his purpose in bribing her with cake.

Had anyone asked Carver which opera he saw that night, he would never have been able to answer.

Nine

As Molly carried a pitcher of water up the stairs one morning for her ablutions, she encountered old Mrs. Bathurst on the narrow landing, signaling to her in some urgency.

"What is it, madam? Are you all right? Is something amiss?" She wondered if perhaps the lady had endured another visit from a debt collector, for they seemed a frequent menace in that house, worse than flies on a butcher's market stall. Molly had already protected the old dear from one scrawny, greasy-haired menace a few days previously—chased him down the stairs with her slipper and a crochet hook.

Mrs. Bathurst's gnarled fingers pulled on Molly's shawl. "Come into my room, my dear. I have something to show you."

Molly left her jug inside her own room and then hurried to her neighbor's. Mrs. Bathurst told her to shut the door. "Come. Sit." She gestured to a small settee with a torn horsehair cushion and then began searching inside a cupboard, muttering under her breath. Molly had never before been inside Mrs. Bathurst's room, and she found it quite comfortable, full of furnishings that, like the old lady herself, had seen better days and possibly known a lifetime of scandalous secrets. Not that Molly listened to gossip. If it could be helped.

"I have come to a decision," said Mrs. Bathurst. "It's time I put things to use. I'm not long for this world, and I can't abide the thought of the bailiffs taking everything when I'm gone. Duns ransacking my treasures to pay bills they *claim* I have not paid. Aha! Here they are." She took three carved wooden boxes from a shelf in her cupboard and placed them reverently in Molly's lap. "These were given to me by a lover many years ago, when I was younger than you are now, Miss Robbins." She smiled, lowering to the seat beside Molly. "He was a very fine man, a Hungarian prince."

Molly looked at the boxes. They were quite plain on the outside, the carving simple but cleanly done.

"He adored me, you know. Ah, but it never lasts."

"No, I suppose not." She tried to keep the disapproval out of her tone, for she liked Mrs. Bathurst. It was impossible not to like a person who often wore shoes from two different pairs on her feet just because she "felt like it," claimed to have lived before as Boadicea, Queen of the Iceni, could recite love poems in Russian, and put crumbs out for the birds on her window ledge every day without fail, because she believed they were the souls of lost loved ones come to say good morning to her. Mrs. Bathurst was a victim, however, of two widely disparate natures. One day she was full of the joys of life and singing from the mountaintops; the next she was down in the deepest gully of unhappiness. Molly always made an effort to cheer the lady if she encountered her on one of those bad days, but it was very hard work and often frustrating.

Today, it seemed, Mrs. Delilah Bathurst was merry and in a mood to reminisce.

"How long ago it was, and yet I can remember his face as if he stands there now, by my window." The lady's eyes fogged over. "I have kept those boxes hidden away for too long. It is time to share. You, I think, have the sensitive eye to appreciate them."

"They are beautiful, madam."

"Open them, my dear. The real treat is held within."

Molly clicked open the first lid and discovered that the box was decorated inside with a pattern of small ebony and mother-of-pearl tiles, like a chess board. Within each ebony square there was a violet flower made of tiny gemstones.

"The boxes, you see, Miss Robbins, are made to look quite ordinary on the outside, but within they hold special treasure, secret surprises of great beauty."

"They are exquisite, madam!" Molly opened the other boxes and found more bejeweled interiors, intricately designed patterns that had kept their brilliant color because they so seldom saw sunlight.

"And now they are yours, my dear."

"Oh, Mrs. Bathurst, I could never—"

"The moment I saw your clever hands at work, I thought of these boxes. Hidden treasures, you see. Not much on the outside, but glorious artistry within. Only those privileged to see inside can enjoy it."

"But surely there is someone else more deserving—"

"No, indeed. My mind is made up. I have my memories, and they must be enough. My sister, who does not have a true appreciation of my treasures, would pawn them for cake to feed the neighborhood. There is no other relative to whom I can entrust these pretty things. I had a son once, but he is lost to me now. At least let me go to my grave, Miss Robbins, knowing I have thwarted the bailiffs who would take everything I ever loved and leave me to be buried with naught but the clothes upon my back. As it is, I daresay they will have the silk stockings off me before I'm cold, and the rings from my fingers, even if they have to break the bones to get them."

While the lady ranted and raved about these ghostly tomb robbers, as if they waited now in the corner of her room, counting the minutes until she expired, Molly ran her hands over the boxes, her mind already churning with new ideas for her designs.

Finally, as the lady's words slowly registered, she looked up. "You had a son, madam?"

"Thirty years ago at least." She lowered her voice and glanced anxiously at her door. "I could not keep him. He was taken from me."

"By whom?" Molly was indignant at the idea of anyone taking a child away from its mother.

"I daresay it was just as well, my dear Miss Robbins. In my state, what could I give the boy?"

"I see. It happened after you were widowed. You must miss your husband, Mrs. Bathurst."

"My husband?" She chortled. "My dear, I'm afraid there never was one in my case. The son of whom I speak was conceived on the wrong side of the blanket, as they say. But there was a dear naval colonel named Bathurst with whom I enjoyed many pleasant afternoons. Sadly, he lost his life at the Battle of Copenhagen. My sister, finding me enceinte some months after, thought it fitting I should play the part of his widow, since he was not around to deny it."

"Oh."

"You see, my sister, although the younger, has always taken charge of me."

"But could you not go to the colonel's family for help? Surely they would want—"

"He was not the father of my child."

She should, perhaps, have seen that coming. Mrs. Bathurst's cloud was a colorful one, to say the least. But this story tugged on Molly's heart, for she could see the lady's sorrow when she spoke of her child. It was a sudden spark of something real among all the whimsical, far-fetched tales.

"Do you know where your son is now, what became of him?"

The lady tilted her head, and a dreamy expression melted over her features. She laid a hand on the carved lid of the box Molly held in her lap. "He is better off than you and I, to be sure. He lives in a beautiful house and is never troubled with fleas in his mattress. I saw him only last week, in a carriage with a lovely young lady. I knew him at once, for he is very like his princely father."

Another fantastical story from her new friend's varied repertoire. It was far more likely that her poor child was placed in an institution of some kind, like so many unfortunates. Like poor Frederick Dawes or dear Rafe Hartley, she thought.

But Mrs. Bathurst did not want to talk more on the matter, and her chatter veered off in a new direction—as it did frequently. "Now, did I tell you, my dear Miss Robbins, about the time I was pursued through the maze at Hampton Court by Admiral Lord Nelson *and* the Duke of Wellington at the same time?"

"No, madam, you did not."

So the lady began her improbable tale of reckless abandon among the hornbeam hedges, and Molly listened, growing impervious to shocks. Until she formed a friendship with Mrs. Bathurst, Molly had always assumed the fault for a lady's ruin lay entirely with the man who pursued and seduced her. Now she understood that women could be equally to blame, equally tempted. Some of them quite enjoyed it.

Try as she might, Molly found she could not disapprove of the indefatigable Mrs. Bathurst or the lurid, implausible stories that made her happy, any more than she could scowl at Frederick's methods of staying afloat. Her mother might have warned her against acquaintances such as these, but Molly knew they were not bad people. Now she lived among them and saw how there were many different sorts of struggle in the world. She had been sheltered from much of it, firstly having grown up within the protection of a large family, then having the good fortune of meeting Lady Mercy Danforthe.

Thoughts of Mrs. Bathurst's lost child plagued her. Those institutions were little more than breeding grounds for crooks. She'd seen abandoned young boys—like the one who'd caught Carver Danforthe's notice recently—who worked the London streets as pickpockets, their faces grubby, and with no shoes on their feet. Most workhouse boys were not as fortunate as Frederick Dawes, who had good looks, street-smart charm, and artistic talent to carry him along. Or as lucky as Rafe, who had concerned family to take him in and offer a helping hand.

Mrs. Bathurst's fiction of what happened to her child was much more palatable than the probable truth, of course, and if fantasy brought comfort to the old lady, who was Molly to spoil it? A dose of reality would not cure her illness and would only sink her into the depression that was never far away on the other side of a fragile wall.

The social debut of Molly Robbins's Designs for Discerning Ladies occurred at the Royal Academy of Art on the occasion of the annual exhibition, during which Lady Cecelia Montague was seen sporting a blue lutestring ensemble of such a new style that it made the Society column of *The Times*, as well as an article, complete with sketch, in *La Belle Assemblee*.

Molly slowly read the description when Frederick—with toast crumbs on his chin and a paintbrush tucked behind his ear—ran up the stairs to show her the article.

As reported by an eager eyewitness, Lady Cecelia's garments were cut with smooth lines that might almost be considered severe and masculine. But they contained a cunning surprise—a bright damask-print underskirt, visible only in teasing flashes as she walked. The sleeves, it was shockingly observed, were quite peculiar in that they simply followed the shape of the arm, rather than provide it with any bulbous curves, epaulettes, or wing-like protuberances. Only a small fanned pleat in the same fabric as the underskirt was used to widen the cuff over Lady Cecelia's hand and to make an upright collar, which rose all the way to her proud chin. The collar itself was revolutionary among a sea of broad wings.

Never before thought of as particularly tall or graceful, Lady Cecelia was now considered "swanlike." There was not an ungainly puff or needless ruffle in sight. In a form that was either old-fashioned or daringly new—no one seemed certain either way—the bodice was molded to her figure and yet miraculously succeeded in masking flaws previously noted by critical observers. Now, when those same eyes looked to find fault in her shape, they saw only an elegant line and a woman confidant that she looked her best.

It was, for all concerned, a triumph.

Soon after this event, Baroness Schofield was spotted at a private ball in a very simple spring-green sarcenet gown. The understated design revealed a surprise however, for as she danced, lifting her wrist and with it one side of her train, a concertina of pleats opened to show a trail of tiny ribbon roses and white embroidered daisies scattered in a seemingly haphazard pattern down the material and across the back of her skirt. Almost as if, as one witness proclaimed, they were spilled there by fortuitous accident. The same daises were sewn into a single strip of ribbon that circled her neck in place of grander jewels.

At the ball, a gentleman was overheard to declare that the Baroness Schofield could put that Season's fresh young debutantes in the shade. She was apparently so thrilled by this that she sent a bouquet of tulips to Molly's lodgings the next day, carried by her lady's maid, who dutifully and without the slightest enthusiasm, related all the details of the successful evening. There was a problem however.

The card left with the bouquet was written in a messy hand Molly recognized at once. It was the same handwriting she'd witnessed almost daily, for twelve years, on letters left upon the hall table at Danforthe House whenever the earl was done with his morning correspondence.

At least no one else would know. She could safely show off her flowers as if they did indeed come from a satisfied client.

Meanwhile, young debutante Lady Anne Rothespur was delighted by the reaction to her lilac silk walking gown with embroidered frog clasps across the bodice and waterfall pleats revealing diamonds of patterned muslin down the back of the skirt. For once, she told Molly, even her brother had approved.

"I do believe even Danforthe thought I looked very well in it," she exclaimed when she called at Molly's lodgings to thank her. "He very nearly gave me a compliment, and Danforthe never gives a compliment. My brother says he can't understand why women flock to him, because he's invariably rude to them."

Molly was caught unawares by the mention of that name. The Earl of Everscham had lurked in the back of her mind, safely tucked away where he could not distract her, but the chattering young lady brought him back out of hiding.

"Of course, Danforthe is heinously handsome, so I'm told." Lady Anne wrinkled her nose. "I just cannot see it, having grown up thinking of him as more of a brother. Ever since I can remember, he and Sinjun have been close. They met at school, you know."

"Oh?" She tried not to appear too interested.

"Danforthe stood up for my brother against some

dreadful bullies, and they were friends from that day on. Sinjun says Danforthe was always protecting those weaker than himself. Do you think him handsome, Miss Robbins?"

She delayed coyly. "Your brother?"

"Jumping Jacks, no! Carver Danforthe. Would you say he is handsome?"

Molly was folding a pattern, her head bowed over the table. "I have heard him described as such." She hesitated. "Although I always considered his nose rather...large." One had to find something to criticize, she thought.

But it was pleasing to learn how he once protected other boys from bullying at school. It made her warm inside, even a trifle dizzy. Must be because she had not eaten yet today.

"Yes, quite true about his nose," Lady Anne replied. "Women tend to put up with his bad behavior rather more than they should, considering the lack of an elegant nose. Why do you suppose that is, Miss Robbins? Why do they let the blackguard get away with it?"

"I really cannot imagine."

"I heard that a young woman once dropped to the carpet in a dead faint just because he spoke to her at a party," Lady Anne exclaimed, turning now in tight spins as if she practiced dance steps. "And he only mentioned the decorative fruit she wore in her hair. Told her she had a very nice pear. That was enough to make her swoon. He does seem to have a curious effect on the ladies. I suppose he can be rather intimidating."

"He's really just an old bear who likes to hear himself growl."

Lady Anne paused her bouncing and collapsed like a tower of cards, laughing breathlessly. "Now I shall always think of Danforthe as a great, silly old bear at the circus, showing his claws and growling." The laughter continued as she gave Molly a tight hug, dispensing with formality and proper reserve, then hurried to the door with her usual speed. As happened on all her visits to Molly's lodgings, Lady Anne's governess awaited her outside with the carriage, not wanting to enter the building and having fruitlessly tried to discourage her charge from doing so. Halfway to the door, Lady Anne suddenly spun around again.

"Oh, Miss Robbins! I almost forgot! I meant to ask if you ever attend concerts at Vauxhall Gardens. There is one on Thursday, and I am eager to go, but my brother refuses to take me. He says I cannot go without a chaperone, but my damn governess says concerts give her a headache. I wondered if I might persuade you to come with me?"

"Well, I have never—"

"Do say you will, Miss Robbins. I will be dreadfully crushed and sent into an abysmal state of depression if I cannot go. I have thought of nothing else but the concert for three nights together, and you will be very good, steady company. Danforthe says you are the most pious person he knows."

She sincerely doubted he meant to flatter her when he said that, but the young lady was adamant, her eyes so innocent and beguiling that Molly hesitated when she should have made a polite excuse. "I'm sure you must have someone to escort you there, Lady Anne."

"Not a soul, I swear! Please say you will come. Miss Forde is to sing. Although I would rather see a magician or Madame Lamotte's feats on the flying wire, I am told Miss Forde is very good. The walks there are very pleasant, so I hear, and we need not sit and listen to the orchestra if you would rather view the pavilions. There is art by Mr. Hogarth and Mr. Hayman. You will appreciate the elegance of the sculptures, Miss Robbins. It will inspire your work."

She laughed at the young girl's eagerness. Lady Anne, as she'd already seen, paid little heed to conventional manner or to the division of class. Her behavior was unapologetically rambunctious, her excitement for life quite infectious. Although Molly had wondered at first why the girl was not reined in as others of her status would be, she soon came to realize it was all good-natured, unaffected spirits, and really, who would have the heart to crush them? Her brother must be the kindly and patient sort to put up with her tireless bouncing. Indeed, nothing bad was ever said of Sinjun Rothespur. Molly had heard members of his household staff refer to him as an honest and fair fellow. It showed that Carver did have some good judgment in the people with whom he spent his time.

She glanced again at the vase of flowers he'd sent her. Perhaps she had been too harsh, too quick to take offense when he sent his mistress to her for a gown. He had merely been trying to help her.

And apparently she was not his first case either, if what Lady Anne had told her about Carver defending her brother against school bullies was true.

The grumbling old bear had a soft side after all. She'd always suspected it, but never dared place much hope behind the thought. There were many ideas she had about him that were no more forged in reality than Mrs.

Bathurst's tales of princely lovers and rumpy pumpy in the maze at Hampton Court. But as long as they remained merely in her head, they could do no harm.

Her imprudent fondness for the rakish and reckless Earl of Everscham must remain like the interiors of Mrs. Bathurst's boxes, hidden away where only she knew they existed. A secret in her heart.

"Please say you will come to the concert, Miss Robbins!"

"Very well. I suppose I can go as your chaperone, if it is agreeable with your brother." Molly had no other social engagements, and although she was busy with her work, a few hours off would do no harm. Besides, she was curious about the gardens, of which she'd heard much, and there would be fashionable people there to watch.

"Of course it is agreeable to Sinjun!" Lady Anne rolled her eyes dramatically. "Anything that gets my brother out of chaperoning me is more than agreeable to him! I shall send the carriage for you at half past five on Thursday. What fun we shall have! Oh"—once again she paused on her way out and came back to where Molly stood—"and do bring that sweet young man who lives here. The artist fellow."

"Frederick Dawes?"

"Is that his name?" the young lady replied, batting her lashes with all the nonchalance of a fox watching a chicken through the fence. "I saw him on the stairs when I was last here. He seems very amiable."

So that was it, thought Molly. The lady had caught sight of pretty young Fred and came up with this scheme to meet him. "I will ask Frederick, Lady Anne. If you would like me to bring him."

"Please do. I am so looking forward to it!"

Molly waved her off. As soon as the merry young girl was gone, she took much of her skipping excitement with her, and a pinch of panic set in. What the devil was she going to wear?

❧

"Do pay attention, old chap," Sinjun Rothespur exclaimed. "This is the third time you seem to have forgotten your turn."

Carver pushed himself away from the paneled wall and stared at the billiard table in which he had absolutely no interest. He didn't even know the score and wouldn't have been playing had a cue not been pushed into his hand, as it was every Wednesday at approximately eight o'clock in the evening. This game was a standing appointment at Skip Skiffington's house for three months of every year since he turned eighteen. It was also a form of protest against the hostesses of Almack's, who insisted gentlemen wear knee breeches instead of long trousers to the balls there in the evenings. Carver had once declared that he would never be seen in knee breeches, and his close group of friends followed suit. Thus they made their own evening's entertainment on Wednesdays, relishing the wearing of their "unacceptable" trousers.

"Where is your head, Danforthe?" his host demanded with less gentle cajoling than Sinjun.

"As you see, it resides upon my neck, where it always is."

"Appearances can be deceiving," Fletcher Covington, Duke of Preston, remarked with a sneer.

Carver moved around the table for his shot. "Occasionally I have things on my mind."

They all laughed, and he felt quite offended by it.

"Will you ride north with us for the glorious twelfth, Danforthe?" Skip asked.

"When have you ever known me to participate in the grouse season?" He'd never been much of a hunting, shooting, fishing sort of man. His passion lay in breeding horses for racing, although he kept that mostly to himself. When his friends went off to shoot grouse, he usually traveled to Sussex and spent time at his stud there on the estate. It was really the only thing that took him back to the estate, which he still thought of as belonging to his father. His custodianship was only temporary anyway.

"We thought you might venture north this year for once," Skip replied with a playful grin.

"Oh? And why is that?"

"Break the usual routine. Hide out."

Carver glared at Skip. "I don't follow. Hide from what?"

The plump and garrulous Fletcher Covington—puffing out a cloud of cigar smoke—explained with a leer, "From your sister's fiancé, Danforthe. Lady Mercy's country adventure is so widely talked about, it will doubtless find Grey's ears the moment he reaches port. Then there will be hell to pay. Lady Mercy doesn't appear in any hurry to come back to civilization, does she?"

Carver let them enjoy their chuckles for a moment. "My sister visits with family friends in Norfolk." It had become his answer to anyone who inquired.

"But Grey will be back from his tour abroad by

August, Danforthe. Thought you might go into hiding until the storm blows over, once he finds out what your sister's been up to."

"Thank you for your concern, gentlemen. I'll brave the storm head on."

Sinjun, who had not joined in the teasing, now said quietly, "Grey might not be much to contend with, but his father is an old curmudgeon, always looking to sue somebody."

"Let him try." Carver shrugged. "Hiding won't help, will it? He doesn't have to find me to file a suit."

"If I were you," Covington opined loftily, "I'd drag that troublesome sister of yours back to London by the scruff of her neck, whip her backside, and lock her up until Grey fetches her."

But Carver wasn't the sort to strap his sister to a chair and feed her gruel, even if he had threatened it in the past.

"Your sister should have married me when I asked her," added Covington, punctuating the remark with a low burp. "I would have tamed her by now."

Skip roared with laughter. "She would have had *you* tamed, Covey! Look how she puts Danforthe in his place and squares him away."

"Too late now, in any case. She missed her chance with me, and when Grey throws her over, she needn't come begging for another chance at the wicket. I don't want her after she's been rolling around the farmyard with her peasant lover. Who would? You'll be landed with your sister now for the rest of her life, Danforthe. Should have been more vigilant. We all told you."

A pall of uneasy silence descended over the billiard table. Everyone present, possibly including a drunken

Covington, now knew the conversation had gone too far beyond teasing.

"My sister knows what she does," Carver muttered, passing the cue chalk to Sinjun. "If there is anything I've learned about women over the years and particularly of late, it's that they do have minds of their own. For better or worse." He studied the table, preparing his next move. "I'm sure she can handle Grey." Mercy was a formidable force when in motion.

"I suppose you have other matters to tend," Skip muttered slyly. "Like your dowdy little seamstress, eh?"

"My what?"

"Your sister's former maid, Danforthe. We all know what you've been up to with her, bridging the class divide."

Carver glanced over at Sinjun, who looked apologetic and then turned away guiltily to chalk his cue.

"I was shocked when I caught a glimpse of her," Covington proclaimed. "Cecelia Montague pointed her out to me on Oxford Street. Not what I expected at all. Not your usual pursuit. Quite a mopsey."

"Miss Robbins is merely a business associate," he replied, low.

"Really?" Covington snorted. "She must have turned you down then."

"Certainly not." Carver leaned over the table to aim his cue, took his shot, and landed a ball in the side pocket.

"Well, how about a wager, Danforthe?"

"A wager?" He looked up, his attention caught on the sharpened edge of Covington's tone.

"Get the grim little seamstress into bed by the end of the month. If you can."

"*If?*" he scoffed.

"Should you fail in your mission, let's say…you give me your new barouche. If you win, I'll give you that hunter of mine you've been admiring."

Sinjun had strolled around the table, and now he whispered behind Carver, "Don't do it, old chap. He's not worth the aggravation."

But Carver's temper was pricked. "Is that all you want of mine, Covey? I rather got the impression I had something else you wanted. Not still after my sister, I hope. Not still licking your wounds from her?"

The other man's eyes narrowed. "No. That smart carriage will suffice. In addition to the dent in your obnoxious pride."

Carver noted his opponent's puffy fingers and bloodshot eyes. "I'm afraid it's out of the question," he said.

"Aha! So you know you cannot win."

In past pursuits, he'd never actually been in any doubt of his chances. But this was new, different. There was nothing predictable about it, nothing safe, nothing usual. He'd begun to want sight of her each day and to feel cheated when he failed in catching a glimpse, for then he wondered where she was and with whom. Was it because of the challenge she'd laid down in her contract? She'd told him he couldn't have her even before he gave it any thought. But whenever she stood before him, her calm eyes drew him closer and hinted at more passion brewing inside, waiting for him to drink. He grew hot when he thought of their kiss, when he remembered the sweet taste of her soft lips. The clean scent of her soap, the fresh air caught in her hair, the light blush of her cheek. Even her knees, always hidden from him and kept in a tight grip, had become objects of fascination to him lately.

He wondered at the strength of his desire for her. Very strange, very troubling. They were all right— Covey, the baroness—she was absolutely the very antithesis of the women he usually pursued. Truth was, she'd impressed him with her gumption. Few people ever rendered Carver speechless and powerless. Few people ever left him wanting more of their company, even if they would only take the opportunity to insult and shout at him.

"Miss Robbins," he muttered finally to his waiting friends, "is a woman deserving of respect. She has more determination and purpose in her than you've ever known or will know. Leave her out of your wagers."

"Getting all honorable, eh?" Covington scoffed. "It seems your sister is not the only Danforthe with a taste for humbler dishes."

"Shut up, Covey," Sinjun muttered.

"Gentlemen," exclaimed Skip wearily, "can we turn our attention to the game at hand?"

Carver shrugged it off and took his next shot. It failed, and the ball bounced off the side baize. Covington's face was smug as he prepared for his own turn.

Molly Robbins, Carver realized, had affected him deeply. At first he'd thought this was merely a flirtation like any other, the thrill of a challenge and a chase, but he knew now it was something beyond that. Here he was standing up for her, wanting to protect her, defend her.

His anger had mounted not at Covington for the foolish wager challenging his pride, but at himself for letting this fancy get beyond his containment and his comfort.

He must get to the bottom of this fascination somehow, or it was in danger of making him look a fool. The dissolute Earl of Everscham had a reputation to maintain.

Ten

HARD AT WORK BY THE LIGHT OF TWO SAD CANDLES, Molly was almost startled out of her drawers that evening by another impromptu visitor.

Shown up to her rooms by a ghostly white, unusually mute Mrs. Lotterby, Carver Danforthe appeared in her doorway, fully clad in evening clothes. "Good God, woman," he exclaimed, wasting no time on pleasantries, "how can you possibly sew by this light?"

She squinted at him until the black-and-white blur slowly transformed into his familiar tall shape. "I conserve candles," she explained shakily. "Do come in, your lordship."

"Can't stay long," he muttered, striding forward and sweeping off his hat. "Thought I'd better investigate the workshop in which I invested."

"Well, this is it." She waved her arm about. "As you see, it is quite ordinary. Like me." Her pulse scattering like spilled pins, Molly made some attempt to tidy her table and then gave up, realizing the futility. This time, it seemed, the street outside was not enough for him, and he came all the way in. She could not keep him out.

He shot her a dark look and began a slow

promenade of the room, his footsteps loud on the old wood and not much muffled by the threadbare carpet she'd purchased. He was too large for the space.

"Although I am not an expert in matters of propriety—being only a simple country girl—I have also been under your sister's tutelage for some years now, and I do believe it would not be considered wholly proper for you to be here, your lordship." Mrs. Lotterby had withdrawn, but there was no doubt she waited in the hall or at the foot of the stairs, listening for snippets of their conversation.

"What?" he snapped at her, still moving up and down the room.

"For you, a single gentlemen who is not a relative, to visit me alone."

He gave a quick half shrug, half shake, dismissing her qualms as if she were being ridiculous merely to raise the thought. "Don't you have help with the sewing? You cannot possibly manage every stitch yourself."

"I can assure you I do manage." She had no choice. An extra pair of hands would take money from the profits, and she was not yet making enough to afford it. Why try to explain, she mused. The Earl of Everscham would never understand the concept of working oneself into a state of exhaustion out of necessity. "Mrs. Slater, a lady who lives below, occasionally lends a hand."

He didn't appear to be listening. Finally he came to a halt and stared at her cluttered worktable. Then he looked at Molly, his hard gaze inspecting her so thoroughly she felt as if she'd fallen prey to an extremely effective pickpocket. "I thought this was a boarding house for young ladies only. It seems there are men residing here."

She was surprised he'd bothered to find out. "Mrs. Lotterby was unable to lease all her rooms, and it left her purse light. When Mr. Frederick Dawes inquired about lodgings, he was quite desperate, so she took him in. He is a very kind and gentle man. He's an artist, an excellent painter. The only other male here, excepting the landlady's good husband, is the brother of another tenant." Since she had nothing good to say about Arthur Wakely and his foot, she kept silent on that score.

He frowned. "I shall speak to Hobbs about this. What could he be thinking to send you here? Even worse to imagine I would condone it."

"But you did."

"Only because the situation of the place was misrepresented to me."

The late hour, the shock of his visit, and a steadily increasing headache made her short-tempered. "Indeed it was not. How could it be misrepresented to you when you asked me nothing about it? You had ample opportunity." She wondered why he made such a fuss about it.

"I asked Hobbs if it was all ladies, and he deliberately equivocated. Yes, now that I think of it, he was most evasive when I asked for details of the place. Acting very shiftily about it. Anyone might think he kept a treasure chest of stolen loot here and didn't want me to find out."

Molly decided she was too tired to argue further. "Whatever you say, your lordship," she muttered wearily. "You are always in the right."

"Hmmph. Don't hurt yourself by admitting it." He turned in a circle and then paused to give her another, louder, "Hmmph," probably meant to curl her toes in her slippers. "Why did you call off that wedding, Mouse? I knew it was a foolish idea in any case, and I assumed you merely came to your senses finally. But did my sister have anything to do with it?"

The unexpected turn of conversation surprised her, shook her out of her drowsiness. "Not at all, your lordship. Indeed, she wanted me to stay and marry Rafe. She was most angry with my decision."

"Are you certain?"

"I think I have known Lady Mercy long enough to read her moods, your lordship, and know when I have displeased her. As I always knew when I'd displeased *you*." Both the earl and his sister made no effort to conceal their hot tempers when roused. She should thank him for the flowers he sent, she thought, following his gaze to the vase that brightened one corner of her room. But she was supposed to believe they came from the Baroness Schofield. Admitting she knew otherwise might lead to even further awkwardness. Better it went unsaid.

He fidgeted with his hat brim. "Did my sister"—he struggled, his voice full of tension—"converse with Rafe Hartley?"

Molly kept her voice low, sensing every ear in that house was listening. Even Mrs. Slater's baby had ceased its wailing. "I asked her to speak to him for me, to explain why I couldn't proceed. Lady Mercy has always been braver than I."

Carver's lips twitched in the slight spasm of a thwarted smile. "I wouldn't say that. She's just louder. True courage does not need to be bolstered with noise and bluster. But you know that, Miss Robbins."

It felt as if he'd reached over, moved a curl of hair from her forehead, and stroked her cheek again.

"If my sister has embarked upon an ill-advised affair in the country with Rafe Hartley, what would you say to it, Miss Robbins?"

It took her a moment to recover her voice. "If she and Rafe...?" Such a strange idea! And yet, she supposed it was possible. Vastly different, totally unsuited people sometimes fell in love. Or one of them did. Stupidly. Knowing reciprocation was impossible.

Molly quickly shook off those thoughts about her own predicament and tried to concentrate on what he'd suggested about his sister.

She wanted Rafe to be happy, whatever he did with his life. The same for Lady Mercy. Truly, what right did she have to judge where others found love and happiness? She thought of Mrs. Bathurst across the landing, surrounded by her treasure trove of keepsakes, all she had left of past loves. Opportunity came and went in life. Before one knew it, old age descended. She supposed joy should be seized wherever possible.

Having thought for a moment, she said softly and earnestly, "I would say good luck to them, your lordship. Life is short and pleasure hard come by."

She had an image, suddenly, of her mother pulling her up out of the long meadow grass by one hand. *"For pity's sake, dozy child. Clouds are white, and that's all there is to it."* Poor woman, not being able to see the many colors around her, wearing blinkers like the plow horses, and bending under her yoke. Molly was sorry—bitterly sorry—for her mother now. If only she had been able to see and understand how much more there was to life. How much more color. All those different shades that made life interesting, challenging, and ever changing.

"Then you are not in love with him?" the earl demanded. "With Rafe Hartley?"

She swallowed. "No. Not in that way, but I hope always to be his friend."

He was looking at Frederick's two empty glasses on the window ledge. There was a little wine still left in one of them. "Are you content here, Mouse?" he asked, sounding strangely forlorn suddenly.

"Of course. This is my dream, and I am fortunate I have the chance to live it."

He swept the small room with another doubtful frown.

"I know it might not seem much to you," she added. "But to me it's a palace. Truthfully, I am happy here, and the people are very kind."

"Good." He cleared his throat. "Good."

Molly waited, hands behind her back, head on one side. "Was there anything else, your lordship?" Perhaps he thought there was more to look at, other than that one room and the dark cupboard beyond, which masqueraded as her bedchamber.

"No…no, just passing, and the thought occurred." He stole another glance at those wine glasses by the window and then studied a sketch she'd been working on earlier, turning it toward him with one hand, his fingers splayed like a giant spider.

"I hope you like it, your lordship."

His brows rose. "Me?"

"It is for the Baroness Schofield."

She saw his jaw tense. "I see," he muttered. "Very nice."

"You approve?" Molly hoped he would realize it was her way of making an apology for the things she'd said about his morals and his mistresses. All things that were not her business. No one in this world could afford to throw stones, whatever their houses were made of, and she knew that now, having felt the intensity of temptation in his presence. Having let herself dream of him at night in her narrow, hard bed, keeping his borrowed silk handkerchief under her pillow. It smelled of him. And of cake. Two of her favorite scents.

Again he fixed her in a thoughtful stare that made her pulse falter. Despite her stout bones, she felt in considerable danger of melting whenever he looked at her that way. "I approve," he said.

"I am glad of it, your lordship."

He looked again at the design she was sketching before he came in. "I wonder where you come by your ideas, Miss Robbins." His voice was halting, uncertain. Was it possible that he felt the awkwardness of this late, impromptu visit as much as she, the victim, did? She'd never seen him unsure before. "I know little about fashion, but even I can see you are talented," he added.

This praise pleased her more than any other. "I never know from where the ideas will come or when. Inspiration can strike at the oddest times." Here again, on this subject, she felt solid ground under her feet, and she was bolder. "I like to observe people, places, architecture…nature. There is beauty to be found in almost anything."

He ran a fingertip along her line of charcoal on the paper and smudged it. "I see. That is why you stare at me with those searching, all-knowing brown eyes. You study me too, eh? Do I inspire you?"

"Sometimes. I suppose you do. Your sister, too, has

been an influence upon me. She is a daring clothes-horse, never afraid to try something new."

His eyes simmered. "You changed the subject deliberately to my sister."

"No, I—"

"You said you find beauty in everything, Miss Robbins. Does that include me?"

On her windowsill, the candle flame fluttered, just like her pulse. His uncertainty before had turned now to silky surety, the flirtatious path he knew so well.

"Yes," she said, realizing there was no point in denial. It was probably written all over her plain and silly face. "You do possess a certain wild beauty, your lordship. As you are, no doubt, aware."

"Wild?" He winced. "I'm not sure how I feel about that."

"Me neither," she confessed with a sigh.

He considered this for a moment, foot tapping against her worn scrap of carpet. "Will you not ask me if I find you beautiful, Miss Robbins?"

A half laugh, half gasp bubbled out of her. "I know what I am."

"I don't think you do."

She looked down at her feet.

He had promised not to flirt with her. He'd signed that contract. But she might have known a promise meant nothing to Carver Danforthe. She gambled on a rake, and she was losing.

Molly wiped a hand across her brow, a weary gesture he must have noted.

"I will say good evening then, Miss Robbins. I've kept you too long." He bowed smartly and strode out. How polite he was tonight, she thought, allowing herself a little smile. They could be civil now, it seemed. Even the wild beast made an effort.

She closed the door behind him and then, freshly inspired by his strange visit, she picked up the charcoal and began another sketch.

But scarcely a minute had passed, and he was back again, banging on her door. When she opened it, he stood there, his brow creased in confusion.

"Thank you for the flowers," she blurted before he could even speak. It had been burning there on her tongue, her heart wracked with guilt for not acknowledging the unexpected thoughtfulness of his gift.

He seemed to be studying the charcoal she held in her fingers. Slowly his dark gaze lifted to her face. "Do you have my handkerchief? The one I lent you when I stole cake for you, madam?"

"No," she answered so swiftly it took her breath away. "I lost it." He wasn't getting it back she decided in the blink of an eye. Besides, he had many handkerchiefs. Why would he need one back? It was all she had of him.

"I see. How careless of you."

"If I find it, I'll return it, your lordship." *Oh, such a filthy liar she had become.*

He half turned away and then back again. "By the by, you made a mistake on that contract, Mouse."

She squinted. "I don't think I—"

"Tomfoolery. You should have checked the spelling."

"Oh?"

Towering over her in the doorway, he had to bend his head or else hit his brow on the crooked lintel. "Since it is spelled incorrectly, that makes the clause null and void."

"I'm quite certain a word misspelled is not enough
to—"

"You may confer with a man of the law, of course,
if you don't believe me." He glared down at her, the
challenge clear in his fierce expression. "Ask Hobbs."

Naturally. Ask his faithful minion to confirm. Why
not? "You came back just to tell me this?"

"I did."

"It seems a dreadful waste of your time, when you
must have more important matters to tend." Her heart
was overexcited, racing too fast.

"How I waste my time is up to me, Miss Robbins."

"I suppose so. You must be very good at it by now."

His eyes widened. "And there was nothing more
pressing at this moment than correcting you." A
warm, teasing light simmered in his lightened gaze.
"And your addlepated contract."

"An addlepated contract *you* signed."

"Under duress."

Slightly breathless, she laughed. "Duress?"

"It was early. I was unprepared." He propped
his shoulder against her doorframe. "As you knew I
would be."

She felt easy in his presence suddenly. It should have
been odd and uncomfortable to have him there, leaning
in her doorway, but she was no longer his servant, was
she? She was Miss Margaret Robbins, her own woman.
Lady Anne, who had never known the old Molly,
called her "bold." She had her own life now and could
do as she pleased. So she pondered the hard set of his
jaw and said, "You didn't shave today. Your lordship."

"Well observed, Mouse."

"Lady Mercy would be appalled."

"Lady Mercy is not here."

Alas. None of this would be happening if she *was*. Molly would not be commenting on the state of his chin scruff, and Carver would not be visiting her lodgings in the dark of night if his sister was present to prevent it.

"Well, I just wanted to point out your spelling error, Mouse. While it was in the forefront of my mind."

"Sakes, yes. We know how briefly thoughts remain there."

He scratched his cheek, and she knew the little hairs must be itching. She'd bet five pounds it was all shaved smooth again by morning. He made no move to leave.

"Do not burden your mind further with the idea, your lordship. I'm sure you have many other thoughts waiting for their turn."

"You infer I can have only one at a time?"

Molly fought hard to prevent her lips curving. "You are a man, your lordship."

He shook his head. "I see your new success has gone to your head, Robbins. Pride comes before a fall." Now he made a small movement that suggested he was ready to depart again.

"Speaking of falls, did Larkin get the grass stains out of your breeches?" she asked hurriedly.

Carver relaxed against the doorframe once more. "He did."

"Good."

"Your concern for my breeches is misplaced." His eyes lightened even further, distinctly mischievous. "The knees beneath them were more severely wounded."

She looked down at the items in question. "One should take greater care when one goes out *riding*, especially in advanced years."

"And young maids," he replied swiftly, "should take better care with their spelling."

Pushing away from the doorframe, he took the charcoal from between her fingers, turned her hand over, and began to write on her palm.

"T…O…M…F…O…O…"

She couldn't breathe suddenly. His gloved hand holding hers was firm, steady. She prayed to all the saints that he would not feel her tremble, but surely he must. The Earl of Everscham was holding her hand. Holding *her* hand. The charcoal tickled across her palm, the lines already smudged by unladylike perspiration.

"L…E…"

Molly knew she ought to pull her hand away and stop him at once, but if she didn't let him keep her hand, where else might he write his letters? She feared to imagine.

"R…Y. There. Now you know how to spell it, Mouse."

She glanced down at the word with which he'd marked her skin in giant letters. Unable to get them all on her small palm in one line, he'd made three-and-a-half lines, some of the letters riding up her wrist. With his free hand, he turned her chin up to face him.

"And now, just so we are clear about the definition too…"

It seemed to take forever for his lips to reach her. His height, of course, necessitated a low stoop. Molly had plenty of time to avoid his mouth, more than enough time to know his intention. But she tipped her head back, and her lips met his.

She closed her eyes. His fingertips stroked along her jaw and down the side of her neck, where he would feel her hectic pulse fluttering. His firm lips took that kiss from her ruthlessly, as if he expected a fight but meant to have what he wanted regardless. Stubble pricked her cheek, chafed slightly. His tongue delved into her mouth, tasting her slowly and yet not tentatively, just exploring at his own pace, relishing what he found. His hand around her fingers tightened until she almost yelped. Would have too, if his kiss had not taken complete possession of her capacities just then.

Never had she been kissed like this, so she had nothing with which to compare it, but she needed nothing. This was the best and yet the worst thing that had ever happened to her. It was fear and thrill, pleasure and chastisement, all rolled into one. It was everything she'd never hoped to feel, and yet everything for which she'd ever yearned.

At last she was released. Her lips throbbed and felt swollen. Molly raised her eyelids, but daren't look at his face.

"Margaret." He cleared the huskiness from his throat with a sharp cough. "Margaret, perhaps you will do me the honor of reading this." He took a folded paper from inside his coat. "This is my copy of your contract, with a slight amendment. If you feel so inclined...sign it." He passed it to her. "Remember, as you just said to me, *life is short and pleasure hard to come by*. I leave our future pleasure in your hands, Margaret." One bow, and he was gone again.

In a daze this time, she closed her door and leaned against it.

Tomfoolery. The word he'd written upon her palm stared up at her in accusation.

She'd just been branded by the Earl of Everscham.

Molly didn't need to read the paper in her hand. She knew what he wanted from her, and it wasn't his silk handkerchief.

Eleven

THE FOLLOWING MORNING, MRS. LOTTERBY BROUGHT
a jug of hot chocolate with two cups on a tray to
Molly's room, claiming to have made too much and
looking for a partner to share.

"My Herbert hasn't the taste for it, which is just as
well, for it makes him giddy one moment and sleepy
the next. I thought perhaps my favorite tenant might
like a cup." She beamed.

"That's very kind of you, Mrs. Lotterby," Molly
replied, clearing a place on her table, knowing exactly
why the landlady was there. May as well get the questions over with. "I suppose you are curious about my
visitor last night."

He had called her *Margaret*.

"Who? Oh, dearie me, no. I'm sure it is no business of mine." But the lady quickly settled herself into
the most comfortable chair and proceeded to pour the
hot chocolate. "I do not pry into the private *affairs* of
my tenants."

It was a good thing, thought Molly, that there was
no lightning strike at that moment. One of them had
just told a giant fib, and the other was about to do so.

She accepted the cup from Mrs. Lotterby and warmed her hands around it, for last night had been chilly and damp, with this morning's sun yet to reach her southerly facing window. "The Earl of Everscham is my former employer, Mrs. Lotterby. I didn't want you to get the wrong idea. He made me a small business loan. Our connection is purely professional."

"Well, I'm sure I never thought otherwise, Miss Robbins. I said to my Herbert, I won't hear a bad word about that hardworking young lady upstairs, and he agreed. We all have our burdens to bear and our secrets, to be sure, but I would never hold them against you, whatever anyone suggests. Let he who is without sin cast the first stone."

"Who would suggest anything about me?"

"One hears rumors, my dear." Mrs. Lotterby squirmed in her chair as if she had an itch it would be indelicate to scratch publicly. "The Earl of Everscham has a certain reputation. An innocent young lady like yourself may not be aware of it." She made a clicking noise with her tongue and twitched her head, reminding Molly of a large hen looking for a place to lay an egg. "Not that I listen to anything he…not a word of it…not to pay it credence"—she glanced meaningfully at the floor—"but one can't help what enters one's ear holes."

"Mrs. Lotterby, I may not be so worldly as some other ladies about this town, but I am not naive. Just because I don't indulge, doesn't mean I am completely unaware of sin and debauchery. I have no doubt you mean Arthur Wakely has been making suppositions about me."

"He does tend not to approve of you, Miss Robbins."

"I've noticed." Molly raised her voice to shout so that the man listening beneath the floorboards would hear clearly. "Rest assured, I don't approve of him either."

Somewhere below them a door slammed.

When Mrs. Lotterby laughed, her entire body shook with the tremors of her merriment. "I've seen it all before, you know. With my sister." She jerked her head in the direction of Mrs. Bathurst's room across the landing. "Scarlet isn't a bold enough color for my sister's past, let me tell you. Has she shown you her magpie's nest of trinkets? She hides it all away, keeps it close, as if ghosts from her past can save her from the harsh realities of the here and now." Despite the grim subject matter, still her tone was jovial and uncomplaining, the voice of one who accepted her lot in life but had time yet to worry about those who hadn't found theirs. "That's what happens to a woman who lets herself be used and thrown away. One misstep can ruin, forever, her chance of a respectable life and a good marriage. But would my sister be told? No indeed. Now all those fine gentlemen she once knew have gone, and she takes her comfort from laudanum and her pleasure from cursing at the bailiffs."

"She told me of her son, Mrs. Lotterby. It troubled her greatly, I'm sure, to give him up all those years ago."

The landlady had been about to sip from her cup, but the handle slipped from her finger. She looked up, blinking rapidly. "Gracious, she hasn't spoke a word about him in years. What made her bring that up again? When did she…see…?" Mrs. Lotterby twitched her head as if she was too irritated to shake it properly.

"You must not pay heed to all she says, Miss Robbins. My sister lives in a world of her own fancy."

"But it was true she had a child?"

"Indeed. Poor little bastard. She could do nothing for it and came to me for help. I was not married then and saw no prospect of it, being only fifteen, plain and poor, or I would have taken the child in myself and raised him as my own. But we did what was best for him. The only alternative."

"The workhouse?" Her heart chilled at the sound of the word.

Mrs. Lotterby was silent for a moment, her gaze falling on one of the little wooden boxes that her sister had given to Molly. Finally she answered, "It was the only thing to be done."

"I'm sorry for her."

"My sister was always a dreadful romantic. She imagined herself in love, but he was a rake. You know how those gentlemen are. He scarce thought of her again afterward, when it was all over and done and he'd had what he wanted."

Molly stirred her chocolate. Not keen to discuss gentlemen rakes, she said, "Your sister fears the duns will come and steal away all her possessions. Is her debt so very great?"

"My dear Miss Robbins, we are all in a state of debt," the landlady exclaimed. "One cannot get out of bed in the morning these days without incurring a debt. But that is no excuse to forget pride and dignity."

"Of course." She couldn't agree more.

"I know how such a handsome gentleman, as were here last night, can steal his way into a young girl's heart and more besides." The lady shook her lace-capped head, arched her little finger, and sipped her chocolate. "It happens all too oft, my dear. All too oft. I would never presume to interfere, and passion leads us all down a treacherous path from time to time. My sister has suffered ill luck, but she has also been prone to bad choices. The best I can do is advise you, my dear Miss Robbins, to take care. While you're under my roof, I promised that nice Mr. Hobbs to look after you, and so I shall. Always look about you with both eyes open and keep your head on straight."

Mrs. Lotterby's words were a timely warning. Molly settled her worried gaze on the unfinished designs laid out on her table. After Carver's kiss last night, her thoughts were too scattered for work, forcing Molly to set the sketches aside. Not a stitch had been sewn this morning, for she'd been daydreaming out of her window and thinking about his amendments to their contract. She'd lost valuable time, thanks to improper behavior. Not just his either. How quickly she had fallen into wickedness, let her sinful yearnings take control. It was a blow to her pride. She was no better than Fanny Tucker, a dairymaid back home in Sydney Dovedale, who was said to let any man kiss her behind the haystacks for a penny.

Mrs. Lotterby peered above the rim of her cup and said cautiously, "I meant no offense, Miss Robbins, only to warn you in a gentle way. I hope I put it rightly."

Molly managed a smile. "You did, madam. I quite understand your concern."

"I'm sure you're far too wise in any case. Not like my poor sister, who fell at the first charming smile. She never had many wits about her."

They enjoyed their chocolate together and spoke no more on the matter of Carver's late-night visit, but her connection to the noble Danforthe family was evidently a point of curiosity for Mrs. Lotterby, as it was for some of Molly's clients, who poked slyly at her for tidbits of information. Which she never gave. The earl's appearance at her lodgings in the small hours would only add kindling to the fire, but rumors of that nature didn't bother him. He was not the one who had anything to lose from the speculation.

Once Mrs. Lotterby had gone, she poured water into her washbasin and, with a great sense of sad ceremony, Molly scrubbed the remaining charcoal smudges from her hand.

⁂

"But, my lord, I do not have any nieces," Edward Hobbs exclaimed, peering quizzically through his round spectacles.

"Hobbs, my good man, I am well aware of this."

"Then, how——"

"You are about to *acquire* two nieces." Carver had woken that day with an idea. Since it didn't happen often, he'd decided to make the most of it immediately and ridden straight to Bishopsgate to find the family solicitor in his cluttered office. He must do all in his power to take away all Molly's other troubles and leave her free to have only one. Him. "You will find two able seamstresses and send them to Miss Robbins to assist her."

This made Hobbs sit up straight and remove his spectacles. "Miss Robbins? The lady's maid?"

"That's right. You will make up some tale." Carver waved his hat about. "Tell her your nieces are visiting from the country and they require experience—an apprenticeship of some sort."

"I thought we were done helping the lady's maid, my lord? Was she not declared to be an ingrate of the highest magnitude?"

"Yes, but I'm willing to overlook it." He was surprisingly willing to overlook a vast deal in her case. He'd let her speak to him in ways no other woman dared, except his sister, but he liked seeing her smile as she did last night. The sweet timbre of her rare laughter still tickled his nerve endings this morning.

Each time he looked at her now, he discovered something new. Like a rose, she blossomed, her petals opening, releasing sweet, soft damask perfume and revealing an exquisite blush-pink center that he wanted to claim for his eyes only. Never the possessive sort before, Carver now had this unconquerable idea that she belonged to him.

He sincerely hoped his kiss had given her something else to mull over before she made a mistake with her artist friend.

Halting sharply, he stared at the wall, thinking of that kiss. Her lips were incredibly soft, her tongue timid. There was a vulnerability underneath that melancholy exterior. Something warm, preciously guarded, a little spark of naughtiness shining through the dolorous piety. But she was a maid still, he was certain of it. Thank god.

He resumed his circling patrol of the solicitor's office. "What she needs is a better place to live. Finer accommodations, where she can have a separate workroom. A little shop front perhaps. That house you found for her is damp and unhealthy."

"It is no worse, my lord, than many places in which the London masses—myself included—must live."

"But she's so slight of build. And not long recovered from a cold."

"Are *you* quite well, my lord?" the solicitor inquired. "You seem a little lively for this early hour, and…contemplative."

He stopped again. Yes, he was feeling remarkably awake and alive this morning. Determined too. Perhaps there was magic in Margaret's lips, as well as her sewing fingers.

"I will look into the acquisition of these nieces, my lord," said Hobbs gravely.

"Excellent." He could rely on Edward Hobbs to get things done. "By the by, have you had any word from my sister?" Mercy, he knew, relied on Hobbs as much as he did.

"Just a short note to assure me she is in fine health, my lord."

Carver nodded. His sister was evidently happy in the country, enjoying her stay. Her latest letter to him, apart from another brief, terse lecture about his possible interference in Molly Robbins's decision not to be married, was full of merry news about the Hartleys. Nothing too serious or solemn, everything light and benign. She claimed to have undertaken several matchmaking missions there, and he knew his sister liked nothing more than matchmaking. She was a terrifying romantic. Although, oddly enough, she had embarked on her own engagement to the Viscount Grey with dreary practical considerations and not the even the most meager of romantic illusions.

"Demanding that she return to London," said Hobbs quietly, "would probably make her stay away longer, my lord."

"Quite so."

"But I do fear we might have a problem with Viscount Grey when he returns from Italy."

"Grey? If he cannot manage my sister and her ways, I would suggest he find another, much more dull and predictable woman to marry. He's destined for a life of disappointment if he thinks to wear the breeches in a union with Lady Mercy."

He didn't want his sister throwing herself away on a man like Grey. Marriage was a dreadful, permanent thing, as he'd commented to her several times in an effort to make it sink in. Marriage wasn't a game. It was the end of all games.

In the country, perhaps, she would have her awakening.

And if she chose to stay there with Rafe Hartley? A few months ago he would have been horrified at the thought, but Margaret Robbins seemed resigned to it, and her gentle words of tolerance echoed through his mind today. She was not in love with Rafe, and she was not angry with Mercy. She wanted only their happiness. It was a vast relief to hear. Carver would not want her to suffer a broken heart because of his sister's antics. Or over that foolhardy farmer.

I would say good luck to them, your lordship. Life is short and pleasure hard to come by.

Everything sounded simple and sensible when she said it. Her words were never knotted up and complicated with false bluster. She spoke from her heart, always, even when angry.

"'Tis a pity, my lord, that you did not go into the country with Lady Mercy, as I advised," said Hobbs quietly. "I wonder why you did not."

Carver smoothed a fallen lock of hair from his brow. "I don't like weddings, Hobbs. You know that."

The little man nodded. "I daresay you would have liked that one even less than most. Had it taken place."

On his way out of the office, Carver paused and frowned over his shoulder.

Edward Hobbs looked down at his papers. "I mean to say, my lord, Miss Robbins has become—"

"I knew what you meant, Hobbs, and you are right. I chose not to attend the wedding because I didn't care to watch Miss Robbins make a permanent mistake with her life. That's all."

"Of course, my lord, to suggest there was anything more than that involved in your decision to stay away would be quite absurd."

Carver stared hard at the other man, who carefully avoided his gaze. "Yes. It would."

"She is merely a former lady's maid."

"Indeed."

"A young lady you dismissed many times as plain, and perhaps even sinister in her manner."

"There is something troubling you, Hobbs?"

"Not at all, my lord. Nothing troubles *me*."

When Carver finally walked out and closed the office door, he heard his family's solicitor whistling an extremely merry tune. It was the first time he'd ever heard Hobbs whistle. Clearly the man was feverish, or drinking too much too early in the day.

Twelve

PLEASE DO NOT LET HIM BE HERE.

Molly was not sure which deity she prayed to. Was there a patron saint of seamstresses, she wondered?

For the concert at Vauxhall Gardens, she wore a muslin gown of robin's egg-blue with a matching pelisse. It was simply cut, as were all her clothes, but Frederick Dawes had agreed the color was especially flattering, and the raised diamond pattern on the sleeves and bodice, while not too evident in daylight, would be picked out by the gas lamps in the park and give the material an added luster.

"You look very pretty tonight, Miss Robbins," Lady Anne exclaimed, bubbling over with excitement as they left the carriage and walked to the grove between the pavilion and the orchestra.

Molly took this with a pinch of salt, since her young companion scarcely focused on one thing for more than a few seconds and seemed to think most things were "pretty."

"And what lovely pearls!"

"They were a gift from Lady Mercy Danforthe," she replied, raising a hand to touch the small earrings

she wore tonight and then the single row of pearls at
her throat. She'd never had an opportunity to wear
them before and was still getting accustomed to them.
But already her companion was chatting to Fred and
looking elsewhere, the pearls forgotten.

They walked up a double flight of stone steps to the
stately pillars of the pavilion. Molly barely had time
to take in the colorful scene and admire the passing
array of fashionable gowns before Lady Anne, craning
her neck, gripped her by the elbow and said, "Let us
walk this way," and dragged her down again at a very
purposeful pace. Molly would have preferred to stand
a while and simply enjoy the parade of fashion, but her
companion could not be still, of course, and Frederick
went willingly with her bidding.

Molly began to wonder what the young lady was
up to. Lady Anne was clearly on the lookout for someone. It would explain her reticence to be escorted by
her brother or her governess.

Their feet crunched along a winding gravel walk,
taking them away from the orchestra and onto a path
lined by lofty trees that formed an arch overhead.
Through them the gas lamps cast an intermittent, lazy
glow, and Molly saw couples dawdling along, moving
in and out of the shadows.

"I think we should go back to the pavilion,"
she muttered, trying to retrieve her arm from Lady
Anne's. "Miss Forde is surely soon to sing."

"But there is an obelisk in the meadow beyond,
Miss Robbins. We cannot come to Vauxhall Gardens
without seeing it. Surely, Mr. Dawes, you will agree."

And then a heavier footfall joined them on the
narrow, gravel lane, and they both spun around.

"Danforthe!"

"Lady Anne, I thought I recognized that bouncing, clumsy gait." His eyes did not immediately go to Molly. He smiled for Lady Anne. "Does your brother know you're rambling freely about, unleashed?"

The girl stuck out her small chin. "Yes. He said I could come if I had a chaperone, and since you recommended Miss Robbins to us in the first place, he trusts her. He said you have a very great opinion of Miss Robbins."

Carver's smile widened. "Don't tell her that. It will only go to her head."

Molly wondered how old one had to be not to suffer blushes, and she wished that year was beyond her now, even if it meant her hair would be gray. She'd always known he must have sent Lady Anne to her as a customer, but to have it confirmed at the top of the girl's lungs and see Fred's knowing grin from the corner of her eye was almost more than she could bear.

She felt duped by Lady Anne, who had flattered her into thinking she was wanted there for her companionship. Now her thoughts were thrown up in the air like a handful of jacks.

Introduced to Frederick, Carver shot the younger man a brief glance of disdain and sighed. "I thought your latest pet artist was that wet fellow with the red hair and weak chin, Lady Anne."

She giggled. "Oh, Danforthe, that was Miles…poor Miles." She put a finger to her lips and gazed into the distance for a moment. "He was very sweet, but not nearly as talented as he thought. I'm afraid his knees were much too knobbly."

"Ah."

"He also had sweaty palms."

"Tragic."

"It was! Mr. Dawes, do walk with me. I should love to hear your opinion of these statues up ahead."

Thus Molly was suddenly the object of Carver's stern appraisal as he held out his arm. "Walk with me, Miss Robbins. It seems we are both superfluous to the people with whom we came."

She squinted down the path to see whom he might have come there with, but the crowd was a blur in that muted light, and she could not recognize any faces. Her eyes were strained by sewing for so many hours, and she had not realized how badly they deteriorated until now. Carver, she thought glumly, would always be recognizable. Even if she was blind, she would know him if he approached. Her skin prickled at the sound of his deep voice.

"I must stay with Lady Anne," she replied firmly.

He nodded. "We'll both stay with Lady Anne. To watch her morals." Molly looked askance and saw his tongue bulge against his cheek.

The lady in question had already skipped on ahead, dragging Fred with her, so Molly had no choice but to walk with the scandalous menace. "I had no idea Lady Anne Rothespur was a patron of the arts."

"She's not," he replied. "She's a collector of pretty things and of pretty young men to adore her."

"Oh."

"Girls of sixteen," he muttered, grim, "cannot be trusted."

She looked up at him. "The same might be said of some gentlemen who are no longer sixteen, your lordship."

"I assure you, Miss Robbins, I can be trusted."

Sighing, she finally placed her hand lightly on his arm. It was easier to do so. Less awkward than walking side by side, especially since he kept altering his pace and his stride, making it difficult for Molly to keep up without looking as if she'd imbibed too much punch.

"No argument to that?" he pushed softly.

Struggling to remember what he'd just said, she was distracted by the heat of his arm, the hard muscle beneath her hand and his sleeve. "I know you, remember? How is the baroness?" Aha. She was pleased with herself for that recovery.

"Well enough."

She studied his fine profile as he looked away down the path after Lady Anne and Fred, who was laughing at something his companion had said. "Will you tell the Earl of Saxonby about this?"

"About his sister and your artist? That lanky, fish-faced boy?" He huffed. "It is nothing of concern. Lady Anne is madly in love with some new fellow every week. It never lasts. It is never serious. As soon as he paints her with a crooked nose or a squint eye, she'll send him packing."

Molly turned her gaze back to her feet. *It is never serious*. No. Just like *his* affairs. "But Lady Anne's brother has brought her to London to find a husband. He won't be pleased to hear of her spending time with a young man like Frederick Dawes, who is amiable but not marriage material for the sister of an earl."

"Lady Anne knows what is expected of her. Eventually she will find some portly fellow with deep pockets and marry him." Carver added, "Some old chap who will never manage to keep up with her but will adore every curl upon her head. Hopefully, for his sake, he will be hard of hearing. Until then, she is like a child running rampant through a bakery, taking a bite of all the wares." Before she could accuse him of being remarkably casual about Lady Anne's behavior, he added softly, "No harm will come to her. She has me and her brother to watch over her. We always have, and we always will."

"You are close to the Rothespur family."

"Since boyhood. Then Sinjun lost his father not long after I lost mine. The misfortune of having little sisters to manage brought us closer."

She supposed no one would dare misuse Lady Anne with those two gentlemen guarding her. Especially Carver, who could be very fearsome when he chose. After all, even Molly felt safe when he was beside her. Safe from everything but him, of course.

Shooting another shy glance upward, she said, "Just as you once watched over her brother? At school?"

"Yes."

"You saved him from bullies."

"Hmm."

"That was a kindly act, your lordship."

"Hmm."

A little color had crept up over the high collar of his coat.

"You are reluctant, I think, to admit yourself capable of good deeds." She spread her fingers a little over his arm, relaxing her hand.

It was a softening she regretted in the next moment, for he took advantage of the lapse. Suddenly he drew her into a shallow alcove between the trees and changed the subject. "Have you reviewed the amendments to our contract, Margaret?"

His eyes were pure silver, gleaming brighter than the gas lamps along the alley. The panther was poised to pounce upon the mouse. He had trapped her there.

❧

She was solemn, the lamplight barely enough to touch the side of her face as it tipped upward. "I have, sir."

"And?" How cruel she was to make him wait. Carver's hands found her waist through the soft fabric of her gown. He bent his head until his lips were almost upon hers.

"I cannot become your mistress. It is not the life I want for myself."

He stared down at her, a castaway again.

"I am sorry if you are disappointed, sir," she added. "I do hope we can continue as acquaintances, with no hard feelings."

"Are you quite mad, woman?"

"Possibly." She pressed a gloved finger to his lips. Then, having turned him down flat, she smiled, ducked out from the alcove, and walked onward, leaving him to follow. Her step was jaunty as she looked back over her shoulder, still smiling sweetly, and said, "Look how the trees arch overhead. It's almost like walking down an aisle, don't you think? Isn't the music lovely, your lordship?"

So was she, he thought churlishly, quickening his stride to catch up. More than one pair of masculine eyes had turned her way as she passed them, and there was no mistaking the open admiration. Damn and blast. He'd arranged all this to get her to Vauxhall Gardens, and now he owed Lady Anne a new bonnet for this service.

"Miss Margaret Robbins." He joined her, breathless. "What can be the meaning of running away from me?"

"Purely self-preservation, your lordship."

So she *was* tempted. "I suppose that's a start," he muttered. Again he took her hand and tugged her aside. She gave a small yelp that went unheard by the younger couple, who continued their stroll up ahead. This time he held her more firmly in a niche beside a small fountain. "Acquaintances, Miss Robbins? Is that all you mean to offer me?"

"Is it not enough?"

"Certainly not. I'm a grown man, not a boy." He would not be relegated to "friend" alongside Rafe Hartley and her artist neighbor.

She groaned and tried to slip out of his grasp. "Did you ask Lady Anne to bring me here this evening? Was this all *your* plan?"

He didn't respond to that question. Didn't need to. She was too clever not to know the answer. Although it was not his idea to invite that artist fellow along; that was all Lady Anne's decision. "Miss Robbins, you must be aware of the honor I am willing to bestow upon you. Any other woman would—"

"I do not mean to be rude, sir, but yet again I must remind you that I am not like those *other women*."

He drew her closer. Margaret glanced anxiously down the path in the direction of Lady Anne, so he turned her face back to him again, made her look at him. "Let me be candid, Miss Robbins," he said quietly, his fingers on her cheek. "I want you. I want you because you are not those women. I have need of you. Have you any idea what you've done to me?"

"Oh, I wish I knew what I'd done, sir, and then I could be sure to stop doing it."

"Don't push my patience, Miss Robbins. I won't be toyed with."

"That makes two of us, your lordship." She tried pulling away again, but he kept her firm, his hand moving behind her head, fingers trying the neat pins that held her hair in place tonight.

"Perhaps I am still too subtle." He frowned fiercely. "I intend to make you my mistress. I will give you a full wardrobe, a house in Town, complete with staff—anything you desire." His other hand moved to the small of her back. "Carte blanche."

She was staring at his mouth; her eyes were almost sleepy, confused. Finally she said, "I appreciate the frankness, your lordship, and the extreme generosity. But I could not possibly accept the post of your mistress."

The smile which had begun to tug at his lips now wilted.

"I must ask you, sir, not to importune me again in such a manner as you do this evening. As you did when you came to my lodgings. It can do neither of us any good whatsoever."

"You said yourself, Miss Robbins, life is short and pleasure hard to come by. Yet you deny yourself that pleasure now with me, out of a wasteful sense of propriety?"

"Someone in this town ought to be proper."

"Unfortunately for me," he muttered wryly, "it has to be you."

She looked pensive. "Do you think it's easy being a good person in this town?"

"I'm not asking you to be a bad person. If you were anything other than what you are, Margaret Robbins, I would not want you so very much."

Her brown eyes widened, and he thought he saw a tear forming. How tempting it was not to throw her over his shoulder and run away with her, there and then. Instead, he must be satisfied with holding her trapped for as long as he might get away with it. He was surprised, in fact, that she had not wriggled away again yet or stabbed him with something sharp.

"But being with you would change me," she whispered. "Would it not?"

"It might change *me*." Carver spread his fingers against her spine, urging her the last little distance closer. He needed her body against his. There was nothing else for it. "I *will* catch you, Mouse. I shall not give up. Let this be your warning."

The scent of his shaving soap surrounded her, along with his strength, the potent masculinity he wore with such confident ease. "One kiss," he whispered.

"Then you will release me?"

"Yes." It was another fib, of course, like before, in his carriage. He wanted more than a kiss. So did she. So much more.

She went limply into this improper embrace, felt every hard, vital inch of muscle of his body against her, separated merely by a few garments that suddenly seemed only to heighten her desire rather than make any barrier between them.

Slowly his lips claimed hers, and he held her closer still. She sensed the latent power in his hands, but she was not fearful. Far from it. His kiss breathed new life into her and filled her with vigorous spirit.

Her fingertips inched up his chest and found his neck, then, tentatively, his jaw. Smooth tonight. Warm. Oh, she hadn't meant to touch him, but she did. Molly ran her fingers along the sharp line and heard a low sound escape from somewhere deep inside his body. He'd almost lifted her off the ground; her toes barely touched earth.

As their lips parted, he whispered, "Come to me, Mouse."

"I cannot. I will not be another of your conquests."

"You are nothing"—his voice broke with frustration—"nothing like them."

"But I would be treated just the same." The words flowed out of her now as if his kiss had unlocked their chains. "I would soon become just what they are, and once you were bored with me, what then? What would I have left?"

"You will have anything else you desire, Margaret."

But that was a lie too. He could not offer her what she truly needed. He could not give her all of him. The Earl of Everscham and a dressmaker? They would be laughed out of every Society drawing room. And even if that did not matter—even if they could somehow survive the ridicule and the scandal—how could she trust that his heart was hers? That in time his eye would not wander, along with his affections?

At Danforthe House there was glass case containing a perfect model of the naval ship *Victory*. It still had all its sailors, canons, barrels, and sails. Lady Mercy had told her that it once belonged to an elder brother who died in childhood. Carver was not allowed to play with it or even open the glass case, which is why all the pieces remained intact. As a boy, he could only look at it. She always thought how terribly sad that was.

But that was the way he had learned to keep his heart safe too. Away from the touch of anyone who might cause it harm.

So she must remain sensible. "Please let us walk on, your lordship. Folk will notice, and I'd rather not be seen cavorting in dark corners with a notorious rake who treats women with less concern than he treats his boots and no doubt leaves them just as worn down."

"I see you have grown bold, Miss Robbins, since you left my employ. You are full of thorns with which to prick me."

With an arch smile, she replied, "Thorns, indeed! Do you think it was a bed of roses working in your household, having to hold my tongue every day for twelve years? I have wounds of my own."

"And now you have found your voice to retaliate."

"Yes."

"I see." He released her hand. "No wonder you couldn't wait to escape my house. Such a tyrant I must have been. I'm shocked you did not poison me with cyanide in the wine or smother me with a pillow while I slept."

Molly laughed gently. "It was tempting on occa-sion." How strange it was to be talking and teasing with him like this. A few months ago she could never have imagined herself to be this playful in his presence, but she liked it. There was no getting around the fact.

He was looking at her oddly. "How can I tempt you now, Margaret?"

Her heart thumped wildly, and the more she tried

to ignore it the worse it became, more forceful and insistent. Just like him wanting her attention, her submission.

"They say the prize most worthwhile is hardest won," he muttered.

Don't look into his eyes, she told herself frantically. *Don't let him trap you again.* "I don't suppose you've ever worked hard for anything," she replied saucily, trying to lighten the mood.

"Until now."

Pretending not to hear that last comment, she finally succeeded in leading him out of the niche and back into the striped light of the walk. "Don't look so depressed, your lordship. We can still be friends— share conversation." Yes, she wanted that. She wanted to keep talking to him now that she'd begun at last.

"Conversation?" he exclaimed, clearly horrified.

"Don't you ever talk to women?"

He cursed under his breath and then grumbled, "Not upright."

Torn between shock and amusement, she was still considering how to reply to that when a loud voice pierced their quiet moment.

"Is that you, Danforthe?"

❧

Carver groaned inwardly.

Fletcher Covington, the Duke of Bloody Preston, marched toward them down Druid's Walk—more commonly known as *Lover's* Walk—swinging his cane over the gravel and making more noise than a coach-and-four. Carver was aware of Margaret slipping away, putting herself closer to Lady Anne, partially hiding in shadow. He didn't look at her, guessing she would not care to be introduced to Covington, and not wanting to share her anyway. He was permitted too little of her company as it was.

"What are you doing here?" the other man demanded, squinting and puffing as he drew near. "Not with the Baroness Schofield, tonight, I see. You should take care, Danforthe, or someone might steal the lovely lady away from you."

He coughed sharply, swallowing another curse. "I am here to escort Lady Anne Rothespur. She wanted to attend the concert."

Now Covington spied the young sister of their friend and bowed, pressing the tip of his cane into the gravel. "Charming! Charming! Of course, yes, I do remember Lady Anne." Then his sly gaze slid to where Margaret stood by an arching yew tree. Her study was restricted to her shoes.

"This is my friend Miss Robbins," Anne blurted and then went on to introduce Frederick Dawes, but Covington took no pains to hide his disinterest in the latter.

"Why, this must be the skilled dressmaker of whom I hear so much." He grinned at Carver.

"Yes. Quite. I believe Miss Robbins is a very talented and successful designer and seamstress." Carver put his hands behind his back and assumed a careless, casual pose with his feet apart.

"Interesting. Interesting! Yes, indeed."

He didn't like the way Covington was looking at her. Leering might be a more apt word.

"And here we all are on Lover's Walk," the duke pointed out, tapping his cane on the gravel. "Surely the ladies won't mind if I join you. Or am I interrupting the cozy foursome?"

For a moment no one spoke, and then Margaret said, "I think we should go back toward the pavilion and find chairs, Lady Anne. You won't want to miss the rest of the concert." Taking the young girl's arm, she led her back the way they'd already walked.

Carver was thwarted. His plan ruined, he could only watch and admire from a distance. It did nothing to diminish his growing desire for her. If this was indeed her scheme to seduce him, render him her slave, it was working.

Thirteen

FOR THE DUKE OF SUTHERLAND'S BALL, MOLLY HAD
six gowns to finish, and each one must be unique and
charming. With only the well-meaning efforts but
very poor skills of Mrs. Slater to cause more hindrance
than help, she feared never being finished on time.
And then a miracle occurred. Mr. Edward Hobbs sent
his young nieces to her. Introduced as two parson's
daughters from Aylesbury, Emma and Kate were
speedy, efficient, and tidy needlewomen. Arriving
in London to visit their uncle, they were eager for a
chance to make use of themselves.

"I did not know you had any family, Mr. Hobbs."
She'd never suspected it, because he devoted all his
time working for the Danforthes, getting them out of
various scrapes.

"I do hope the girls are adequate," was his only reply.

Adequate? They were lifesavers.

They came to her lodgings early every afternoon
and stayed often until past midnight. Mr. Hobbs sent
a carriage to bring them to and fro. The extra hands
meant that she required less from Mrs. Slater, but the
lady still came up to help with the trimmings, bringing

her noisy baby with her. Frederick called in some evenings, but she was too busy to stop work and chat with him. Sometimes he made sketches of the ladies at their work, surrounded by a flurry of muslin, silk, and taffeta.

Mrs. Lotterby braved the steep, crooked stairs at least once a day, bringing little treats for Molly and her assistants—hot chocolate and apple dumpling if it was cold out, lemonade and caraway seed cake if the weather was warm. Discovering that Molly shared her fondness for marzipan, the landlady bought some for her whenever she could. A pig being fattened for honorable slaughter at the harvest feast could not have been better cosseted.

Meanwhile, across the landing, Mrs. Bathurst's haven of memories fed Molly's mind with inspiration, just as heartily as Mrs. Lotterby fed her stomach. From the colors of her old moth-bitten ball gowns, to the tarnished gleam of her rings and chokers, Mrs. Bathurst provided Molly with a glimpse into another world, a place inhabited by lusty Hungarian princes, somber British Naval heroes, fiery-tempered Russian Cossacks, a tough-skinned Highland gillie, and two romantic Italian sculptors.

At night, Molly sat up with a few lit candle stumps and sketched creations that, come the next morning, would surprise even her. Mrs. Bathurst exclaimed that only a woman conversant with the skilled touch of an amorous lover could design gowns as she did, but Molly assured her that she simply had a very good imagination.

Danforthe and his contract amendment remained in her thoughts, hovering over her like a great

black-haired bird of prey. Despite her own resolve and
Mrs. Lotterby's gentle warnings, Molly's stubborn will
had begun to pull in a wicked direction, stirred by his
kiss and the touch of his hand around hers.

He had called her *Margaret*. For some reason that
seemed more wickedly intimate than any other word
he might have used.

❧

In the last few days before the ball, Molly and her assistants spent their time traveling from house to house,
making final fittings and discussing accessories for
their clients. The very last scheduled fitting was that
of Baroness Schofield, who, as she was hooked into
a striking buttercup-yellow gown with short puffed
sleeves, inspected her image in a long mirror and
exclaimed crossly, "Yellow? But I never wear yellow
in the evenings. Not since I was a girl."

"Then it will be something fresh and unexpected,
madam."

With a heavy theatrical sigh, the baroness exclaimed,
"I don't like it, Robbins. It makes me look jaundiced."

"But in candlelight the effect will be quite different."

"I think I know what colors suit me, Robbins, and
this does not. No, I cannot get used to it. Also the
bosom is not cut low enough. These crisscross ribbons
on the bodice crush my curves too severely. Ugh! I
just cannot get beyond this dreadful color."

Molly felt her assistants growing fidgety. The baroness had expressed no such doubts before this, and
she'd had several fittings. There was only one day until
the Sutherland's ball, and while that left time for final
adjustments, it did not leave much time for an entire

new gown. Color was not something that could be altered with a few careful stitches.

"And these sleeves," the woman gestured impatiently, "look childish."

Childish? Molly swallowed a hot spur of anger, but it smarted in her throat. Nothing she ever designed could be called childish. This was a gown she had specifically made thinking of Carver Danforthe and what he would like his mistress to wear. She politely suggested the lady might like to consider the gown a little longer.

"No. I don't like it." With one quick move, the woman tore the sleeve from the bodice. "You'll have to start again. Nothing yellow, for pity's sake, Robbins." She dropped the ruined sleeve to the floor at Molly's feet. "The entire world knows a woman over twenty should never wear yellow for a ball. Not in Town. Perhaps in the country dullard's village that spawned you it was acceptable. Here it just won't do." Stepping down from her stool, she put her foot directly on the torn scrap and walked on with her lady's maid. "Help me get out of this atrocity of a gown, Peters. I'm feeling quite nauseated by so much bile yellow."

Molly stared at the woman's back.

"Oh, and, Robbins"—the baroness turned to look over her shoulder—"I like to look young, but I'm not a girl. This does nothing for my figure. If anything, it hides the bosom, which is one of my best features. We're not all flat across the top like you. A rare and expensive orchid would be more appropriate for me than a common buttercup."

"But the Earl of Everscham approved the design.

He prefers buttercups to cultivated flowers." It came out of her before she could bite it down and force it back into that secret vault where she kept everything she knew about him, everything she'd stored away in her mind's scrapbook.

The baroness had very sharp green eyes that never warmed, even when she smiled. Today they left Molly's face with ice burns. "I think I know what *he* likes."

She curtsied, her gaze lowered hastily to the torn scrap of sleeve. "Of course, madam."

The other woman came back to where she stood. With one long finger she raised Molly's chin until their eyes met. "What do you mean, he approved the design? When did he see it?"

"I meant to say that his lordship would approve it, madam. I feel certain of it."

"Well, you're wrong. You do not know him as I do. You never could."

"Of course not, madam."

The baroness made her voice soft and silky as the purr of a well-fed cat stretching on a sunny window-sill. "You're so plain, Robbins, such a grim little face. Perhaps you ought to take this gown and make something out of it for yourself. Yellow might lift your features. If anything could. Not that you have any use for a ball gown, of course." She sighed, her gaze drifting down to Molly's small bosom. "Poor thing." With that she walked away again, dismissing her with a pert, "Peters will see you to the door, once she's helped me out of this disastrous creation."

Leaving that house, Molly was seething and hurt, but by the time she arrived back at her lodgings, the feelings had mellowed somewhat. It could not be easy trying to keep the earl's interest, she supposed. His mistress must be aware of the tenuous place she held in his life, and with a new batch of debutantes on her heels, that would draw anyone's nerves thin.

"What shall we do?" Emma asked as they laid the rejected gown across the worktable and gathered around it like mourners at a funeral.

"I say we spit on it," said Kate, "and tell that hussy to go to the ball in her drawers."

Molly couldn't help but laugh at that. "Come, girls, let's not be downhearted." She put her arms around them both. "We must look at this as a challenge."

She told herself that not every design would be a success, not every client would love her work. Until then, she'd been fortunate, meeting praise at every turn. But the baroness had reminded her of how quickly favor could be lost as well as won. Favor in all its forms.

❦

Carver attended the Sutherlands' ball with Sinjun and Lady Anne, who, despite her annoying qualities, had become a useful conduit to the company of a certain frustrating dressmaker.

"May I say, Lady Anne, you look very lovely this eve-ning," he assured her while a liveried footman announced their names to the folk gathered in the ballroom.

"I know that's what a gentleman is supposed to say, Danforthe," she replied merrily, "but I also admit you are right on this occasion too. I have no qualms about confessing my loveliness, and it's all due to the wonderful Miss Robbins." She dropped his arm and gave an excited twirl in her blush-pink gown. "She is thoroughly brilliant. I only wish I could keep her all to myself."

He knew the feeling.

Sinjun came up behind them. "I see the Baroness Schofield in fine fettle this evening. Covington seemed to think the two of you are on the verge of parting company."

Carver pretended he didn't hear and swept Anne off for the first minuet. Dancing had only one use in his mind. It was an excellent disguise, a meaningless exercise performed while one hatched the most fiend-ish plots of seduction. He'd never been a great dancer, but lessons forced upon him in boyhood ensured he did not make a complete ass of himself on these occa-sions. His sister had also done her best to chisel and carve him into a better dancing partner—all part of her campaign to get him married off. A pointless effort on her part, but she insisted on it.

As they joined the other couples, he noted all the usual faces, and thought to himself, not for the first time, what a strange ritual this was. Everyone gathered in one place to dress up, show off, and usually make sizeable fools of themselves before the end of the evening. For fifteen Seasons he'd walked this path, tolerated every tedious moment.

"Oh, lord!" Anne exclaimed. "I must have caught my sleeve on the carriage door. I thought I felt the stitches pulled! Now my lovely beads are coming unraveled."

He followed her panicked gaze to where a few tiny pink drops scattered from her arm, down her skirt, and across the dance floor.

"Excuse me." She released his hand. "I must find Miss Robbins and see what she can do." Turning before she had even finished her sentence, she slipped away through the other dancers, and he watched her go.

Amazing what one could achieve with the ring on one's little finger, while pretending to place a gauze shawl around a lady's shoulders as she exited his carriage. Although Margaret must have sewn those beads on damn tight, for he'd expected them to start falling sooner.

Noting a few hopeful faces eyeing him eagerly above fluttering fans, he picked up the fallen beads and made a hasty retreat from the dance floor.

≈

Molly had promised herself not to look for him, but as soon as she took her turn at the crack in the dressing-room door, her tired, misty gaze traversed the bright crowd for a certain tall figure with very dark hair.

Oh, there he was. She caught a tense breath. Carver Danforthe was always a fine sight in his evening clothes. While she watched, he steered a young lady in a minuet. Pink gown. Was it Lady Anne Rothespur? Her eyesight was not cooperating, so she fumbled for her spectacles—a new cross to bear, but sadly a necessary one—and put them on. A series of very bad headaches had sent her, at Mrs. Lotterby's urging, to see a physician who insisted on the spectacles, much to her dismay.

Ah, yes. It was Lady Anne. A vast improvement on his usual partners. As she watched the couple dancing, it occurred to her that Carver Danforthe really ought to marry. Despite his oft-stated disdain for the institu-tion, his estate needed an heir. Lady Anne was full of life and did not appear to have a single affectation or mean bone in her body. She would make him a charming wife. If Carver did marry, thought Molly, perhaps it would finally help her conquer these unsuitable feelings for him. Feelings that continued to grow inside her, despite determined neglect.

The couple had not danced long, when the young lady suddenly turned and headed directly for the annex room, which served as a dressing room for the ball, filled with lady's maids waiting to fix the inevitable tears and stains their mistresses would soon bear. Molly quickly backed away from the door rather than be caught spying.

A few footsteps later, and Lady Anne dashed into the room. "My beads! I'm so dreadfully annoyed with myself, but I caught my sleeve on the carriage door, and now…see?"

"Don't fret, your ladyship." Molly assessed the damage through her spectacles. "We have some extra thread and beads in case of this very eventuality."

"Thank the Lord! You are a treasure, Miss Robbins. It's my first dance of the evening, and only with silly old Danforthe."

She was just about to thread her needle when she heard someone else enter the room behind her, and the atmosphere suddenly had a new bite to it, like the taste of unexpected ginger spice in Mrs. Lotterby's marmalade when one expected only sweet, bland orange.

"Oh, sir, you shouldn't be in here," someone exclaimed. "This is ladies only."

"But I reclaimed Lady Anne's beads. Will they not buy me admittance?"

Her heart raced at the clear, deep sound of his

voice amid the cluster of females. Hastily removing her spectacles to slide them out of sight, Molly pricked her finger and silently cursed herself for that pathetic vanity. But she got on with her work, even with something closed tight around her heart, squeezing. Whatever it was—whatever she was tempted to call it—the feeling had no mercy, just like his kiss.

"Miss Robbins." His hand was stretched out to her, palm up, showing her the fallen beads. "Will these help?"

"Danforthe, you shouldn't be in here." Lady Anne laughed. "Were you trying to see ladies in their petticoats?"

"Perhaps," came the wicked reply.

No one dared make any move to throw him out. Instead, they surrounded him with a churning sea of agitated breathing—outraged sighs, nervous giggles, and heaving bosoms. At times like these, Molly despaired of her own gender. He'd be disappointed if he ever thought his nearness would corrupt *her* into a quivering trifle. Having assured herself of her own utter indifference, Molly resumed the struggle to thread her needle. A most problematical enterprise without spectacles.

As she reached for a bead in Carver's warm, outstretched palm, she missed. They were very small, and the surface was shiny.

"Here," he said, "let me." He took one of the beads and held it for her. Somehow she got the point of her needle through the miniscule hole. "How lucky, Miss Robbins," he observed softly, "that you are here."

She said nothing, eager to preserve the proprieties under these strange circumstances. Just because one person misbehaved didn't mean they all had to, as her mother would have said.

"Give the beads to me," Lady Anne whispered. "Your presence is upsetting everyone, Danforthe. You really are too naughty. What are we going to do with you?"

"I am on tenterhooks to find out."

"Danforthe!" Lady Anne exploded in giggles that shook her shoulders and thereby made Molly's task even more trying. She slowed down, afraid of pricking the fidgeting young lady with her needle.

"I have wandered into a land of Amazons," the earl teased. "And we all know what the Amazon warrior women did to the males they encountered."

Playing right into his hands, Lady Anne demanded to know what they did.

"Why, they used men for only two things—body strength or seed for propagating the species. In short, slavery and breeding."

A ripple of dizzy laughter danced and skipped through the small room, and Molly felt the heat rise several degrees. Trust Carver Danforthe to speak of matters that the high-born, unmarried young ladies in that room should know nothing about. Must be in his cups, she thought with a terse sigh, staring hard at her blurred stitches.

"I'm sure Miss Robbins would have made a very fine Amazon queen. See how stern she keeps her countenance, despite all attempts by the lone male present to make her smile. See how savagely she wields her skillful needle, weaving her web. No man would get beyond her gates without capture. He would find himself bound up in her threads." She felt him moving around her. Very close. "While she decided what to use him for. Slave or mate. Both perhaps."

"Danforthe, you are the very worst! Stop teasing

poor Miss Robbins and let her work." But even as she admonished him, Lady Anne could not keep the laughter out of her voice, and it rather sounded as if she sweetly corrected the bad habits of a little lapdog, not the saucy words of a rake.

Molly pursed her lips and took back her earlier thoughts regarding Lady Anne's suitability as his wife. The girl was too young, too giddy to put him in his place. He needed a slap with a rug beater, not a tickle with a feather duster.

"Am I troubling you, Miss Robbins?" he inquired, leaning over her shoulder.

"Certainly not," she replied crisply.

"There. See?" She heard the sly grin in his voice. "Miss Robbins is not troubled, and she's the most important Amazon here, I think we can all agree. Without clothes created by the likes of Miss Robbins, you'd all be naked and at severe disadvantage for battle against the intruder in your midst."

His fingers casually moved the pleats of Molly's skirt.

Goose bumps rose on the nape of her neck, under the stray wisps of hair that had escaped her topknot. She feared he would see. Oh, she wished someone would throw the rake out. If only Lady Mercy were there, but alas, she was flitting about the countryside, leaving her wicked brother to his own devices. Chaos. Utter chaos.

He was determined to seduce her, it seemed. Each time they met, he wore away at her resistance a little more.

"Are you ready for another?" he asked. His hand moved her skirt again, surreptitiously brushing the thigh beneath.

"What?" She couldn't think, could barely take a breath.

"Another bead, Miss Robbins."

"Yes…thank you, your lordship."

He proceeded to thread another bead onto her needle. "You look flushed, Miss Robbins, and your hand, which I've heard described as infamously steady, appears to tremble."

"The room is overheated." She accidently met his gaze full on while raising her eyes from Lady Anne's shoulder. Somehow he held her there, just with the ravenous, demanding intensity of the look he gave her. "And so are you," she muttered under her breath. "Too hot."

"Too hot? I am indeed. We can't all have ice water in our veins, like you."

The injustice of that remark caused her to stick her needle too far. Lady Anne yelped, and Molly apologized profusely.

"Danforthe, now you have upset Miss Robbins!" Lady Anne cried.

"Nonsense. I am only teasing. Miss Robbins should acquire a sense of humor."

A few other ladies had now entered the annex room, ostensibly to have hems and sleeves tended to by their own seamstresses and maids, but very probably to see what Danforthe was up to. Molly wondered where the Baroness Schofield might be. She took a step to the side, inching away from his body heat.

Just two more beads, and she'd be done, but Carver was not helping her cause. In the act of passing her a bead, he fumbled and dropped it.

"Oops!" he exclaimed. "I'll get the blasted thing."

He disappeared in a hasty crouch, while Lady Anne Rothespur joyfully assured him he was a clumsy oaf.

The dressing-room door swung open again, and a blast of much-welcome cooler air swept Molly's brow. The clipped tones of Carver's mistress quickly followed the breeze, almost as if her own thoughts had summoned the woman.

"Goodness it is crowded in here. Robbins, for pity's sake, make haste. You've made a dreadful botch-up of this seam. It's too tight, and I can barely breathe."

Molly looked for the baroness, but without spectacles, her overworked eyes were slow to see which of the new faces was the one calling to her. She felt the room begin to tip on one side. Had her eyesight worsened in just these last few hours? Or was it merely the heat of the small room and her nerves suffering the pressure of this grand occasion?

"Robbins!" the baroness snapped again. "Are you deaf as well as mute, girl?"

The woman did not care that she was busy with another client. Nor had she seen Carver Danforthe on his hands and knees between skirts, searching for the dropped bead.

A swift hush descended over the room, but if the baroness took note of it at all, she probably assumed they were all in awe at her grand appearance. "I swear you are the slowest, stupidest, most trying seamstress I've ever had the misfortune to encounter." She turned to the woman on her right and laughed coldly. "First she tries to drown me in bile yellow, and then stuffs me into a gown that was evidently measured to fit someone else, because she was too lazy to make a new one for me. Thought I wouldn't notice. I really cannot understand the sudden appeal of this dull, jumped-up lady's maid. I don't know why I wasted my money."

"But you didn't, did you, Maria?" Carver suddenly stood upright. "It was my money. Or my ancestors' money, since I've never actually earned any."

Molly thought she would faint. His fingers skimmed her sleeve. She dare not look at him, but kept her gaze on Lady Anne's white evening glove.

The silence, like the heat, was heavy, suffocating, but no one left the room. This was too interesting now, of course.

⚜

He saw the spite in Maria's eyes, glistening like shards of ice forming with unnatural speed over pond weeds.

"You owe Miss Robbins an apology."

Her pouty, unnaturally red lips parted, and she squeezed out a gasp, part scornful laugh, part sheer outrage. "I most certainly do not. Every word I just said is the truth. She tried to put me in a horrid yellow gown, and I—"

"Enough," he growled, and the room froze. "Miss Robbins." He put the last bead into Molly's hand and watched her fingers gather around it. Standing close to her in that crowded room had a most rousing effect on his body and his senses. There was one particular curl against the nape of her neck that he felt an almost overwhelming urge to kiss. Then he wanted to press the tip of his tongue very lightly to her skin. It was, he supposed, her innocence that drew him in, rejuvenated the lusty spirit in a jaded old rake like him. Pursuit had grown tiresome in recent years, and he was seldom intrigued enough to go to great lengths for a woman. Until the Mouse started scratching at his walls, making her presence known, so he missed her when she was not there.

He liked looking down into her large brown eyes and seeing all the questions spinning and darting about. The ideas swimming through her mind intrigued him.

But hers were the only eyes not watching him now.

"Lady Anne." He bowed to his friend's sister. "I will see you when Miss Robbins has put you back together, and we will, I hope, resume our dance."

"Certainly, your lordship."

Carver left the room, not looking again at his mistress. He knew she followed him out, her slippered feet rushing along in his wake. "How dare you speak to me as if I'm a child in need of reprimand! And in public!"

Paused at the margin of the dance floor, he spun around to face her. "How dare you speak that way to Miss Margaret Robbins." Several faces in the crowd looked over at them, forcing Maria to draw herself up, bosom out, earrings dancing with the tremors of her restrained wrath.

"She is a servant," she hissed, her teeth gritted in a smile as false as the color in her cheeks—a youthful blush he now knew to be the work of carmine rouge. "Perhaps you forget."

"Yes, I've seen how you speak to your servants, Baroness Schofield. It is not how I speak to mine."

Her eyes flamed, the icicles melting. Soon he suspected she would try tears again. She readied them, like an actress rehearsing her role. "It must run in the Danforthe family, this desire to play below stairs."

Carver's hands formed fists at his side, so tightly

clenched he almost lost the feeling in them. "I beg
your pardon?"

"Just like your sister with her farmyard diversion,
you choose to dally with a commoner. I've heard
that men of a certain age are often drawn to girls like
Robbins. It makes them feel as if they have reclaimed
their youth, makes them the conquering hero again—
looked up to and swooned over by a chit of a girl
who owes everything to them. I put up with your
other fancies, but now I am supposed to tolerate this
perverse dalliance of yours too?"

"By no means would I expect you to *tolerate* anything, Maria," he replied tightly. "You are welcome
to absent yourself from my company any time you
desire. That—as I'm sure you can appreciate, having
suffered so many years of your husband's tiresome
company—is the beauty of not being bound in
matrimony." He turned away from her and walked
through the guests standing around the perimeter of
the dancing.

Again she followed. "Robbins is paid for a service.
Is it too much to expect a gown I can wear?"

"You seem to be wearing that one."

"It is much too tight at the bosom. Look."

Knowing full well what she was up to, he wouldn't
look at her. "Perhaps you have gained weight, Maria.
That, so I hear, happens to women of a certain age."

That silenced her for a while. She deserved that
arrow, he thought angrily. Not only for the way she
insulted him, but for how she spoke to Margaret.

"And for your information, madam," he added
eventually, "yellow happens to be my favorite color."

"Well, how was I to know?"

The same way Margaret had known, he thought. By not being absorbed in herself. By taking note. By caring enough to know.

"Are you going to dance with me?" the baroness demanded.

He stared at her. "No," he said eventually. "You and I have danced our last. I am clearly not the partner you wanted. If you find yourself obliged to tolerate me, I cannot fulfill your needs, and you, madam, cannot fulfill mine."

Her face was white with fury.

He bowed. "Good evening."

❦

"That was quite a scene," Lady Anne Rothespur remarked as the two angry people departed. "She's very brassy. What does he see in her, I wonder?"

Molly threaded the last bead into place. "A beautiful face, an elegant form, and a very full bosom, no doubt," she muttered drolly.

"Men can be such tedious creatures, easily distracted by bright objects. My brother is just as bad. I've decided I shall marry a bookish man who doesn't care at all for looks. Then he won't be tempted to run off or keep a mistress."

"A sound idea, to be sure."

Lady Anne looked over her shoulder. "What about you, Miss Robbins?"

"Me?"

"Have you no plans to marry? Frederick Dawes told me you ran away from your groom at the altar. Did he have a wandering eye too?"

"I decided to devote myself to a career instead,"

Molly replied, jabbing her needle into the pincushion at her wrist. "There is no place for a husband in
my life."

"But you will be an old maid."

"Yes, thank goodness. A *happy* old maid."

Lady Anne looked doubtful.

"I am content with my choice," Molly assured her.
"Not every woman is made to be a wife."

"Jumping Jacks, Miss Robbins! To resign yourself
to spinsterhood at your age. It's a mistake."

Molly merely smiled.

Suddenly Lady Anne spun around to face her fully,
the skirt of her gown fanning out. "I wager you have
a secret love."

"Gracious no." The more aware she became of
the heat in her face the worse it felt; the higher her
temperature climbed.

Hands on her waist, the romantically inclined
young girl surveyed Molly with sparkling blue eyes.
"I always knew there was something about you.
Something brewing inside. Carver is right. You have
a very devious look about you, Miss Robbins."

"I assure you there is no man in my life. Not in that
sense. Goodness it is hot in here."

"Perhaps he is promised to another, or there is some
other awfully tragic reason why you keep him secret. I
suppose you have closed your heart to others because
it is reserved only for him, and you will love him unto
death." She placed a gloved finger to her lips. "Is he
young or old? Fat or thin? Dark or fair? Are his teeth
evenly spaced? Is he good humored? Does he dance
with elegance or charge about like a ram in a field of
ewes? Does he ride adequately?" Leaning closer, she

giggled behind her fan. "Is he ravishingly reckless in the saddle? Does he drink too much port? Does he have horrendously hairy knuckles? I hope, for your sake, he looks well in knee breeches. There is nothing worse than a bandy-kneed beau."

She laughed at the young lady's odd jumble of ingredients for a worthy suitor. Caught up in it for a moment, still giddy about the way Carver defended her before his mistress, she decided to play along. "He is old. Too old and set in his ways, I fear. He is very ill humored, dances badly, and drinks far too much."

"Gracious!" Lady Anne laughed and then said slyly, "Then you really must be in love with Danforthe to see beyond all his faults."

Horrified, Molly could only stare dumbly at the young woman before her.

Much to her relief, the teasing was ended almost immediately when Lady Anne's brother came to the door, looking for her.

"You needn't worry," was her tormentor's parting remark, "I shan't tell a soul your secret, Miss Robbins. As long as you save all your best, most delicious designs for me."

Appalled, she watched the mischievous lady exit the room on her brother's arm. Until that moment, she'd thought Lady Anne quite naive and uncomplicated, a sweet girl but prone to making a vast deal of noise. Alas, it seemed she misjudged the young woman.

She knew other folk in the dressing room eyed her curiously, wondering at the way the Earl of Everscham spoke up for her. Intent on ignoring the incident, Molly replaced her spectacles and tidied her sewing box. But the music filtering in from the ballroom made her feet tap and her petticoats swing in a manner most unusual for her.

It wasn't long before news of a quarrel and a pair of thrown diamond earrings reached the annex room. The Earl of Everscham, so the eager gossip went, had finished with his mistress, and she retaliated by scoring his cheek with her diamonds.

Of course it was never considered a good party without a little drama, and it was not the first time Carver Danforthe had been the cause of it. Nor was it, so the gossips exclaimed gleefully, the first time a woman had thrown jewelry at him. After all, said one stout lady standing near Molly, he was known to always give his mistresses a piece of very fine jewelry as a parting gift whenever he ended an affair.

~

When Molly eventually went to her bed that evening, after describing the ball in enough detail to satisfy her fellow residents at the house, she expected to sleep almost immediately. It had been a tiring few weeks leading up to the ball. But as she lay down, her mind still raced excitedly, unable to settle. While her body was drained, her head and heart were too full.

Carver Danforthe and his teasing had knotted around her mind like an invasive weed slowly taking over the garden of her good thoughts. *You might change me*, he'd said at Vauxhall Gardens.

Could she? Did she even want to?

Lying on her belly, Molly hugged her pillow tightly and tried her damndest to cast him out.

It was a futile exercise. When she did finally fall asleep, he was there in her dreams, waiting for her under an arbor of thorny roses. She felt herself smiling, holding her pillow even closer, melting into it and into his strong arms, helpless and losing control. But not nearly as angry with herself as she should be.

Fourteen

WHEN MRS. LOTTERBY RECEIVED NEWS OF A WINDFALL coming her way on the death of a relative, it took her several days to recover from the shock. The unexpected influx of coin was enough to pay for repairs to the old leaky roof and provide other much-needed maintenance to the house, so it must indeed be a sizeable inheritance, as well as unexpected.

To celebrate, she organized a picnic in the park, and all her residents attended, except the unpleasant Arthur Wakely, who had apparently packed his bags and left in the middle of the night. Not even his sister knew where he'd gone, and nobody cared enough to find out why. Mrs. Bathurst's health had taken a turn for the worse quite suddenly, and she would have stayed in bed, had Molly, who thought the lady was simply giving in to a mournful state of mind, not persuaded her to join the party.

"It won't be the same without you, Mrs. B. Who will entertain us with stories if you don't come?"

"Quite true, my dear," the lady eventually conceded. "I suppose the sunlight won't kill me any faster, will it?"

The weather held out for the excursion to Hyde

Park, and Molly anticipated a restful afternoon under a parasol, seated by the lake and sipping lemonade. Frederick made them all laugh and kept young master Slater occupied by threatening to throw him into the Serpentine. Mr. Lotterby fell asleep with his mouth wide open, and his merry wife, in between swiping at flies to keep them away from his face, fussed over her tenants to be sure they ate plenty.

"Miss Robbins, you are in need of sustenance, I'm sure. Do have a tart, and give me your opinion. Take two or three, indeed, for you are all bones and very little flesh. When winter comes, you'll welcome a few more layers. I know when the cold winds set in, I'm grateful to have my Herbert. At least then he is of use. But you'll have no one to keep you warm at night."

It was not a reminder she needed. "I'll procure a warming pan for coals."

Mrs. Bathurst leaned over the proffered plate and, ignoring her sister's chiding, palmed three tarts with the efficiency of a magician. "You need a man, Miss Robbins," she said.

"I'm sure I'll manage well enough without one."

"Nothing can take the place of a man in one's bed. A warming pan does only so much. And it is likely to cause a fire if one leaves it in too long." She snorted and nudged Mrs. Slater. "A man can cause the same conflagration, but in that case, the fire in one's bed is welcome."

The young widow flushed scarlet, and Mrs. Bathurst teased her.

"Now don't be coy, madam. You know of what I speak. That noisy child of yours was not found under a gooseberry bush."

In ladylike embarrassment, Mrs. Slater moved away to wipe sticky jam from her greedy son's cheeks. As the subject of children was raised, Molly glanced at Mrs. Lotterby and then at her sister. She'd given a great deal of thought to the matter of Mrs. Bathurst's baby and decided something ought to be done about it, before it was too late to manage a reconciliation. Secrets were all well and good—they had their place— but she would not stand by and see her friend fade away and die, never having met her own son.

"Mrs. Bathurst, you said you recently saw your son, now fully grown. Did you never approach him?" She did not believe, even for a minute, that the missing man was now a fine gentleman who traveled in grand carriages with beautiful ladies of high society, but if Mrs. Bathurst had truly seen him, it must have been somewhere not far from their lodgings.

"Goodness, no." Mrs. Lotterby spoke up for her sister, who still had a mouthful of jam tart. "Why would she approach him? What could she say? How would such an encounter be managed?" She turned to her sister. "You did not tell me you thought you had seen him, Delilah. Why would you think it and not tell me?"

"You took him from me all those years ago," Mrs. Bathurst replied primly. "I daresay you would keep him from me still. My own child wrenched from me."

"Nonsense. I did what was best, as you well know." The landlady seemed deeply wounded by the accusations of her sister. "If the Good Lord wanted such an encounter between you and your child, Delilah, he would arrange it. We must put our faith in the Almighty to know what is best."

Her sister gave a deeply saddened sigh. "Then he

and I shall never know each other. That is my punishment, I suppose, for a life of sin. I'm sure he would
not wish to know me as his mother, in any case. Such
a disappointment I would be."

"It was for the good of the child," Mrs. Lotterby
muttered, brushing crumbs from her bosom. "We
made that choice together."

Molly thought about the choices people made.
Her choice, for instance, had been work and business
over marriage and a family. Resigned to the life of a
spinster, she had forfeited her chance to be a mother
when she ran away from the altar back in April. Had
she stayed and married Rafe Hartley, she could be
expecting a child by now and eventually given birth
to a curly haired, rosy-cheeked baby, who would look
at her adoringly while she sang to it.

Now that would never happen. Her choice was to
remain alone, unburdened by a husband and children,
but one day, she too—like Mrs. Bathurst—could sit by
this lake, pondering her past and regretting the things
she once gave up. She knew some success with her
designs now, and it was a very sweet feeling, but it had
not yet made her whole. Perhaps Arthur Wakely was
right, and there was something amiss with her because
she chose her work over a child.

Or perhaps not. Young master Slater wobbled over
to her, snatched the last bite of jam tart out of her
hands, and smeared it over his own newly cleaned
face. Children, she remembered with a sigh of relief,
were not all golden-curled cherubs with pink cheeks.

"Frederick is painting your portrait, I understand?"
Mrs. Bathurst asked as they watched the boy toddle off
after a butterfly.

"Yes." She'd finally agreed to it, just for some peace. "I cannot imagine what he wants my picture for, unless to scare crows from a seed bed."

The lady laughed croakily. "A lack of vanity can be just as bad as too much, you know."

"I know what I look like."

"You know what *you* see in the mirror. When Frederick has completed his portrait, you will know what others see when they look at you. That is what scares you, young lady. And do not frown, Miss Robbins. When you are not aware of being watched, you are in danger of becoming almost pretty, but the moment you feel eyes upon you, out come the spikes—just like a hedgehog."

She supposed it was an improvement on a mouse. Or was it?

"Frederick is a very talented fellow," added Mrs. Bathurst as she looked wistfully over at the man walking by the lake with Mrs. Slater. "A fine young man indeed."

Molly followed her gaze and studied Frederick Dawes with a new thought taking root. Was it possible that when Mrs. Bathurst mentioned seeing her son fully grown and riding in a carriage with a fine lady, she spoke of Frederick and his benefactress? Mrs. Bathurst's son would be about the same age, and Frederick had spent his childhood in the workhouse.

Surely it was merely coincidence. A great many children, sadly, grew up in workhouses. She had let her imagination run away with her. In a place the size of London, Mrs. Bathurst's son could be anywhere. He might even be abroad by now. Or deceased. It was merely her own desire for neat ends and clean designs that made Frederick into a potential long-lost son.

An open barouche rumbled by the lake, following the meandering curve of a gravel horse path. Molly had watched it for several moments, squinting without her spectacles, before she recognized the passengers, and one of them noticed her.

Lady Anne Rothespur raised a hand and waved violently, calling out her name with the usual excess of vitality and lack of decorum. The barouche slowed to a gradual halt just a short way on. Now the lady twisted in her seat, beckoning rapidly.

Mrs. Bathurst peered through a crooked pair of opera glasses. "You'd better go and see what they want, my dear. Two very fine-looking gentlemen! Gracious me, and it is not even the fashionable hour, but that is a very grand barouche indeed. If I were twenty years younger... oh, but you, of course, have no interest in men. I had forgot you are resolved to spinsterhood. Pay me no heed."

Molly clambered to her feet, brushing crumbs from her skirt. The people in the carriage watched her approach, and behind her, she knew that her friends did the same.

"Lady Anne." She curtsied with some difficulty, for the ground between her friends by the lake and the people waiting in the carriage was an uneven, grassy slope.

"Miss Robbins, such a fine day, is it not? How glad I am that you get out in the fresh air and do not spend all your waking hours slaving away at work in that dingy little room."

Carver Danforthe hitched forward on his seat, stiff and unsmiling. "Miss Robbins, you will join us for a ride around the park?"

"We have plenty of room," said Lady Anne. "If you wouldn't mind sharing a seat with the Earl of Everscham." She lowered her voice. "He is, as you know, quite obnoxious company, but you needn't speak a word to him, and I shall poke him with my parasol if he gets out of hand." The young lady punctuated this comment with a wink that Molly would rather not have seen.

"Thank you for the offer, but I am with my friends, as you see." Gesturing to the people by the lake, she saw Carver glance over, his eyes very dark. "We're having a picnic," she added.

His lip quirked sulkily. "So I see. Well, don't let us keep you from your *friends*." The last word, if it had teeth, would have bitten her. Her heart ached when she saw the mark on his cheekbone, the wound from his spurned mistress and her thrown diamond earrings. It was true then; he had given the baroness up.

Lady Anne also looked at the people by the lake and smiled, twirling the parasol over her shoulder. "Oh, there is that darling young man, Mr. Frederick Dawes."

Carver flung himself back into his seat with such force that the Earl of Saxonby looked at him in surprise. Abruptly, Carver shouted to the coachman, "Drive on!"

The barouche rumbled away at speed, wheels kicking up gravel. Lady Anne waved as they rounded a bend and vanished from Molly's sight.

❧

"You're in love with her," said Sinjun, his tone incredulous.

"I beg your pardon?"

"Your very aspect when my sister mentioned that artist chap…the way you defended her to Covey. The way you sat up when you spotted her there by the lake. Now it all makes sense—the bloody mood you've been in of late. I've never seen you like it, man."

"Don't be tedious, Rothespur."

But he felt Sinjun's eyes boring into him. "Remember, I've known you too long."

Lady Anne moved her parasol to look at her brother. "What can you mean, Sinjun? Danforthe in love?" She guffawed. *"With Miss Robbins?"*

Had they conspired to make him feel like a fool exhibited in the stocks, they couldn't have done it better, but Sinjun had a habit of saying whatever was on his mind in that moment, and his sister did the same, always much louder than required. Often she was so very loud, Carver wondered if she'd been thrust down a well as a child.

"Your brother has a wild imagination and a romantic constitution," said Carver, stretching one arm along the back of his seat. "He is prone to moments of mad supposition."

"He is? I've certainly never noticed." She arched her brows high, and he caught the twinkle of mischief dancing in her eyes. "But I pity you, Danforthe, if it's true. Miss Robbins is much too good and sensible to become one of your damn doxies."

Her brother turned his head to glare at her. "Anne! Where on earth did you learn a word like that? For goodness sake, don't say it in front of Mama, or she'll blame me."

"Which word? Damn or doxy?"

"Both."

"Separately or together? I do love a bloody good alliteration, and damn just makes everything so much more definite."

Carver put a hand to his mouth and coughed, but his amusement did not last long when she turned her attention back to him. "You're the very worst sort of man for Miss Robbins," she shouted to be heard above the hooves and tumbling wheels as they clattered over a stone bridge. "A positively gruesome prospect for such a pleasant, sweetly mannered lady. Besides, she despises you heartily. I fear you quite waste your time, if that is why you wanted me to bring her to Vauxhall Gardens. She has nothing good to say about you."

"No doubt." He frowned hard.

Lady Anne closed her parasol and poked her brother with the end point. "See. You've got it all wrong. Miss Robbins is quite obviously in love with that delicious artist fellow. I knew she had a clandestine lover."

"Well, the artist is certainly more appropriate for her. Younger and more handsome too. Don't fancy your chances there, old chap." Her brother smiled knowingly at Carver and tipped the brim of his hat with his cane.

Thoroughly annoyed by this travesty of misjudgment—Sinjun's, Anne's, and the Mouse's—Carver pursed his lips, crossed his ankle over one knee, and became excessively interested in the shape of the clouds overhead.

A certain pinch-mouthed, judgmental seamstress rejected all that he could offer her and preferred to spend her spare time with gaunt, pretty young men who daubed paint around on canvas, did she? He realized he was drumming his fingers on his thigh and grinding his teeth so hard they hurt.

"Don't fret, Danforthe." Lady Anne exhaled with a heavy sigh, eyes shining. "I don't suppose it's a lost cause yet. You'll just have to try harder, won't you?"

He glared at the girl and wondered when, exactly, she'd stopped being so flighty and vacant-headed. Clearly she wasn't nearly as dense as he'd assumed.

But she was wrong if she thought hard work would scare him off. "There are things in life worth making an effort for," he replied grumpily. "Even I can put myself out for a good cause."

Sinjun and Anne looked at him in considerable amazement and curiosity. He took superior pleasure in ignoring them both for the remainder of the journey.

The solicitor took Molly to view an empty shop on Bayswater Road near Oxford Street.

"Can I afford it, Mr. Hobbs?" She tried not to show too much excitement.

"The lease is quite within the budget, Miss Robbins, and there is a very pleasant room above, which would make a little retreat for you, some additional living quarters."

"I would not wish to leave Mrs. Lotterby. I am among friends there."

"Naturally, but if I were you, I would furnish the room above and use it for consultations with some of your elite clientele. Far less wear on your boots, not to be dashing about town in all weathers."

"But my clients expect to be waited on, Mr. Hobbs. What will they think of having to come out to see me, rather than the other way about? They will think it most irregular."

Mr. Hobbs gently reminded her that the upper classes were an easily influenced lot who liked nothing better than to get "one up" on their friends and neighbors. "You need only convince them that this is the new, fashionable idea, and that if they do not come, they're missing out on something. They will converge upon the place in no time. The sign of true success, Miss Robbins, will be making them come to you. It will become a mark of status to be brought *upstairs at Miss Robbins's shop.*"

"I suppose so," she muttered doubtfully, still wondering if she could afford the place, trying not to get ahead of herself with too many grand ideas. But Mr. Hobbs was a man of sound business sense, and it was well worth listening to his advice; certainly it would be favorable to have a tidy, clean, dry room in which to meet clients. Meanwhile, the room on the ground floor of the shop would be the place where all the work happened. She would have no more clutter in her lodgings at Mrs. Lotterby's and could invite her friends for civilized tea and chat without making them sit among scraps and pins.

"Imagine the sign above this window," Mr. Hobbs urged: "Miss Robbins's Designs for Discerning Ladies. Yes, I can see it now in gilt paint. Very tastefully inscribed on a black oval, I think. Don't you?"

Oh yes, she could see it clearly too as he described it.

Thus Molly was persuaded to lease the shop. With Mr. Hobbs's assistance, she acquired furnishings for the new space, but kept it fairly sparse and open, preferring clean lines and airiness to greet her clients, rather than too much decoration that would detract from her designs. The walls were white, creating a simple background upon which she could show a few samples of fabric from the nearby haberdasher. Beside the swathes of silk, satin, and muslin, she hung sketches of her designs, and around the room there were small, carefully arranged groups of comfortable chairs where clients could sit and ponder their choice, or read a magazine while awaiting a consultation.

Her assistants were ecstatic.

"As much as I enjoyed the coziness of your other lodgings," said Emma, "I think this workroom will be far superior."

"No more wailing baby below," added Kate, hands clasped for joy. "No more unholy stench rising up from the alley on warm evenings. No more Arthur Wakely tut-tutting at us while trying to see up our skirts as we mount the stairs to your room."

"Should have kicked dust in his eye. That's what I always did. Oh, and once I threatened to drop an iron on his foot."

The girls laughed.

"In any case, he seems to have disappeared for now."

"Good riddance."

Despite Mr. Arthur Wakely's tiresome existence and the inevitability of his return one day, Molly had grown to love Mrs. Lotterby's house and the other people in it. They were, in a sense, her new family, and so were these two young girls whom she thought of as her angels. They'd laughed with her, worried with her, and celebrated with her, surrounding Molly with their warm-hearted light until she, too, glowed with it.

Standing in her new shop, Molly looked around and felt as if she ought to pinch herself. How could so much good fortune and success have come to one poor, plain little girl from Sydney Dovedale? From hard work, a determined spirit, and good friends, that's how, she told herself with a firm nod.

But she couldn't help fearing it might not last, that someone, somehow would decide she didn't deserve this and take it all from her. For when a person went up and up, sooner or later they had to come down. The Molly Robbinses of the world were not meant to find their way up into such lofty heights.

❧

Whenever she had a moment to spare, she sat for Frederick's painting. Although he seemed pleased by the progress, he refused to let her view his work. "When it's complete, you may see it then," he assured her grandly.

She asked if he'd ever considered painting Mrs. Bathurst. "Now there is a lady with character in her face. An entire lifetime of expression."

"True. But who would buy a painting of Mrs. Bathurst?"

"Who would buy mine? I sincerely hope you don't think to sell it."

He looked smug. "We'll see."

Molly drew the conversation back to Mrs. Bathurst. "She is a dear old lady and admires you very much."

"Of course she does. Everyone adores me. I am adorable."

There was something in his expression that reminded her of Mrs. Bathurst. The more she looked, the more evident it became. "You said you have no family still living, Frederick. Where was the workhouse in which you grew up?"

"St. Giles Cripplegate. Why? Do sit still. That's the third time you've fidgeted, and it's not like you at all."

Molly fixed her gaze on a point above his easel. "Would you like to meet your mother?"

"My mother? What for? I've nothing to give her. I'm not a fat, rich, famous artist yet."

She sighed. "There is such a thing as love, Frederick. It comes free of charge, but it seems to be so easily dismissed in this town. Folk are too busy for love."

"Love does not pay the bills or put food on the table. Unless it's the sort of love sold in a dark alley outside a gin shop for sixpence."

"Frederick!"

He laughed. "And you're a fine one to criticize, Miss Molly Robbins. What time do you spare for love, eh?"

She dismissed it with a haughty shake of her head, but he was right, of course. If she was not careful, she would become as hard-hearted as the other people there. Had she not closed her heart inside one of those boxes? She meant to guard it, protect it from harm, but it longed to be set free, to love where it wanted, where it needed. Keeping her heart shut away was as cruel as it would be to keep a lively creature like Lady Anne Rothespur trussed up and locked in a room. It might keep the young lady out of trouble, but it would surely cause her pain and change her for the worse.

Pensive, she wondered what had become of Carver lately. She hadn't seen him since that day in the park. Had he given up his pursuit at last? Now, when she held his handkerchief to her face at night, she thought his scent was fading. Tears threatened, but she forced them back, felt them scalding the back of her eyes.

Fred promised to unveil her portrait at Mrs. Lotterby's next dinner party. Despite the nonchalance with which she'd approached the ordeal, Molly was on tenterhooks that evening, wound up with anticipation. However, when they all gathered in Mrs. Lotterby's parlor, the painting revealed was not of Molly. It was a portrait of Mrs. Slater and her son.

Curbing her disappointment, she declared herself glad that he'd finally followed her suggestion and painted the young widow. "You did great justice to her eyes, exactly as I knew you would, Frederick."

"It was damned hard to get the boy to sit still," he muttered to her as they sat at the dining table. "I had to bribe him with treats. Aren't you going to ask me what happened to your picture?"

"I assumed it came out so badly that you burned it in Mrs. Lotterby's fire," she replied curtly.

"No. I sold it to an admirer."

"Frederick Dawes, don't fib! Who on earth would buy a picture of me?"

"A gentleman who desires to remain anonymous. As if you cannot guess his name. As if we do not all know it by now after his midnight visit to your room."

Molly's face was now warm as toast and could have melted butter.

"He paid a high price, or I would not have parted with it. Now I can pay off all my debts and still have coin with which to celebrate my first sale. He was most generous. For an aristocrat and an old man."

"Oh, Fred. I wish you had discussed it with me before you sold my portrait."

"Why? You said many times that you didn't want

to see yourself." He shrugged, utterly unconcerned. "I don't know why you fret so."

She couldn't put it into words, but somehow the thought of Carver Danforthe being in possession of her picture felt rather scandalous. It was almost as if she could feel his eyes studying her closely, as if part of her soul was captured in that portrait and was now his prisoner. There was no mistaking who had bought it, of course; she didn't need to hear his name.

"Can't imagine what you see in him," Frederick added slyly. "Apart from the coin, of course. I suppose I can't blame you for that. He's been very generous to all, because of you. Because of his desire for you."

"What can you mean? Generous to whom?"

The others were all seated now, and her pulse was too brisk, her breathing unsteady. Frederick looked pointedly around the table, and she followed his gaze. Mrs. Lotterby had put on a large spread that week. In fact, all her dinners that past month had been more extravagant than usual. Ever since the mysterious bequest left to her by a never-before-mentioned relative.

Frederick was very smart that evening in a brand new waistcoat. Molly had not noticed it earlier. Occasionally he checked the time on a new fob watch, the gleam of gold bright in the corner of her eye. As wine loosened his tongue, he flirted with a blushing, giddy Mrs. Slater, who had come out of her shell since the welcome, unexplained disappearance of her brother.

Fortune seemed to have turned lately in favor of her friends. Mrs. Lotterby's sudden influx of coin for repairs and a new roof was just the beginning of it, and where did it end? Was even the delightful absence of Arthur Wakely part of this same pattern of fortuitous occurrences?

Finally to be considered, there was Molly's new shop in the Bayswater Road. Mr. Hobbs had assured her she could afford the lease there, in addition to her rent at Mrs. Lotterby's, with only a few small adjustments to her budget. But how could that be? She had been blinded by her own excitement and a willingness to believe in miracles.

Blind to a great many things.

She'd even begun to wonder about the provenance of her "angels," those two young parson's daughters supposedly from Aylesbury and sent to her by Mr. Hobbs. Was anything in this town ever what it appeared to be?

That evening at dinner, Molly went through the motions without hearing a solitary word anyone said. She knew she had to do something about this. Better take charge of the situation—of him and of her heart—as best she could, before he sneakily took all the control out of her hands.

Fifteen

SHE STRODE BOLDLY UP THE FRONT STEPS OF
Danforthe House the next afternoon and tugged
hard on the bell cord. Richards opened the door and
almost toppled backward to see her standing there at
the main entrance.

"I've come to see the earl," she said calmly. "I trust
he's out of bed by now."

"Robbins, you cannot just—"

Molly pushed her way by him and into the house.
"Please fetch him. I'll wait in his"—she turned
slowly, considering—"his library." And with that,
she marched into his lair, leaving a complaining, irate
Richards in her wake. As she'd said to him before, let
the sullen butler pick her up and toss her out into the
street. If he dared. She knew his back would never
take the strain.

The library curtains were open, afternoon sun
streaming across the earl's empty desk. A faint scent
of candle wax, old leather, and wood smoke lingered.

Her gaze rummaged over the shelves of books
with their gold-patterned spines. So many words of
wisdom. Had he read any, or were they only for show?

It seemed a lifetime had passed since she stood before him in this room, her boots leaking, her feet wet, asking him to sign her contract. Trying her damndest to ignore those pangs of desire for him. Thinking they might go away.

The fireplace was dark today; an embroidered screen was set before the hearth with a hunting scene leaping across it. Above the mantel was a painting of the earl's mother, a handsome woman with copper curls the same as her daughter's. She looked down at Molly, a very slight smile lifting her lips, green eyes hard and bright but not very warm. The background was full of sweeping strokes and not much definition. One got a sense of a nervous, rushed artist hurrying to capture that face, as if he knew his subject was too impatient to sit for long.

Behind her, the door opened, and she turned.

"Why did you do it?" she demanded at once.

He stood inside the door in his shirtsleeves, evidently fetched in haste and sparing no time to put on a jacket. Slowly, he closed the door. "Do what? What am I accused of now?"

"All those things for my neighbors. I know you gave Mrs. Lotterby money for repairs, and you bought my painting from Frederick Dawes." She paused. "Perhaps you got rid of Arthur Wakely too." She wouldn't put it past him. "Where is my painting? What have you done with it?"

"Come with me, and I'll show you."

"Come with you where?" She straightened her spine.

He laughed and shook his head. "Trust me, I'm not going to corner you in a dark cellar." His eyes gleamed with a sudden flame. "Not today, in any case."

Striding to the bookshelf, he pressed one of the fat tomes, and there was a sharp click. A small door opened to reveal a secret chamber beyond. All her years in that house, and she'd never known of its existence.

"This is where I keep my treasures," he said. "A man has to have some place to keep his secrets and go where no one can find him."

He led her into the little room. It was shadowy, dusty. Since he had no candles, the only light came from the library window, and that barely reached. But there she saw her picture. It took her a moment to be sure it was her, but she recognized the old gray pinafore first, and the pincushion tied around her wrist. The face did not have much likeness at all, she thought. The expression was quite mischievous and naughty. Not at all serene and sensible, as she'd expected—or as she saw herself. Mrs. Bathurst was right; it was unsettling to see how differently she was beheld by others.

"As you say, he's quite talented, your painter."

She looked at Carver. "He's not *my* painter." How small her voice sounded suddenly.

He bent his head toward her, and she thought he looked vulnerable, younger. "Good."

Molly felt her pulse fluttering wildly. She swallowed, stared at his lips, and murmured, "Why did you buy the painting? He told me you paid a great deal of coin."

"Until I can have the person herself, the image must suffice. It was some comfort."

Slowly she opened her reticule and took out the folded contract. The one he'd amended. His gaze drifted down to the paper in her hand and then back up again. "Is that—?"

"Hush."

A slow smile lifted one side of his mouth. "Margaret—"

"I didn't say I signed it, did I?" She had to let him know he couldn't have it all his way. Since watching his lips tempted her own to misbehave, Molly looked instead at his flannel waistcoat, at his hands, his shoulders— anywhere but his face. "What happened to Arthur Wakely?" As much as she disliked Arthur, she wouldn't want to think anything too desperate had occurred.

"He's enjoying an extended stay at a sanitarium on the coast of Kent. For his foot."

"Oh. How clever of you to know."

"I'm much more clever than I look. And you're much less stern than *you* look."

Molly glanced again at her picture. Was that really her? The woman in the portrait was very composed and sure of herself. "I don't see any other treasures in here," she remarked. "Is this all you have?"

"I threw the others out to make room for you. You are the only treasure I need."

She tried not to be too pleased. *Remember, Moll, this is how he seduces women. He's good at it, well practiced. Don't think this is anything out of the ordinary for him.*

But how funny he was with his little secret room. It reminded her of Mrs. Bathurst with her "magpie's nest," as the landlady called it. After a few moments, her eyes grew sore from staring in the dim light, and Carver led her back out into the library.

"I've done many things in my three and thirty years that I shouldn't, Margaret," he said softly. "Let me have this one thing I needn't regret. This one good thing in my life. You."

There was nothing she could say to that and,

fortunately, the contract would suffice as her answer, since words failed. She put it slowly into his waiting hand.

Carver didn't open it immediately to see whether she'd signed his amendment. Instead, he clasped her fingers, drew them to his lips, and kissed her knuckles. "Whatever your reply to me, Margaret, my feelings for you, my desire for you, will remain."

It was still unbelievable to Molly that he should feel this way for her. But why did she think herself undeserving?

She was no longer a girl; she was a woman free to make decisions, free to look at all the colors in the clouds. And she had a heart that persisted in wanting above her station, inconvenient as it might be.

Suddenly Carver put his hands around Molly's face and lifted it for a kiss so full of want that the battered remains of her virtuous shield crumpled.

He'd known she would come to him sooner or later, to argue about his "meddling" again. She was too clever not to realize he was behind it all eventually. Never before had he put so much effort into a seduction, but he liked doing things for her, and he wanted to keep doing them.

Her sweet lips parted tentatively, and he slipped the tip of his tongue inside until it touched hers. She did not withdraw. Her eyes were closed, dark lashes fanning her cheeks. Her skin was warm silk under his palms. Slowly he moved one hand to her shoulder, spread his fingers, and slid them down to the front of her gown. He heard the hitch of her breath, felt a slight tremble, and then he closed his hand over her left breast. Her heart was beating so hard, in unison with his.

A slight arch of her spine pressed her shape into his hand, and he squeezed gently, cupping the firm apple through her gown and stays. She was small, but a perfect fit for his hand. Heat stirred his blood, raw need mounting quickly, but he must be patient.

She'd come this far, and he didn't want to chase her away again.

Reluctantly his lips left hers. He drew his fingertips slowly across her bosom and up over her lace fichu to the hollow at the base of her throat. Her neck was so slender. He kissed her there, beneath the line of her jaw, and caught a taste of sweet perfume—rose oil if he was not mistaken.

They did not say another word. What was there to be said? They communicated with their lips, their eyes, their hearts.

When she was gone, he unfolded the contract and looked for her signature beside his amendment, where he had drawn a line through her "No Tomfollerie" clause.

And there was the sweet sight of her name.

Margaret.

"What can I possibly wear that won't make me look like a former lady's maid?" she demanded of her assistants.

Emma ran to the storeroom and brought out the buttercup gown once rejected by the Baroness Schofield. The two girls held it up to her, and before she could make any but the feeblest of protests, they had proclaimed her, "Perfection."

Back at the house, when she announced that she'd

received a formal invitation by messenger to dine with the Earl of Everscham, she expected a barrage of questions. Instead, she received eager donations from all the female residents. Mrs. Lotterby, after an anxious lecture about being sure to eat well and not drink too much wine, was kind enough to loan her the use of the hipbath in the scullery and some perfume distilled by her own hand from rosemary, sage, and damask rose petals. Mrs. Slater dressed Molly's hair for her, and Mrs. Bathurst happily contributed the finishing touches from her cupboard of treasures—gloves, fan, and a shawl that smelled only faintly of mothballs.

"'Tis a pity you have no diamonds to wear," the lady whispered as she helped her into the gloves, which were a little big for her slender arms. "But I daresay he will give you those in time."

"I cannot think what you mean, Mrs. Bathurst," she replied. "It is only dinner."

"There is no such thing, my dear, as *only dinner*, not with a man like the Earl of Everscham."

A little knot of panic tightened in her stomach. When she tried opening the fan with one flick of her wrist—the way she'd seen it done before—she not only snapped a strut, but somehow managed to jab herself in the eye. Her gloves kept dripping down her arms, and she couldn't get accustomed to the weight of hair piled up on her head. A simple, braided knot was far easier to manage, but this arrangement made her feel unbalanced and top-heavy. The treacherous slither of pins already warned that her sophisticated new style was not long for this world.

"You must talk to him of current events," Mrs. Bathurst advised. "Try to avoid politics and religion, however. No man wants to talk with a woman about those subjects. Do you play or sing, Miss Robbins?"

She shook her head.

Mrs. Bathurst looked aghast, and then shrugged in resignation, "Well, I daresay you are resourceful enough to think of some way to entertain him. Good luck, my dear. Come and see me in the morning. I long to hear all about it."

She wanted to ask so many other questions, but there was no time.

When the carriage arrived, sent from Danforthe House to collect her, she stepped up and glanced back over her shoulder. The three women clustered under the old lantern in the doorway, watching as if she was royalty. As Frederick had pointed out, all the residents in the house had benefitted from the earl's interest in her. She felt quite a responsibility not to let them down now. It scattered her nerves quite dreadfully.

What did one do with a man? The most knowledge she had of men and what they wanted from women came from observing and eavesdropping on her brothers growing up. But they were always very mysterious, deliberately speaking in terms she did not understand. Once they'd gone to a fair in the neighboring county and paid a shilling to watch a gypsy dancer in a tent. As far as she could make out, they'd watched her spinning about with seven veils, which they'd enjoyed immensely, but to Molly, it seemed an awful lot of nothing for a shilling. And she didn't have any veils.

Good thing she wore her best silk drawers, she thought as the carriage sped away, taking her into the gathering dusk. She certainly needed them tonight.

The footman who opened the door to her was new, and therefore did not recognize her as a former servant in that house, but Mr. Richards, the butler, knew exactly who she was, of course. His haughty, forbidding demeanor trebled with every step as he led her across the tiled hall, opened the drawing-room door, and announced her name in cold, dispassionate tones. Evidently he didn't mean to look at her at all, and when she said, "Good evening, Mr. Richards. So nice to see you again," he tripped, stubbing his toe. His eyes flashed down at her, and his lips bent in a half sneer, but he made no reply.

Molly entered the room and found Carver standing with his back to the hearth, waiting for her.

"Thank you, Richards," he said. "Please tell Mrs. Jakes we're ready to eat."

Behind her, the door swept closed with a soft thud, shutting out her old life, and with it, her innocence.

Miss Margaret Robbins was a vision cast in gold, a goddess.

The moment he heard the bell, he felt the beat of his heart quicken, and when she appeared, air left his lungs too rapidly. It took him a moment to recover.

She wore a stunning yellow gown that flowed softly around her figure, defying the trend for wider skirts. The color made her skin glow, bringing a sunny summer afternoon into his house at seven in the evening. Her soft brown hair was piled up in gentle curls, some of which meandered down the side of her neck and lay upon her shoulder. Which he intended, very soon, to kiss.

"You came." What a stupid remark, he thought instantly. For some reason, his tongue had lost its smooth wit when she walked into his drawing room. He must remember he was in control tonight. He had gone to a great deal of trouble for this singularly difficult young woman, and she'd better appreciate it.

"I might have known," she muttered, looking around the drawing room. "Are there to be no other guests?"

"I need no others." Carver strode to where she stood, took her hand, and raised it to his lips. Her gloves were wrinkled, falling down her arms. Apparently she did not use her earnings to buy items for herself very often.

"I must congratulate you on the acquisition of your new shop, Miss Robbins."

He heard her heavy sigh. "I knew the rent seemed impossibly low, but Hobbs was so convincing!" She sounded nervous.

So was he, and unaccustomed to the sensation. Carefully, he slipped the loose glove down her arm and off her hand. When he lifted her fingers to his lips this time, there was nothing in his way. "Why did you call off your wedding and come back here?"

"You asked me before, and I told you," she replied, breathing hard as he let his mouth play over her bare fingers. "I came back here to pursue my dream."

"Is that all?" He had to know the truth, had to hear it from her lips. "Margaret?"

She swallowed, and a small sound, part sob, part cry of anguish came out of her. "You know, of course. You said yourself you are much more clever than you appear."

He pressed a gentle kiss to her knuckles. "Tell me."

When he felt her trying to tug her hand away, he tightened his grip and moved his kisses to her wrist. The hunger inside him grew in leaps and bounds, but his appetite was not for Mrs. Jakes's dinner. Carver had no idea how he was going to make it through five courses before he might enjoy a sample of his new dish. The anticipation of all that was to come had set his blood on fire.

"*Tell me*," he urged again, his voice hoarse.

Her eyes were large, darkened by his shadow as he leaned over her. "I came back here to follow my dream. But..." She closed her eyes, sighed, opened them again. "I came back here...for you. To be near you. Any way that I could. I hope you are happy now you made me say it!"

It was all he needed to hear. Carver lowered his mouth to her trembling lips and kissed her, greedily drinking down the sweet honesty of that reply, claiming it ruthlessly.

Bare hands pressed to his shoulder, she pushed back. "Richards! I hear his footsteps."

A second later, the drawing-room door opened again, and the butler announced cheerlessly that dinner was served. Apparently the Mouse had good ears, he mused. Of course she did.

She took Carver's arm and let him lead her across the hall and into the dining room. At his orders, it was set intimately—two place settings facing across the width of the table instead of at far opposite ends. There were minimal flowers, but an extravagant array of candles, because he knew how her eyes were strained in poor light. She wouldn't wear her spectacles in front of him. Fool woman!

He held a chair for her, and she sat.

"I did have a few questions about the contract," she said suddenly. Then she smiled up at him. "Don't worry. It will be painless. Just some items I would like clarified."

Painless? That's what she thought. He was already hurting.

Stiffly, he walked around the table and sat. After the soup was served and the wine poured, he gave the footmen a signal to retreat. "And your questions?"

"What do you mean by the word *exclusive*?"

"It means none other."

"I know what the word means. I just wanted to be sure that was what *you* meant. I didn't want to misread it."

"Of course."

"But I know your reputation. So is this word only for me, or for you also?"

"Certainly. For both."

She frowned.

"You have my word, Margaret. I want no one but you." Damn woman! She made him say it. Forced it out of him, just as he'd forced her to admit why she came back to London. To him.

Her eyes brightened with surprise.

"Any other questions?"

After studying his face a moment, she blurted, "When do we begin? Do I share your bed tonight?"

His hand shook, and he spilled some soup on his cravat. Immediately, she took her own napkin, wet it with her tongue, dashed around the table, and proceeded to clean up the spot.

"I had planned to borrow Rothespur's hunting lodge,"

he muttered, looking at her hand, then her face. "It's only a day's ride…but…" If she was eager to begin, there was no cause to delay. "If you are ready," he continued, watching her attack his stain, "then, yes." He cleared his throat. "We may proceed tonight." He was aching for her. Truly in some agony to possess her completely.

"Then I have only one term I should like to add," she said quietly. "Something you overlooked."

Eyes narrowed, he studied her face in the candle-light. "Oh?"

"A date of termination, of course. We must have one of those. All contracts must."

He wasn't sure about that, but she sounded very certain. Why not agree, if that was her only demand?

"Very well. As you wish. An end date."

"It would be for the best," she replied evenly, returning to her chair. "I think until September, don't you? When the leaves turn."

Six weeks. Plenty of time, he thought, to get this out of his system. She was right; it was all very sensible to have a date of expiration. That way there would be no clinging from her, no dreadful scenes when it was over. Quite a civilized arrangement, really. Everything under control. He was glad of that—of her eagerness for pattern and structure—because he'd felt severely in danger of losing control lately when it came to this woman.

"You're not going to ask me to play the pianoforte, are you?" she demanded suddenly.

"Ummm…no." That was not something he had in mind, he mused.

"Good. Because I can play only one tune. 'Sing a Song O' Sixpence.' Your sister taught me, and that was as far as our lessons ever progressed."

He laughed, relaxing finally. "I can promise I will never make you entertain me with music." There were plenty of other things he had in mind, however.

Between each course, Richards and the footmen returned to clear plates and bring new ones. As always, they were brisk and efficient, but the butler's disdain moved in waves down the table, all directed at the former lady's maid. Molly did very well in pretending not to notice, but she must have. She was very intuitive. Not that Richards made any attempt to hide his disapproval.

Molly ate every morsel and sent her profuse thanks to Mrs. Jakes at the conclusion of each course, but the best Richards could manage was a sharp twitch and a mumbled sound that could have been anything. Finally, the dessert was set before them, and Carver was amused to see his guest's eyes grow even wider. Although she had, only moments before, declared herself "full to the brim," she soon found a little more space for Mrs. Jakes's famous pineapple tart.

"I never saw a pineapple until I came here," she told him as the door closed again behind Richards. "When the crates came from the Everscham estate hothouse and Mrs. Jakes told me to get one out, I was almost afraid of it. A big ugly thing like a giant pinecone with spiky leaves and prickly bits."

"Prickly bits?"

"Well, I thought they were prickly. It looked as if it might attack me."

"Were you afraid of me too?" he teased.

She licked her fork. "No. You don't have any prickly bits."

"Oh, but I do."

He watched her tongue wet her lips as it chased after the last pastry crumb. Discreetly, he repositioned himself beneath he table. "Will they attack me?" she asked.

"They might." They wanted to right then. On the dining table. He'd never felt such a savage lust before. But she was a maid, he reminded himself yet again, and he must proceed carefully.

Even so, she didn't look too concerned by the possibility of his prickly bits. "When is Lady Mercy coming home?"

Ah. "I do not know." He'd had a visit from Viscount Grey earlier that week, insisting that he do something about his sister's behavior, so he'd written to her. Apparently Grey's father was eager to seek financial reparations if the engagement was called off. But if Grey was incapable of standing up to his own father, Carver knew he'd never survive marriage to Mercy.

"She could come back at any moment."

"So?"

Molly lowered her voice. "What if she finds me here?"

Carver wiped his mouth on his napkin. "Allow me to worry about that." It would be his business what he did with his sister's former maid.

"She would be furious with me, and with you, your lordship."

He pushed his chair back and stood, knuckles resting on the table. "My sister, I suspect, is in no position to question you or me about our sleeping arrangement."

He watched her swallow. "Oh?" Her eyebrows knotted themselves in confusion. "Aren't you angry with her?"

"I am."

"You don't look it, or sound it."

He shrugged. "No point in wasting the effort until she comes back." Besides, he was glad of his sister's absence at that moment. His own selfish needs took precedence. Although he never allowed Mercy's disapproval to prevent his affairs before, this time many things were different. Including the maidenly target of his seduction, who was currently sitting at his table, licking her fingers, and watching the remains of pineapple tart with an extremely lascivious glint in her soulful brown eyes.

She ought to be looking at him that way, not at the tart. Soon she would be. He'd teach her.

"Are you certain, Miss Robbins, that you wish to go through with this?" he exclaimed impatiently.

She paused, a finger between her lips. Slowly her eyes lifted to meet his, and the finger popped out of her mouth. "You may as well call me by my first name, don't you think?"

He couldn't tell whether she delayed on purpose. "Very well. Margaret…are you sure about this arrangement?"

Head tipped back, she appeared to be surveying the grand chandelier and carved ceiling medallion above it, as if she'd never noticed it before. "I suppose so," she muttered finally. "If I must."

"What?" Now he began to get annoyed. "You suppose?"

But then the Mouse twitched her nose, and the beginnings of a smile tentatively moved her lips. "Only teasing, your lordship. Do get a sense of humor."

Sixteen

HE CARRIED HER OUT OF THE DINING ROOM AND ACROSS the hall. To her relief, the staff were all below stairs, and no one saw. Not that he would care. Carver Danforthe was accustomed to getting what he wanted and never troubled himself too much about propriety. His sister was the one who liked everything in its proper place.

"How many other women have you carried like this?" she asked.

"None."

"For some reason I find that hard to believe, your lordship."

He carried her along to his room at the end of the passage. The door was ajar, and he nudged it open with his shoulder. "I can assure you, I've never needed to carry a woman to my bed before."

She frowned. "Why carry me then?"

"I rather got the impression you might suddenly make a run for it. You've made a habit of scuttling from me. Like any mouse." There was the hint of a smile. "And shouldn't you call me by *my* name now?" He dropped her to his bed and immediately shrugged out of his evening jacket.

Propped up on her elbows, she watched him stride back to the door and close it. "I'm not sure I can."

"Why not?"

Molly screwed up her face. "It sounds...odd." She didn't think she'd ever be able to call him "Carver." It wasn't the sort of name one could say in the throes of passion. "I'll think of something to call you."

He grimaced. "No doubt you will." He was unbuttoning his waistcoat, and suddenly the reality of their situation and what she'd agreed to become hit her like a hard slap across the face. *It* was about to happen. She was about to descend into the abyss she'd carefully stepped around all this time. *Oh, Ma, what must you think of me?* She'd tried to fight it, hadn't she? But her heart would have its own way, and it turned out to be far stronger than her head when it came to this man. She'd decided at last that they would have their moment together. Why deny herself the pleasure? But she'd insisted on an expiration date for their arrangement. That way he would not grow bored with her, and for Molly, there would be no painful wondering when the axe would fall.

"Aren't we going to have conversation?" she asked.

He pulled his shirt over his head, and she forgot about the abyss and her mother's warnings. "About what?" he demanded.

She knelt up on the bed and reached for him, placing her palms against the firm planes of his naked chest. "Current affairs."

His eyes narrowed. "Do you want to talk about current affairs?"

"Not really."

"Me neither. We'll save that for next time."

There was no backing out now. She'd signed his contract amendment. It was done and dusted, kippers and custard. As her father would have said. She hadn't thought of her father for a while, she realized. Her mother's memory was the dominant one. But her father crept in now with his quiet smile, and she felt his hand on her head, momentarily sheltering her from the sun's heat on a summer's day as they walked to church. She must have lost her bonnet that day, or refused to wear it. "*Molly, Molly, sweet and jolly*," he'd sung to her in a low voice and then whispered, "*Look at that pretty blue sky*." And he'd lifted her up, as if she could touch it if he held her high enough. Her mother, walking ahead, had looked back and shouted at him soon after to "*put the child down, for pity's sake, before you drop her*."

But Molly remembered she was laughing, enjoying the warm air on her face, her pudgy hand reaching up for that beautiful blue sky above them. She wasn't in the least afraid.

Her father had appreciated the colors of life. Perhaps that was where she got it from and why her mother was always so irritable with her when she spoke her "dozy" thoughts aloud.

Carver was leaning over. "Kiss me, Margaret."

"Is that an order, my lord?" A thrill rushed through her when she saw the urgency of his need written plain upon that darkly handsome face. This man wanted her. He wanted plain Molly Robbins. And badly.

It was a powerful feeling to know this. She'd expected to hate herself for being weak and giving in, but in fact, she felt stronger than ever, knowing the extent of his desire for her. She could reach for it now and hold it in her hand. Quite literally.

His lips hovered over hers, and as she fell back to the bed, he followed her down. "Yes. It is an order," he whispered.

She lifted her face to his and let her lips caress his mouth. He was heavy, but it was not unpleasant to feel his body stretched over her, his hard thighs moving against hers. Buckskin against silk. He stroked her face, her neck, her bosom, and wherever his fingers went, his lips followed soon after.

"Tell me what to do," she whispered, but her hands were already stroking his manhood through his clothing, moving instinctively, exploring.

He lifted his hips to toss her skirt and petticoats upward, and then discovered her drawers. Apparently they pleased him. Glancing down, she saw he was already stripping his breeches, and the organ that protruded took her by surprise. Raised with so many brothers in a one-room cottage, she'd seen the male appendage before, of course, but never had it looked like this. Thick and tall and stretching even as she watched.

With his large hands, he tugged her drawers off, but left her stockings. She lay back, trying to compose herself, but that effort was soon abandoned when he touched her intimately, tenderly, and his warm fingers began a trembling exploration of her body. He lay beside her now, resting on one hip, fierce dark eyes watching his hand and then her reaction to it.

She squirmed, getting hotter, a wicked flame leaping to life in that part of her where he concentrated his steady, rhythmic strokes.

"Oh." She closed her eyes and felt his lips on hers again, devouring her hungrily this time, savagely. Her spine arched as shivers raced through her.

His palm possessed her entire womanhood now, the heel of his hand exerting slight pressure. And then his finger slipped inside her just a little, just enough to make her gasp into his mouth.

He moved that fingertip within her.

"How long I've waited for this," he whispered, kissing her chin as she arched and pressed her head back into the bed. "A great deal of want has built up in me, but I'll try to be gentle."

She moaned. "Do you think you're the only one with want? I have more than you. You've had ways to release yours."

A soft chuckle warmed the side of her throat as his lips traversed downward and his tongue lapped over a sensitive point below her ear. "Shall we see who wants more?" His finger moved deeper inside her, and then he added another. "How much of me do you want, Margaret? Tell me."

But the waves of heat washing over her and through her made any speech impossible just then.

His hand stilled.

"More," she cried out.

"Oh. More?"

"Yes!"

Slowly he resumed his fondling, but only with his fingertips now at the crest of her sex. "I might have known you'd be a demanding mistress."

Molly opened her eyes. "The worst you've ever known," she assured him solemnly. "Are you certain you can handle me?"

He laughed, kissed her bosom through her gown, and proceeded to quicken his strokes between her thighs. His breathing deepened, and she felt his phallus pressed to her hip. The thought of what he meant to do with that soon sent her over the edge into blissful oblivion.

Pleasure seized her. It began in the very core of her being and shot outward like the rays of the sun. She was burned by it, left breathless and quivering. His hand continued to hold her until she moved herself against his fingers, pushing for more.

"More?" he chuckled deeply.

"I warned you," she gasped.

He knelt up on the bed and gestured for her to do the same. She waited impatiently while he tackled the hooks and laces of her garments. In her peripheral vision she watched his thigh next to her own, the hard muscle moving under the skin and the rough dark hairs of his body. At last, freed of her gown, stays, and petticoats, she lay back. Clad only in her transparent chemise and stockings, she somehow felt even naughtier than she would if she was naked in his presence. "Don't throw it on the floor," she admonished him. "Have you no respect for my work?"

He paused, the buttercup gown bunched in his fist, about to be consigned to the carpet.

"It took hundreds of hours to sew that gown," she said, exaggerating only slightly.

"Then you are right, my dear Margaret." He shook it out and laid it reverently over a nearby chair. "From now on I shall treat your gowns with greater care."

"See that you do."

He came back to the bed and crawled on all fours

to where she sat up in a nest of his pillows. First he kissed her toes, then her knee, then the ribbon garter around her thigh. His hands slid under her, pulling her down the bed.

"Mind my hair!"

Apparently he didn't care about the careful arrangement of curls on her head, for he buried his face between her thighs. Thus, she very quickly forgot about Mrs. Slater's hairpins too.

Melting into his bed, she gazed up at the ceiling until her sight fogged over, and then she closed her eyes. Never had she known it was possible to feel this way, to know this much happiness. But as he lavished her with his full attention, her world was transformed. She went from hard-working, tired seamstress to pampered princess in just those few moments.

"Margaret," he groaned, moving over her again, parting her thighs with his knees. "I hope you are ready. I can't wait longer." His lips closed around her left nipple, tugging through the lace chemise, not waiting to remove it.

She grasped his shoulders, silently assuring him of her own swelling need.

And then she felt his manhood against her inner thigh. It was rampant, hot steel.

"Is this what you want, Margaret?"

"Yes."

"Are you sure?" His voice was even deeper than usual. It left goose pimples across her skin, made her pulse race. "Here it comes."

A moment of panic stalled her breath, but a sharp, startled exhale was pushed out of her in the next second as he thrust with his strong hips and her body opened around that forceful sword. Had he cleaved her in two? Perhaps.

But now he was half sheathed, paused there, the effort to restrain himself causing a slight tremble, beads of sweat breaking on his brow.

Molly stroked his shoulders and slowly slid her hands down his back to grasp his taut, hard backside.

"I want all of you," she whispered, spreading her fingers and squeezing his buttock muscles. "All of you."

He groaned and swung his hips again as she thrust with hers. Thus he claimed her fully at last.

Carver had never known the like of it. The woman who had played the meek, prim, disapproving miss for years suddenly transformed into a wildcat in his bed, insatiable and possibly untamable. Not that it would stop him from trying.

She was a delectable surprise, a luxurious treat. He forgot himself completely and was overtaken by primal urges never before experienced. The voice screaming in his head to withdraw from her body before he spent was fiercely ignored. Another first that night. She, of course, was too naive to know when the moment was upon him, and even if she had, Carver suspected nothing would have stopped him. Such a need had built up in him over the course of the last few weeks that it over took his usual sanity and willpower, beating it into the ground. He slid his hands under her bottom, lifting her body to meet his remorseless thrusts in that moment of sublime madness, wanting to fill her with his seed. To claim her fully for himself, and damn the consequences. So he did.

He was Carver Danforthe, the Earl of Everscham, and he always got what he wanted at any cost.

The tiny, nagging, guilty doubt squeaking away in the back of his mind—that thing some folk called a conscience, could go to hell. She was his now, and in that moment, it was all that mattered.

Finally sated, he gathered her in his arms and encouraged her to rest.

"I'll have to leave soon," she murmured. "I can't stay all night. What will Richards think?" Soft feathers of her breath swept and tickled across his chest as she talked, still wide awake and full of vitality. When he drowsily warned her that she would be sore and tired that day, her reply was a stubborn, "I don't feel it."

He kissed the top of her soft curls, which were now a disorderly mess and spread all over his wide shoulder and the pillow. "Sleep a while, Mouse."

She wriggled in his arms. "You've gone all soft." Her hand was exploring his penis.

"That's what happens when a man is spent."

"Have I worn you out?"

"I fear so."

But it was a very good feeling to be so exhausted. He slid one hand down her back and cupped her small bottom. Was this how it felt to have a virgin? His need to protect her, keep her close, had just multiplied. It was an onerous responsibility.

"I'll recover," he muttered.

"When? Soon?"

"Tomorrow." He yawned and patted the cheeks of her bottom.

"It's tomorrow now."

Oh, Lord, had he made an error thinking she

should be as easily entertained as other women he'd known? But then she laughed and kissed his chin. "I suppose I ought to let you rest, Danny."

"Danny?"

She nestled back down again into the curve of his chest. "That's what I'm going to call you. It's my name for you."

He was ridiculously pleased by this development. "I've never had anyone make up a name for me before."

"Good. Can I have some more pineapple tart later?" Three gentle sighs followed, and then she was snoring.

⚜

Molly woke abruptly and lifted her head from his chest. To her horror, dawn light drew claws across the sky through his window, and a loud, imperious voice approached his door at speed.

"For pity's sake, Richards, don't drag my trunk along the floor. I may as well carry it myself if it's too much for you. Is my brother in?"

"Yes, my lady."

"Well, I suppose it's too early to get him up. I'll see him later today. I'm absolutely drained and could make use of a good few hours of sleep myself…" The volume gradually decreased as their footsteps passed his door and moved on down the hall.

Molly sat up and was half out of bed before his hand sprang to life and captured her wrist. "Where are you off to, Margaret?"

"It's late," she exclaimed, fraught. "Or early. Oh, goodness." What had he made her into? A creature like him, unaware of the proper time and living by his own strange clock? "Your sister has returned, and I must get out of the house at once. I should never have stayed so long."

Carver sat up, scratching his head and yawning. "No need to worry. Richards won't bat an eye. Come here and kiss me."

Such a request was hard to refuse. He looked even more handsome that morning, she thought. Rumpled and drowsy and warm from his bed. So she slid back for a kiss. He rolled over, pinning her body beneath his, surprising her by suddenly becoming alert when, only moments before, he seemed barely awake.

"I'm not ready to let you leave yet," he growled.

There was no possible way she could accommodate him again that morning, for his warnings to her had been justified. What she needed now was a soothing bath for her aches and pains. Fortunately, he knew this and kept his beast at bay, contenting them both with a kissing game that involved their mouths on various, extremely sensitive body parts. Last night he'd pleasured her many times in that fashion. This morning she learned how to do the same for him.

"Much more entertaining," she said with a smile, "than my playing the pianoforte for you."

He grinned. "But I still want to hear 'Sing a Song O' Sixpence' one of these days."

Finally he conceded that it was time for her to leave. He washed her with towels dampened in his washbasin and then helped her dress.

"I can leave by the servant's staircase."

He argued with her about it, but she won. Carver rang the bell for Williams the coachman to take her home, and after one last kiss, she hurried off in her fine buttercup gown. No other servant was encountered, luckily, and she slipped out of the house, witnessed only by Williams, who had probably seen enough ladies leaving that house in the small hours to never blink an eye.

Since this was not a cheering thought, she abandoned it and concentrated instead upon controlling the giddy, shameless-hussy excitement keening through her body from head to foot.

He rang for his valet and took a bath before going down to breakfast. His unusually early appearance on the stairs caused a fright for the housemaid, who was still sweeping them, and she shrank against the wall, looking as if she wished for a hole to open up and swallow her.

"Good morning," he said cheerily, at which point she swayed, clutched her dustpan, and almost toppled over completely.

Carver strode into the breakfast room and greeted the footmen similarly. Neither knew how to react, but one of them managed a shaky smile. The dour-faced butler entered as he was helping himself to grilled trout from the chafing dishes on the sideboard.

"I hear the prodigal sister has returned, Richards."

"Indeed, my lord. She arrived very early and did not wish to wake you."

"Good." Carver moved on to the cold veal pie and some plump, tasty-looking sausages. His plate full, he took his seat and flipped open a napkin.

"Shall I pour the coffee, my lord?"

"No. I can do it."

Suddenly the door swung open, and there was his

sister in a simple emerald-green morning dress with a pinafore over it and with her hair tied up in a fringed scarf. She looked as if she planned to move furniture and clean floors. Or possibly herd sheep. All that was missing was a shepherd's hook. He stared at her for a moment as he chewed, wondering if this was another new trend that had passed him by. "If that is a nod to Marie Antoinette, aren't you a little late?"

"Very amusing, Carver." She glanced at his plate of food. "You'll get fat if you eat that way when I'm gone."

"I'm exceedingly famished this morning," he replied with a smirk. "Worry not. I'll exercise it off later." Wouldn't she be shocked to learn with whom? He was feeling rather mischievous this morning, ready to seize the day.

So much to do. Things to plan for Margaret and their six weeks together. Six weeks sounded a considerable time—at least as long as his lengthiest relationship in the past, but there were many things he wanted to share with Margaret, and she could not devote her time solely to him, of course. Which was inconvenient, but he supposed he could work around it. A woman with other things to do with her day—things other than getting dressed, arranging flowers, or discussing menus with her cook—was a novelty he would try to get accustomed to. He'd have to share her, no doubt, but if he wanted her, he'd get used to it. Wasn't forever, was it? Wielding his knife ruthlessly, he sliced another sausage in two, spearing it on his fork and thrusting it into his hungry mouth.

"I suppose you've been up to no good while I was in the country, Brother dear." His sister sat at the table with some toast and proceeded to butter it thickly. "At least the roof is still on."

"Before we talk about what I've been up to, we should discuss your antics."

That washed some of the brazen color out of her cheeks. She flashed her lily-pad eyes at Richards. "You may leave us."

The butler bowed, gestured to the footmen to follow, and all three servants left the room.

Mercy poured the coffee for them both. "Molly Robbins told me that you offered her a loan to start her business." Aha. So she was going on the attack to deflect his accusations even before they came. He might have known it. His sister was a cunning creature who always managed to maintain the self-satisfied air of a do-gooder, despite the lapses of which he knew her capable.

"That is correct," he replied.

"I could have loaned her the money. Why would you do such a thing for her? Since when have you had any interest in my friend? Or in dressmaking?"

"She didn't want you to loan her the money, because she knew you'd meddle."

"How dare you!" She grabbed her knife and began slathering yet more butter on her toast without looking at it. "You made that up. She would never say that."

"Well, she did. So there."

"I shall get to the bottom of this now I'm back."

"Yes, I'm sure there are a great many things demanding your attention, since you've been so long away." He filled his mouth with the second half of sausage.

She sat tall in her chair. "Ask me what you want to know," she exclaimed with an air of wounded nobility, as if she was in the dock and somebody had the audacity to accuse her of picking pockets.

"Did you enjoy your visit to the country?"

"Yes."

"And you left the Hartleys well, I hope?"

"Yes. Mrs. Hartley has just discovered she's having another baby. Long after she and her husband had given up."

"Excellent. Delighted to hear it." He washed down his food with a thirsty gulp of coffee. Then smacked his lips with bad-mannered relish that made her exhale in disgust.

"Don't be sarcastic, Carver."

He looked up, wounded. "I'm not! I meant it. I'm very happy for them. The Hartleys are good people."

She stared as if he'd just streaked naked around the breakfast table. "Since when have you cared about the Hartleys? Aren't you always saying how dreadful it is that they remain so sickeningly in love at their age?" Then she frowned. "Are you still foxed from last night?"

Oh yes, he was foxed, he thought, amused. Well and truly drunk on Miss Margaret Robbins. "If it causes you to shout at me, Sister dear, I shall say nothing more about your precious Hartleys and their strange insistence on populating the world with more of their sort."

"Ah, there's the brother I know and adore." Then, after a pause, she demanded, "So is that all you want to know about my extended visit?"

He considered carefully. The fewer questions he asked her, the fewer she would have any right to ask him. "For now." He wiped his mouth on a napkin. "I think I'll have some more of those splendid sausages."

His sister frowned again. "Carver, you are acting most peculiarly."

"Why? Because I'm eating sausages?"

"Because you're up so early. And dressed. And smiling. In a friendly way as opposed to your usual menace."

"Perhaps I'm turning a new leaf."

She slumped in her chair, apparently disappointed by his lack of curiosity. "Your letter said Grey was returned and anxious to see me."

"Yes. May as well save your explanations for him, Sister." He winked. "Better hope they're convincing."

Seventeen

Thus began the two lives of once-harmless Molly Robbins. There was the spinster Miss Robbins, a quiet, bespectacled seamstress; then there was Margaret, mistress to the Earl of Everscham and a young woman of fiery passion, who, after a lifetime of self-denial, quickly and thoroughly gave herself up to wicked pleasures. Somehow she kept the two lives balanced. Or so she thought and hoped.

Carver wanted her to move into a house he would lease. She'd adamantly refused.

"I will stay right where I am," she said.

"But it makes it very difficult for me to visit."

"Then you must use your imagination, Danny." She kissed his cheek. "I know you have one—even if it is not as wonderful as my own—and with your resources it shouldn't be such a challenge. One would think you never had to make much effort for your past affairs."

"I didn't," he muttered, sounding bewildered.

Taking pity on him and conceding partially to his demands, she made the room above her shop more comfortable with additional furnishings and spent some evenings there, where they could meet in private. There was a fireplace where she could boil water for tea, and Carver bought her a chaise lounge with several soft cushions. Occasionally she pretended to faint upon it so he could revive her with his very special and ingenious talents.

But when he bought her jewelry, she made him return it. "Where on earth will I wear that?" Rings and bracelets, she explained patiently, would get in the way of her sewing.

He wanted to take her to the theatre, but she declined. Being seen with him publicly was out of the question. As things were, she could still maintain the fiction of their relationship being a professional matter only. No one had any proof otherwise, as long as they were careful.

Not that he seemed to worry about what people thought. He sent flowers every day to her shop, until there was almost no room to move around, and then she persuaded him to send them once a week instead. Emma and Kate watched her coyly whenever he found an excuse to come into the shop, but they were too much in awe of the earl and too fond of Molly to speak a word of speculation about it.

"My friends wonder what has become of me," he said to her one evening. "I am never at the club or the opera, and haven't seen a single horse race this season."

"You should go, then. I don't wish to keep you from them."

"Do I not keep you from your friends too?"

She thought about it and admitted that he did. "But it cannot be helped. After all, there is a limit to the time we have."

He took her hand in his and squeezed. "We should bring them together."

"Bring what together?"

"Our friends."

"Good Lord, no!"

"Why not?"

"Danny, it just wouldn't work, and you know it. Far better that we keep our worlds separate."

"I don't understand you," he replied after a moment. "I thought you were a great champion for progress." He tickled her palm. "Perhaps only if it serves you, eh, Mouse? Don't you want me to know your friends? Are you afraid of what they will tell me about you?"

Molly didn't know what to say. In truth, the thought of meeting *his* friends terrified her. She could put on an act for clients in her shop, but to meet those people socially was still far beyond her. Despite the level of success she'd attained, it had only been a few months since she left her post as a lady's maid. She had no formal education and suffered a tendency to fall mute again in large crowds. Her confidence had improved vastly, but she was not yet brazen enough to walk into a High Society drawing room and dazzle the guests with her witty repartee.

Eventually she said, "I would rather spend this time with you alone." Then she slipped into his lap, wound her arms around his neck, and kissed him. "I don't want to share you." This seemed to please him, and he soon forgot the conversation.

It was easy to fall under his spell and let herself believe this was more for him than just another affair. But when she was alone again, sewing at her table, squinting through her spectacles, that other fairy-tale world vanished, and with it her foolish, carefree smiles. She might be brave enough to call him Danny now and share intimacies of a sort she'd never imagined in all her maidenly daydreams, but he was still the Earl of Everscham and a rogue of the highest order.

They had until September; she forced herself to remember that.

Lady Mercy came to see her at the shop and took a tour of the upstairs room, which Molly had carefully furnished to masquerade as an innocent old maid's bedchamber and sitting room, rather than a scarlet hussy's den of lasciviousness.

"You have changed so much, Molly. I barely recognize you." The visitor dragged a reluctant Molly into the light to examine her more closely.

"It's just the spectacles."

"Don't be silly!" Lady Mercy removed the articles from Molly's face. "Are you sure you made the right choice to return to London? You do not regret it?"

She shook her head. "I've never been happier in my life." It was true. When she was with Carver, she was madly happy and content. In fact, the pleasure of his company threatened to overshadow the enjoyment of her success in business, but she supposed that giddy flush would fade in time, and she would soon be back to herself. It was simply that it was new, she thought. Her love affair was a sparkling, exciting new present, and she relished it while she could. "Now you are returned, my lady, you must let me make you a new ball gown. You will have need of at least one."

Lady Mercy dropped her hands and turned to look through the window. "I'm not planning to stay in Town."

"But, my lady, I thought—"

"I am not going to marry Viscount Grey."

As these words fell softly from Lady Mercy's lips, she turned and looked at Molly. Her wide eyes were pensive, shining with tears such as Molly had never seen there before. "Did you not, at the very least, think to answer Rafe's letter?" her former mistress demanded abruptly.

Molly could not think what the lady meant. Rafe had not sent her anything lately, other than a list of provisions he meant to buy. She'd never known him to be forgetful or scatterbrained, but she could only assume he'd addressed it to her in error. "How was it to be answered, my lady?"

"Pen and ink," came the curt reply.

When Molly told her what her former fiancé's last letter had contained, Lady Mercy stared. "It was *what*?"

"It was a list of items." Molly went to her dresser drawer and took it out to show her. She'd kept it with the intention of sending it back, but then so much had happened in the last few weeks that she'd completely put it out of her mind.

Lady Mercy read the blotted list of everyday provisions and then crumpled it in her hand. "Wretched man! I thought he had written to beg for your return to Sydney Dovedale."

"My lady, I know Rafe was never in love with me. Not that way. As much as I care about him, my fondness was sisterly rather than that required of a wife."

"It seems I was wrong about so much."

Molly hastened to assure her she was never wrong. Except in this instance.

Suddenly Mercy wiped her damp eyes on her glove and sniffed. "My brother has agreed to finance your enterprise, has he not?"

"He has, my lady. But I am repaying him. Every penny."

She groaned. "For pity's sake, after so many years of friendship, I think we can safely dispense with the formality of my title. Can you not call me by my name?"

Eventually Molly agreed, and her friend laughed. The tears soon dried. "Come"—she held out her arms—"embrace me, Molly, for I have a very hard task ahead of me. You are my oldest and dearest friend and, prepare yourself for a shock of severe magnitude, but I think perhaps I should ask *your* advice for once."

"Mine?"

"I'm going to be married."

"I thought you said—"

"To Rafe Hartley. If he'll have me."

Now that new chaise lounge was truly needed. Molly dropped to it like a dead pigeon from a church spire. Carver was right then to suspect his sister and Rafe.

"It seems we are both at a crossroads, Molly. You have chosen your way by staying here, and now I choose mine by leaving. Our lives will never be the same again."

Although extremely curious to know all that had happened to her friend in the country, Molly chose not to ask. After all, she wouldn't want her former mistress probing too deeply into her own arrangement with Carver, would she? Mercy would most definitely never approve.

After waiting a few seconds, the lady put her hands

on her waist and exclaimed, "Aren't you going to ask me anything either? Gracious, I expected to be bombarded with questions, but everyone is silent and mysterious as the blasted grave."

"Don't sound so disappointed." Molly chuckled dourly. "I think you'll find your absence has caused quite a stir, and you will have more than your share of questions to answer when people hear that you're quitting London Society to become a farmer's wife."

"I daresay. But don't *you* have anything to ask? Like my brother, you seem remarkably reticent to quiz me. There was not the slightest interrogation from Carver. In fact, he was rather like a fat, contented, overpampered tomcat when I returned. I could almost see the cream upon his whiskers."

"Oh." Molly hesitated and looked down to hide her smile. "I wouldn't want to pry, my lady. I mean…Mercy."

"Why ever not? I would have no scruples about prying into your life. *If* there was ever anything worth prying into."

Molly raised her eyelashes again, wondering if she'd just heard a tone of mischief in her friend's voice or whether she'd imagined it, and she found Mercy regarding her with a distinctly naughty, impish gleam in her eyes.

Something had changed between the two women since they were last together, and Molly had a very good idea of what it might be. Best not raise that subject just yet, even though it had brought them closer.

Instead, she sat to pour the tea and asked politely, "Would you care for an almond tart?"

Mercy walked over to sit beside her. "Only if it comes with a little gossip and scandal, Molly Robbins."

They sat—or rather, sprawled—on a blanket by the
hearth, and he watched her sketching, fascinated as
ever by the ease with which her charcoal flowed in
graceful lines across the paper. Her long, slender hands
barely left a smudge. When she was absorbed in her
work, Carver had to restrain himself from distract-
ing her, but she looked so lovely this evening in the
lace-trimmed nightgown he'd bought her, with her
hair falling in a long braid over one shoulder, that he
was tempted beyond all endurance. The soft curve of
her cheek demanded the caress of his finger. The tip
of her tiny nose required the lick of his tongue. The
dark, teasing shadow of her nipple, swaying slightly
against the lace as she sketched, begged sweetly for
his lips.

"Danny, mind my sketches," she protested mildly
as he crawled across them, almost spilling their wine
glasses.

"Damn the blasted sketches," he muttered, reaching for her breast, cupping it gently in his palm.

"I knew you'd be a terrible distraction."

"I've waited at least half an hour for your attention."

She laughed, rolling her paper aside. "An entire half
an hour? Sakes, what can I be thinking to make you
wait that long?"

"Don't do it again." He slipped his other hand
under her nightgown and between her satiny thighs.
"I am the Earl of Everscham, you know."

She stretched out with a pleased sigh, her hands
reaching to pull his shirt up and over his head. "To me
you're just Danny."

That, apparently, was how she dealt with their situation. He didn't mind if it helped her to pretend he was not her former employer. Whatever worked to his advantage. Scruples would never get in his way, and he didn't care a straw what she once was. All that mattered was the here and now, and at this moment, she was everything he needed. Carver lowered his mouth to the pointy nipple that pushed at the front of her nightgown. She giggled. Ticklish, it seemed, tonight. He kissed along the curve of her firm breast and then upward, under her arm. Another giggle, and this time a squirm too.

Slowly his forefinger stroked the warm cleft of her womanhood, where she was already moist, clearly as eager for him as he was for her.

He returned his mouth to her breast and nibbled around the dark circle, causing that little point to sharpen and press up through a hole in the lace. The taste of her skin always reminded him of honey and cream, a treat his nanny gave him as a boy. But she was a man's treat. He let his tongue slip back and forth over the blushing pink bead and heard her breath quicken. She began pulling apart the braid over her shoulder, releasing a soft lavender scent with each freed lock. The fragrances she wore were never overpowering, but just enough to leave a trace on his body, and he never wanted to wash it off.

Closing his lips firmly over her teased nipple, he sucked and felt it pucker then swell. It only added to his own arousal, knowing how he pleased her. With fingers clutching at his hair, he was further lost. Her legs climbed around his hips.

"Hurry," she gasped out.

In just moments, she went from ignoring him to begging for impalement. The woman needed some patience, he mused. But how could he correct her when he was equally hungry?

Her fingernails scraped over his scalp; her heels dug into his lower back. "Oh, hurry."

Carver sat up, extracting his body from her lusty clutches. She'd made him wait while she sketched a sudden idea that came to her; therefore, he would now make her wait, even if it delayed the consummation of his own need.

Her eyes opened, glaring hotly up at him. "What are you doing now?"

"Aha, the meek seamstress can be quite imperious in her demands when she chooses."

"I'll go back to my sketches then." But before she could wriggle away, he pinned her down again. Looking around in haste, he spied a box of trimmings on the floor nearby. Reaching for it, he grabbed a long white feather. "Lie still, Mouse. Any movement you make—any sound you make—will send me back to the beginning."

"I don't—"

Carver silenced her with a finger to her lips; then he began a thorough exploration of her body with his feather, starting at the soles of her feet.

As he'd promised, any little squirm or moan sent him back to her toes. Consequently, it took him several minutes to finally reach her inner thighs. When he ran the tip of his feather over her pink, roused flesh, he saw her lift her bottom but chose to ignore it. Her arms were stretched out at her sides, her fingers curling in the blanket. Again he let it go and did not punish her. Twice more he ran the feather over her private crease, brushing it slowly from side to side, watching her bud darken and blossom. Then he concentrated his teasing on the very crest of her nether lips, finally sliding it between them. The next time she exhaled a throaty groan and one of her hands flew out, spilling a glass of wine, he couldn't overlook it—knew she was too close to her peak—and was forced to return the damp feather to her toes.

His own excitement mounted with each pass of the feather over every inch of her smooth skin, and just to relieve some of his own need, he decided to follow the path of that feather with his lips. When he reached the apex of her thighs again, she was ready to fall over the edge. He drank from her greedily, relishing every sparkling drop, and when he knew she could bear it no more, he covered her body with his and entered her at last, allowing them both the release and completion they so badly needed.

They lay together on the chaise that night, watching the fire smolder in the hob grate. Carver wrapped her in his arms, not wanting to leave yet, and too content to speak. She, too, was silent but awake, her head on his chest, allowing him to tangle his fingers in her loose hair. His wandering, thoughtful gaze stumbled over the abandoned sketches again.

"I am jealous of your talent, Mouse," he confessed suddenly. "I wish I had one."

He felt her gentle laughter rocking his body. "You do. A very special, very lovely talent."

"Well, naturally." He smiled. "But beyond that. I'd like to be more than your plaything, you know, woman."

She turned her head, resting her chin on his chest.

"Forgive me if I lack understanding, but you are a titled peer of the realm."

"Hmmm." He twisted a lock of her hair around his finger. *Only by accident—by tragedy*—he thought, grim. If his brother had not died, Carver would have been worth even less in his father's eyes. But then perhaps his father would have been content to leave him alone and let him be whatever he wanted, do whatever he chose with his life. The flash of a memory came to him, a hand flung through the air holding a cane. He felt the sting. It made his eyes water, but he didn't cry out. That would have made his father even angrier. So he bit his tongue until he tasted blood.

"What's the matter?" A fearful, wary look had come into Margaret's wide brown eyes.

"Nothing. Nothing is the matter." He gathered her into his arms again and held her tight. While he was with Margaret, he wanted to think only of light, happy things so she would remember him always in a cheerful way. He was her slave, intent on her pleasure, never wanting a solitary rain cloud to spoil the mood between them.

The moment of darkness passed, and he was soon absorbed again in rediscovering all her ticklish spots with that feather. Doing what *he* did best.

Eighteen

"CARVER DANFORTHE IS VERY, VERY BAD, AND WHEN he's not wicked, he's awful."

Molly could now agree with that giggling, tipsy young lady once overheard and never forgotten. Her lover was not accustomed to using much discretion when it came to his affairs. Simply put, he did whatever he wanted and got away with it. Since people thought the worst of him anyway, he saw little cause to bother putting on a mask. He took great delight in teasing Molly, making her blush when they chanced to meet in public.

"For my sake, Danny, do make an effort," she urged. "I don't want the whole world to know about us."

Although he always agreed with great solemnity to try to ignore her, he would apparently forget that intention the next time they ran into each other.

Her business was growing, and a Molly Robbins Design, thanks largely to her devoted patron, Lady Anne Rothespur, had become the most sought after object for many of the new crop of debutantes. But despite her success, she was still frequently traveling around Town almost daily. Some of her wealthiest clients had not yet become accustomed to the idea of visiting her shop for fittings and consultations, so she remained a well-known face to the drivers of hackney carriages, and a familiar visitor to the finer homes of Mayfair, where Carver and his circle of friends were also known to gather. With increasing regularity, she found her secret lover lurking in wait to open a door for her, and on more than one occasion, he miraculously recovered a pair of gloves she'd mysteriously misplaced soon after entering a house.

"Miss Robbins, do allow me to walk you out," he would say, popping up before her like a suspiciously gallant jack-in-the-box.

This, apparently, was his idea of "discretion."

And his mischief knew no boundaries. One afternoon while Lady Cecelia Montague deigned to pay her shop a visit, Molly was alarmed to see Carver dismounting outside. There was no time to hide or put the "closed" sign on the door. He swept in, loudly jangling the bell above the door, and making everyone look over. There were several other ladies in the shop that day, in addition to Lady Cecelia, and naturally they all knew who Carver was, if only by sight. When he saw so many faces, he seemed almost surprised, as if he'd expected to have her all to himself. Molly hastily drew Lady Cecelia's attention back to the designs in the book she had spread open between them. She hoped he would come to his senses and leave again when he saw how busy she was.

Her hope was in vain.

Hat under one arm, Carver Danforthe strolled around the room, pretending to admire swatches of velvet and muslin, occasionally tipping his head to chirping clusters of curious ladies.

As the only male in the place, he caused a considerable stir again, bonnets turning to follow his progress, some of the bolder ladies smiling as they bobbed like pigeons. After a while, it occurred to Molly that he was enjoying himself. This became more evident when he proceeded to pause and loudly grant his sartorial advice to some of her customers, sounding very like his sister as he offered his opinion on which color they should choose or which style of sleeve.

"Lady Allen you have such strong, noble shoulders. I would suggest a smaller puff, of about so long, and possibly something in magenta."

The ladies listened with mouths agape, drinking it all in, but Molly very much doubted he knew the difference between magenta and peacock blue. He was merely spouting words he'd heard from her or his sister. Sly, mischievous man! Of course he knew how to flatter them.

"Mrs. Shadwell, that emerald green would be most becoming on you, but only for evenings. The summer sun would surely be too harsh for it."

He soon had the ladies eating out of his hand. They chortled and pecked around him, feathers preened, chests pushed out, little beaks nibbling eagerly on his advice.

Since he was being a disruption to the calm order of her shop, Molly finally left Lady Cecelia with her designs and walked across the room to ask him what he required there.

"Ah, Miss Robbins." He beamed at her. "I was planning a present for a very special lady of my acquaintance. I am told you are the very best mantua maker in London these days."

She was aware of Lady Cecelia's dark hard eyes watching every move. "That's very kind of you to say, your lordship." Hands folded before her to keep her fingers from fidgeting, she looked up at him. "What sort of present did you have in mind?"

"An evening dress, I think."

"A ball gown?"

"No. Something"—his gaze swept down over her like a warm shower of rain—"for an intimate affair."

All around her, skirts rustled, and she heard sighs expelled into the heated air.

"Intimate?" she murmured, fixing her gaze on a point to the left of his shoulder.

"Yes, for only one guest to enjoy, Miss Robbins."

One of the ladies gasped, and another broke into giggles.

Molly kept her countenance. "I see."

"Something entirely in lace with ribbons all the way down the front."

"Ribbons?"

"To be tied. And untied."

After all the previous excitement stirred up by this menace, it had now gone very quiet in the shop. All the ladies were straining to hear, absorbing every naughty word he uttered.

"Closely fitted to the lady's shape," he added, his voice low, slightly husky.

"Not too closely fitted," she replied. "You will need room for a garment beneath, if this item is to be all lace."

She made the mistake of returning her attention to his face just as he grinned slowly. "But that is the point, Miss Robbins. There will be nothing beneath it."

She knew her lips had parted, but no sound emerged. Behind her someone whispered the word "indecent." Or was it her own inner voice disapproving?

"Could you show me some samples of lace?" he asked. "I'd like to be certain it has the right pattern. Nothing too cluttered and busy."

Because then he wouldn't be able to see through it so well. Oh, no. She knew exactly how his mind worked. It was his voice inside her head, trying to make her flustered. Finally she found her words and her wits again. "I haven't much lace to show at present, but I will order some and make a sketch for you. Perhaps next time you come in you can bring the lady with you. I'll need her measurements, of course."

"She is slender, but tallish. I would say she is about your size, Miss Robbins."

She swallowed. "Do bring her in."

His grin widened.

One of the elderly ladies nearby muttered that it sounded to her like a dress in which someone would catch cold. Her younger companion hid a smile behind her glove and turned away.

"I do appreciate your patronage, your lordship. Thank you for coming." Molly moved aside, hoping he would get the hint.

Eventually he did. But as he moved by her, he replied, "You needn't thank me for coming, Miss Robbins. It is always entirely my pleasure. And I'll come again soon, no doubt."

She looked at him, her lips pressed tight. He was the very limit. Hat back on his head, he left the shop, and she found herself at last able to breathe again.

Returning to Lady Cecelia, she thought her face was

composed again, serene. A swift, sly wipe of her hands
on her skirt disposed of the dampness on her palms.

"I hear you've made an enemy of the Baroness
Schofield, Miss Robbins," the lady remarked casually.
"She spent the entire evening railing against you at
Almack's. What can you have done to her?" Her expres-
sion suggested she knew exactly what Molly had done.

"I believe we had a difference of opinion on style,
your ladyship."

"Perhaps it was not a difference that came between
you, but a correlation."

"I don't follow, madam."

"A similarity in male protectors." Lady Cecelia's
laughter felt like the sharp, brittle pricks of icicles.
"Don't look so appalled, Miss Robbins. I could hardly
care less about the baroness—a cheap and tawdry creature. Mutton dressed as lamb. She got above herself, in
any case. Serves her right that the earl threw her over.
I am not the only one relieved to see her back in her
place. If she continues to speak ill of you, I guarantee
you'll be rushed off those little feet of yours with new
orders. Now do tell me you intend to make something
for me in that new patterned silk over there. I absolutely cannot live without it."

Molly recovered, somehow, and hurried to fetch
the silk.

As days passed and more customers ventured into
her new shop, Molly realized that some came merely
to see a curiosity, like a two-headed calf at the fair. Sly
sideways glances caught her with sudden jabs and then
hurriedly withdrew to study her designs instead.

"Who cares if they come because they're nosy?"
said Kate with enviable, breezy confidence. "They'll

stay for the gowns, won't they? They know you're the best in all London. Whatever brings them to the shop, it will be your skill that keeps their custom."

Molly hoped it was true, but self-doubt crept in and would not leave. It was easy for Kate to be careless, for none of this would affect her once she went home to Aylesbury—or wherever she truly came from. There was no going home for Molly Robbins.

"I am honored that you can spend a few hours with me tonight." Sinjun grinned. "Your obsession has kept you busy these past few days."

Carver relaxed in the chair, legs stretched out and crossed at the ankle. Obsession? Yes, it was a good word for what she had become. "I have to let her rest sometimes, don't I?" He missed her tonight, but she had a gown to finish and told him in plain terms that she did not wish to be disturbed. He supposed he ought to abide by her wishes, and anyway, she would have her assistants with her at the shop.

"Quite true. Although you can always rest when you're dead." His friend ordered brandy from the attendant, who quickly retreated to fetch it. "I hear your sister's given Grey his congé."

"I believe it was a mutual decision," he replied cautiously. "No hearts broken."

"And what now for Lady Mercy?"

"She's gone away for a while. Can't say I blame her, with all those tongues stabbing her in the back." He wasn't about to tell anyone that she was making plans to return to the country, or that he'd given her his blessing. Truth was, he couldn't be very angry with her about Rafe Hartley, since he was misbehaving quite severely with Rafe's former fiancée. It was a tangled web from which he felt no inclination to extract himself.

"It's a good thing she's gone, Danforthe. I can't imagine she was very amused by your latest dalliance."

Carver merely shrugged and folded his newspaper.

"Do tell me what you find to do all those hours with your Mouse, holed up in her shop," Rothespur continued with an arch smile. "I don't mean the physical, of course. That much is obvious."

"Then what the blazes do you mean?"

"Conversation, for instance. What on earth can you find to talk about?"

Carver tossed the paper down and waited while the attendant delivered their glasses on a silver tray. Then he sat forward. "Sometimes we don't talk at all. I simply enjoy her company." He tried to explain but couldn't find the right words.

"She's had no formal schooling?"

"No. A year or two in the small village school, I believe."

"No tutors or governesses? No other instruction of any kind?"

"Since her family needed the wage she earned, they were hardly in a position to send her away to school, or hire a music tutor. I daresay they thought dance instruction might be ever so slightly superfluous." He took a large, decidedly uncivilized mouthful of brandy. The heat seared his throat, leaving his voice frayed and rasping when he added, "She appears to manage perfectly well with her natural talents."

Sinjun rubbed his eyebrow with one finger and

shook his head. "I just wonder what you can have in common when you're upright."

He scowled. What exactly, he thought, had a governess, a French dance instructor, and a year at an expensive finishing academy done for Sinjun's sister, Anne? Sweet and lively as she was, the girl could be annoying as a squeaky coach wheel on a long journey, and she still frequently burst out with odd remarks to unintentionally embarrass her brother. Anne Rothespur couldn't hold a conversation about anything without getting distracted by a butterfly or a pair of diamond earrings across the room. His Mouse, on the other hand, always gave her full attention and absorbed what she heard. "We manage," he muttered, curt. "She's very intelligent and charming, as a matter of fact. Quick witted."

"I didn't mean she is in any way stupid, Danforthe. No, of course. She's certainly smart enough to have seduced you. She has you by the nutmegs, to be sure." He chortled loudly, and Carver's scowl deepened.

Yes, she had seduced him. Somehow. With her cunning wiles. She'd made a pattern for his seduction just as skillfully as she planned her designs. He knew that. She took control of their situation with that contract, but when they were in bed, he had the upper hand. There she was still the novice, still his eager pupil. The thought stirred his blood, quickened his pulse.

"But it's not as if you can take her out anywhere, can you, old chap? I suppose that's why you stay locked away with her out of sight. Meanwhile, here I am, stuck with Skiffington and that dreadful bore Covey for company. If you deemed her rather more presentable, her company wouldn't be taking you away so much, and we'd all get to discover her charming quick wit."

He seemed to infer there was something to be ashamed of about Margaret—as if Carver hid her away on purpose. "I did suggest to her recently that we get our friends together for a small evening party."

Rothespur looked alert. "Excellent." Amusement rippled through his blue eyes. "Why don't I ask Anne, and we'll host a gathering in Hanover Square. She's wanted to have a small party, something to cut her teeth on, so to speak, as a hostess. And she's very fond of your seamstress. I'd like to meet this young woman who has you so much in her thrall. Meet her properly."

Carver took another hasty swig of brandy. Sinjun was right; it was time he brought her out in public and showed her off. He didn't want anyone thinking he was reluctant to do so, and she surely wouldn't want that either.

❧

She shrank away. "No. I don't want to. I can't. It's impossible."

"Margaret, it will be a quiet, intimate evening with friends. There is nothing to fear."

"I'm not afraid," she answered immediately, her face ghostly pale.

He told her to invite some of her own acquaintances, if that would make her more comfortable. "My oldest friend wants to meet you properly—socially. You'll like Sinjun. He's a very proper, well-behaved gentleman. Not like me."

"But I won't fit in. It will be awkward, distressing."

Carver put his hands on her waist and drew her close. "Why not ask your friends if they would like to attend?"

"They won't want to. I know already." Her stubborn little face was closed off, turned away. Like a child avoiding her bath, he mused.

"Just ask them, Margaret. For me." Gently he kissed her brow. "I thought you would want to be a part of my world."

"I like things the way they are."

"What happened to '*life should move forward, my lord, not lie stagnant*'?"

She looked at him again, studied his lips. "I have noticed, sir, that although you accuse women of employing selective senses, your own memory retains the things I say only when they might be used for your own advantage."

"I'm a member of the House of Lords, sweetling. I'm well trained in subjective hearing."

That earned him a tiny smile and then a willful shake of her head. "In any case, I spoke of our arrangement. I prefer the secrecy. Perhaps it matters little to you, but I don't want the entire world to know about us."

"Of course not. These are a few of my close friends. You and I will simply be two guests among others." He kissed the tip of her nose. "You must trust me, Margaret, I will keep you safe. I would never put you in harm's way."

Her eyes flashed up at him. "But you did already. Our very first night together, remember?"

As if he might forget his unfortunate failure to withdraw from her body before he spent. It was the first time in his life that had ever happened, and his dratted conscience hadn't shut up about it ever since, despite every effort to silence it. He was appalled by his lapse, wondering at the depths of this spell she'd cast over him. "You are right, Margaret. I was careless that first night, but it won't happen again." He added with a sudden grin, "Certainly not in the Earl of Saxonby's drawing room. Although it might liven up the party though, don't you think?"

She groaned.

"It would definitely make the Society pages," he teased, feeling her tension melting away, her soft, reluctant chuckles drifting against his jaw as she leaned her head on his shoulder. "Would there be illustrations of our wicked embrace to accompany the story?"

"I expect so, Danny. Vastly exaggerating your dimensions."

"How could they possibly exaggerate my dimensions, Mouse?"

"True. They could not make your *nose* any larger than it is in life."

They both laughed at that, although he tried not to. She got the upper hand with him too oft as it was, with her cunning, circuitous drollery.

He held her for a moment, enjoying the soft warmth of her body in his arms and the smart trot of her lively heart pressed to his chest. Then she said, "I don't need you to protect me from your friends, Danny. I can stand up for myself. We country girls are bred from hearty stock, and I have very strong bones."

"I know. Look how you stood up to me."

"Until I succumbed to temptation," she muttered wryly.

"Yes. There is that." He kissed the top of her head. Her rich brown hair slid silkily against his lips and caught on the rough hairs of his chin where he hadn't shaved today.

"I was once a good, honest woman, but I let you despoil me, and now look at me."

Carver leaned back. "*You* seduced *me*, Mouse."

She denied it, as always. "What did I know of seduction? I was an innocent. I was a maid, and you ruined me."

Although she spoke teasingly—or he hoped she did—Carver had begun to feel remorse about that. He had, in fact, greeted several new "feelings" of late, and all thanks to her. Feelings, he'd always said, were the domain of hysterical women. He couldn't understand it. She evidently did not belong with Rafe Hartley, and it wasn't as if he'd stolen her away on his horse. It was her choice not to marry. But two uncontestable facts remained: he'd taken her virginity, and he'd never before been any woman's first experience. It was a tremendous responsibility, he now discovered, to ruin a maid.

"Don't fret, Danny. I went to your bed with the full knowledge that there would never be a marriage." She looked up at him with large, vulnerable eyes and expanded black velvet pupils. There seemed to be a question hanging there, but for him or for herself, he wasn't sure.

"But I have treated you well, have I not?" He didn't think she had cause to complain, for he was sweeter to her than he'd ever been to anyone.

Her lashes lowered, and he saw her bottom lip indent where she tucked it under her teeth for a moment.

"Have I ever made you regret our contract?" he asked again, an uncomfortable, nagging sensation pulling on his nerves like the cold hands of beggars in the street. What did she want from him now? With the baroness, or any other woman in the past, he would know what she was thinking at once. Not so with Margaret.

"I do not regret a thing," she whispered.

"So you will come to the party?" he urged, drawing their conversation back to his purpose before she could distract him any further from it. "I'll make certain there's pineapple tart."

She pushed her way out of his arms and sat on her chaise, staring into the fire, hands clasped on her knees. "I won't know how to act, what to do. I'll always be more at home in a poultry yard than a drawing room."

Carver flipped up his coattails and sat beside her. "Then I'll teach you."

"You?" She snorted.

"I can tell you all you need to know, young lady. All the tricks."

"I'm not sure I need to know your sort of tricks, Danny."

"Hush, woman." He took her clenched hands and separated them. "Pay heed."

She looked at him, her chocolate eyes brimming with skepticism.

Carver kissed each of her palms and returned them to her lap. "Now, first thing to remember, always wait to be introduced to a gentleman before speaking to him or dancing."

"There won't be dancing, will there?" Two hot dots of pink appeared on her cheeks.

"Perhaps not, but when attending a small, informal

gathering, one never knows. And never dance with the same man thrice at—"

"I am not utterly ignorant of etiquette," she exclaimed, suddenly churlish. "We have manners in the country too, you know, Danny."

He sighed. "Of course."

"We are not a mindless rabble, just because we don't count in the eyes of the beau monde."

"I didn't mean to suggest you were."

"What am I allowed to talk about? What do I do with my hands? These are small things that will single me out for mockery. How do I sit? What do I look at?"

She cared very much about the details. He might have known from seeing her at work with a needle. "Very well, surly madam. The most important thing to remember is don't fidget. Always be composed. A lady's hands should move gracefully, not flap about like fins. She should enter a room neither too quickly nor too slowly. She should greet the hostess first and, when invited to do so, she should sit—elegantly, like a fallen leaf, not a lump of custard—with her knees together, slightly to one side. Listen to the conversation of others and take your cues from them. You might make a flattering remark or two about the decorations and furnishings in the room, but not too much. Everything in moderation. Do not be self-conscious. Be yourself. If you believe you belong, others will too."

"All sound and practical advice given with ease by a man who has never felt out of place in his life." She was quite beautiful when she forgot to be plain, he mused. It was not the cultivated, highly maintained look of the women he usually knew. It was utterly natural, unmanipulated.

He laid a hand on her knee. "When you are with me, you can never be out of place. No one would dare mock you in my presence."

"How nice. I daresay they will not hesitate to do so the moment I leave."

"Oh, and your friends never do that, I suppose," he replied dryly, sliding his hand along her thigh.

"I'm sure there is a law somewhere, Danny, about not bringing people of different ranks together."

"Too late," he whispered, leaning close to lick the warm, scented space behind her ear.

She pouted. "And kindly remove your hand. I'm positive *that* is not proper etiquette."

"No. but it's the Earl of Everscham's rule. You're my mistress, and I do with you as…" he kissed her nose, "…I…" he kissed her chin, "…please." Finally he found her lips, and fortunately for him, she had no further argument.

Nineteen

ON THE EVENING OF THE ROTHESPUR PARTY, MOLLY was able to recruit Mrs. Slater and Frederick Dawes to attend with her. A bad cold kept Mrs. Bathurst in bed, and Mrs. Lotterby had volunteered to watch young master Slater.

Frederick's carefree manner and dashing confidence was such that he could enter a drawing room anywhere, charm the occupants, and make himself at home before the first sherry was drunk. On the other hand, there was bashful Mrs. Slater, whose manners were either self-consciously rigid, or cowed and timid. Molly knew it would be a struggle to make her talk at all in exalted company, but the sad lady admitted she had not enjoyed an evening out since her husband's demise. It was plain to see the time under her controlling brother's thumb had left her unsure of herself and discouraged, so downtrodden that any confidence she once knew was severely stunted. Molly thought it would be a good deed to bring her to the party, and with Fred to do all the talking, they would both be saved from having to do much of it themselves.

When they arrived at the Rothespurs' house, Lady

Anne dashed over to greet her, excited about playing the hostess at her very first party. When introduced, Mrs. Slater was duly declared to possess "enviable cheekbones," and Frederick—already known to the hostess, of course—was quickly ambushed with a commission.

"I want you to paint my portrait, to immortalize my first Season, Freddie."

Freddie? Bemused, Molly looked at her friend, who replied with a smile, "I would be happy to oblige, Lady Anne."

Satisfied, Anne tucked her arm under Molly's and led her farther into the drawing room. "My brother had chosen an awful old fellow to paint me. My eyeballs were so offended by the sight of him that they could barely open in his presence. He had hairy nostrils, his breath reeked of onions, and he complained that I never sat still enough—can you imagine such a thing? So after I met Freddie, I said I would sit only for him and no one else. I do hope you don't mind."

"Why should I mind?"

"I didn't want you to think I might poach your pet away from you."

Molly replied with mock solemnity, "Lady Anne, I can pass him on to you with impunity. As long as you keep him well fed and watered and clean out his cage."

"Good gracious. It is quite a liability to look after an artist."

"Indeed, your ladyship."

Carver, who had crossed the room to greet her, added wryly, "The creative soul is never an easy one to keep domesticated."

She shot him a look that she hoped would urge him to behave. He duly kissed her hand very politely, so no one but she would note the wicked gleam in his eye as his lips lightly stroked her knuckles.

Apart from Lady Anne, the Rothespurs' drawing room was inhabited by males until Molly arrived with her friends. They were introduced to the other gentlemen present, all of them looking at her with great interest. Then she was seated beside Mrs. Slater on a small, dainty sofa, and after answering a few questions about their journey across London that evening, Molly let Fred take the conversation, which he did painlessly and seamlessly. Fortunately, he and Lady Anne were both chatterboxes, and for the first quarter hour, theirs were the voices most often heard. Occasionally Lady Anne's brother spoke up to rein her in discreetly, and Lord Skiffington interjected the odd comment, which seldom had much to do with anything, but Carver spent those first moments simply watching Molly across the room with his potent, heated regard.

When Lady Anne opened the instrument and invited the ladies to play, Mrs. Slater suddenly perked up and accepted the challenge. Until then, Molly had never even known the lady knew how to play a note, but Mrs. Slater turned out to be far more eloquent on the pianoforte than she was with her speech. Her fingers moved over the keys with great dexterity, and she was soon absorbed in her playing.

Well, it was really no surprise that she'd never known about the widow's musical bent, thought Molly, for there was no instrument at Mrs. Lotterby's house, and no room, or coin, for one. But she had surely been a terrible friend for never bothering to know about Mrs. Slater's accomplishment. Until then, the struggling, widowed young mother was little more than a sad shadow in the corner of her eye, a victim of unhappy circumstance, and someone to be pitied. There was, of course, more beneath, if one bothered to scratch the surface, but Molly had been too caught up in herself to take the time. A woman did not disappear just because she married, lost her husband, and then had a baby. Mrs. Slater had been someone before all that happened, someone with hopes and dreams and laughter in her life. Someone who took music lessons and learned to play beautifully. Yes, indeed, it was important to scratch beneath the surface if one meant to properly know a person.

While sitting at the instrument, the lady's entire demeanor changed from meek and browbeaten to composed and confident. Molly supposed—like her own ability with needle and thread—music was a way to express thoughts and ideas she could not put into words. The poor lady must have suffered dreadfully for the lack of an opportunity to exercise her skill, for it would drive Molly insane if she could not sew or sketch her designs.

Glancing around the room, she was glad to see everyone paying attention and admiring her friend's playing. Very proud and pleased for Mrs. Slater, she made up her mind to purchase a small spinet for her as soon as she had enough money. What was the good of her own success if she could not share it with her dear friends?

Beginning to feel as if the evening would not be nearly as uncomfortable as she'd imagined, Molly's spirits improved, and she lost some of her own reserve, but not enough to attempt a tune on the pianoforte.

Watching the faces of Carver's friends, she wondered

how many knew the truth about their relationship. They were gracious to her, very civil. Lady Anne's brother clearly made an effort to put Molly at her ease, smiling pleasantly and angling a few subjects in her direction without questioning her pointedly to make her the center of uncomfortable attention. He had also, she soon discovered, provided pineapple tart, just as she'd been promised.

She soon decided that Sinjun Rothespur, Carver's oldest friend, had a likeable, unpretentious manner and an endearing smile. As for Lord Skiffington, he was the typical rakish blade, bent on pleasure. The sort that never properly grew up. Yet he was tolerable and not at all stuck-up. On his best behavior perhaps, she thought.

When Lady Anne took over the musical entertainment, it only allowed them all to appreciate the superiority of Mrs. Slater's playing. Their young hostess had a heavy hand on the keys and distinct lack of rhythm, but what she lacked in certain areas she made up for in sheer determination and bravado. Frederick offered to turn the music for her, and soon he was singing along, a born show-off, while Lady Anne thumped away at the pianoforte, her ringlets bouncing, eyes shining. Molly watched them together and saw two lively, spirited young people who might be in very real danger from each other.

Better have a word with Fred later. Wouldn't want him getting his heart broken, and it was doubtful the Earl of Saxonby would let his young sister fall in love with an artist. She glanced slyly at Mrs. Slater, for she'd harbored some romantic hopes for the pretty widow and handsome, merry Fred, but the lady watched him now with a kind smile and seemed to be enjoying the dreadful noise as best she could, tapping her foot in an effort to keep time even when there was no discernible beat to the playing.

Alas, mused Molly, one could not make love bloom where there was no seed. On the other hand—she looked for Carver—one could not stop love growing in places where it should not either.

Oh, where had he gone? He was no longer in the chair where he had sat moments ago.

Suddenly a large hand tapped her shoulder, and she turned her head to find him behind her, having apparently moved across the room while she was watching the entertainment. His lips moved in a slight smile as he looked down at her. There was no word exchanged, no need for any. The tender touch of his fingers on her bare shoulder spoke an entire soliloquy. However, Molly refused to let her imagination run away with her again. Just as it had in regard to Fred being Mrs. Bathurst's long-lost son, her mind was eager to sew neat seams around the facts. She might want to believe Carver was in love with her, but her wishes didn't make it so. Even if he was capable of such a feeling, what good would it do? She was still a dressmaker, and he was an earl. Their love could flourish only in shadow.

But tonight she felt connected to him in a new way. A deeper way.

It was as if they were alone together in that room.

The glorious sensation lasted just five more minutes.

When the doors opened, everyone seemed surprised. The music stopped abruptly, and Lady Anne rose from the instrument to greet her new guests. A hollow silence fell over the room, unnatural and sinister as cockcrow in the afternoon.

※

"Covington. I thought you were otherwise engaged," Rothespur exclaimed.

"I decided to come after all. You know the Baroness Schofield, of course."

It was a good thing Sinjun had the ability to play perfect host and hide his thoughts, for Carver knew his were written all over his face at that moment. His gut tightened, as did his jaw. His teeth began to hurt.

Fletcher Covington walked into the party with Carver's former mistress on his arm, smirking like a man who just won a fortune on the Epsom Derby.

Carver would have left at once, but Margaret laid a hand over his fingers, where he'd placed them upon her shoulder moments before, and when he glanced down at her, she shook her head very slightly. Her color had risen, but she was composed, her eyes calm, her hand steady.

She was right, he thought, why should their evening be cut short? He had finally drawn her out of hiding, and the last thing he wanted was to see her run back again into her mouse hole at the first sign of trouble.

Everything was going so well. Until now.

After a slight delay, their trainee hostess, Lady Anne, scrambled to welcome the new arrivals, but a crisp chill had cut through the atmosphere of the room. The baroness made her disdain for Margaret and her friends quite obvious.

"Ah yes," she murmured. "You are that seam-stress...Roberts, isn't it? The runaway bride who jilted that poor country lad because she had bigger fish in her net."

Furious, Carver stepped toward her, but again a subtle movement from Margaret prevented him from making a protest.

The baroness chortled. "Don't mind me, just a silly jest."

"No one else is amused," Carver replied, curt.

"I can't think why. I know you love a good joke. Perhaps it's amusing only if it's not at your expense, Danforthe." She looked at Margaret again, her eyes narrowed slyly. "You're quite flushed, Roberts. Must be the heat of the evening. I do hope I have not said anything amiss."

"Not at all," said Margaret quietly. "I am flattered you remember me at all, madam." Clearly she had more poise in the face of rudeness than he did, he thought, and his admiration for her leapt another few steps that night.

The baroness entreated them all to continue the party. "Don't let me disturb you. Please, play on Lady Anne." She and Covington swept away to be seated.

Carver caught Sinjun's eye and read there a silent, hapless apology. He shook his head, gesturing that it didn't matter, even though it did, of course. There was no doubt that Covington had done this deliberately, springing Maria on the party to create maximum disruption, but it was hardly Sinjun's fault. He couldn't have known, or he would have prevented it. Covington picked his moment well, because Lady Anne was such an untried hostess and would probably not have any idea how to handle the situation—even if she had an inkling of her guest's discomfort—while

Sinjun was the peacemaker, always wanting everyone to get along and avoiding confrontation.

Now Anne continued her playing, and they all sat stiffly, pretending not to feel the tremors of discontent filling the room.

⤷⤶

A light supper buffet was served. Although a footman offered, several times, to refill her glass, Molly only sipped her wine, anxious not to lose any control. She felt as if she was being tested tonight and would need all her wits about her.

The large ruby earrings swaying in the Baroness Schofield's ears every time she gave that shrill laugh seemed to flare in the corner of Molly's eye, drawing her attention when she would rather look at anything else. The woman kept touching them too, then letting her fingers drift down the side of her elegant neck. Finally, when Lady Anne politely asked about them, she explained they were a recent gift from an admirer, and she threw a pointed glance at Carver.

Molly looked at her lap. Of course they must have been a parting gift. She knew he always gave his ladies jewelry when he moved on. But each time the baroness ran her fingernails down the side of her neck, Molly thought of Carver's hands once following the same path. Touching that woman as intimately as he lately touched her.

When Mrs. Slater gently asked if she was all right, Molly forced a smile, not wanting to spoil anyone else's evening. Fred and Lady Anne seemed to be the only guests who were not troubled in some way by the late arrivals. Their hostess was possibly oblivious to the fragile air and undercurrent of drama. Fred was his usual entertaining self. Thank goodness for Fred, she mused glumly.

At one point, the Duke of Preston, who had escorted the baroness into the party, began a conversation about horse racing. It was nothing Molly could take part in or, indeed, have any possible interest in. But as talk turned to wagers lost and won, the baroness suddenly raised her fan to her lips, caught Molly's eye, and then leaned over to Lady Anne and whispered in her ear.

The young lady instantly glanced over at Molly too, so she knew—had she been in any doubt—that the whisper was about her.

She raised a hand to her hair, anxious that it should not let her down by unraveling to her shoulders, as was its tendency whenever Molly was agitated. The room seemed very large suddenly, but there was not enough air in it. Like one of those bitter cold mid-winter days when the breath was sucked out of one's chest. Her body was shrinking into the upholstery of the sofa, her veins freezing and cracking.

A low giggle slipped out between Lady Anne's gloved fingers as she held them to her rosy lips and exclaimed in a gasp of part horror and part amusement, "*Danforthe won her in a wager?*"

All other conversation faded away. The baroness fanned herself rapidly, beaming from one ruby to the other. Everyone now looked at Molly.

"Is that true?" Lady Anne demanded. "Jumping Jacks! How positively scandalous. And yet so like you, Danforthe."

She couldn't feel anything. Sinjun Rothespur looked mortified, but the Duke of Preston, who had clearly imbibed too much liquor even before he came to the party, bellowed with laughter. "Not exactly the case. He didn't win her in the wager. Miss Robbins *was* the wager."

Molly couldn't look at Carver, who still stood behind her. If his good friend Sinjun was not staring at the carpet and wiping sweat from his brow, she would not have believed the nasty remark. Rothespur's guilt-wracked countenance, however, suggested it was true, and then the duke added, "Seems I owe you my best hunter, Danforthe." He blew out a cloud of gray cigar smoke and coughed. "You worked that one in record time."

Although only the duke was laughing, that sound echoed around the drawing room until it felt as if they all laughed. She was surrounded by faces that were either embarrassed for her or ready to mock. Even Lady Anne, of whom she'd grown fond, was looking as if she didn't know whether to laugh or frown.

"You know that's not true, Covington." Carver's deep, angry voice passed over her head while Molly sat very still and straight, unable to move or even swallow. "Apologize to Miss Robbins. Now."

"You always said you could have anyone you wanted," the duke replied. "So I challenged you to get her into bed. Next thing I know, you're canoodling with her at Vauxhall Gardens."

"I never accepted your stupid wager."

She saw a movement in the corner of her eye and knew Carver had sprung forward, but Sinjun Rothespur jumped up from his seat and put himself in the way. "I think you'd better leave, Covington."

"Why's 'at?" The portly drunk slurred, "'S the truth. The damn truth, I say."

The baroness stood and closed her fan with a snap. "I'm quite ready to leave. I've never been to such a dull party. Really, I thought it might at least be interesting in a morbidly curious way—a novelty—but I was wrong. It seems the poor can be just as tedious company as some immensely rich folk of our acquaintance." She sauntered to where the duke sat and offered her elegant hand to help the corpulent fellow to his feet. "Let's leave, Fletcher darling. We've done our part for charity this evening. If he chooses, Danforthe can pander to that talentless little seamstress and prop her up with every penny of his fortune. That doesn't mean we all have to treat her as if she's something other than what she is."

Mumbling under his breath, the tipsy duke got up and let her lead him to the door, only a few paces ahead of Sinjun, who signaled to a footman to escort them out, and even fewer paces ahead of Carver, who would have caught them at the door if his friend did not waylay him seconds before he made contact with the Baroness Schofield's arm.

Molly was relieved he didn't reach her in time. The last thing she wanted was to see him touch that woman, even in anger. After all, had he not said to her once that there was only a slender leap from anger to desire? She would much rather he ignored that woman from now on. That was surely punishment of the worse kind for a creature who wanted to be the center of attention however the place was earned.

But tonight she'd done her damage successfully. The villains had stayed just long enough to fire their cannon, and now they sailed away, leaving their victims to pick up the pieces.

❧

Carver took Margaret and her friends home, after another half hour of everyone trying to act as if nothing unpleasant had taken place. Lady Anne, at her brother's gentle urging, had apologized to Margaret and made several indignant exclamations about the rudeness of Covington and his guest. The young lady had been an unwitting pawn in a cruel game, and the baroness knew exactly what she did when whispering her vulgar lie into the inexperienced ear of the loudest squeezebox in the room. Margaret said very little in the carriage returning to Mrs. Lotterby's house. Her artist friend made a valiant effort to keep the silence from becoming oppressive, but even he lost breath by the time the house was in sight. When the carriage drew to a halt, her two friends went inside, leaving them alone for a moment.

"You do know that was a lie. There was no wager, Margaret."

She studied his face, her own countenance giving nothing away, closed off from him again. "The baroness told Lady Anne that she heard every word of it while you played billiards."

"Then she heard half of what happened. I never took that wager. It was Covington acting like an ass, and I never took him up on it."

She nodded, but her lips were pressed tight, well guarded again.

"I daresay Maria's vanity wouldn't let her believe I threw her over for you unless there was some game involved."

"I daresay," she muttered, her shoulders wilted, her eyes forlorn.

"If you let her upset you, she's won," he added.

"Yes." But her voice trembled, and he knew she'd been deeply wounded by those spiteful remarks at the party. She might have strong, capable bones, as she liked to say, but she was not made to withstand the force of those cruel blows. Margaret was more fragile than she liked to think.

He curved his hands around her face and lifted it so the lamplight gave him a better view of her features. If those were tears in her eyes, she wasn't letting them fall, but the sight of several shining droplets caused his heart to ache. He never wanted to see her unhappy. Never. He kissed her. Right there in the street. It was dark, but for those few street lamps, and he did not care who saw anyway. "Tell me you believe me, Margaret."

"I believe you."

Thank god she was too sensible to let Maria's words cause a rift between them. "Let there be no misunderstanding," he choked out under his breath, "that woman will pay for causing you any pain or embarrassment."

Her eyes widened. "I would rather you say or do nothing to her. Don't engage her in the quarrel she clearly wants to have."

"But she cannot be allowed to get away with it." His fury against Maria Schofield had frozen into a great solid block of ice in his gut where it sat heavily and would never thaw out again until he'd said his piece to that witch. He was equally incensed by Covington's behavior—bringing her to that party for one purpose only. Their malicious strike against his Mouse would not go unpunished.

Margaret straightened the collar of his coat.

"Please let the matter rest, Danny," she whispered gently. "I want it forgotten." Her hands tidied his white scarf, and she paused a moment to look at the initials sewn under the fringed hem, running her finger over the stitches. He was relieved to see her smile, even if it was rather a sad one. "I'm putting my past behind me and moving forward. You must do the same. Promise me."

He swallowed hard. She looked so young and vulnerable tonight in the light of the gas lamp. Her eyes were full of unshed tears, but they were brave too, fighting, determined.

His own temper had been raging hot, but her words were soothing, calming.

"It's just about us," she said. "You and I. That's all that matters."

Carver's heart slowed its beat, and he felt several stone lighter suddenly. She was right. What else mattered?

"Yes, of course." He gave her another kiss before she walked away, and he watched her pass under the hanging lantern that lit the doorway of the house.

His heart always hurt when she walked away, he realized. He found himself seeking ways to make her stay longer in his embrace, delaying the moment when that pain would come. How sweet she was, yet not naive. Margaret would never act the way Maria Schofield had done tonight. She had no meanness in her, no spite.

Knowing this made him want to earn her respect. He wanted to hold her, protect her, make her trust him. He never wanted to see tears of sadness in her eyes ever again.

He looked up at the sky and took a great breath of

the warm night air. Was this how it felt to fall in love? How would he know?

Frankly, it terrified him.

Twenty

THE ORDERS FOR ASCOT KEPT HER BUSY. LADY ANNE Rothespur, anxious to make amends for the unfortunate scene at her party, brought all her young friends to Molly's shop, and for several hours, while they skipped about among the pattern cuttings and reams of fabric, she could barely hear herself think.

"I do hope you can forgive me," said Lady Anne. "I really must learn to curb my tongue and not spurt things out the moment they come to me."

"Impulsive spirit often comes with youth. And you are not the one at fault."

"But I feel wretched, Miss Robbins."

"Please do not concern yourself a moment longer. The incident is already gone from my mind. Wiped clean."

Lady Anne looked pensive, squeezing her gloved palms together, little chin wobbling indignantly. "That frightful rum doxy! When I see her again, I shall set her straight."

"I think the less said about the entire matter the better, Lady Anne. When a woman feels…affection… for a man, she must take the bad with the good. And no one"—she sighed—"no one is perfect."

The girl nodded slowly. "My brother says Danforthe has changed, however. He drinks and gambles much less and never goes out now."

Molly would like to think she had a hand in his reform—if it was more than a passing phase—but it seemed unlikely that her presence in his world could make such a difference. His presence in hers, however, continued to improve not only her life, but the lives of those around her.

Mrs. Lotterby's house was no longer drafty and damp, Mrs. Bathurst's health was tended by the Danforthe family physician, and a tearful Mrs. Slater was presented with a brand new spinet, which was just small enough to fit in a corner of her room by the window.

One evening as the lovers lay together on the chaise in her little room above the shop, Molly told Carver the sad story of Mrs. Bathurst's child and asked if he might help find out what happened to it. The lady's health was deteriorating, despite the care of Carver's learned physician, who bled her daily with leeches and tried all manner of new medicines. Molly worried that Mrs. Bathurst would soon depart the mortal world, and the only thing she could possibly do for the lady now was to find her lost son.

"London is a very large place," Carver replied drowsily, threading his fingers through her hair.

"I know. But I thought the Earl of Everscham could do anything."

"You are, it seems, the only person who believes that."

She smiled, lifting her head to kiss him on the lips. "Am I not all you need?"

"Yes," he replied, not smiling. "You are everything I need."

Molly laid her head down again on his wide, warm shoulder. "Her son was born about thirty years ago, and poor Mrs. Bathurst never saw him since. I should hate for her to die and never even hold his hand once. Never know what became of him."

"I daresay he was far better off without her."

Molly raised her head again. "How could you say such a thing?"

He looked surprised. "An unwed woman cannot raise a child. Look at your friend Mrs. Slater. She has troubles enough, and her child is at least legitimate. A woman who keeps the product of an affair is making a grave mistake. For herself and for the child."

She stared. He was so somber and certain, his words left her chilled.

"Wherever the son is now," he added, "I doubt he would care to have his life set asunder by the discovery of his birth mother. They would be strangers after all this time. Boys are resilient creatures, and they can survive a great deal."

"I do not agree." Once, not long ago, she could never have said those words to his face. As his servant, she had keep her opinions tucked away. She suspected that not many people ever dared disagree with him. "What do you know of boys, little children?"

"Plenty." He seemed about to say more, then stopped himself and altered course with a smile. "I was one once."

But she very much doubted his childhood had been anything like that of Mrs. Bathurst's son.

He tilted his head against the arm of the chaise. "It surprises me that you are so fond of that lady. She was a courtesan, you know, and you have always been so prim. I would not expect you to approve of her at all."

"How can I be a hypocrite? I'm a fallen woman now too."

He blinked, and his eyes narrowed. "But you are not the same. Your situation is different."

"In what way?" she demanded, annoyed that he could be so apparently callous about Mrs. Bathurst's situation and overlook her own.

"Margaret"—he stroked hair from her cheek and looped it behind her ear—"you will never be passed from man to man as she was. You belong to me."

"Only for now."

His mouth tightened. He said nothing, just stared at her, his features half in shadow. Firelight couldn't quite reach and only teased her with glimpses.

She was so accustomed to the planes of that handsome face now—to seeing it almost every evening. Her world without him would be a lonely one. She'd given too much of herself in a temporary affair.

When it was over, she would be just like Mrs. Bathurst in many ways—all but one, for she had no child, of course.

"Margaret? You've gone very pale." He sat up, concern lining his brow, his hands reaching to steady her shoulders. "Don't be upset," he said. "I'll see what I can find out about Mrs. Bathurst's son. If you wish it."

She thanked him, but the curt way in which he had dismissed the idea of Mrs. Bathurst's child needing her in his life stayed in Molly's mind, stuck there like a splinter.

Two days later, while trying on bonnets at a shop on Oxford Street with Mrs. Slater, she chanced to see the reflection of Lady Cecelia Montague over her shoulder in the mirror. She was with a small group of women, and one of them had glanced Molly's way.

It was a quiet shop, making it easy to pick out the occasional word from other conversations, and Molly heard Lady Cecelia's words clear as a bell ringing a death toll.

"Yes, that's her, over there. Everscham's whore."

The picture in the mirror became blurred. Her fingers lost their grip on the silk ribbons she'd been tying under her chin. All the breath and blood seeped out of her as if she'd been stabbed in the back by a cruel dagger.

She closed her eyes and saw her mother turn her back, and her father's hands dropping her out of the warm blue sky.

Had the milliner not approached at that moment to ask if she liked the bonnet, Molly would have toppled from the stool on which she sat. Instead, she waited for the uneasy spell to pass, her hands gripping the display table, shame and humiliation streaking a wide path through her.

Finally she opened her eyes and managed to reply that she thought the bonnet did not suit her. Then she left the shop with Mrs. Slater at her side and Lady Cecelia's voice rattling around in her head.

Everscham's whore.

It might as well have been painted on her forehead in scarlet letters. The way he'd once written TOMFOOLERY on her palm.

Everscham's whore. That was what the world now thought of her.

He was at his club that evening when a message was put into his hand, informing him that a young woman desired an audience. Since women were not allowed inside the club, he had to step outside to meet her. The moment he saw Margaret's face in the light of the gas lamps, he knew something was amiss, but she gave him no time to ask what. A few fat spots of warm summer rain had begun to fall, already making the silk ribbons of her bonnet stick limply to her shoulder.

"I'm afraid I cannot continue," she said, words rushing out, scrambling over one another. "This is not what I came to London to be. I have let myself down. I do not blame you, sir. I'm sure it will never trouble you to conduct a private affair in public, but I'm afraid I cannot endure it. This must end now." She abruptly handed him a small packet. "The remaining payment of your loan, sir."

Carver waited a moment, thinking he must have misheard. Her hands were clasped again now, and her face solemn. The spark of hope for him was gone from her eyes, and he felt a hard pit in his stomach. "Most amusing, Mouse. What's the trouble? What couldn't wait until I saw you later this evening?"

"I cannot see you this evening, sir. Or any other." Her eyes were dull, unblinking.

"I don't have the pleasure of understanding you."

"Certainly you do. I am calling a halt to the foolishness upon which we embarked."

It sounded as if she got that from a book, he thought. Or had rehearsed it all the way there. In the next beat of his heart, she turned and was walking away. Just like that. As if she had a right to leave his presence without so much as a by-your-leave.

He trotted down the steps and followed, not caring about the rain that fell harder now. "Miss Robbins, you forget something."

She kept walking. "I doubt it."

Carver sped up and stepped in front of her. "Our contract. We still have one fortnight."

"I am canceling the contract." Head down, she walked determinedly around him, but he followed again. "I have put up with more than enough gossip about you and me," she added hurriedly, staring at the wet pavement. "It must have been a moment of madness when I agreed to your contract. I thought we could be discreet and civilized, but I see that is impossible for you. Now my success is blighted. They are calling me your whore."

Margaret walked faster now, not looking back. Carver, standing in the mellow glow of a street lamp, could not think what to do to stop her. He only knew that he could not let her leave. She would not be permitted to abandon their agreement. He was hurting. Badly. She did this to him.

A hansom cab clattered down the street behind him, and he quickly raised his hand to stop the horse.

He leapt up. "Follow that woman," he yelled. "Don't let her out of your sight." Whatever he had to do to keep her longer in his arms, to keep her safe and himself from hurting for as long as possible, he would do it. Regardless of whatever "civilized" rules she hoped to cling to. Besides, she was the one who had called him wild.

He didn't care much for "civilized" he decided.

She heard the hooves galloping after her, but thought it was simply someone in haste to get out of the rain and rushing along the street. The last thing she could have expected was an arm swooping down like a hook, claiming her around the waist and scooping her off her feet.

With a cry of alarm, she found herself dragged into a moving carriage and held prisoner. "Get off me," she squealed, swinging her fists and heels.

"Never," he shouted back at her as the vehicle continued on at its reckless speed. "You owe me a fortnight, woman. Two blasted weeks, and I'll have them. Every minute of them."

"What are you going to do?" she exclaimed, breathless, her bonnet knocked off her head. "Keep me locked in your cellar, fool man?" How typical of the rogue to think he could manhandle her like this.

"No." His eyes flared, savage and determined as he loomed over her, pinning her to the rocking seat. "I'm taking you into the country with me."

"What?"

"We're going to the Sussex estate, where I shall have your full attention."

The Earl of Everscham wanted her attention and apparently meant to get it, no matter what he must do. Once the shock had worn off, she was rather thrilled by the prospect. And then quickly ashamed of herself for being so. She resumed her wriggling, although she knew that even if she got free of his arms she could hardly leap out of a racing cab without cracking her skull open on the cobbled street. "I'm not leaving

London. I have a business to run, orders to fill. You've distracted me long enough already. Let me go, foul beast! Release me at once. How dare you?"

"The contract, madam. You signed it, remember? There is no out clause."

"Well, I just put one in it."

"Don't be absurd."

"You changed it. So can I."

"Indeed you cannot. You will see this through to the bitter end, damn you, woman! You walked back into my life and turned it all arse about face, just when I thought I was rid of you."

"I turned *your* life arse about face?"

"Ladies don't say arse."

"Arse! Arse! Arse!" she screamed.

"Oh, that's right. You're not a lady. You're a country ragamuffin! I briefly forgot with all these airs and graces you've adopted." He was clearly lacking breath, and she suspected he'd made this decision on the spur of the moment, but his countenance was that of a man satisfied with his actions. There was definitely a wicked smirk pulling on his lips, even as he struggled to keep her from squirming and kicking. Twisting around, he wrestled her into his lap and closed his arms hard around her.

"Fourteen full days to go," he muttered. "Only then may you leave me."

"You're being ridiculous!"

"Tsk, tsk! You forgot to call me your lordship, Mouse," he growled, his breath hot against her brow as he held her captive in his lap.

"You're being ridiculous, *your lordship*."

"I am forced to take these dire measures. This is

how the landed gentry dealt with difficult women once. It's in my aristocratic Norman blood."

"For pity's sake!"

"Pity? *Pity?* What is this pity? Never heard of it. They don't teach us that at Eton or Oxford either."

She groaned. He was impossible. "What *do* they teach you?" She was instantly sorry she asked.

His lips curved against her brow, and he whispered, "Shall I show you here and now?"

"Certainly not!" But it was too late, and her words did not come out as stern as she meant for them to be. His mouth already moved to her cheek and then the side of her neck. She felt the slight graze of his teeth as passion ran away with him as speedily as the horses' hooves charged down that rain-washed street. There in that rattling carriage, he devoured her, and she realized, perhaps for the first time, the full extent of his powerful strength. Tonight the beast escaped and took her with him.

Twenty-one

HE ALLOWED HER TO WRITE INSTRUCTIONS TO EMMA and Kate about managing the shop while she was gone, and then a letter to Mrs. Lotterby. Not wanting the landlady to worry, she wrote that something unexpected had called her into the country, but she would return in September. She was not permitted to send for her own clothes or any other items, except for the lace gown he'd ordered her to make. With the ribbons to be tied and untied at his leisure.

"Won't Mrs. Lotterby think it strange that this is all I take with me?" she demanded.

"If you require anything else, take it from my sister's chamber," he snapped. "She left plenty behind."

If she required anything else? Apparently he expected to keep her in a state of indecent undress.

That same evening they departed London for Sussex and the Everscham estate. Despite the circumstances of this sudden trip, Molly was curious to see the place. She'd heard about it from Lady Mercy but had never seen even a picture. Perhaps she would learn more about Carver once she'd visited the estate. It might explain a lot of things, the way taking a cover off a clock showed her the workings with all the little cogwheels. She knew he made only brief visits to his birthright, and there were obviously reasons why he stayed away for long periods. Reasons he didn't care to discuss.

In the carriage, he barely spoke at first. When it grew light enough, he read his paper or stared out of the little window. After his treatment of her in that same carriage mere hours earlier, it was plain he meant what he said when he vowed to make the most of their remaining days. She was quite certain she had bruises already flourishing after his crude manhandling. But he had not escaped entirely unscathed, she thought with sharp satisfaction as her gaze found the little mark on the side of his neck just visible under his tall collar. Part kiss, part nibble. A brand left in response to those he'd given her. A mark of her frustration, her passion, her sense of helplessness that she found herself in such a predicament. She, Molly Robbins, of the very little harm.

"People here will know we shared a bed," she said on the first evening when he took a room above a rowdy tavern.

"So?" came his sharp reply. "What business is it of theirs?" He kicked off his boots and undressed with careless haste. When she took time to pick up his discarded clothes, fold them neatly, and place them on a chair, he grew impatient. "Make haste, woman. Come to bed. I don't want to fall asleep before I've had you tonight."

"How romantic. It seems you left your charm in London, my lord."

"But you were impervious to my charm anyway."

"Of course I was. That's why I never gave in and let you seduce me."

"Woman, cease fussing with my clothes and come to bed. I have something else requiring your attention."

When she still delayed, he got up, strode naked to where she stood, raised her over his shoulder, and tossed her onto the bed. If the good landlord below had not known before what was happening in his most costly chamber, he certainly knew then, by the creaking and yelling coming from it. She rolled over and off the other side of the bed, taking umbrage at his high-handed manner.

"Get back here, country ragamuffin." He rolled after her, ready to chase her around the bed. Until he stubbed his toe and cursed.

"What's the matter, Lord Lazybones, Earl of Idiocy? Too old to keep up with me?" She ran, laughing. Her captor had demanded she wear that indecent lace gown tonight, and now she knew he would be teased and tormented with glimpses through the material as she skipped out of his reach.

But he wasn't putting up with that for long. Abruptly, he leapt across the mattress to catch her, dragging her back to the groaning, protesting bed, and securing her there with a knee on either side of her hips.

Slowly, he set about the slow untying of each satin ribbon, beginning at her throat.

"This is for your insubordination in running away from me," he murmured as the first bow slid open under his fingers. "This is for the names you called me." There went another knot.

Molly arched her spine, breathing hard, each fall of soft, sensuous ribbon kissing her skin, tantalizing.

"This," he continued, working another bow free, "is for each time you bite your lip to drive me mad with desire, when you know I can't act upon it in a room full of people."

She looked up at his face in amazement. Surely she never did such a thing. Not Molly of the very little harm.

"This is for the pert pucker of your mouth, used to make me think of kissing you when you pretend you don't want me to have any such thought in my head."

Oh, dear, had she done that deliberately? It didn't sound like her.

"This is for every devious flutter of your long lashes that lure me in while I'm not supposed to notice you. This for the scent you wear behind your ear, which is not supposed to make me yearn for a taste. And this...this..." His fingers had just released the bow at her navel, and now they skipped back up to her chin. "This..." He pressed on her lower lip, opening her mouth a little. "This is for me."

Carver kissed her now as if she was his last meal before execution, and his hands were trembling. He was needy and demanding. May the Good Lord help her, but she didn't mind it. He parted her thighs, even with several ribbons still left knotted, and entered her swiftly. She clung to his hot shoulders and dug her fingers into his hard flesh.

"Mine," he groaned into her hair.

Just for now, she thought.

That night she studied his sleeping profile by the light of the August moon through the window. Dark lashes twitched against his cheeks, and his lips moved as he talked in his sleep. Giving commands to her no doubt. His need for her was puzzling. He gave her far more than she could ever give to him, yet he was intent on completing their month together, resorting to these extreme lengths of abduction.

He treated her like a piece of property to be mishandled and brazenly taken from the street just because he needed her. Molly knew she ought to make an attempt to get away, but he would simply chase after her. Better to get this contract over with, and then he would have no further excuse to waylay her. Then they could both go on with their lives as they were before this happened.

Molly flirted with the idea of telling anyone they met on the road that she'd been kidnapped and was held against her will. What would he say to excuse himself? At a toll-gate, she decided to find out and complained to the keeper's wife that the Earl of Everscham had manhandled her into his carriage and spirited her away as his prisoner.

The good lady laughed uproariously and nodded, then went back to her knitting.

At an inn outside Guildford, she considered confiding in the barman, who seemed a jolly, helpful fellow, but the idea passed as soon as a plate of food was put before her. She'd never been so hungry in her life.

Since he'd made no advance preparations for the trip, he'd packed only one small trunk for himself and had not even spared a moment to bath and shave before they set off. At the first roadside inn, he'd sent a message back to Edward Hobbs in London and another on ahead of them to his land agent, but those were the only letters he wrote, the only warnings he gave anyone.

They passed through Surrey and entered the county

of West Sussex, where the countryside rolled along outside the coach window in a pleasant patchwork of fields and woodland. The estate, he informed her stiffly when she inquired, covered more than six hundred acres at the foot of the South Downs.

"How lovely it sounds," she said.

"Humph," was the reply.

When the coach carried them over a bridge across the River Arun, she knew it was not much farther. Molly's excitement mounted, as did her trepidation.

"They will be shocked to see you at the estate," she muttered. "Will they know who you are?"

He glared at her.

"They might think you a beggar at the gate and turn you away." She laughed curtly. "You don't look very noble in your current state. More like a desperate highwayman."

"I can assure you they'll know me."

He was right. A stout fellow at the gatehouse waved them on without hesitation when he saw the fine coach and roan horses approach. Several workers they passed along the wide gravel drive removed their hats and bowed respectfully as the coach rumbled by. There appeared to be a large number of children among them, little boys with happy, ruddy faces, who had less restraint than the elder workers, and leapt up and down, waving at the coach. The estate workers, she concluded, must be a fertile bunch.

Tall oaks and chestnuts flanked their route, shading the horses from the melting afternoon sun, and still they traveled onward for what seemed an interminable amount of time. Molly sat back in her seat, not wanting to seem too impressed by the extent of her heartless kidnapper's domain, but after a while, her natural curiosity drew her forward again to admire the lush scenery.

Through the sentinel trees, she watched fat, woolly sheep grazing contentedly on a great swathe of lush green. Beyond them, another quantity of beech trees, and then sweeping fields, folding one into the other. Eventually, surrounded by a dry moat and raised up on a slight hill, the house itself came into view with the pink and copper sunset falling behind it. Her pulse quickened, overtaking the horses' hooves. The structure in the distance was more of a castle than a house, a vast rambling structure with wings built on over the years, each one showing its age by the amount of ivy claiming its walls. At the very center rose a round medieval tower fortress, the sort of place in which one expected to find skeletons of forgotten prisoners.

"Goodness," she exclaimed. "Do people often get lost in there?"

"Yes," he replied solemnly. "My grandfather had a valet in 1756 who was last seen heading for the west wing. Occasionally, on still, windless nights, one can hear him wailing as his footsteps trail haplessly in search of an exit."

Molly shook her head, and at last, his lips cracked in a small smile.

"You might lose me too," she warned.

"Not a chance."

A little shiver fluttered over her skin as if he'd whispered in her ear.

The horses clattered to a halt before the main door, where a short line of servants waited to greet their arrival. "What will you introduce me as?" she demanded, flustered again.

"Miss Margaret Robbins, of course. What else? Perhaps you prefer Madame Fifi La Roux?"

That was not what she'd meant, but there was no time for further discussion. He leapt out first and helped her down, lifting her with his hands around her waist when she would much rather have descended by her own power.

A stocky, weatherworn fellow stepped forward, hat in his hands. "My lord, how pleasant to have you home again."

"Thank you, Phipps. This is Miss Margaret Robbins, my honored guest. Miss Robbins, this is my land agent, Phipps."

Honored guest. Well, that was respectable enough. A wave of relief swept over her so rapidly she felt the gravel move under her feet. A long line of household staff waited to be introduced, and a tall, angular woman, dressed all in black with a ring of keys at her waist, stepped forward to take over the greeting. As if Phipps might not be trusted to do it properly.

"This is my housekeeper, Mrs. Martindale. She will answer any questions you might have and show you where to find whatever you require. Mrs. Martindale has lived here since the first foundation stones were laid."

The woman's dour countenance did not change. "I certainly have not, young man. Take that back at once."

Surprised to hear him addressed in such an informal way, Molly glanced at Carver and saw him smile. "Well, you know where all the skeletons are buried, and we Danforthes have plenty."

"Yes." She conceded with a stern nod. "That much is true. Welcome to the estate, Miss Robbins. As his lordship said, I can answer any questions you might have. Always come to me, not to him, for he will fill your head with dreadful, shameless lies about this house. He has quite a vivid imagination."

Molly's surprise continued. "He has?"

"Oh yes. There is no limit to the gruesome ghost stories he can conjure up."

Carver quickly drew her onward, taking the steps three at a time with his own long stride and almost causing her to fall on her face. "Don't dally, Miss Robbins," he exclaimed crisply.

"Why the haste? I have plenty of questions to ask Mrs. Martindale."

"I'm sure you do."

"And you don't mean to let me ask them."

"You're my prisoner and captive, Naughty Mouse," he reminded her with a whisper that caressed her cheek. "You'll do as I say, or I might have to tie you up in my dungeon."

"Nonsense, you haven't any dungeon. Lady Mercy told me."

"Aha, but I do. So there! She wouldn't even know about it, being a coddled girl. If you don't believe me, try my patience and see where it gets you." His large hand slid down to her bottom and, out of sight of the others, stole a sly squeeze.

She snorted with laughter, unable to hold it in, even though she feared this made her a terrible wanton hussy, every bit as wicked as he claimed her to be. But almost immediately, she fell into awestruck silence, for they passed into the cavernous main hall. Stretching to the left of the entrance, the vast room held a massive stone chimneypiece, decorated with heraldic shields and rampant lions. A beautifully carved staircase led up to the second floor, but her wide eyes went at once to the enormous portraits hung on the dark paneled wall directly facing the entrance vestibule.

The woman she recognized from the smaller portrait of his mother in Carver's library in the London house, and the man in the companion painting she guessed must be his father, the previous earl. Now she understood why he'd said the locals would know him and not mistake him for anyone else. The resemblance was startling.

"We'll save the tour for later," Carver muttered, still rushing her along by the arm. "Eat first. Food, if you please, Mrs. Martindale."

"You will find the table set in the dining parlor, my lord."

The servants dispersed rapidly, and he took her down the length of the grand hall, through a wide Tudor door, and into an equally impressive chamber with another fireplace and a vaulted ceiling from which hung an iron wheel full of candles. The long trestle table had been set in readiness for their arrival. Apparently they would dine without service, and she was glad of it. She wouldn't want to make a pig of herself on the first night and in full view of the staff. Her mouth watered pitifully at the delicious scent of roast beef and thick, rich gravy. Oh...and if her poor sight could be relied upon...Yorkshire pudding. She was ravenous again already. Must be nerves, she mused.

There was something satisfying about watching her eat. She'd begun to fill out in a very pleasing way, and Carver was no longer afraid that a strong gust of wind might blow her out of his hands. She consumed the supper with gusto, despite the fact that she must have been tired after their journey. Not to mention unsettled by her strange surroundings.

He supposed he ought to feel shame at the way he dragged her into the country with him, but how else was he to keep her to himself? He'd wanted to take her away from London and the bitter-tongued gossips, and he had to act quickly. No time for thinking. There was a vast deal of confusion in his mind, and the only thing that smoothed out the tangles was to have her in his sights, by his side.

"It's late now, but tomorrow I'll take you around the estate," he told her. Then it occurred to him that he didn't even know if she could ride. Well, they could always take out the small curricle, or even the steward's gig. He knew Phipps was anxious to talk with him about repairs to some of the tithe cottages, as well as the main house itself. Why not take her along with him? If he left her in the house, she might start mending and cleaning his garments.

"When was the last time you stayed here?" she asked.

"Last autumn, with Hobbs, but I haven't stayed for any length of time since I came into the title." He speared another slice of beef on his fork.

"Why?"

"I prefer Town."

"Why?" She stared through the candles, her eyes very large and full of wonder. Glad the spark was back, he allowed her to question him, as he never would tolerate it from anyone else.

"More noise, more people. After my father died, this place was too quiet, too large and empty."

"And I suppose there were too many responsibilities to face here."

In the process of cutting into his slice of beef, he stopped and glowered at her. "That was not the point." It was not responsibilities that chased him out, it was ghosts.

"Oh? I thought perhaps it was entirely the point."

"I face my responsibilities. You have no idea."

"I don't suppose I do"—Margaret turned her gaze to her plate—"since you never share your serious thoughts with me, or your problems. I'm not important enough to be told anything."

Carver reached for his wine and then stopped, fingers curling into a fist on the table. "I suggest you tell me your theory of why I stay away, then. I can see you have one, and I'm on tenterhooks to hear it."

When her plush lashes lifted, her eyes were warm. "Forgive me, Danny, but I've seen you abdicate responsibility over the years—handing it to Hobbs or even to your sister. When forced into action, you can be decisive. Look at us now, for instance." She waved her knife. "We wouldn't be sitting here if you hadn't suddenly decided to drag me off the street. But until it's an absolute emergency, you do your very best to avoid decisions. And for the most part, it works well for you, because there is usually someone else there who gives up waiting and makes the choice for you."

He did not interrupt, but let her speak, let her get it all out. Her voice was soft, mellow, very pleasant, and never shrill. He didn't even mind when it insulted him. Quite possibly he could forgive her anything, he realized, appalled by the thought.

"It's not your fault that you've been spoiled and cosseted, protected from making decisions. You can't help being born an earl. You are lucky to have blindly devoted, loyal servants like Edward Hobbs in London and Mr. Phipps here. Not to mention a sister who is more than happy to direct your life and would even pick a bride for you, if you let her. I daresay if I was born with people to do everything for me, I, too, would have become lazy and complacent." She smiled and continued her meal, apparently satisfied with her saucy little speech.

Trouble was, the impertinent madam was right. He had been lucky, and yes, he had escaped responsibility on several occasions, neatly sidestepping to let it land on the shoulders of faithful Hobbs or his meddling sister, Mercy.

"But I mean to change all that," he said suddenly, making her look up again. "That's why I'm here now. You'll see."

"Will I?"

He cleared his throat. "I have been afraid to make mistakes in my life."

She put down her fork. "We all make mistakes, Danny. That's how we learn."

"Indeed."

She beamed.

Once again he realized how different she was than any other woman he knew. At times she made him feel…stupid…humbled. And then she lifted him up again, a new man.

He could not remember why he'd ever thought her plain.

"So tell me some of your horrid ghost stories," she urged, eyes twinkling under her lashes.

"Where should I begin? Shall I tell you about the third Earl of Everscham, who murdered his wife with a wood axe and still chases young maids around the upper floors with his bloodied weapon? Or shall I begin with the story of old shepherd Bob, killed by a savage wolf and left for all eternity to seek his lost sheep in the low meadow whenever there is mist in the valley?"

"Danny! I didn't know you had it in you."

Pleased that he managed to amaze her, Carver continued regaling his prisoner with bloodthirsty tales while she filled her stomach with roast beef, eating enough for a woman twice her size.

Mrs. Martindale returned with a large candelabrum to lead them up to bed. To Molly's surprise and relief, she was given her own chamber, a very large one with a four-poster bed and windows that she was informed overlooked the rose garden. Dusk was loosening its grip on the sky by then, and it was too dark to confirm the view for herself, but the housekeeper assured her a very pretty garden awaited below.

"It was the Countess of Everscham's favorite place," Mrs. Martindale explained as she moved around the room, lighting more candles. "She spent hours tending those roses. Sadly, I don't have the time to devote to it, but then I never had green fingers. The gardener, Jenkins—although a capable fellow—is somewhat dismissive of decorative gardening and puts more of his time into the home farm. His expertise, as he will proudly tell you, is in vegetables, for one will never starve as long as one plants vegetables. I'm afraid he sees flowers as less than useful and beneath his dignity."

Molly answered at once that she would be happy to tend the roses while she was there. The housekeeper looked at her sharply, as if suddenly seeing her in a new light. "Well, that would be most useful, madam. If you're sure…"

"Certainly. I am happy to help in any way I can."

For a few moments, as she unpacked her trunk—filled with Lady Mercy's clothes, which were all too short for her—she was aware of Mrs. Martindale's stern regard closely observing all her movements. Then the housekeeper asked if she was in need of a maid to help her.

"My girls have not had a vast amount of experience in tending to a lady, for his lordship has never brought a guest such as yourself with him when he visited before, but I'm sure they would be adequate. I can send them up to you, if you desire it."

"Oh no, Mrs. Martindale I can manage. Thank you."

"Very good, madam. When would you like to be awakened in the morning?"

Molly had never needed to be awakened by another person in her life. She was usually the first one up and often the last to bed. The only morning heralds she'd known were the pigeons outside her window in London, or the cockerel in the yard outside her family's tiny cottage in Sydney Dovedale. "I'll wake myself, Mrs. Martindale. I'm sure I'll be too excited to oversleep. I'm looking forward to exploring the estate."

Again the older woman looked at her oddly, inclined her head in a half bow, and then left the room, closing the door with a gentle thud.

Molly tested the bed by bouncing lightly on the edge and found it comfortable but firm. There was a faint odor of mothballs, but she supposed that was inevitable, since she'd been told by Lady Mercy that the house was mostly shut up all year round. A dish of potpourri beside the bed helped sweeten the air, and a fire had evidently been lit earlier in the grate to chase away the damp, for there was a lingering hint of wood smoke. All these efforts made just for her. She was quite overwhelmed by it.

Mrs. Martindale had said he never brought anyone like her to the house. Whatever that meant.

She peered through the drapes at a star-filled sky. The moon seemed larger than it did in London. How quiet the land was too, she thought. Just a soft owl hoot somewhere in the distance. She supposed if she had lived all her life in London and known only the noise and smells of the town, it might have been eerie to hear her own breath and her own heart drumming. But she, of course, was raised in the country. She was not the grand lady of Town that Mrs. Martindale had expected.

A sudden click behind her brought Molly out of her reverie.

Her kidnapper, wrapped in a velvet-trimmed bed robe, carrying a candle, appeared through an opening in the wall paneling.

"I thought you were the lost valet or the third earl with his wood axe," she quipped, her pulse skipping.

He set his candle on the dresser. "I would hope you'd make more noise and protest than that if it was someone other than me, Miss Robbins, appearing in your bedchamber in the still of night."

"Perhaps," she chirped. "Depends how handsome he might be."

Slipping off his robe, he tossed it to her bed, and she watched the silver drift of moonlight caress his fine musculature. He was very confident in his nudity. Why would he not be? He'd had bouquets of beautiful women sing his praises in bed.

"Turn around," he whispered, crossing the floor toward her. "Since you have no maid, I must undress you tonight."

So she let him unhook her gown and untie the laces of her stays. "You are fond of your secret doors," she muttered. "I suppose you have them all over this house."

"They are the invention of a previous, very resourceful Danforthe." She felt his lips on the nape of her neck.

"A house this old must hold many secrets."

His breath tickled her shoulder. "It certainly always felt that way. As if the adults kept things from me."

"I suppose, because you were an only child for ten years, you were left to amuse yourself."

"Yes. There were no other playmates here, just ghosts, secrets, and mysteries. I was always fond of mysteries. That's what first drew me to you, Margaret."

She scoffed. "There's no mystery about me."

Her clothing fell away, and then his hands slid her

drawers down. "On the contrary, you are all mystery, all dark hidden places and buried treasure."

Molly laughed. "There is nothing hidden from you anymore." He had kissed and caressed every part of her body. What could there be left for him to claim?

He led her away from the window. "Now I have you all to myself. No work. No other people to interfere—yours or mine."

She raised a hand and ran her fingers through his midnight hair, just as she'd imagined doing for so many years. "Mrs. Martindale wonders about me. I suppose you can lift a girl out of the servant's hall and take her upstairs with the fine folk, but she'll always be a downstairs sort of girl."

"Only if that's what she prefers." As her hand drifted down the side of his face, he turned his head and kissed her palm. "Do you?"

In all honesty, Molly wasn't sure where she belonged anymore. Here she was, living the superior life with her aristocratic lover, wearing Lady Mercy's clothes and being waited on. She couldn't turn her nose up at it. What woman didn't want to be pampered like a princess in a fairy tale at least once in her life?

"Tonight," he whispered, "you're my upstairs lady, and I'll be your downstairs fellow."

She chuckled. "Danny, I don't want you to be my servant."

"Why not?"

"It wouldn't suit you."

He made a wounded face. "I always thought I'd look rather splendid in footman's livery."

He would too, she thought, chagrined. "But you'd

have to do what people said. All the time. And keep your opinions to yourself."

A deep crease wrinkled his brow. "Ah."

"Precisely. Far better you stay as you are and just be…pretty."

"Pretty?"

Molly struggled to remain solemn. "It is what you do best, your lordship." She turned and walked to the bed. "*One* of the things you do best," she added, sliding under the coverlet and holding it for him.

After a slight delay, he followed her to the bed. "So what you're saying, Miss Robbins, is that I'm little better than a plaything for you."

She looked at him somberly. "Why would you want to be anything else?"

He paused, shook his head, and then slid his warm hand over her breast. Her nipple pricked instantly to attention. "Since I'm here solely for your entertainment, Miss Robbins"—he bent his head to kiss the little peak—"you'd best make the most of me in the last days we have left."

"I intend to." Not that she needed any encouragement, or warning about time passing them by.

His fingers tickled downward, over her stomach. "So tonight I am the servant to do your bidding. Where shall I begin?"

"That's a good place. Down a little farther."

"You want me downstairs, my lady?"

She sighed as his hand slid between her thighs. "Yes. Just there."

Slowly he kissed his way down her body, following his fingers. "As you wish, my lady."

The damp tip of his tongue trailed across her skin

and then delved down to tend the heated little flame darting and pulsing at her core. Molly writhed and stretched, excitement racing through her from head to toe. "You're a very good servant below stairs, my darling Danny. Most obliging and efficient."

He couldn't answer because he was busy lapping over her sensitive flesh with steady, possessive strokes of his masterful tongue.

"And your attention to detail is becoming...quite... ex...excep...exceptional." A short while after this, she gave up speech herself. At least the sort of decent conversation that made any sense.

Twenty-two

IN THE MORNING SHE WOKE TO FIND HIM SPRAWLED OUT on his stomach, taking up most of the room, snoring loudly into his pillow. Molly knew she should have been tired too, but she wasn't. Not then. As she'd said to the housekeeper, there was too much to explore.

Half an hour later she was descending the grand staircase, eager to tour the house at her own pace, without him rushing her along, letting her see only what he wanted to show. This was her chance to pry.

The sun was bright that day, a cloudless sky stretching overhead, blue never ending, but inside the house it was cool, corners swathed in shadow. She stood a while in the hall, staring up at the large portraits of the previous earl and his wife. They grimly stared back, wondering, no doubt, why a mere dressmaker thought she had any right to observe them with such a searching perusal. Molly thought that if she was the countess, she would want to be painted with her husband, not separately. It would have made for a sweeter study. But from the look on the fourth earl's face, he didn't care much for sweet.

Feeling the chill of his stern regard, she eventually

turned and walked out into the sunny day. Barely had she taken two steps across the gravel when a young foxhound ran by with a ball in its mouth, and the small whirlwind following it almost took her off her feet.

"Sorry, missus!" the boy shouted.

Instantly she recognized that bright freckled face and stopped him. "What are you doing here?" It was the boy pickpocket who used to run around the streets with his friends in London. The same boy who once impressed Carver with his knowledge of horses.

"I live 'ere, missus." He didn't seem to recognize her at first. "I've got to catch my pup." So she let him go and watched as he ran after the foxhound. A moment later she spied the gardener with his wheel-barrow, heading around a corner of the house. Molly quickened her pace to catch up with him and ask about the boy.

"That's young Tom, Miss Robbins," she was told. "He's one of the boys his lordship took in to work with the horses. You'll find there's a lot of 'em about."

She learned that Carver provided shelter on the estate for many transplanted boys from the streets of London and other towns nearby. They were all learning a trade. Not only that, but in some cases their younger siblings had also been brought to live on the estate grounds. Tom's little sister, Susie, was in training with the housemaids. A small, wide-eyed girl, too shy to speak, she reminded Molly of herself.

The children were healthy and happy, well shod, eager, and clearly looked after by the staff under whom they worked. Over the next few days she met many of them, and talking to each one was like peeling back the magician's curtains, behind which the true Carver

Danforthe had kept his secrets. He rarely spoke to her of these tasks he'd taken on. He was a man who made light of good deeds, and praise in any form made him shrug and itch and fidget, as if he had a shirt full of stinging nettles.

But he could hide from her no longer behind his beastly guise.

"Does your sister know about all your work here with the children?" she would ask him later.

"Good Lord, no. Why would I want her sticking her oar in?" And when he smiled in that mischievous way, Molly knew he took great delight in doing all this without his sister's knowledge. How he liked his secrets, his hidden treasures.

"I wish other people knew the truth about Carver Danforthe," she said softly.

"Why? What do you mean? Who cares what they think?"

But she longed for others to know the real Carver and to value him as she did, not to dismiss him as just another entitled, dissolute rake. It hurt her heart to think that he was not appreciated for the good things he tried to do.

"What's this?" he demanded sternly, standing over her and raising a finger to wipe a few droplets from her lashes. "Where is all this water coming from, young woman? It will not do. I won't have it."

She sniffed. "I'll cry if I want to."

"Indeed you will not." He cupped her face in his hands and lifted it for a kiss. "It's not in your contract."

❧

He strode out to the stables, ready to instruct the

groom on finding a sidesaddle for Margaret. He knew there must be one that had belonged to his mother or his sister somewhere about the place. But his guest was there before him and chatting amiably in the cobbled yard with the young men who tended the stables. She must have been up with the lark. Her face was flushed with good color, and she did not appear in the least weary. Irrepressible youth, he mused.

When the grooms saw him and snapped to attention, she swiveled around excitedly. "There you are. I've been waiting."

He should have reprimanded her for speaking to him that way before the grooms and stable lads, but in the next moment, he had something else to worry about. She held her skirts up with one arm and, using the aid of a mounting block, swung herself up onto one of the hunters. There she sat proudly astride the beast without a saddle but with the ease of an experienced rider.

"Have we no sidesaddle?" he muttered, quite certain he should not approve. His father certainly never would have, but then his father would have approved of absolutely nothing about Margaret Robbins, a stubborn, independent woman with rebellious ideas about life.

"I don't need one of those," she replied, gathering the reins in her gloved hands. "I'm a country girl, your lordship. We are made of stronger stuff. I'd much rather ride like this."

And showing off an improper length of shapely leg above her riding boots, he thought churlishly. The grooms were doing their best not to notice, but one of the young stable lads had just dropped a hay fork on his foot, prongs first.

"Do hurry," she exclaimed, turning her horse toward the gravel path that led from the stable yard. "You did say the estate is six hundred acres, and I'll never see it all if we don't start soon."

Apparently she'd taken him literally when he said he would show her the estate, although he'd really intended to take her around only a few scenic spots. Trust Robbins to insist on seeing every detail.

A second hunter was saddled and ready for him, so he mounted with no further delay, deciding there would be time enough later to lecture her on the indecency of riding bareback and astride.

But as he caught up with her, he couldn't resist teasing. "You were once so prim and prudish, Miss Robbins. Yet here you are displaying your legs in a most indecorous fashion. What has become of you?"

She turned her head to look at him. "You corrupted me, Danny."

He very much doubted that. The naughty Miss Robbins was there all along, hiding in his wainscoting. But it was likely she didn't know herself back then and was still discovering her own capabilities just as she helped him find his.

Carver took her around the fields that day. Harvest would soon be upon them, and the swaying wheat was high and golden. He showed her the orchards, where workers picked fruit and stacked baskets and boxes as high as themselves. He also took her to visit the cottages bordering the estate and introduced her to several tenants. If it was any other woman, he'd known he would never have let her greet his tenants, and she would very probably not have wanted to. But Margaret displayed a keen interest in everything they saw that day, and Carver took quiet pleasure in watching her talk easily to the farm laborers and their families. There was no uncomfortable condescension, for she saw herself as one of them, and they, after the first surprise, were happy to invite her into their homes.

Phipps rode out to meet them at the tithe cottages to discuss repairs recently undertaken, as well as those that were still required. Although Hobbs had reported to him regularly on the state of his tenants' cottages, Carver had been content simply to throw money at the problem. Now he opened his mind to the idea of more substantial changes and developments, rather than hasty fixes.

"Let's get new thatch on all the cottages and renovate," said Carver. "Not just those that are damaged. An ounce of prevention is worth a ton of cure."

Phipps looked pleased in a quiet, undemonstrative way. "Very good, my lord."

The sun was high, the air warm and flowing with the fragrance of late summer, and riding with Margaret at his side, he felt a deep sense of pride in the estate. He showed her the places he'd played as a boy, including the ditch he fell in when learning to ride.

He told her for sympathy, but of course she laughed. And how he loved to see her laugh.

In the afternoon they stopped to let the horses drink from a brook and enjoy the shade of a willow. Carver took her inside the threshing barn, where dust beams danced in the air, gilded with gold from the sun's rays that filtered through the old planks. Stacks of hay bales were stored there now, but very soon the barn would be filled with activity once the harvest was underway.

"The people seem pleased that you are here," she said. "You should come more often and stay longer."

"I should." He was looking at her as the tiny speckles of light hovered and darted around her face. Ten days left. For the first time in his life, the clocks were moving too fast.

But how could he make her stay longer? They'd both agreed to that contract, and she wanted to go back to her work. He could not keep her from it—it wouldn't be fair, knowing how she loved it and how successful she was. Besides, he did not like more permanent relationships. A man should be free to come and go, not let himself be pinned down. There were many other women out there, and devoting himself to only one would be a mistake. What would become of him then, if she fell ill and died or left him or didn't love him as much as he loved her?

Suddenly he was frozen to the spot, his feet like lead in his boots.

Loved her. Did he?

Was it possible, after all these years of avoiding any tenderness of feeling, that he, Carver Danforthe, fifth Earl of Everscham, had fallen in love with his sister's lady's maid? *Former* lady's maid. A woman of incredible talents. A woman who looked at him as if he was worth looking at, worth more than his bank account and his title. Worth caring for.

"Margaret."

"Yes?"

How did one say these things? His sister would have plenty of advice, but she was not there. She was off gallivanting in the Norfolk countryside with her farmer.

He wanted to keep Margaret Robbins in his house

and never let her out of his sight. It was a dangerous thought, an impossible, potentially ruinous need, and he must be rid of it at once for the sake of his own sanity.

"From now on you will ride sidesaddle like a proper lady," he said, barely listening to his own voice, watching only the disturbed speckles of sunlight. "And have some modesty when mounting before the grooms."

A very slight frown crossed her brow. "I told you I prefer to ride without a saddle."

"It is not a matter for debate. I am the master here."

Her gaze lowered to his feet.

"It is also for your safety when riding about the estate." His own mother had died after a hunting accident, when she boldly took a blind leap over a hedge instead of passing through a gate. An example of an obstinate woman coming to harm because she insisted on doing things her way. He could not have anything happening to Margaret.

"Very well," she replied, but the surly downward bend of her lips warned Carver that she would not pay heed to his warnings. The wild streak he'd recognized in her long ago was even more evident now that she'd come out of her shell. Bringing her out of London had also changed her demeanor, as if she felt more at home in the country. He had foolishly not considered that possibility when he brought her there. "Are there any other rules I must follow?" she demanded crossly.

"I'm glad you asked. Yes. Plenty."

"I'm sure." One eyebrow curved like a bow, ready to release an arrow. Possibly poison-tipped.

"The most important one is that you will do as I say. At all times."

"And if I don't?"

"If I catch you riding astride again, you'll find out. Won't you?"

She pursed her lips and folded her arms, very unladylike.

"Now smile, Margaret. That's an order."

"So I'm *your* servant again?"

He didn't answer. He couldn't, because he didn't know what she was anymore.

Rather than smile, the hussy stuck out her tongue, deliberately antagonizing and taunting him into action. He took a step toward her, and she leapt around a beam, dodging his reach. Stripping off the burden of his riding coat, he followed his mischievous playmate in and out of the hay bales and around sturdy beams. She was laughing now and breathless, as was he. It was twenty years at least since he'd played a game like this, but suddenly he was a boy again with a lifetime ahead of him. No mistakes yet, no regrets. No sadness. Just the dizzy pursuit of a pretty woman whose hair had fallen loose down her back in glorious, tumbled mahogany waves that tempted his fingers.

She tripped over a hay bale, and he followed, landing heavily on her. She didn't appear to mind as he tugged her skirts upward without ceremony.

"Oh, sir, don't tear my gown," she wheezed, panting.

With a low growl, he swept her warm hair aside and nipped the back of her neck gently in his teeth. "Be still then, and submit to your master's desire, wench." Already his hand crept up over her stocking tops and garters.

"Oh, sir, be gentle."

"Why should I?" He stroked the curve of her

bottom through her drawers, his mind filled with images of Margaret riding astride in that reckless fashion, showing her stockings off. "You must be punished for your defiance."

"I'll be good, sir. From now on."

"Yes, you will." He spanked her, not too hard.

"Ouch. You rotten bugger!" But he noted the lift of her hips and the little wriggle, deliberately taunting. The catch in her breath, and even the way she gripped the hay bale with her fingers, told Carver she was enjoying herself.

"Now, now, wench. That's no way to address your lord and master." A second spank followed, and then he laid his hand over her bottom, fingers splayed, demonstrating ownership. "Promise me you will not show your legs again to any other man."

She rested her upper half on her elbows, her chin cupped in her palm. "I'll have to think about it."

For that she got a third spank, a little harder this time. "By all means keep me waiting," he growled, resting his hand on the heated swell of her right cheek, pressing his groin against her as she spread her thighs over the bale and tried to keep her balance. "I can spank you till the cows come home."

Finally she sighed. "Oh, very well then."

He gently squeezed her bottom. "Very well then what?"

"I won't show my legs to any other man."

"Better, wench."

"Are you done with my punishment, then?"

"Not quite." Carver positioned himself swiftly, unhooked his breeches, and angled his erect manhood through the slit in her drawers, unable to wait another second.

She gasped in surprise and delight. "If I'd known this was to be the punishment, I would have misbehaved much more often."

Bending over her again, his groin flush to the back of her thighs, he whispered huskily in her ear, "You'll be the death of me, Margaret Robbins." She giggled as he rocked forward. He couldn't get enough. Neither, it seemed, could she. Perhaps, he mused, death by desire was her design for him after all. She was merciless.

Twenty-three

THE DAYS PASSED, ROLLING GENTLY BY LIKE A STEADILY bubbling stream. On some mornings she watched Carver with the horses on his stud farm. She liked it best when he was unaware of her presence and she could spy on him in secret. He had a gentle way with the animals, and when he rode around the paddock in his rolled up shirtsleeves, a peace came over his face that she had rarely seen at other times. There was no haughty superiority when he conferred with his grooms about a sick horse or a pregnant mare. He laughed easily, worried openly, listened and advised without sarcasm. She even saw him slap his blacksmith on the shoulder once as they shared a joke, which she could not hear but strongly suspected was not fit for her ears anyway.

As she'd promised the housekeeper, Molly took a long basket and a pruning knife into the rose garden most afternoons, while Carver was busy with Phipps or meeting with people who came up from the village to discuss their problems. Molly could see that he was much more efficient and effective in his role than he thought he was. People may have feared and respected his father, but she heard from the staff how much they liked and trusted Carver.

Rising early every day, keen to make the most of every moment, she explored the house and country-side, finding ways to help Mrs. Martindale and the maids as much as they would allow her. Once, as she approached the kitchens, she heard the cook and housemaids discussing her.

"That young lady is just what he needs. Pity he'd never marry her, of course."

"Why not?"

"Why not? You daft 'apeth! She's just a lady's maid. Done well for herself, and no mistake, but not of the caliber he must marry. She's got no title, no breeding, and no family fortune. In any case, his lordship has always said he'll never take a wife."

"But he needs an heir for the estate."

"He has cousins enough to inherit. And he doesn't want children. I heard him say once he is not cut out for fatherhood."

Molly stepped back farther into the shadow behind the door.

"Aye, well he had a hard childhood in this house, trying to fill his father's shoes *and* make up for the loss of an elder brother. Then after the tragedy of losing his parents, being left to look after his little sister. 'Tis no surprise he avoids marriage and doesn't care to have any children of his own. Oh, but those awful cousins! Not one of them is half the man he is, and it'll be a sad day when one of them takes the reins of this place."

To Molly's relief, the housekeeper must have entered the kitchen from the outside door at that moment, for she silenced their gossiping immediately, and they all got back to their work.

She waited several minutes before she walked in to greet them, not wanting anyone to know she'd overheard.

Although she already knew Carver's views on marriage and fatherhood, it wasn't any less painful to hear his staff talk of it.

Of course, he had enough children to deal with now, did he not? Those he rescued from the rough streets of London. Ironically, the man who did not want children of his own took on the children no one else wanted.

The roses in his mother's garden were overblown at that time of the year, although with a careful pruning, Molly thought some of the plants might yet enjoy one more late bloom before the weather turned. She tidied and trimmed diligently, putting shape back into the twisted vines around the arbors. She raked up dead leaves and fallen petals, delivering them in a small wheelbarrow for the gardener's disposal. She even mended the broken bird feeder and stocked it with scraps from the kitchen. Slowly she brought the neglected garden back to life.

As she strolled along the narrow paths, drinking in the thick, sweet fragrance, she felt serenity and contentment settle over her. Sometimes, when coming upon the pleasant surprise of a stone bench or a wooden seat under the leafy arbors, she sat for a spell and found herself nodding off. It was unheard of for her to take naps during the day.

Perhaps this life of leisure was already rubbing off on her, she mused.

The rose garden occupied an area behind the south-facing side of the main building. It was enclosed by rugged stone walls on three sides and the hothouse on the fourth. A pretty wrought iron scrollwork gate led into the pleasant sanctuary, but kept out the sheep that wandered freely all over the lawns. With a gentle squeak, that rusty gate warned of any other visitor soon to approach, and today it brought the house-keeper, Mrs. Martindale, who came looking for her.

"Tea is served, madam, in the green parlor."

The green parlor, it had been explained to her during a tour of the house, was the sitting room where the countess once greeted visitors in the afternoons. There were French doors that opened onto a sunny paved area and overlooked the vast green lawns. The room itself seemed to have been preserved exactly as it was when the countess was alive, and Molly got the sense that dust covers were removed just at the last minute before the carriage brought them up to the entrance steps. Molly felt honored even to sit there, let alone have tea served to her within its elegant, refined walls, but she was hungry again, and there would be dainty, sugary little cakes. For such treats, she could overlook the fact that she really had no right to be there.

"Thank you, Mrs. Martindale. That sounds lovely."

The housekeeper was looking around at the newly trimmed bushes and the arbor, which no longer sprouted wayward tentacles. "My, you have been busy, madam. I knew you came out here every afternoon, but I hadn't realized how much work you've done."

"I have to find something to do with my hands, or I'd go quite mad," she confessed with a sigh. "I'm afraid a ladylike life of leisure is not for me."

"So I see." The lady finally cracked a smile. "We must find more things to keep you entertained."

His lordship was managing that quite nicely, she thought wryly, but pushing that fact aside, she leapt at the chance to be useful. "If there is any sewing to be done, I'd gladly help."

"I'm sure I can find some, Miss Robbins." The woman paused. She seemed about to turn back to the house, but changed her mind. "It is very good to see his lordship smiling for once. To hear his laughter. It seems we have you to thank for this."

Molly felt her cheeks flush. "I don't know how much of a part I play in it, but I am glad if he is happier." Gathering her courage to be curious while she had the ear of someone who might actually give her information, she added, "I have heard his childhood here was quite sad, Mrs. Martindale."

The housekeeper glanced over at the gate and then, assured of their being alone, replied, "Indeed. He struggled so for his parents' affection, but they were both taken from him while he was relatively young and his character not yet fully formed. It was very hard."

"I'm sure. And his elder brother also died here." She'd never dared ask Carver about that. It felt rather sneaky to ask the housekeeper behind his back, but she was desperate to know more. His childhood in that house had been much on her mind of late. Almost as if she saw and heard ghosts sometimes, just as he'd warned her she might.

"Yes." Mrs. Martindale glanced over at the rusty

gate again. "The firstborn child was only two when he passed on. It was devastating to the earl and countess. Especially the countess. She took to her bed for a month or more, and I feared she was inconsolable at the loss of her son. The physician said she may not have another child, so there was great fear for the future of the estate, you see. The previous earl had no love for his cousins—had borne a grudge against his uncle for many years—and did not want the place falling into their hands." There was another uneasy pause, during which Molly felt as if even the falling rose petals clung on a moment longer, fearful of missing something. "And then, along came the second boy, and all was well."

"It was lucky there was another son to inherit."

"Most fortunate indeed." The other lady began to move away. "I must see if I can find that mending for you, Miss Robbins."

When Carver found Molly in the green parlor later that day, she was occupied with a basket full of mending, so absorbed in it that she forgot to remove her spectacles until it was too late, and then she fumbled, dropping them to the carpet.

"What's all this?" he demanded, gesturing at the wicker basket by her feet.

"It's called work. Don't worry, it's not contagious."

With her toe, she tried to push her spectacles out of sight under the chair, but he stooped, picked them up, cleaned them on his sleeve, and handed them to her. Quite casually. As if it was the most normal thing in the world and he'd known about them all along.

"I suppose you ate all the cake again. Any more tea left at least?" He dropped into a chair beside her, pursed his lips in a tuneless whistle, and reached for the newspaper.

It suddenly struck her as vastly amusing. Here they were, like an old married couple, sitting together and having tea. The lady's maid and the nefarious rake. What an odd pairing.

Ouch! She'd pricked her finger. Hastily she slid her spectacles on and got back to the mending. Other mistresses would probably spend their afternoons in floaty lace and feathers, waiting about for him and with nothing else to occupy their time. She, however, was not like that and couldn't be even if she tried. In a way, he had just silently acknowledged the fact. Sitting about on her backside, waiting to entertain a man, was the last thing she'd do, and he knew it. Just as she knew he wasn't thinking of her every minute of the day.

Oh well, it couldn't all be about the lust and the passion, could it?

"What are you laughing at, Mouse?" he muttered, shaking out his paper.

"You."

"Of course, what else?"

It was comfortable to sit quietly in that little parlor with him. Almost too comfortable. Perhaps she *ought* to get up and do the dance of the seven veils for him. That thought made her laugh even harder.

But as she bent over her sewing, she felt a sudden hot wave of nausea. If she wasn't careful, all that sweet cake would make a reappearance.

"Tell me about your cousins," she said after searching for subjects to take her mind off the strange churning going on in her stomach. "I've never heard you or Lady Mercy talk about them."

"Probably because they are all obnoxious brats."

"A Danforthe family trait, isn't it?" she teased coyly.

"Most amusing, Miss Robbins."

"But one of them will inherit this estate."

He sighed. "Felix. The son of my father's cousin, and the biggest bore you would ever meet."

"Won't you be sorry to leave everything to him then?"

"I've never looked at it that way. The estate has never really been mine." He paused. For a moment she thought he would not speak further on the subject, but he took a breath and plowed onward. "It belongs to the Everscham name, and it goes to the next male Danforthe. I am merely the current custodian."

His eyes were black, cold, looking away from her. She thought of all the improvements she'd seen and heard of him making over the last few days. "But you will make your mark," she said. "You have already."

"Have I? I daresay my father would be surprised to see the place still standing."

"Well, you are not him. We all try to live up to our parents' expectations, but we still have to make our own way in the world. If we did not, if everything always remained the same and we never learned anything from our time on earth, there would be no point in us being here, would there?"

Finally he turned his eyes back to her, and they warmed slowly, steadily. Until they were almost pure silver, polished and shining in the afternoon sun that lit that comfortable parlor.

Molly felt another sudden burst of nausea. She'd meant to smile back at him but found she couldn't. That fluttering sensation deep in her belly did not go away. Later, she managed to slip away to the privy, and there she purged her sickness without anyone knowing.

It soon returned.

She hoped it would go away, but with a steady, inexorable rhythm, the heated waves of sickness continued. She sat in her chamber, fingers screwed tightly around his handkerchief—which was never far from her possession these days—and tried to quell the panic. Molly Robbins, fallen woman, was now, almost certainly, with child out of wedlock. Molly had done her best to conceal the truth from herself, but she knew enough about pregnancy, having witnessed her mother's constant toil, to recognize the signs that heralded a new brother or sister. Her descent into the abyss was complete. Frederick Dawes had warned her, had he not? The sinful Town would get her in the end. And so it did.

But it was too late for weeping and thrashing her pillows about. The problem must be faced with a practical mind, a steady hand, and a straight stitch.

Carver had made his feelings plain on the matter of unwed women keeping their babies, but she knew at once that she could never give hers away. If she discussed the matter with him, they would argue. It would spoil their last few days. Molly did not want him to think she expected his help or more of his money. She was old enough to know what she risked when she signed that contract with him.

The next day, when she expressed a desire to stay in rather than ride out with Carver, he seemed mildly disappointed but accepted her choice without pushing the issue. He kissed her forehead before he left, and Molly went back to her basket of mending.

She took another tour of his house, this time by herself, wanting to keep a picture of the place in her head, hoping that when she was far away she would recall every corner. Sadness almost overwhelmed her at the thought of leaving, but she had to put aside her own feelings and remember that life would go on. His life without her, and hers without him. They'd had this time together, and it was better than nothing. It must be.

Twenty-four

"THE YOUNG LADY WAS MOST DETERMINED, MY LORD." The housekeeper hurried along at his side. "I did advise her against it, but she had the idea in her head and could not be dissuaded."

"I'm sure you did your best, Mrs. Martindale. She's a stubborn creature." They came to the attic steps, and he called up them, "Miss Robbins, kindly come down here."

No reply. He took the candelabrum and slowly mounted the steep, narrow steps. The attic of the house stretched the entire length of the oldest section. The rafters rose in a low point, requiring that he bend his head to fit under, and as he stepped cautiously along the old beams, he took care to steer around the thick, straggling spiders' webs that swayed in the drafts. There he found her, with a solitary candle, kneeling among the dusty old coffers and hampers, looking at some faded baby clothes and broken toys.

It was inevitable, he supposed, that the Mouse should seek this place out. She was not afraid of the dark or spiders, and thumbed her nose at the idea of ghosts. Supernatural spirits should probably be more fearful of her, he mused.

"Good Lord." He hunkered down beside her as she found a doll with no arms or legs. "I believe that was my sister's. She was very hard on her toys, as you can see."

"At least she played with them." She tilted her head. "I understand you weren't allowed to play with yours."

Again he was struck by how much she knew about him, things no other woman ever bothered to find out. "Some of them. I didn't have much of a boyhood. It was expected that I follow my father about and learn how to manage the estate. There was never much time for games."

"How sad." Her gentle sigh teased the flames of his candelabrum as he set it down on the flat lid of a trunk.

"I made up for it as an adult. It sometimes seems as if I've done nothing but play games ever since I turned eighteen." He added dryly, "As I'm sure you'd be the first to agree."

She nodded. "If your older brother had lived, he would be the earl."

"Indeed."

Suddenly she reached out and took his hand. Her slender fingers knitted through his larger ones. It was almost as if she feared he might run away from her. "You don't remember him?"

"I was born after he died. I was the replacement heir. It was the only reason they had me."

Her wide eyes looked wet. She seemed pale and fragile today. "It is tragic when a child dies so young. It must have been terrible for your parents."

He did not usually talk of these matters, but with her clever fingers so tightly wound around his own, he felt calmer, better able to view the past without flinching. "Yes," he admitted softly. "They adored him, by all accounts. I'm afraid I turned out to be a very sorry substitute."

Margaret shuffled around on her knees. "Don't say that. I'm sure they loved you just as much. Why wouldn't they? You were their son too."

But he doubted they ever felt the same for him. He knew his parents must have been wary of loving another child after their tragic loss. That was one way to explain his mother's distance and his father's resentful manner, which—thanks to a violent temper—too often descended into cruelty.

Shortly before the end of his life, his father had warned Carver never to give all of himself in a relationship. *Only a glutton for punishment leaves his heart unguarded.* All these years later, Carver remembered those words, but now they seemed more bitter than wise.

He squeezed her hand and then feared he might have crushed her bones. He was a great clumsy oaf. Should never have—

Suddenly, Margaret leaned forward and placed a warm kiss on his cheek. With that one small gesture he was lost and found, all at the same time.

Nothing else mattered at that moment but her happiness.

"Margaret, I—"

"Look," she said. "There is a large box here, and I can't get it open. Will you try?"

Try? He would have broken it open with his own thick head for her, he mused. But that was fortunately not necessary. After he wrestled with the lock for a few moments, the lid broke free, and they gained access to contents that must have been hidden there—by the thick lacing of cobwebs—for thirty years or more. At least as long as Carver had been living.

With all the determination of an intrepid, fearless adventurer, Margaret eagerly dug around inside, her entire top half disappearing for several moments. Then, with a cry of delight, she brought something out into the candlelight, cleaned it on her skirt, and held it up for his perusal. It was a wooden box with an intricately carved lid.

"Must have belonged to my father," he muttered.

She stared at it for a moment and then very slowly eased the box open, as if afraid something dreadful might spring out at her. Inside was a colorful pattern formed of miniature tiles, like a Roman mosaic.

Carver explained, "He used to collect them. I'd forgotten, but now I recall seeing boxes like this when I was very young."

Margaret bent over the box in her lap and was silent.

"What is it?" he demanded.

Slowly she turned it to show him the interior. "Love birds," she whispered.

"So it would seem." He smiled, but she still stared at the box. "Margaret, your spectacles need cleaning." They were wet with tears and smudged with dust. He hated to see her cry, and he'd told her this many times, but she continued to defy him.

She handed the box to him and rooted around inside the large chest, where she found two more similar boxes. Each one brought a small gasp of amazement from her lips.

"If you like them, you can have them," he said, trying to understand what made her so excited. They were pretty enough, he supposed. For boxes with nothing inside but pictures. He would rather have found something real inside.

At last she took off her glasses and wiped them on her sleeve, but she was very pale, her hands unsteady. "Where did your father get these?"

"I don't know. His travels, I expect. Why?"

She shook her head. "Mrs. Bathurst has some just like them. *Just* like them."

"The old Cyprian living in your boarding house?"

"Yes." She took a deep breath. "Her lover gave them to her. She called him a princely lover. Perhaps I took her too literally."

"Well, that's odd. But I suppose there were other boxes made."

Margaret raised her eyes to his. "I suppose so." There was such gravity in those three words that he held her gaze for even longer. "This house keeps a lot of secrets," she whispered.

"Yes. I'm sure there are dusty boxes all over this attic."

Suddenly she said, "Have you ever been to a workhouse, Danny?"

He didn't answer directly, because he didn't want her to know yet that he'd visited the institution at St. Giles Cripplegate, in search of her friend's lost son. Since he had no results yet to report, he said nothing. Instead, he took her hand and kissed it. "I suppose you would love me more if I wasn't an earl. If I was born in a workhouse."

She was looking at her hand where his lips had been. "No," she said softly. "It wouldn't be possible."

Although he would like to imagine she referred to the impossibility of loving him more, Carver got the sense she was thinking of something else entirely and not listening to him at all. That was the trouble with women who thought. One could never be sure exactly what was in their mind. One could certainly never control it.

 ⚜

She placed the boxes on the dresser in her chamber. It could be nothing. Mere coincidence. But those coincidences were building up.

Carver looked a lot like his father; nothing like his mother. Mrs. Bathurst had said, quite clearly, that she saw her son recently—knew him after thirty-odd years—with a fine lady in a carriage. How would she have known him, unless he looked just like his father? And Mrs. Lotterby had never actually admitted to taking the baby to the workhouse for her sister. Now that Molly thought of it, that had been a story all of her own making after hearing Frederick's tale put thoughts in her head. All Mrs. Lotterby had said was that, "*We did what was best for him. The only alternative. It was the only thing to be done.*"

Had his father, afraid the countess would never bear another child after the death of the firstborn, taken his illegitimate son and raised it as his legal heir? Lady Mercy was born a decade later, and she was, by most accounts, a surprise to everyone, but as a girl, she could never have inherited from her father. If anyone knew Carver was bastard-born, he could not inherit the title or fortune either, so the deception must have been very carefully covered up. It would take great secrecy and the care of devoted servants. Like Edward Hobbs. Who had known of the boarding house and taken her there when she needed a place. It all began to fit.

Oh, but she shouldn't think that way. It was wrong to cast supposition on people who were not alive to defend themselves. And what business was it of hers?

Her pulse was racing. For the first time in days she forgot the sickness that plagued her.

Carver was the Earl of Everscham, and that was all there was to it. Perhaps it was merely wishful thinking on her part that he was someone else, someone with whom she could have spent the rest of her life.

The next day Carver sat at the desk in his father's old study and unlocked the top drawer. He took out a small leather box and lifted the lid. A diamond-and-sapphire ring gleamed up at him from the dark velvet lining. It had been his mother's, passed on to her by the women in her family. Since her death, it had sat in that box, in his father's desk, waiting to be placed upon another living finger. Carver had always thought he would give it to Mercy one day, but she wouldn't want it now; a ring like this was not made for the hand of a farmer's wife. It was fit for a countess. His wife.

Marriage. He'd seen good men fall to it before and sworn he never would. He had an ongoing bet in the book at White's that said Sinjun would be the first of their small group to marry. He'd wagered ten guineas on it.

Good Lord, he was sweating!

With trembling hands, he snapped the box shut. He couldn't do it. He would not subject himself to permanent, chafing bondage. But after closing the drawer and locking it again, he tapped the small brass key in the palm of his hand. Couldn't seem to put it away.

He got up, walked around the desk, and sat down again.

It was a momentous decision, the most important one of his life. No one else could make this one for him. Not Hobbs, not Mercy. Certainly not his father's ghost.

No rush, was there?

Still twenty-four hours left.

❧

The last night was upon them. They dined on lamb and minted potatoes—one of Molly's favorites. The conversation was light, neither apparently having much to say, but both feeling the importance of not falling into ominous silence, and so searching for easy, frothy subjects.

"You must be looking forward to returning to London and your business," he said to her finally as the candles burned down and it was impossible to avoid the passing of time, the slow, inexorable march toward their parting.

She smiled. "Yes."

Molly had seen his fingers toying with a small box he kept in the inner pocket of his coat. Her good-bye gift, no doubt, she thought gloomily. Did he not know her well enough by now to realize she seldom wore jewelry? But Carver Danforthe was a creature of habit. Naturally he would present her with some gaudy piece of jewelry to send her on her way. She hoped he would forget about it. In fact, the entire thought of saying good-bye was likely to bring her out

in a nervous rash. Her arms already itched in anticipation of the dreaded moment. If there was any chance
of doing so, she would much rather simply sneak away
at first light and sidestep the wretched formal adieu.

Oh, there went his hand again—sneaking inside
his coat to feel for that little leather box. She couldn't
bear it.

In a desperate move, she flung out her arm and
knocked over her glass of wine. "Oops!" She leapt to
her feet as a blood red stain bloomed on the tablecloth.
"How clumsy of me."

A footman hurried over to remove the glass, and
Carver was very calm, assuring her there was no need
to clean the stain immediately.

"Oh, but there is," she cried. "Wine will stain
irreparably if it is not tended at once."

"Please sit, Margaret. There is something I—"

She began removing dishes and plates, carrying
them to the sideboard.

"What are you doing, woman?"

"The cloth must be removed and cleaned."

He reached for her hand and caught it. "Margaret.
Sit."

"I am not a foxhound." She tightened her fingers
into a fist so he wouldn't feel the perspiration on
her palm.

"I have something to give you."

Her heart was beating so hard she couldn't breathe.
"No."

He frowned. "No?"

"I don't want it."

His eyes darkened, as if puzzled by her reaction. His
grinding jaw told her he was frustrated too.

"I don't want it," she repeated, softening her tone. "Don't make this harder than it is, I beg you."

Carver watched the footmen folding the cloth and removing it. He had released her hand, and she returned to her chair. Her face was pale, her eyes wary.

He'd always known her business was important to her, but surely she would not reject his proposal. Or would she? He knew how determined she was to succeed and make her own way in the world. She'd run away from one wedding already, so what made him think she would agree to another?

The idea of marriage was not something he had fully embraced yet—he knew only that he didn't want her to leave him, and an engagement was surely the proper thing. A solid commitment.

Ah, commitment. That word was enough to strike a bolt of panic through his heart. Perhaps he was merely feeling desperate. It must pass. Surely.

It did not take much to discourage him from the idea of proposing, and her ambivalence about marriage did not help disperse his own fears. In the past, Margaret had proven herself sensible and intuitive. If she shrank away from marriage, it was probably for the best. She was dedicated to her work, but the woman he married would become the Countess of Everscham, and it would be most unusual to find a countess running her own business. He hadn't thought things through enough. Probably, he thought morosely, because he'd never been in this position before. Never been in love.

It was a wretched state.

The woman who held his foolhardy heart and all the cards in her hands sat meekly waiting for the syllabub, her eyes averted, her face solemn again. It was dangerous to give one woman so much power over him and his happiness. How did it happen that he became enamored of her? Over the past five months she had turned his world on end, but where it began he couldn't say. Although he'd been a stranger to gallantry for most of his life, he understood now that loving her as he did, respecting her talent, he must let her return to London and live as she wanted. Keeping her trapped at his side would not make her happy, and therefore it would not make him content either. He wanted what she wanted, even if it would cause him pain to let her go.

"I hope you continue to know success in your business," he said finally. "I wish you every good fortune."

Her lashes swept up, and he saw her relief and her gratitude, fierce and warm. "Thank you. And I wish the same for you. Always."

They made love that evening with a new tenderness, and they did not speak another word. He held her in his arms until she gave in to dreams. Then he lay awake and listened to her gentle sighs, feeling her heart beating against his chest and the softness of her hair under his hand. Her hands and feet often twitched when she slept. That was the signal that told him she was far into her dreams. It was a strange sensation to be this intimately familiar with another body. He'd known his share of women, of course, but in the past he'd always kept a certain distance, going through the motions, keeping up a reputation for wickedness that prevented any marriage-minded matron from pushing her daughter at him. It had become too easy to breeze along, not caring, not thinking too deeply about the woman—sometimes *women*—in his bed.

He'd always thought that to let one in too far would be unmanly, a sign of weakness. If he closed his eyes, he could see his father seated at one end of the long dining table, his mother at the other, neither speaking. They went through the motions too, in a marriage that joined property and wealth but not hearts. He could not recall witnessing a single kiss between them, not even a hand held. His mother's green eyes had observed her husband with polite coolness, unless, of course, it was one of those days when she'd angered him by doing something against his wishes. Then those eyes boiled with fury, emitting sparks to burn anything unfortunate enough to be in her path. The loud part of the fight went on behind closed doors, but the silent part continued long after, a menacing tension hanging over the house sometimes for days.

It often seemed to Carver as if his mother went out of her way to be defiant, to rouse his father's foul temper and sharpen her own. Almost as if it was a game to her. When he saw his father's tears at her funeral, he was shocked. It was the only time he saw the earl weep. After that, his father spoiled little Mercy, who was the physical image of her mother. It was as if he thought to start again, make up for the past. And Mercy, only five when the countess died, idolized their father, thought him above reproach.

For years Carver had resented the fact that his sister got all the good attention, and he realized that now as he held Margaret against his body and pondered his feelings as he'd never dared before.

He'd been afraid of so much, avoided coming to the estate because of all those terrible memories of anger and seething resentment. But having brave, fearless Margaret there with him had changed things, brought new light to the darkest corners. She had inspired him in so many ways. Made him want her approval, her smile. Made him want to step out of the shadow behind his father's towering ghost and be his own man.

He used to laugh scornfully at other men who made besotted fools of themselves over some bit of petticoat. And here he was, hoisted on his own petard. In his case, it was even worse. Margaret the Brave firmly refused to devote herself to his bed. She was a working woman with a sensible head on her shoulders. Too good for him.

Oh, he'd taught her to be more playful, yes, but she was still, at her core, the decent, honest, and honorable Margaret Robbins. Despite her fears, he had not changed her for the worse. She deserved now to be set free, as he'd kept her long enough. If it caused him hurt to let her go, that was his own fault and part of his reformation.

When he woke the next morning, she was gone. He learned that she'd taken his coach only as far as the turnpike, and there boarded the mail coach back to London.

The sudden loss, although he'd prepared himself for it, was unbearable. Simply put, his world was not the same without her in it.

As he ate breakfast alone, Mrs. Martindale placed a large vase of roses from his mother's garden on the sideboard behind him. "That young lady certainly worked miracles in her ladyship's garden. Brought it back to life in the short time she was here. Some folk have that special touch, of course." She sniffed. "Sadly, I never did."

"Margaret Robbins has very clever hands," he muttered. "A lot of clever parts. All of them astute enough to run away from me."

"Evidently. Of course, if you had any functioning parts above the breeches, you wouldn't have let her go."

He turned to admonish her for that remark, but she was already moving through the door, making a hasty escape herself, and slamming it shut so hard that several petals were shaken loose from the roses and drifted slowly to the floor.

Twenty-five

SHE SPENT THE NIGHT AT A COACHING INN ON THE London road. As a young woman traveling alone, Molly was the target of several lewd glances, and while attempting to enjoy a supper of game pie, she noticed that one such glance came from a face she recognized. Arthur Wakely. Apparently he did not know her at first, but after eyeing her fine garments for several minutes across the crowded dining room, he finally looked harder at her features, and her scowling countenance must have tipped the scales of recognition.

Contrary to her hopes, he got out of his seat and crossed to where she sat. "Miss Robbins, what good fortune that we should meet."

There were few things she would be less likely to think of as fortunate. "I hope your stay in Kent was beneficial. Are you returning to London?" She pitied his poor sister, if that was the case.

"I am indeed. I must say you are looking very well."

It might have been the expected response to thank him for the compliment, but his greasy, smirking manner was in danger of turning her tender stomach on its end again. "Excuse me, sir. I am tired and must retire to my room."

"Oh, but I thought we might talk a while." To her horror, he reached across the small table and gripped her wrist. "I should like to catch up on all the news of our shared acquaintance."

"I have nothing of interest to tell you."

"How pert you are, Miss Robbins. Always so prim and pious. But I know what you are." He leered at her, leaning closer until she inhaled an unpleasant waft of his drunken breath. "Seamstress, indeed. I know the truth about you."

"That I am a hardworking woman of business, Mr. Wakely?"

"Hardworking you might be. But your business is not what you pretend. I always suspected it, and now I see you all dressed up like a hussy, waiting for a gentleman here in this inn, I know the truth, don't I?"

"A hussy?" She thought with amusement that Lady Mercy would not like to hear her gowns referred to in those terms.

"Your business, Miss Robbins, is managed on your back." He curled his slimy finger against her pulse. "And I ought to find out just how hardworking you are for myself."

A spark of panic shot through her. Traveling alone was a dangerous enterprise. There was no one in the inn whom she knew or trusted, no one she could go to for help. But the fear was short-lived. She did not have just herself to protect anymore, did she?

She smiled at him. "How is your foot, Mr. Wakely? Which one is it again that gives you trouble?"

He looked startled for a moment and then slurred an answer. "The left."

"Ah. This one." Molly moved her own leg swiftly

under the table and stomped her boot heel firmly on the infamous foot.

Arthur Wakely released his grip on her wrist and shot up out of his chair, howling and cursing. Faces turned to observe his strange dance, and several folk laughed loudly at his performance.

She stood and shook her head. "You really must take better care of that foot, Mr. Wakely. I hope you won't be too embarrassed by your actions tomorrow when you are sober. Good evening to you."

There was to be one final epitaph for Arthur Wakely. In the morning, while boarding the coach for the next leg of her journey, she saw him again, but this time in the company of a short, stout, noisy woman with a severe countenance, who seemed to do nothing but shout orders. Molly watched in amazement as a shockingly humbled Arthur struggled to load the woman's large trunk onto the mail coach without a word of protest. She'd never seen him so cowed in the presence of a woman. As the journey toward London progressed, she learned from his stern companion's constant complaining that Arthur had met her while she was his nurse at the sanatorium in Kent, and she had, somehow, cornered him into marrying her.

As Molly realized that Mr. Wakely had met his comeuppance at last, she couldn't help smiling at her reflection in the window of the coach. Carver and his good deeds, she mused, swallowing a chuckle. Sending Arthur Wakely off to that sanatorium was perhaps one of the greatest of all.

❧

The post arrived in Sydney Dovedale—or rather it charged through on its way between Norwich and Morecroft, pausing just long enough by the ancient oak at the crossroads to collect and deliver letters for the village residents. On this day in the midst of September, as the leaves began to fall, gold and fragile, the mail coach brought not only parcels and communications, but a prodigal returned. Miss Molly Robbins alighted from the crowded, swaying vessel, carrying one small trunk and a hatbox.

No one was there waiting for her, because no one knew she was coming. Two little boys, knocking acorns from the oak with long sticks, stopped what they were doing to inspect the arrival, and then, finding nothing of interest to them, resumed their assault on the old tree. Only a handful of others were there to meet the coach, and they, it seemed, did not recognize her in her new clothes.

Except for Mrs. Flick, the village busybody, who was possibly as ancient as that noble oak under which she took shelter, but whose eyesight was remarkably sharp.

The black-garbed old woman took one look at Molly and tripped, stumbling over her own walking cane, in such haste to hobble away and be the first to spread tidings, before anyone else saw the unexpected arrival in the village.

Molly let her go, even gave her time to get there ahead of her. Ambling down the leafy lane, she was in no particular hurry to face the questions that would undoubtedly greet her return. She breathed in the familiar, misty autumn air and tasted the bitterness of bonfires in the fields, the muskiness of damp, dead and rotting leaves. Two gray carthorses looked up from their grazing as she passed. Did they recognize her, she wondered? Looking ahead, she saw a soft mist settled over the jumble of cottages down in the valley. She stopped a moment, setting her luggage down in the lane to catch her breath and straighten her bonnet.

Well, there was her old childhood home. She had thought she could never go back there. She was about to find out if it was true.

She walked on, head high atop her strong bones.

Carver arrived in London and immediately heard from Sinjun that Margaret Robbins had mysteriously vanished. Lady Anne had booked several fittings at her shop and been attended each time by the assistants, neither of whom seemed to know where their mistress had gone.

"I do think she might have told me," the young girl pouted. "I am surely her very favorite customer. Why would she up and leave without a word of good-bye?"

Edward Hobbs explained that Molly had paid him a visit shortly before she departed London and asked him to keep an eye on the business during her absence.

"But how long does she expect to be gone?" Carver demanded.

"She did not say, my lord, but I was given to assume a matter of several months, perhaps even a year. Apparently she is still designing and sending her work to the shop for the girls to make patterns."

It was all very odd that she should leave her business in the hands of others. Carver knew her well enough to suspect something most dire must have occurred to drag her away from it.

"My lord, there is another matter of importance," Hobbs added, peering somberly through his spectacles. "The issue you asked me to look into, regarding the child sent to the Cripplegate workhouse."

"Yes, yes," he replied impatiently, still worried about Margaret.

Hobbs hesitated and then, with a most unaccustomed flourish, stuck his quill into the bruised apple by his ledger. "I think, my lord, we had better visit the boarding house together. It is time the truth was out, for I've been burdened with it long enough, and in light of recent...developments..." Hobbs slipped his arms into a patched coat. "If you come with me now, my lord, all will be revealed."

Lady Mercy sat across from her, trying to come to terms with what Molly had just said.

Molly waited, giving her friend time to digest the fact that she had come home to have a child. It was not an easy thing to tell anyone, and she supposed it would be no easier for Lady Mercy to hear and absorb it.

"Are we to know the father of the child?" her former mistress demanded.

"I would rather not say."

Molly knew she must step with caution. If Lady Mercy heard the truth, she would instantly write to her brother.

"I came home to have my child here," she continued, "and I had hoped my oldest friend would understand, even if she could not wholly forgive. But I am prepared to manage alone if need be."

"Nonsense! You will certainly not go through this alone. It is not your fault, Molly."

"Oh, but it is. I am to blame. I knew what I did. I knew the risks full well." She referred to more than the chance of a pregnancy; she meant also the jeopardy in which she'd placed her heart, but she said nothing of that.

"I wonder why you didn't remain in London or travel to some other town, like Norwich," Mercy remarked, her eyes gleaming shrewdly. "One would imagine it easier to obscure a pregnancy among people one hardly knows and in a large town. Instead, you came back here to this small place, where we all know one another's business and nothing remains secret for long."

In fact, Molly had considered Norwich, but in the end it was peaceful Sydney Dovedale that called her home. She wanted her child born here, where the air was not clouded with soot, where the pace of life was slower, gentler, and where her own mother had raised so many babies.

Sydney Dovedale had its drawbacks, but also good points that far outweighed the bad. She planned to return eventually to her work in London and take her child with her, saying it was a relative left in her care. Other women managed without a husband, and so would she.

Suddenly Mercy's demeanor softened. She reached across, grabbed her friend's cold hand, and squeezed. "Don't fret, Molly, of course I'll help you, and I am glad you came here to have your child. In truth, I would have been angry if you did anything else. No one can take care of you so well as I. Worry not. I shall manage everything."

Molly smiled and bore it all stoically.

Lady Mercy's marriage to Rafe Hartley was planned for October. It was to be a small affair with just a handful of guests, but Molly was unable to ascertain whether the bride expected her brother to attend. When she inquired about it quite casually, Mercy replied that Carver was invited, but whether or not he would see fit to attend such a scandalous marriage was up to him.

"Carver has never been very fond of weddings, because they mean he must smile and be pleasant to people—oh, and he says folk at weddings have a tendency to corner him with questions about when he intends to have his own." She laughed, and Molly tried to smile too.

But Carver was unpredictable. One never knew what he might do. Especially now that he was rising from his bed earlier in the day. It gave him so many more hours with which to cause havoc.

Eventually she decided that if he did come, she would be civil and act as if there was never anything between them but a business loan. She did not want anyone taking her baby away from her, and she certainly didn't want Carver feeling as if he must make any form of recompense to her or the child. He didn't want marriage or children. He'd always made that perfectly clear. And she didn't want a husband. She wanted her independence.

Visits to her brothers and sisters passed awkwardly. They teased Molly for her "fancy" clothes and manners. The best cups were put out when she came to

tea, and the children were squeezed into their uncomfortable Sunday best, forced to keep clean and tidy for
the duration of her visit, which won her no admirers
among the youngsters either.

Their wariness multiplied at church one Sunday
when Molly appeared with a just-picked bunch of
late-flowering toadflax tucked in her bonnet, an
eye-catching display that caused Mrs. Flick to accuse
her of "gaudy peacock vanity, and on the Sabbath
too!" Apparently she ought to be ashamed of herself,
but really, why would God not want to see a beautiful sprig of His own creation in church? So what if
"dawdling" and stopping to pick wildflowers from the
verge had made her late for Parson Bentley's service?
So what if it was a startling yellow and a little too
abundant—almost covering one entire side of her
bonnet? So what if it was unusual for Molly Robbins
to draw attention to herself? So what, as Carver would
say, who cares what they think?

They could all get used to the new Molly Robbins,
and that was all there was to it.

She let out the seams of her clothes, and as the
weather turned colder, more layers were appropriate
anyway, giving her the chance to hide changes in her
formerly slender figure.

At Lady Mercy's suggestion, she applied to
"Jammy" Jim Hodson and his wife, proprietors of
Sydney Dovedale's most important shop, and they
agreed to sell pinafores, petticoats, and tippets that she
made to stay busy and pay for her board and lodging
with Lady Mercy.

"There is no need for you to worry about that,"
her friend had insisted, but Molly would not hear

of moving in without contributing to the cost of her keep.

On one mellow autumn afternoon, she walked with Rafe Hartley in his uncle's orchard and apologized for jilting him at the altar all those months ago. He merely laughed and thanked her for seeing sense.

"Some things just can't be helped," he said. "Hearts will love where they desire, not often where it is practical."

And she too smiled. "You were always in love with Lady Mercy. I knew there was someone, but I didn't realize it was her. You disguised it so well by thoroughly hating her, out loud, at every opportunity."

He shrugged. "A man has his pride." Then as the laughter drifted off, he bent to gather a windfall apple. "You'll find love of your own one day, Moll." He shot her a sly, sideways glance. "If you haven't already."

Disinclined to talk further on that subject, she snatched the juicy apple out of his hand and walked on.

❧

"Well, it took you long enough to come looking for that young lady," Mrs. Lotterby exclaimed when finding Carver on her doorstep.

"I do not think she wanted me to look for her, madam. She made that clear when she left me."

The woman groaned. "How many years have you lived, sir?"

"Three and thirty."

"As I thought. Then you should know that sometimes women don't mean what they say."

"Yes, I suppose it might make life too easy for men if they did."

The landlady woke her napping husband with a sharp nudge of the elbow, and he sat bolt upright in his rocking chair. "Yon fellow has come for our Molly. Look lively, Herbert. Tell him what you said you would if you ever saw him face-to-face."

Carver stepped into the light of the fire. "I hoped you might know where she's gone. I know she left here some weeks ago."

"She's gone home o' course," Mrs. Lotterby exhaled impatiently, still prodding her sleepy husband.

"Home?"

"To Sydney Dovedale."

"Do you know that for sure?" He'd never have expected her to go back there, but he'd written to his sister just in case. Mercy had replied with a letter full of details about her wedding plans but no news of Margaret Robbins. "Did she tell you that?"

"The young lady was very close lipped and would not say where she meant to go, but it was no great difficulty to come to that conclusion," her landlady answered crisply, hands clasped under her ample bosom, her bright eyes boring into him. "Where else would a poor girl go but home when she finds herself in trouble?"

Herbert Lotterby lurched to his feet, smoothed down a few wisps of thin gray hair, and cleared his throat loudly. "Now look here, young man, that little lady deserves to be loved and looked after properly. She's a good girl, kindhearted and true to a fault. I'll not have her misused. For all you're a nobleman, sir, it won't stop me standing up for her."

"But I would never—"

"We all know what goes on in this world, young

man, but I won't have that little lady treated ill by you or anyone. She's like a daughter to us."

"I certainly—"

"Our Molly is a very special girl." The landlady's tiny husband stepped closer, puffing out his chest. "I demand to know your intentions, young sir!"

Fortunately, at that moment, Edward Hobbs came in and averted everyone's attention. "Mrs. Lotterby, perhaps you would take his lordship and me to your sister's room?"

Her eyes slowly grew rounder. "Oh! You've come to—"

"Yes, madam. I always knew the day would come when he must be told, and recent developments now make it necessary. It is best for all concerned parties that the truth be known to them."

"Well, I have not spoken a word of it, just as I promised his father when I passed the child over to him. Not a word to—"

"Yes, thank you, Mrs. Lotterby, for all that you've done. Will you take us up?"

Hobbs gestured for Carver to walk ahead and follow the landlady up the narrow, crooked stairs to the upper floors of the house.

"I do hope it won't be too much of a shock to her," Mrs. Lotterby whispered, opening the door and stepping aside for him. "It has been so many years."

Carver walked slowly into the room, and Hobbs followed. The door was closed behind them. The old lady lay in her bed, wearing a white lace cap. At the sound of footsteps, her eyes opened.

She looked directly at Carver, and a slow smile lifted her face. Her dark eyes, one moment black and the next silver-gray—just like his—shone with pleasure and more than a little mischief.

"My fine son," she whispered. "So like your father. How you've grown."

He stared at the old woman on the bed, and it felt as if the warped floorboards under his feet were about to give way.

Delilah held out her frail hand.

"Come and sit with me a while. I won't keep you long, young man."

Hobbs silently moved a chair next to the bed, and Carver sat before he lost the use of his legs.

"Now, my dear boy," his mother whispered, "you must tell me how you mean to win that sweet Miss Robbins back."

❧

Carver swept into his library, and with a trembling hand, poured two brandies, passing one quickly to Hobbs.

"You knew. All this time. Why was I never informed?"

"My lord, your father felt he had no choice. When the first son was born, it was a difficult birth, and he was told the countess may never carry a babe to term again. After the boy died, the earl was desperate for an heir, and when he learned his mistress was with child, he decided to make the best of it. If the child was a boy, he would bring him to the estate and raise it as a son of his legal marriage."

Carver suddenly felt no appetite for brandy and set his glass on the desk. He wanted to keep a level head. With his world tipping and swaying, he needed one thing at least to remain stable. Margaret wasn't there to keep him sensible, so he must rely on himself.

Hobbs continued, "I made the arrangements. Delilah and her sister were given the boarding house as a gift and sworn to secrecy. They were too in awe of your father to speak a word to anyone. He did have a talent for striking fear into people's hearts. As you know, my lord."

"Yes. He did it to me quite effectively all my life, with or without a cane in his hand." The solicitor sipped his brandy and sighed. "The countess remained in the country that winter for her 'confinement.' When you were born, I wrapped you up and rode with you through the snow to Sussex, where I put you into your father's hands. Thus it was done."

Carver dropped into his chair behind the desk. "So my true mother has lived in that damp, decrepit house ever since?"

"Sadly, your father made no provision for the lady in his will. He was not a man who thought a great deal about the difficulties of others." Hobbs bowed his head apologetically. "I have done what I could to help the sisters over the years, but my own funds were always tightly budgeted. Thank goodness they are two honest, uncomplicated, kindhearted ladies who would never go back on their word to your father, or they could have demanded much more than he ever thought to give them."

Head in his hands, Carver was slowly coming to terms with his true identity. "Then I owe you much recompense, Hobbs, for taking care of my mother all this time. Something my father failed to do."

"You have done much for them yourself in recent months, even without knowing the intimate connection."

Carver stood and paced. "I did all that for Margaret."

"Yes, my lord, I know."

Falling back into his chair, he linked his fingers behind his head and stared at the portrait of the countess above his mantel. "Then none of this is mine, Hobbs. I am not legally entitled to it." Suddenly he felt a laugh bubbling out of him, but it was a painful one, and there was nothing merry about it. "I always knew, somehow, I didn't belong."

"Oh, do you think so, my lord?" Hobbs raised a thick gray eyebrow. "I always thought how perfectly you did fit."

He snorted. "I never could do anything right in my father's eyes. As for my mother..." He paused. "I suppose I should call her his wife, the countess...she could scarcely look at me, and now I know why. I was a deceit. I was one of those dirty secrets that lurked in shadowy corners of the house. Always fluttering in the corner of my eye."

Hobbs finished his brandy and looked wistfully at the decanter. "Forgive me, my lord, but rather than dwell upon the past, should you not look to the future? Think not of how you came to be where you are, but of what you can do while you're here. Now you have discovered the truth, it is up to you what is done with it."

Hobbs was right. It was all up to him whether he kept the secret. Did he give everything up for Felix, his distant, unlikeable cousin? Did he strip himself of the title and...do what? He would suddenly be an ordinary man. Perhaps Hobbs could make him a clerk in his firm, he mused.

Aha! Margaret Robbins would not run from him then, would she? She would prefer him as a humble fellow, surely.

But if he gave everything up, he would have to forget about funding that school for orphaned boys. Just as he'd found his purpose and learned how to make something good out of his life, it could all be ripped away from him.

As Hobbs said, he had much to consider.

"I've put too much on your shoulders all these years, Hobbs," he muttered, looking up at his friend and counselor. "It's time I took things in hand and stopped throwing everything at you."

"That would be nice, my lord."

There was a pause, and then both men laughed.

One thing Carver knew with certainty: He didn't want to be like his father. He finally had a chance to choose his own future, just as he'd wanted since he was ten.

Whatever he chose, he would be his own man.

Twenty-six

THE WEDDING OF LADY MERCY DANFORTHE AND RAFE Hartley took place in the chapel at Sydney Dovedale where, seven months before, he was supposed to wed Molly Robbins. It was an intimate affair, and the bride wore scarlet.

"What else would she wear?" grumbled that professional scold, Mrs. Flick. An uninvited bystander, she peered over the mossy churchyard wall that afternoon to see the newlyweds emerge under a flurry of rice.

Molly, close enough to hear the comment, replied briskly, "A wedding is a joyful occasion, Mrs. Flick. If you have nothing pleasant to say, I suggest you move on and don't tarry here." But the woman who made an occupation out of shaming others was never easily shamed herself. She glared boldly back at Molly over the wall and pointed with a gnarled finger.

"You're no better than your fine mistress. I always knew she was a pampered, brazen little strumpet with too much to say for herself. But I expected better from you—a girl born and bred in this village. Now we all know why you came slinking back here with your tail between your legs."

Since the weather was bitterly cold that day, Molly carried a large fleece muff for her hands. It was also a useful way to keep her figure well hidden. Not that she showed much yet, but she was so very conscious of it that she sometimes feared it was obvious to anyone who saw her, despite Lady Mercy's assurances to the contrary. "I can't imagine what you mean to say, Mrs. Flick." She'd decided denial was the best policy. The few people who needed to know had been informed, and under no circumstances did Mrs. Flick count as someone who needed to know anything.

"Oh, can't you indeed?" the old crone replied, her mean little mouth gathered tight. "What would your poor mother think of you now? Of course, she never did anything but spit out babes one after t'other. I don't suppose you'll be any different. Although you might at least have got a husband first. There was a time when this village was a good, quiet, orderly place. Now it's sin and damnation everywhere I turn."

Molly sighed. "If it's everywhere *you* turn, perhaps you are the cause of it."

Mrs. Flick drew back, eyes afire with indignation. "Don't talk daft."

While looking over the crone's black bonnet, she watched a coach-and-four pulling around the common. Her heart ground to a halt just as the wheels did. Very few carriages that grand ever came to Sydney Dovedale. The chestnut trees shivered in the breeze, and the first fallen leaves spun under the hooves of those fine horses. The door opened, and even without her spectacles, she recognized the man who stepped down.

Sin and damnation personified. He had come to his sister's wedding after all.

There was nowhere to go. The lych-gate was the only exit from the churchyard, and he was heading directly toward it. Unless she climbed the cobblestone wall and leapt over Mrs. Flick—an amusing thought certainly, but hardly practical in her state—she could not escape an encounter with her former lover.

Coming down the path with her new husband, Lady Mercy suddenly saw her brother by the gate.

"Carver! You came!" She rushed by in a blur of scarlet and embraced her brother as if she hadn't seen him in years.

"Of course I came. Wanted to make sure you went through with it. Can't have you turning up on my doorstep again like a bad penny, can I?" Carver kissed her cheek. "I waited long enough to be rid of you."

From a short distance, Molly quietly observed the greeting. At the sight of him after their weeks apart, her heart bled. She'd had no idea how hard it would be to see him again. She forgot about Mrs. Flick standing on the other side of the wall, until the old crone grumbled again, "Just what we need, another London sinner coughed up on our doorstep. And the worst of the bunch, from all I hear."

"From what you hear?" She was amused by the thought of Carver's reputation traveling all the way to Mrs. Flick's ears. Did it come by carrier pigeon, she wondered?

"Aye. A devil incarnate. A Bluebeard for the way he disposes of women."

"To bear any similarity to Bluebeard, he'd have to marry them first, and that will never happen, Mrs. Flick."

The old woman was still considering this when

Lady Mercy spun around, looking across the church-yard. Spying Molly by the wall, she waved her closer.

"Oh, Carver, here is Molly Robbins. You do remember her, I'm sure."

He turned and bowed his head. "Miss Robbins."

Inside her muff, Molly's fingers were knotted so tightly she thought she might never get them undone again. "Your lordship." She curtsied, her gaze dropping hastily to his boots.

The wedding party moved through the gate, chattering and merry, but Carver hung back, waiting to walk with her. How tall he seemed suddenly. She felt overshadowed by his presence, very insignificant, meek, and mousy again. "Margaret, will you walk with your arm in mine?" He was looking at her large muff as if it might suddenly show fangs and attack him.

She glanced over at the wall, where Mrs. Flick still watched. "I think not, your lordship. My hands are cold."

So they walked side by side instead.

"I bring greetings from your friends in London, Miss Robbins."

"Oh." She kept her gaze on the merry wedding party as it moved away with greater speed than the two of them. It had begun to rain.

"I have a letter for you from Mrs. Slater, and cake from Mrs. Lotterby, to make certain you are eating well." He smiled. "I also bring good tidings of Mrs. Bathurst."

"How is she?"

"Better. Her spirits have much improved now that she sees her son regularly, and he is arranging for her move to the country."

She stopped and caught a frosty breath. "Her son? You found him?"

"Yes." He stopped on the path. "Hobbs was able to locate the man. He had never been very far away, as it turned out."

"Frederick Dawes?" she asked in a frail whisper.

Carver's eyes were gray that afternoon, reflecting the overcast autumn sky. She felt as if she would like to soar in those eyes, the way birds spread their wings against the clouds. "No," he said. "Closer to you."

"To me?"

He held her arms and lowered his mouth to kiss her.

Molly listened for a squawk and a thud, but there was none, so Mrs. Flick must not have fainted at the sight of such remorseless impropriety.

When she finally had use of her lips again, Molly demanded he tell her the truth. "I know you like your mysteries, Danny, but you'd better tell me at once!"

They walked on and came to the lych-gate, where he stopped again to shelter her from the rain. "First, before I tell you the identity of Mrs. Bathurst's son, you must make two decisions."

"Oh, must I?"

"Firstly, shall we marry here or in Sussex?"

Shocked, Molly couldn't find words for several moments.

"And secondly, would you like to marry an earl with a fortune or a humble bastard with nothing but his looks?"

Slowly she tried to make sense of all this. She took one hand from her muff and placed it against his cold cheek. "Are you telling me that you are her son?"

"You knew it, did you not? When you found those boxes in the attic."

Molly fought against the tears that threatened. She never used to be one for tears, but they came more easily these days. "I suspected. But I couldn't believe—"

"So now you have a choice. Which man do you want?"

She thought about it, her fingers trailing slowly over his rough cheek. He must have ridden in haste to be there, for he had not even shaved.

"You're telling me you would give all that up? Just for me?"

With his thumbs he wiped the tears from her face. "I will do whatever you want. I love you. It's pitiful, but there it is. I am at your mercy."

Molly could barely breathe, her heart hurt so dreadfully. But it was a good kind of hurt, she mused. A very good kind of hurt. "I believe, Danny, we are all put on this earth to try and raise ourselves up. To become something more than what we are when we start."

He nodded, his eyes watching her face carefully, lovingly.

"So how could I ever ask you to take a step back for me?" A gentle breeze rummaged through her petticoats and pulled on her damp bonnet ribbons. "Besides," she added with an arch smile, "I might be a simple country mouse, but I'm no fool. I'll take both men, including the rich one, if you please, sir."

Carver looked down at her and broke into laughter. "Greedy minx. I might have known. You did tell me once before that you wanted me only for the money."

She too laughed, all her worries of the past few

months falling away like gilded leaves from the chestnut trees around the common. "Well, there is something about me that you *don't* know, Danny."

"Oh?"

"It's another mystery." She tapped the side of her nose with one finger. "Since you like them so much, I'll let you guess. It's your turn."

"Damn you, wench. Tell me, or I'll give you another spanking."

"That's a fine way to talk to your countess." That stopped her dead in her tracks. Countess?

Molly Robbins was about to become the Countess of Everscham. That could not be. She must have fallen and cracked her skull open and be living in some strange fantasy world. Hopefully she could go on living in it and never return to sanity, if her mental state depended on never seeing him again.

She waited for her pulse to settle. Perhaps she should tell him to give up the title, but whichever way they made this work, one of them would have the harder struggle. Better they struggle with the money than without it. As she'd said to him, she may be a country girl at heart, but she was also practical.

Turning her face to him again, she exclaimed, "How could a lady's maid ever be a countess?"

He was utterly unruffled by the thought. There was no hesitation. "The same way a bastard can be an earl. I have no doubt we'll manage." He kissed her hand. "We are quite a team, you and I."

"But what about my business?" Her shoulders drooped. "I don't want to—"

"You'll never have to give it up. I want you to be content, and for as long as you want to sew gowns, I won't stop you. My lady wife-to-be. Sakes, I'll have to get used to that."

"You will. Just as you got accustomed to good deeds."

Rain fell faster now all around them, but the slate arch over the gate kept them dry. The wedding party had disappeared, and even Mrs. Flick must have dashed off for cover. It was just the two of them and the rain. The wind was colder now, but with Carver's arms around her, she barely felt it.

Not just the two of them, she corrected herself; there was another soul to consider in all this too.

"If you're sure you want to marry me, Danny, we'd better do it soon."

"If I'm sure? Why else would I come all the way to this dratted one-horse village, chasing after a pert-faced dressmaker, when I could be home in my warm, cozy bed?"

Suddenly overcome, she flung her arms around his neck, and her muff fell to the flagstones at their feet. "I love you very much. So much I might burst with it one day. My seams feel very loose."

He wrapped his arms tighter around her waist. "But will you still love me when I'm old and ugly?"

She tipped her head back to look at him. "Of course I do."

He laughed. "Most amusing, Mouse." Then he stopped, and his eyes narrowed. "What do you mean, we'd better do it soon? Why the haste?"

She blinked. "We don't want another bastard in the family, do we?"

It took several moments for the color to return to his face. "Are you sure?"

"Quite sure."

"Good Lord," was all he seemed capable of managing.

"Jumping Jacks, as Lady Anne would say." She smiled. "Something else for you to get used to, Danny darling."

Epilogue

AS THEY SIGNED THEIR NAMES IN THE CHURCH REGISTER, Carver was reminded of the first time he watched her write her name, when she brought the loan contract to him on a rainy day last April. He could not have known then, that he was looking at his future wife and the mother of his children, but he always knew there was something devious going on behind that prim countenance.

He should have realized Miss Molly Robbins had designs upon him.

After the wedding, he held her hand and helped her up into the carriage. His sister and Rafe Hartley were there to see them off, along with her other village friends—Rafe's father and stepmother and his aunt and uncle. Molly's siblings came too, all greatly suspicious of their sister's new title, and muttering that she'd better not expect them to curtsy to her.

The horses moved forward, and the carriage wheels bumped over muddy tracks.

He glanced at his wife and saw how she tried to hide her wet lashes, leaning out as far as she could to wave at the vanishing folk through the carriage window.

"You're sad to be leaving Sydney Dovedale and all

the people in it," he said, drawing her into his lap. For once, he would permit her to cry in his presence, but after that, he never wanted to see her unhappy again, and he would make it his personal duty to keep her smiling.

"I am sad," she acknowledged with a nod, sliding a slender arm around his neck. "But I am happy to begin a new chapter in a new world."

"With me."

"With you. With us. No matter what we are, or where."

"That's all that matters," he whispered against her lips. "Just us."

The lane straightened out, and the horses picked up their pace, leaving the village behind and carrying the Earl and Countess of Everscham away under a thinning canopy of copper leaves.

Soon, once winter took the countryside in its firm grip, those same branches would be stark and bare against a bleak sky. But buds would sprout again eventually, and birds would nest there. By the time the next Everscham heir was born, the cherry and apple trees that bordered the lane to Sydney Dovedale would celebrate the occasion with festoons of pink and white blossom. And thus the cycle of life began all over again.

Acknowledgments

I would like to thank my family and friends for their tireless support and encouragement. To Aubrey, Danielle, and everyone at Sourcebooks—your belief in me has taken me farther than I ever thought possible. And to all my lovely readers—without you, none of this would be worthwhile.